Intermezzo

Melinda R. Morgan

Silverton House Publishing • Ogden, Utah

For Bobbye . . .

Intermezzo
Book Two of the Birthright Legacy

TheBirthrightLegacy.com

Copyright © 2013 by Melinda R. Morgan

978-1-60065-029-1
Library of Congress Control Number: 2013911564

Printed in the United States of America
10 9 8 7 6 5 4 3 2 1

Silverton House Publishing
an imprint of WindRiver Publishing, Inc.
3280 Madison Ave • Ogden, UT • 84403-0637

SilvertonHousePublishing.com

Contents

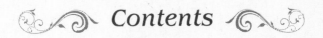

Prologue

The darkened sky that hovered overhead added its seal of regret to the small gathering at the Hastings' family cemetery. Only members of the immediate family and a few close friends attended the intimate ceremony led by Patrick McKay, or as the members of his parish fondly referred to him, "Reverend Pat." The Hastings didn't particularly care for Reverend Pat; his sermons were too rigid and unforgiving. But, despite their dissatisfaction, a Christian burial was of utmost importance to the prominent family, so they made do.

The modest gathering formed a somber circle around a small mound of mud and a grave that would soon give rest to the tiny pine box that held the body of Eleanor Hastings' baby brother. Christopher, once a bundle of endless excitement and unconditional love, now lay cold and still. His death came unexpectedly, and Eleanor's father, Charles Frederick Hastings II, did not take it well. His two eldest sons, Charles Frederick Hastings III and Miles Harrison Hastings, had both died at Gettysburg, leaving Christopher as the only surviving male of the Hastings family. Christopher's premature death meant the end of the family line.

Eleanor stood between her mother and her younger sister and watched as the two men who served as Reverend Pat's assistants struggled to lower the casket gently into its final resting place. Dressed in black, the three Hastings women, each with veiled faces, stepped forward to gather a handful of dirt—now thick as mud—and cast it into the young child's grave. This they did without any outward show of emotion, for such a display would not be proper, and propriety was a way of life among the Hastings women. But Eleanor was not like the other women of the Hastings family, at least not since she had recovered from a fever that by all the laws of nature should have claimed her life. She knew she didn't belong here, and try as she might she could not mask her emotions with the same poise and grace as one would expect from a lady of proper upbringing.

Tears streamed down Eleanor's face and a painful lump lodged itself at the back of her throat. *How could this be fair?* she wondered in silent anguish.

She looked toward the sky, pleading, as if she might somehow find the answer revealed there; but the only thing she saw through her black lace veil was the ominous motion of the clouds that threatened to turn what was presently a light, scattered rain into a steady downpour.

"It figures," she mouthed silently. A bitter taste of sarcasm coated Eleanor's tongue as she lowered her gaze back to her brother's grave.

"Father, we give Thee but Thine own. Take this child into Thy bosom and give him eternal rest . . ." Reverend Pat said as he began the final portion of the service, which led flawlessly into a recitation of the twenty-third Psalm. In a few moments, those gathered around the grave would join in chorus to recite the Lord's Prayer, signaling the conclusion of the service. Then the Hastings family would make its way along the wooded path that led back to the main house.

Death was no stranger to the folks of Marensburg, Pennsylvania, a modest township located west of Gettysburg between Chambersburg and Greencastle. In Marensburg, news arrived with unsettling frequency announcing the latest casualties of the war. The postings always arrived on a Wednesday. Families of soldiers would gather in the town center and search frantically through the list, relieved when the name they hunted for wasn't there. Too often, however, more than one family would learn that a father, son, or brother would never come home, and once again, Marensburg would mourn.

Eleanor longed to give her family and the people of Marensburg hope, to let them know that the war would soon be over and that their fallen fathers and sons had not died in vain; but of course, she could not tell them this. That was against the rules. She couldn't tell them that history books would report that more Americans died in the Civil War than would die in two subsequent World Wars. Nor could she tell them that President Abraham Lincoln would be assassinated in Ford's theater.

Eleanor couldn't tell them these things, *because they hadn't happened yet.*

Just as promised, the sky soon crackled with the sound of thunder and began to dump a heavy, sustained rain on the small party of mourners. Umbrellas did little to protect the Hastings women from the sideways sweep of rain which seemed to shift directions randomly. Christine, now the youngest member of the Hastings family, folded her arm through Eleanor's and leaned close to her.

"Do you think he's happy?" she whispered.

"Who?" Eleanor whispered back.

"Christopher."

Eleanor was quiet for a moment as she fought the urge to shrug her shoulders, something she had learned—and learned the hard way—was never appropriate for a lady.

"I don't believe I'm the best person to ask," she finally said.

"Why not?" Christine asked.

Eleanor's mother turned slowly, but she didn't say anything. Eleanor knew she was listening.

"I'm sorry, Christine, I'm not myself today," Eleanor replied.

Christine nodded. "I know . . . neither am I." She squeezed Eleanor's arm. "But he's in heaven, right? So he must be happy."

Eleanor breathed deeply and sighed. "Yes, I'm sure Christopher would be happy there." It was the best she could do.

A bright flash lit up the atmosphere as several bolts of lightning danced across the sky in rapid succession. A fierce rumbling of thunder followed, shaking the ground around Eleanor and her family. Christine tightened her hold on Eleanor's arm.

"Let's go, Eleanor, please . . ." she begged. "I don't like storms."

Eleanor lowered her umbrella and wrapped her arm around Christine. Rain swept across both their faces as they started back to the house. Lightning zigzagged in front of them as if it were searching for something it had lost on the ground. It frightened Eleanor and made her stop short. She tightened her hold on Christine, who started to cry.

"Let's hide in the trees," Christine pleaded, referring to the woods that surrounded the small cemetery on three sides.

"We're not safe near the trees," Eleanor yelled above the now pounding rain.

"The lightning is too close!" Christine screamed. "We need to hide!"

"Trust me!" Eleanor said, jerking Christine along the path to the house.

Another series of lightning bolts lit up the forest beside them and an ear-piercing crack let them know that the lightning had found a victim. A few seconds later, a large section of a mature pine tree tumbled to the ground. Christine screamed and tore free of Eleanor's grasp. She started running back across the cemetery to where the family had sought cover under a canopy of trees. Eleanor ran after her sister, but before she could catch up she lost her footing and fell into a sinkhole hidden by the dense undergrowth. Christine continued to scream as she ran—unaware that Eleanor had fallen. Eleanor clutched at the ground, struggling repeatedly to get out of the hole, but her heavy wet skirts and the saturated soil prevented her from gaining purchase.

The next series of lightning bolts lit up alternating sections of the cemetery. Headstones hidden in the darkness now jumped into view just long enough to announce their presence and disappear again into the backdrop of the storm. Each flash of light made it more difficult for Eleanor to see clearly.

She clawed frantically at the slushy mud beneath her, trying to release her feet, but each struggling movement forced her deeper into the ground. After several fruitless attempts to straighten herself, she lost what little footing she had and fell face first into a pool of saturated soil. The lace veil that shielded her face was plastered against her skin, making it difficult to breathe.

"Help! Somebody help me!" Eleanor screamed into the wet blackness, but her cries were no match for the angry sky that bellowed continuously with pounding thunder and blinding flashes of blue light. "Please help me!" she sobbed.

"Eleanor!" a man's voice called from the distance, but the violent vibrations of the ground distorted the sound making it impossible for Eleanor to discern who was calling her or how far away he was.

"Beth!" another man's voice called, only this voice came from somewhere beneath the ground. Eleanor struggled to grab hold of anything that might give her enough leverage to pull herself out of the sinkhole.

"Beth . . . !" The voice echoed in the thunder as something wrapped itself around one of Eleanor's legs and started to pull her down.

Eleanor screamed and began to kick frantically against the unseen force pulling her deeper into the earth. "NO!" she screamed, louder this time.

"Eleanor!" the first voice called again; it was closer now.

Eleanor fought, clutching desperately at the ground. Finally, she found something to wrap her hands around; it felt like a large root. She tried to pull herself up, but the harder she pulled the tighter the pressure grew around her leg, pulling her back down.

"Beth! Let go! I've got you."

"Eleanor, hang on!"

Eleanor was being pulled by two forces at once, but which command should she obey? One offered to pull her to certain safety, out of the miry mud that seemed determined to claim her. The other meant letting go of that safety and allowing herself to be swallowed up in the depths of the ground.

The thunder rumbled impatiently as sheets of rain swept across Eleanor's face and arms. She lay outstretched, clinging to life on the one end and fearing death on the other.

"Beth, there's no time. Let go—now!"

For a brief second, Beth—now housed in Eleanor's body—thought she recognized the voice.

But that's impossible, she thought to herself. *Grace is the only one who knows where I am. This can't be right.*

Before she could make sense of what was happening, a man's strong arms wrapped around her and pulled her from the ground. She felt the hold on her leg slip away—she was finally free.

"Hang on Eleanor, I've got you." Eleanor recognized her father's voice as he folded her in his arms and carried her through the storm toward the house.

Eleanor's mother and sister were waiting at the door when her father arrived. As soon as he was in earshot, he began barking orders to the staff.

"Get her bed ready," he said to Mrs. Weddington, their housekeeper. "And get the fire going in her room."

"Bring hot water and rags," he ordered another servant. "Get her out of these wet clothes."

Before she knew it, Eleanor was tucked snugly into bed—dry and safe—and completely unaware of two yellow eyes that watched her from the mirror in the corner of the room.

The Plan
CHAPTER 1

Approximately Nine Months Later...
Early March 1864

Dear Grace,

It's been a long time since we said goodbye in Uncle Connor's basement. I never would have had the courage to leave had I known I'd be apart from everyone I loved for so long. I sometimes wonder if you knew this would happen all along - maybe that's why Jonathan was so against the idea of me traveling. You assured me the night I arrived that my traveling was part of a bigger plan. Why would you say that unless you suspected all along that I was never coming home?

I used to dream about Jonathan. Sometimes the dreams were so real I actually believed I was home. But then I'd wake up and again find myself in Eleanor's bed, imprisoned in Eleanor's body.

"Eleanor?" Christine called from the distance. I couldn't help but smile. Christine had been my saving grace during the past nine months, ever since I arrived in Pennsylvania in July of 1863, just days after the Battle of Gettysburg. I knew she idolized me—that is, she idolized Eleanor—but I was feeling contrary at the moment, so instead of laying down my quill I deliberately ignored her.

"Eleanor!" Christine called again. "Land sakes, ELEANOR!"

I chuckled. Christine still hadn't figured out that bellowing my name from three stories below was not going to elicit a response from me. Ladies do not yell! I know this because embedded somewhere in the protocols of Christine's society, there is an understanding among the upper class that when a woman raises her voice, she exhibits an unbecoming lack of self-control and poise. I'd learned this the hard way, along with several other lessons foreign to twenty-first century girls. And to make matters worse, Eleanor had apparently been the poster child for propriety—at least she was until I came along and inhabited her body.

Had Christine remained at finishing school the way she should have, the head mistress would have disciplined her sharply for her display of impatience. But Eleanor's father had put boarding school on hold for Christine as well as a study abroad program for Eleanor. He felt the money normally spent on his daughters' formal education was needed elsewhere; namely, to support the war effort in providing much needed supplies and ammunition for the Northern troops. Everyone in Marensburg knew he could easily afford to do both, but he didn't want to flaunt his wealth among those who were less fortunate—which was pretty much the whole of Marensburg. I suppose he had a point.

I shook these thoughts from my head and returned to my letter.

I don't dream about Jonathan anymore, Grace. But you know what's even more frightening? Even in my dreams, I'm Eleanor. It's as though Beth Arrington never existed. Perhaps she's just someone Eleanor dreamed up while slumbering in the coma that held her at death's door for so long.

An abrupt knock on my bedroom door interrupted me. Christine! I blew on the ink and put the letter aside, pausing to stare at the handwriting that wasn't mine. Then I decided to dip my quill into the ink for a final note.

By the way, it might interest you to know that I'm engaged. Not officially of course, but it's only a matter of time. I bet you didn't see that one coming, did you?

"Eleanor?" Christine called impatiently from the hallway. "I know you can hear me."

Even through the thick wood door that separated us, I could tell she was panting—she must have run up both flights of stairs. I carefully laid the letter aside and started fiddling with the clips Lucinda Dolan, Eleanor's lady's maid, had placed in my hair earlier. Lucinda was an interesting girl and apparently not well liked by Mrs. Weddington. But then, I sometimes wondered if Mrs. Weddington liked anyone.

I picked up my brush and pulled it through the long curls that hung from the clip at the crown of my head. I never tired of brushing Eleanor's hair; it was the envy of every young woman she met. I stared in the mirror at her beautiful reflection, still awed by the perfect symmetry of her face. I wondered how it would be if I finally did make it home to the twenty-first century. Would I ever be able to view myself as pretty? Or would I long to be as beautiful as Eleanor Hastings for the rest of my life?

"Eleanor, please!" Christine whimpered from the hall. Please don't make us wait any longer."

I could tell by the consternation in her voice that she was about to cry. "Just a moment, I'm coming," I answered in a soft, unhurried voice. "I'm ready," I said, smiling as I opened the door. "Remember sister, a lady always takes her time tending to details. Often, it's the tiny details that matter the most." I tried to sound smug, but the disapproving frown on Christine's face told me I had missed something—again.

"Really, Eleanor," she said with a deep sigh. "I know you're doing this on purpose just to test me, but did you really think I wouldn't notice?"

I stared blankly at Christine for several moments trying to figure out what I'd forgotten, then I looked down at my hands.

"Rats!" I blurted. "Gloves! Good eye, little sister!"

Christine pursed her lips and shook her head in disapproval.

I went back to my vanity and picked up the lace gloves Lucinda had set out for me earlier, and thank goodness she had because I still couldn't get a handle on which gloves were appropriate for which time of day or which type of weather. You'd think after being in the nineteenth century for nine months I'd remember. I chuckled quietly to myself and wondered how many classes at Christine's boarding school were dedicated to the ins and outs of glove protocol. I remembered how my real mother, Hattie Arrington, used to tell stories about her grandmother and how she owned more pairs of gloves than most women owned shoes. I started to roll my eyes at the thought, but quickly caught myself; eye rolling was another etiquette "no-no."

"Aren't you going to post your letter?" Christine asked, eying the letter I'd left on the dressing table.

"What letter?" I asked innocently.

Christine shot me a look that told me I had just insulted her intelligence.

"Oh, that?" I faked a chuckle and quickly slid the letter into a drawer. "That, little sister, is none of your business. Now come, let's not keep mother waiting." I ignored Christine's scornful gaze and motioned for her to lead the way. Christine took a few steps toward the door, then turned around with both hands set firmly on her hips.

"I know where you hide them, Eleanor," she said indignantly.

"Hide what?" I replied, puzzled by her comment.

"You know what." Christine took a deep breath and sighed. "All your 'secret' letters."

"Letters?" I asked, honestly clueless. "From whom?"

"I haven't figured that part out yet, but don't worry, your secret is safe with me."

"What are you talking about?" I demanded.

"Oh never mind!" Christine huffed. "Let's just go." She turned toward the door and marched out into the hall.

"Christine, wait!" I ran after her and grabbed her by the arm. She spun around quickly, her eyes wide.

"What letters?" I shook my head, confused. "What hiding place?"

Christine's eyes filled with moisture. "I promise I won't tell, Eleanor."

My heart swelled with compassion for Christine and I released my hold. "I'm sorry, I shouldn't have grabbed you. But won't you please tell me what you know?"

She searched my eyes for a moment, baffled, and then replied, "I don't know anything for sure, but I caught you hiding something behind the hearth when you didn't know I was looking."

I stared at Christine in amazement but said nothing as she turned and ran down the stairs. I started to follow, then paused and glanced back at the fireplace. Making a concerted effort to concentrate, I searched Eleanor's mind—there was no memory of what Christine was referring to.

Mrs. Weddington and Eleanor's mother, Margaret Hastings, (formerly the wealthy Margaret Irene Hamilton of the Hamilton Estate in Greenburg, Pennsylvania) were waiting patiently when Christine and I arrived at the carriage. Mrs. Weddington took her role as housekeeper on our estate very seriously and seemed to share an unusually close relationship with Eleanor's mother. But from the first moment I met her, I got the feeling she didn't like me—not in the same way she didn't like Lucinda's Irish accent or the ginger hue in her hair that almost glowed bright orange in the sun (her hair irritated Mrs. Weddington for some reason and she forced Lucinda to always wear it pulled back in a tight bun), but in a way that said she didn't trust me.

It was Mrs. Weddington who'd been shocked to find Eleanor still alive nine months earlier, the night my spirit arrived in the nineteenth century and took over Eleanor's body. The night my own body, that is the body of Beth Arrington, seemingly disappeared somewhere between the present and the past. She had entered Eleanor's bedroom in the early hours of the morning carrying a basket of rose clippings. She had expected to find Eleanor dead and intended to spread the clippings throughout the room in an effort to cover the pungent odor of death. Imagine her surprise when she entered the darkened room and found Eleanor standing at the mirror, draped in her long white nightgown.

Mrs. Weddington had walked in at the precise moment I'd come to the realization that my spirit had taken over Eleanor's body. When I'd turned to her, Mrs. Weddington's face had blanched white with fear and the basket of roses she'd clung to fell to the floor. Her ensuing stream of high-pitched shrieks had awakened the entire household. In what seemed like a matter of seconds, a host of perfect strangers had flooded Eleanor's room and then stopped dead in their tracks, paralyzed as though they'd seen a ghost. But as soon as the shock wore off, they'd thrown their arms around me and sobbed—everyone, that is, except Mrs. Weddington.

"Come along girls," Mother called as Christine and I approached the carriage. "We have much planned this morning."

I chuckled. Depending on the day of the week, mother's "plan" was always the same. Today was Wednesday: that meant our day would begin at the Marensburg town square waiting for the latest news of the war and the dreaded posting of casualties. Afterwards, Mrs. Weddington and Christine would deliver fresh bread to the volunteers at the local hospital and visit the less critical patients while Eleanor's mother and I attended the weekly meeting of the Ladies Poetry Club. I wasn't crazy about poetry, but I enjoyed the refreshments and having an opportunity to observe the often-heated dynamics among the women of Marensburg. It reminded me of a Jane Austen movie; and I have to admit, I often found their bickering and posturing quite entertaining.

We were scarcely ten minutes from home, however, when the carriage jerked violently to one side. We heard a loud "snap" followed by a sharp clanking noise and the carriage began to wobble and teeter.

"Whoa . . . whoa!" the driver yelled as he steadied the horses. The four of us braced ourselves and waited while the driver climbed down, muttering profanely at the carriage. A few moments later, he opened the door and addressed Eleanor's mother.

"Beg pardon, Mrs. Hastings. It appears we've a broken wheel here."

"Thank you, Phillip," she said politely. She thought for a moment and then took a deep breath. "Girls, I believe it's a lovely day for a walk. What do you say?"

"But Mrs. Hastings," Mrs. Weddington spoke up, "the girls will soil their dresses."

"Nonsense!" Mother smiled. "The weather is mild for March and the walk will do us good. Phillip?"

"Yes, Mrs. Hastings."

"Help us out of this contraption, please."

Phillip offered his hand as one by one we climbed out of the injured carriage. Mother was the last one out and began walking briskly toward town.

"Come along, ladies," she called. "We'll not let something as insignificant as a broken wheel spoil our day. Phillip, please send another carriage to meet us at half past noon."

"Yes, Mrs. Hastings."

"Now then," Mother began, "if all goes as planned, we'll arrive at the Town Square just after the crowd disperses and still have plenty of time for a glass of lemonade before the Poetry Club begins."

If all goes as planned, I thought, *if all goes as planned. . . .* The words reverberated through my head until I felt slightly nauseated. If all went as "planned" I would have been home nine months ago! But *nothing* was going as planned. My plans to launch a career as a concert pianist died in the car accident that killed my mother, severely injured my left hand, and left me in a coma for nearly seven months.   I was convinced I would never play the piano again. Oh yes, I was the "poster child" for plans gone awry.

Pity party—party of one, I scoffed mentally. That's what my mother always said whenever she wanted to tease me for feeling sorry for myself. My mom had a knack for using humor and sarcasm to spin a new perspective on almost any negative situation.

I miss my mom.

As I continued to walk along the dusty road into Marensburg with Eleanor's family, my mind wandered back over the past year and a half. When I moved to Andersen, Wyoming, the summer before my senior year of high school, my plan was to search for answers regarding the suspicious circumstances surrounding my mother's death. What I discovered was that she possessed information—information so important she was willing to die protecting it. I also discovered that an army of supernatural beings known as Intruders were on a mission to take over my mind and body. Why? Because I'm the offspring of an immortal mother and a mortal father and as such, I hold the potential for *reclamation*—a process whereby my human cells could reclaim their primordial immortal genetic encoding. If the Intruders could gain control of me before my reclamation, they would successfully achieve the one thing they desired more than anything else—a tangible body to house their unembodied souls. But not just any body—a body with the capability of experiencing heightened emotions, unlimited passion, and unparalleled physical abilities. Still, I wasn't the only one the Intruders were after. They were seeking out all those nearing the age of adulthood who they suspected might experience reclamation.

So why send an army of Intruders after just one soul—after me? Because that was Bailey's "plan." I shuddered as I remembered that as the leader of the Intruders he'd developed a sadistic crush on me. Over time, his feelings morphed into a sick obsession. He wanted to unite his soul with mine, two souls sharing one body—an immortal body—because he believed it would make him all powerful, like God.

When Bailey's attempts to seduce me through friendship failed, he'd resorted to coercion—both physical and emotional. Thanks to Jonathan, those attempts were thwarted. But Bailey was determined, and when his last attempt to get to me through my friend Eric backfired, it unleashed a raging anger in him. Eric had died as a result of what Bailey did, but Bailey vowed to return with his legion of followers and finish what he'd begun. And that's how I ended up in the 1800s living in someone else's body.

It was Jonathan's sister Grace who came up with the "plan"—a supposedly fail-safe plan to protect me from Bailey's army of Intruders—the same plan that had inadvertently trapped me in 1864 Pennsylvania. The procedure was supposed to be simple and it was—in theory. Grace would transport me back in time to "hide" me while Jonathan stayed in the twenty-first century to train a specialized group of immortals to eliminate the Intruders' threat once and for all. I was intrigued by her plan—the very concept was irresistible. As the daughter of a scientist, I couldn't pass up the opportunity to explore the possibilities of time travel. And when Grace asked me where I wanted to go in the past, I jumped at the chance to catch a glimpse of Jonathan as a bratty little toddler, years before his reclamation began (as offspring of immortal parents, both Jonathan and Grace would experience reclamation first hand; reclamation was their birthright).

However, only hindsight is 20/20. Looking back now, it's obvious my reasoning wasn't sound. If I had possessed an immortal body, perhaps Grace's plan would have gone off without a hitch; but as I mentioned, I was the queen of plans gone awry. I was only supposed to stay in the past for two weeks, or more accurately, that's all Jonathan would allow. It didn't seem like too great a price to pay to keep me safe. Had Jonathan known that my mortal body couldn't make the journey, or that I would wind up in the body of Eleanor Hastings, his first love, he would have pulled the plug on the whole plan. Right?

I could no longer deny the fact that I was sharing both Eleanor's body *and* her memories. They weren't vivid memories, more like distant dreams, but sometimes I had trouble distinguishing between her memories and mine. Beyond that, we were opposites in nearly every aspect of our personalities. She was elegant, refined, deliberate, and surprisingly aloof at times. I was casual, inquisitive, stubborn, and laughed freely—something Eleanor would never allow herself to do. Yet in spite of our fundamental differences, Eleanor and I shared one passion: we both loved music.

I thought for a minute about her pianos. They weren't like the pianos I was used to playing; they were much bigger and produced a different sound. The one in the drawing room was similar to a pianoforte whereas the one in the ballroom was as grand as any I had ever played. It didn't possess the clarity of sound I was accustomed to, but the acoustics in the ballroom were amazing and the instrument's rich tones resonated with such power that clarity didn't matter. Besides, the elation I felt each time I put Eleanor's perfect hands on the keyboard more than made up for any complaints I may have had about her antiquated instruments. I had spent hours a day sitting at the piano, bathed in gratitude for the chance to play again as a whole person, without any pain or stiffness. Unfortunately, my obsession with the piano had alarmed Eleanor's family (more particularly the servants) because I played every song in my repertoire, including those that Eleanor hadn't learned and others that hadn't even been composed yet.

I can hear Mrs. Weddington now: "It's the devil's music, I tell you. The very devil himself!" She was convinced that only witchcraft or the unsavory works of Satan could have brought Eleanor back to life so unexpectedly. After all, Eleanor had been on her deathbed; the entire family had accepted the fact that her demise was imminent. My spirit had entered her body just seconds before her last breath. It was no wonder Mrs. Weddington eyed me with suspicion and repeatedly complained to Eleanor's mother. Fortunately, Eleanor's mother didn't see the point of humoring Mrs. Weddington's overactive imagination and eventually the accusations stopped.

"Come on, Eleanor!" Christine nagged. "Why do you always insist on being such a slowpoke! We'll never get into Marensburg."

"You leave Miss Eleanor to her thoughts, child," Mrs. Weddington said. (I was surprised to hear her defending me!) "She has much on her mind these days."

"That's right," Eleanor's mother interjected. "The Debutante Ball will be here before we know it, and Colonel Hamilton will be visiting soon." Mother looked back at me and winked.

Ah yes, Colonel Hamilton. Colonel William Carlton Hamilton, to be more exact. I had yet to actually meet the man, but I'd learned a few weeks after arriving that Colonel Hamilton was Eleanor's intended betrothed. From what I could piece together, Eleanor's father had entered into an agreement long ago with one of Eleanor's mother's relatives—some cousin or second cousin or whatever. Supposedly, Colonel Hamilton was a direct descendent of Kristoff Friedrich Marens, cofounder of Marensburg, although Colonel Hamilton and his family were not actual residents of Marensburg.

I readily admit, I have a difficult time trying to keep track of who's who in Eleanor's family. Her father, a Hastings, came from old money. They were one of the first families to settle near Marensburg. Because of his huge estate and multiple connections throughout the East Coast, Eleanor's father wielded a great deal of power among Marensburg's elite. Eleanor's mother, on the other hand, claimed to be a descendent of German royalty two or three times removed. There had been so much inbreeding in the Marens family that I was surprised Eleanor didn't end up with a few extra fingers and toes; but apparently, marrying your cousin was a common practice in many aristocratic families—at least it was prior to the twentieth century.

"Have you and Father decided when you're going to announce Eleanor's marriage?" I heard Christine ask her mother.

"Your father would like it to be a surprise, but I expect it won't be long now."

"Will it be a grand wedding, Mother?" Christine asked with her usual enthusiasm. She was always so eager and happy. I could count on her to shed a positive light on even the gloomiest moments.

Eleanor's mother chuckled. "Oh, I doubt it will be grand by your standards, my dear." She cast a quick glance towards Mrs. Weddington and winked. "In fact, if your father has his way, it will be a private ceremony held in our gardens with few embellishments."

"Oh Mother, he wouldn't!" Christine complained. "Surely he wouldn't dare!"

I couldn't help smiling as I watched Eleanor's mother and Mrs. Weddington try not to laugh. I'd have laughed myself, but every time I heard someone bring up the subject of Eleanor marrying Colonel Hamilton, I got an uneasy feeling in the pit of my stomach. Jonathan had told me very little about Eleanor, other than she was supposed to marry a man she didn't love. I'd presumed he was talking about Colonel Hamilton. That was why Jonathan had been so determined to come back for her—determined to the point of leaving his post without permission—a decision that had cost his family dearly.

As we got closer to Marensburg, Mother shifted the conversation away from Eleanor's wedding and focused instead on a detailed discussion of decorations for the Debutante Ball—which was only a few weeks away. I continued to hang back, content to drink in the warmth of the morning sun and think. *Nine months . . . still no word from Grace, Jonathan, Uncle Connor, or even my crazy cousin Carl. Why am I still here? What has gone wrong? Did Bailey and his legions win? Is that why my blood chills every time I catch a movement from the corner of my eye or sense someone watching me when there's nobody else around?*

"Eleanor? Are you all right?" Christine slowed her pace, allowing me to catch up with her. "You seem troubled."

I glanced down at Christine's innocent eyes. She had sensed early on that there was something different about Eleanor after her illness. It wasn't anything she said that led me to this conclusion; it was more what she didn't say. I couldn't help but detect a sense of longing in her, as though she desperately wanted to reconnect with Eleanor, but something seemed wrong. I often felt a twinge of guilt when I couldn't give her what she desired most—her sister.

I slid my arm through Christine's and smiled. "How can I be sad when I have you around?" Christine grinned and patted the top of my hand.

"Let's skip, okay?" Her young face was eager.

I took a deep breath, pretending to be bothered by her girlish suggestion, then abruptly went skipping down the road with her in youthful abandon.

Just as Eleanor's mother predicted, we arrived in town just after the dramatic posting of Wednesday's casualties, a ritual that started soon after the war broke out. After the bloody battle of Gettysburg, which was only a few miles east of Marensburg, the weekly postings had become increasingly devastating. It was through these postings that the Hastings learned their two oldest sons had been killed.

The mood of the people told us that today was a good day, however. Out of the hundreds of names posted on the casualty list, none were identified as family members or friends. The whole town seemed to breathe a sigh of relief as people went about their daily affairs.

After enjoying some cold lemonade, Christine and Mrs. Weddington left for the hospital while Eleanor's mother and I started for the Poetry Club. As we rounded a corner and approached the post office, I could overhear part of a conversation between two men standing by the main entrance. Normally, I would have ignored them—eavesdropping was not ladylike—but something about the men's conversation struck me as familiar.

"It's like I said," one of the men was saying, "this had nothing to do with the war."

"I say you're dead wrong about that," the other argued. "It's Harrisburg all over again."

"The two attacks are nothing alike!" the first man insisted. "Listen to me, I was there! I saw that poor woman's body. She wasn't just violated, she was—well, I ain't never seen nothing like that, least not around these parts. It weren't the war put that kinda fear on that girl's face."

A sudden chill ran down my spine as the man continued.

"And two more went missing last week just over in Greenburg. I'm telling you, it's just a matter of time before—"

The second man cleared his throat when he realized I could overhear what they were saying and the conversation stopped short.

"Morning Mrs. Hastings, Miss Hastings," both men said, tipping their hats.

I wasn't surprised that the men recognized us; everyone knew who the Hastings were—particularly Eleanor, the wealthy Hastings' beautiful daughter.

Mother and I nodded politely to each of the men without addressing them. They waited until they thought we were out of earshot, then I heard the first man say, "That Colonel Hamilton is one lucky fellow."

"Come along, Eleanor," Mother said, prodding me to walk a little faster. "We don't want to be late to the club."

The Poetry Club always met immediately after the Wednesday postings to read poems and gossip—a lot! The ladies had a predetermined schedule. Besides poetry readings on Wednesday mornings, Fridays were set aside for charity, which meant distributing bread, soup, and fruit to those on the "other" side of town. The younger women spent most afternoons doing lessons, refining their needle craft, reading the Bible, and practicing their music lessons.

I found that life as Eleanor Hastings was definitely not dull since in addition to the weekly routine followed by the elite in general, Mondays and Thursdays Eleanor and her mother made calls and Tuesday mornings they went to the market. Tuesday and Thursday afternoons were their "at home" times, complete with tea and biscuits. Saturdays the family gathered berries, arranged flowers, took long walks, and went riding (there was usually a picnic basket involved). This was supposed to be our "leisure" day, but it often felt like work to me. Sundays we went to church and then gathered for the weekly Sunday luncheon hosted by one of Marensburg's finest.

And of course, mingled among all these activities were dinner parties and bridge nights. Whew! Contrary to what I might have expected, the rich were not idle people. Had they been, father would have used his influence to change things. He firmly believed that idleness was a sin and a tool of the devil, and that those who squandered their precious allotment of time in idle pursuits would find the gates of Heaven locked in the afterlife.

Eleanor's father was not alone in his belief since her mother held to the same value system, one of the few topics on which they both agreed. Eleanor's mother took it a step further, however. Although some of the women varied the weekly schedule a little, she adhered to it strictly, and saw to it that we all did the same. It wasn't enough that we were busy, we had to be busy doing the right things—*right* as defined by Marensburg society, that is. This also involved abiding by a strict code of etiquette when it came to providing charitable service and paying calls. I soon learned that Eleanor's mother had zero tolerance for mistakes when paying calls. She insisted on following the strict letter of the law, not because of any fondness on her part toward the women she visited (some of them she couldn't stand), but because she prided herself on setting the bar high for Marensburg's elite.

Due to Wednesday's rigorous routine, I was tired at the end of the day. But when I was finally alone with my thoughts the longing for my life as Beth Arrington returned, and with it a burden of hopelessness and despair. I retrieved the letter I'd written earlier and suddenly remembered what Christine had said about Eleanor hiding something behind the hearth. I moved cautiously to the fireplace and began fidgeting with the stones, looking for a crevice or an opening, anything that might indicate a hiding place. After several minutes of searching, I gave up my half-hearted effort.

Silly Beth, I thought. What were you hoping to find? *Some secret message miraculously sent from the future?*

My thoughts faded into the orange glow of the fire's embers. I watched as the light from the dying flames danced against the dark perimeter of my bedroom, my "chamber" as Lucinda called it. I chuckled softly to myself and then moved back to Eleanor's desk. I turned up the flame on the oil lamp, picked up a quill, and continued writing.

The night you brought me to the 1800s, Grace, you told me

my memories would fade quickly. Fortunately, you were wrong about that. Some of the details are a little cloudy, but painfully, I've hung onto most of my memories. And that's not all you were wrong about. You and Jonathan assured me that Bailey and his henchmen would never find me here in the past - that I'd be safe here because Intruders can't travel - but Bailey is here, Grace. Don't ask me how I know, I just know. Maybe it's that moment when I catch a glimpse of something in the mirror, or when I sense a quick movement behind me and when I turn, there's nothing there. I don't know, I can't explain it exactly, but I know I'm not imagining it. Bailey's here Grace. I can feel him. Only question is, what's he waiting for? Why hasn't he made contact?

I blew on the ink and waited for it to dry. Then, as I'd done with every other letter I'd written to Grace or Jonathan, I carried the letter to the fireplace and dropped it carefully into the flames.

"Oh, Jonathan!" I whispered softly to myself as I settled into bed for the night. "Where are you?"

Tears ran unchecked down my cheeks. It was too unpleasant to consider the possibilities of what may have happened, and unbearable to accept the only possible explanation that made any sense—that the Intruders had won the battle.

I flipped over onto my side and tried to think of something else—something safe and secure, like the feeling of being in Jonathan's arms. But the harder I fought to remember the warmth of his embrace, the cloudier my memories became as I drifted off into a dreamless sleep.

Mistaken Identity
CHAPTER 2

*F*ree time was not the only rarity I experienced as Eleanor; time alone (meaning without a servant nearby or a chaperone watching my every move) was even rarer than leisure time. Enjoying both at the same time was almost unheard of. I occasionally feigned illness just so I could have some time to myself, but that quickly backfired when Mrs. Weddington convinced Eleanor's mother she should call for the doctor whenever I had an "episode." She still seemed convinced I was hiding something and would check on me repeatedly under the guise of *concern* for my state of health.

On the few occasions when I was able to convince Eleanor's mother to make her calls and travel into town without me, the guilt wore on me so heavily that I had a difficult time enjoying my freedom. I couldn't relish my "me time" knowing that most of the women of Marensburg dedicated their mornings and afternoons to the needs of the war effort. Spending one's free time on selfish indulgences or pursuits was viewed with silent contempt by the elite and outright disdain by those less schooled and polished.

Naturally, I didn't share the town's angst and sense of urgency when it came to supporting the Union army because I had it in the back of my mind that we were on the winning team. After all, in another year the South would surrender and all would be back to normal, right? Knowing the final outcome of the war gave me a unique sense of security, which unfortunately left some with the false impression that I was apathetic to the Union cause. Eleanor's mother covered for me on more than one occasion by explaining that she'd been cautioned by the family physician against exposing me to any stressful activity or disturbing conversations surrounding the war. But I could see the disapproval in her eyes and sensed that she felt I was betraying the family honor by not taking a more active interest in doing my part to support our Union soldiers.

"What if Charles and Miles were the ones benefiting from our efforts?" Eleanor's mother would often remind me. "I cannot bear to think for even a moment of my dear boys out there fighting for our cause without benefit of blankets, clothing, or food. No. The very idea is too awful to consider."

Eleanor's mother was right. Despite the fact that I felt no emotional ties to Eleanor's brothers, throwing Charles and Miles into the debate was always the trump card that sealed my guilt. All I had to do was think of Jonathan and my cousin, Carl, who were both engaged in a very dangerous, very different kind of battle in the twenty-first century. I would do anything and everything within my power to help them if I were back home.

And so I did my part with the ladies of Marensburg society. We visited wounded soldiers at the hospital and wrote out letters for those unable to write themselves. And we sewed uniforms and made blankets and put together care packages for the soldiers in our surrounding territories, as far east and north as Harrisburg, and as far south as Chambersburg and Mercersburg.

Along with supporting the war efforts, members of Marensburg society took an active interest in the political campaign to elect Abraham Lincoln to his second term as President. Though most talk of politics was out of earshot of Marensburg's finer sex, the elite ladies of society prided themselves on doing their part to promote the party. They did this subtly, of course, and only under the direction of their husbands.

With so many external distractions, it was difficult for me to expend much effort in promoting my own cause. There was no doubt in my mind that many of my memories as Beth were continuing to fade, so I decided to keep a personal journal in the hope that as my memories faded (as Grace indicated they would) I might somehow retain some connection with the twenty-first century. It never occurred to me that someone else in the house possessed a key to the trunk where I kept the journal hidden. I could never prove it, but I was certain it was Mrs. Weddington who found it (no doubt while snooping through Eleanor's belongings), and she took it straight to Eleanor's father.

Eleanor's father was not a large man. He did, however, have a presence about him that commanded respect. He stood about 5'8" tall and walked with a heavy limp due to an injury sustained while fighting in the war with Mexico. He sometimes used a cane when the pain became unbearable, but doing so angered him. He probably thought it made him look weak. On more than one occasion, I had witnessed him heave it across the room in a fit of anger and frustration. Fortunately, he didn't have his cane with him when he called me to his office and confronted me about my journal.

I have to admit, though, he had a point when he told me there was no reasonable explanation for such notions to be running through my head. (I mean, how do you explain time travel to someone in the mid 1800s?) He made it explicitly clear that he would not tolerate such appalling behavior on my part.

Mrs. Weddington saw my journal as further evidence that Eleanor was under the influence of a demon. I suppose in a roundabout way she was closer to the truth than anybody realized—not that I considered myself a demon by any stretch of the imagination—but the truth was, I did possess Eleanor's body. So in that sense, Mrs. Weddington was at least half right. Eleanor's father, on the other hand, blamed Eleanor's shameful behavior on willful defiance. I'm not sure which was worse.

"This is an outrage!" he shouted as he threw my journal on his desk.

I stood stunned, intimidated by the bulging veins in his forehead and neck.

"How dare you bring this filth into my house!"

"I didn't br—"

"Silence!" Father roared. "You will speak only when I tell you to!"

"Yes, sir." I lowered my head. I hated cowering before him, but I sensed deep down (perhaps a feeling coming from Eleanor) that I had best not cross him.

"I demand you tell me who is responsible for filling your head with such despicable rubbish!"

I made no attempt to reply—mostly because I couldn't think that fast under pressure.

"WELL?" Father shouted.

"Nobody," I said quietly.

"Speak up child!" he demanded.

I raised my eyes to meet his glare. "Nobody! They are my own thoughts."

"For what possible purpose would you write such . . ." he searched for the right word, "such nonsense?" He picked up the journal and began reading from the first page:

"My name is Elizabeth Anne Arrington. Those who know me and love me call me Beth. I grew up in Southern California, but moved to Andersen, Wyoming, after the unexpected death of my mother. There I met a young man named Jonathan, who I later learned wasn't so young after all. We fell in love, but unseen forces have combined to try and keep us apart. I have traveled from the twenty-first century to Civil War Pennsylvania in order to hide from a group of Intruders who wish to claim my soul."

Father shoved the journal away from him. "No daughter of mine could claim these thoughts as her own. I insist you tell me where such utter foolishness comes from. It's absurd! Why, it's a complete disgrace to this family! Is this the kind of poppycock that goes on in that Poetry Club your mother insists on dragging you to each week?"

"No, Father. This has nothing to do with that. This is just a story I started to write." An idea was forming in my mind. "It's a story about a girl who traveled to our day from the twenty-first century. I only meant it to—"

"It's the gibberish of unlearned trash!" he bellowed. "I'll hear no more of this! Do you understand me?"

"Yes Father."

He glared at me for a few moments before he finally dismissed me, waving his hands at me as if shooing me away.

"Father, may I have my journal back, please?" I don't know what possessed me to ask that question, but you would have thought I had just committed a mortal sin judging by Father's reaction. I thought for a moment that if he didn't relax, his face would literally split in two.

He grabbed the journal from his desk and proceeded to tear out all the pages I had written. He wadded them up and then limped angrily over to the fire and threw them into the flames. I watched as memories of my life as Beth Arrington turned blue in the heat of the fire and crumbled into ashes. He walked back to his desk and retrieved the journal which he then handed to me.

"Yes, you may have it back," he replied. "Only this time, you will produce something worthwhile."

I stared at the leather binder full of blank pages. "I don't understand?"

"You will spend the next several days copying the Book of Exodus. That is a story worth telling."

I didn't bother to ask if he meant the entire book—I'd made that mistake once before when he made me copy the Book of Ruth. I had been uncivil to Eleanor's mother at the dinner table (I'm sure it had something to do with wearing gloves) and Father thought I needed to learn a lesson about loyalty; hence, I'd spent two days confined to my room until I finished copying what I thought was the most important part of the story. When I gave the pages to Father the next evening before dinner, he tore them up and made me start over. Three nights later, I handed him the book in its entirety and was finally granted permission to rejoin the family for the evening meal.

Eleanor's mother deferred all decisions of any consequence to Eleanor's father, including, at times, decisions about how to discipline their children. Eleanor's mother tended to trouble herself only with those issues that involved etiquette, propriety, and her children's schooling. This was a source of much discord between them, and on more than one occasion Eleanor's father had pulled rank and ordered his wife to dole out the discipline.

It really didn't matter who did the disciplining, the punishment was usually the same, and judging by the size of the Book of Exodus, it would be at least a week before I ate dinner with the family again.

A week and a half later, after finishing my stint with Moses and the children of Israel, I was granted my freedom. Father never mentioned the journal again, nor did he acknowledge the fact that anything was out of the ordinary when Mother complained about the large calluses that had formed on my index and middle fingers.

"That's the sign of a worthy scholar, Mrs. Hastings." (He commonly referred to her as "Mrs. Hastings" whenever he wanted to remind her of exactly who was in charge. Mother never seemed to notice or care).

"Well, I suppose nobody will see the calluses so long as she wears her gloves."

Groan. Again with the gloves!

After the journal escapade, I did my best to keep a low profile. I performed my societal duties in town as expected, and when home, focused on my needlepoint, helped Christine with her lessons, played the piano without drawing attention to myself, and generally tried to keep my mouth shut as much as possible.

I thought about rewriting the destroyed pages from my journal but decided against it because I couldn't think of a safe enough place to hide them. I figured it best to seek an alternative strategy for hanging onto my memories of the twenty-first century. But after Christine divulged Eleanor's secret about hiding her letters somewhere in the hearth, I was hopeful I might have another opportunity to write my story after all.

I tried several times to find Eleanor's hidden letters. I don't know what motivated me the most—the hope of finding somewhere safe to hide my journal or the intrigue of knowing that Eleanor had secrets. But regardless of my motives, my repeated attempts to find her hiding place failed. This was a huge disappointment for me. I even tried to force my way into Eleanor's memories, but I couldn't access the thoughts buried deep inside her mind. Frustrated, I decided I had no other alternative but to be patient for I suspected that as the barrier separating Eleanor's memories from my own weakened, it would only be a matter of time before she could no longer withhold her secrets from me. I feared, however, that time was a luxury I might not have; especially if I planned to hang onto my memories of the twenty-first century with any hope of clarity.

The thought came into my mind late one night that if I could possibly earn Eleanor's trust, she might willingly divulge her secrets to me. Regrettably, I knew my only hope of gaining her confidence was if I could somehow manage to keep her out of trouble. Unfortunately, that meant being on my best behavior and playing by the rules. Although it wouldn't be easy, I resolved to become an upstanding model of propriety. I would make sure to be and do everything that the people of Marensburg expected from the daughter of Charles Frederick Hastings II.

I must have played my role well because crotchety old Mrs. Weddington finally seemed to warm up to me and eventually quit muttering about Eleanor being possessed. Winning her over was a huge accomplishment. But there was still Eleanor's father to contend with and unfortunately for me, I knew he would prove to be my greatest challenge.

By the beginning of May, spring growth was in full bloom. I made every attempt possible to spend time outdoors exploring the Hastings' property. Bees worked busily spreading pollen from flower to flower and birds gathered twigs to begin building their nests. Since the fruit trees had managed to survive the last freeze, the air was rich with the odors of cherry and apple blossoms. For the most part, it looked as though fresh fruit would be in abundance during the summer.

Sketchpad in hand, I skipped along a stone path at the back of the estate and headed for a narrow trail that led to a stream on the south side of the Hastings' property. The path was lined by rows of well-manicured rose bushes that were on the verge of exploding into a frenzy of color. It was so beautiful—but the part I liked best was the freedom to roam without bothersome chaperones along. I was free as long as I was back in the house before twilight. Any later and I would have to find a servant, relative, or close friend to accompany me. Needless to say, I was careful to watch the sun.

The first time I explored the path, I was amazed to discover that the Hastings owned all the land down to and across the stream that emptied into a larger river further south. If someone had told me that the Hastings' estate spanned more than one hundred acres, I would have scoffed and said they were crazy; but the truth was, the estate was twice that size, and then some.

Estates boasting such large spreads of land were almost always open to travelers. It wasn't uncommon to bump into a familiar face now and then, but to me they were all strangers. Before the weather turned the previous fall, I had crossed the path of a family on their way to Greenburg who turned out to be cousins of Eleanor's mother. They didn't stop to visit, and I learned later that Eleanor's mother was not too keen on that part of her family. It seems she and her aunt had a falling out over something (no doubt something trivial), and were not on the best of terms.

I continued on down the path but instead of stopping at my usual spot—a felled tree next to the stream where I normally sat to sketch—I decided to stroll further upstream to search for a new view. As Beth, I had zero talent when it came to drawing or sketching; however, Eleanor was a different story. I found that whenever I held a charcoal to my sketchpad, the movements of my hands became automatic—fluid—even poetic. The fact that Eleanor possessed this talent should not have surprised me. Was there any flaw in this girl? It was no wonder Jonathan had fallen for her. I couldn't help comparing myself to her and every time I came up short. I hated feeling this way. I wasn't normally insecure, but I couldn't help wondering what it was about Beth that caught Jonathan's eye once he had known Eleanor's beauty and refinement.

As I walked, I closed my eyes and focused on the sound of the running water. An image of Jonathan flashed through my mind, sitting, knees bent, arms folded around his legs, listening to the sound of the air rushing through the trees at the Upper Palisades. For a brief moment, the vision was as clear as if he were sitting with me now. I held onto the memory as tightly as I could, wishing that I had reached over and touched him that day so I could touch him now in my mind. I struggled to recall the way he smelled, the wave of his hair, and the way I felt the last time we were together when he kissed me on the floor of Uncle Connor's basement. My memories of Jonathan kept me going, yet I feared they, too, threatened to fade with the passage of time.

He'll come for me, I thought to myself. *He promised. He would never leave me alone in the past intentionally.*

The part of me that was Eleanor did not share the longing ache I felt for my family in the twenty-first century. Her thoughts, though weak and obscure, seemed to focus on things like books, music, drawing, and of course, the man she would soon be engaged to marry—although there seemed to be very mixed feelings emanating from her regarding him. I couldn't explain it, but Eleanor was worried about him. I figured it had something to do with the war, but I couldn't shake the sense that there was more to it than that.

Also mingled among Eleanor's thoughts were dreams of her big night—the night she would be formally introduced into society. I sensed that Eleanor was looking forward to that with excitement. As for me, I dreaded it. Not that I didn't enjoy dancing and socializing, but I feared I wouldn't be able to conduct myself according to all the expectations of Marensburg society.

"Eleanor! Eleanor!" Christine's unexpected call startled me. I spun around in time to see her trotting down the path in my direction.

"Be careful Christine," I called, curious that I so often found myself mothering her.

Christine was nearing fourteen years of age and was destined to be as beautiful, if not more beautiful, than Eleanor. But Christine lacked the poise and grace of her older sister, giving herself to more abrupt spontaneity. I couldn't help liking her. It was a shame that she was forced to curb her enthusiasm at nearly every turn, but that was the custom. Christine obviously idolized Eleanor. She watched her every move and mimicked her with precision. But right now, "Eleanor" was not exactly the best of role models.

"Slow down, will you?" I called. I smiled as she tried to hold her hem away from the mass of scattered leaves and sticks that carpeted the ground. She stumbled on a bent root, but caught herself, recovering just in time to catch the bottom of her dress on a protruding dead branch.

"Sakes!" she sighed, frustrated. "Why do you insist on the most inconvenient places to work on your sketches?"

I chuckled and offered her a hand as she approached. "With so many travelers lately, I prefer places off the beaten path."

"Well, you've certainly succeeded," she grumbled. She hitched the hem of her skirt to the side and scooted next to me on the fallen log. Her eyes surveyed the scenery around us, then she looked down at the blank page in my sketchpad. "What are you planning to sketch?"

Without thinking, I shrugged my shoulders.

"Good heavens! Don't let Mother see you do that." Christine's horrified expression made me laugh. "She'll order Mrs. Weddington to take a strap to you." She made a nasty face, imitating Mrs. Weddington's seemingly permanent scowl perfectly.

"I don't think it would matter much with all this padding," I laughed, patting my behind.

Christine opened her mouth but then shook her head. "Sometimes, I don't know what you are thinking."

"Did you need me for some reason?" I asked, changing the subject.

"No. I wanted to watch the travelers, so Miss Dolan sent me out find you. She said I could only come out if I stayed where you could see me."

"Well, you might be disappointed. There haven't been any travelers yet this morning."

"Yesterday, when I was walking with Miss Dolan, there were lots— whole families even. But mostly there were soldiers, way more than usual. They're my favorites. They always look so . . ." she paused, hunting for the right word.

"Anxious?" I offered.

"I suppose," she said, then shook her head. "It's more than that. It's like they've lost something they can never get back."

"Hmm, I imagine they have."

Christine's comments made me think of the soldiers who lay recovering from wounds in the Marensburg hospital. Many of them had a faraway expression in their eyes—pining for home I guessed. The eyes of others were hollow, as if they'd been permanently changed. And they were the soldiers with the less serious wounds. Those with more life-threatening injuries were usually transported to the hospital in Harrisburg.

Ever since Gettysburg, the Union had made concerted efforts to strengthen its position along the southern border of Pennsylvania. This meant a greater number of forts in the neighboring townships and more soldiers positioned in nearby communities. Marensburg, though further north than some of the more vulnerable areas, was among those that had seen an increase of Union soldiers recently. This influx of soldiers made Eleanor's mother particularly happy because in her mind, it meant there were more men who'd be able to attend this season's Debutante Ball.

"You know," Christine said thoughtfully, "when the war first began the boys couldn't wait to run and join, but now . . . it's different."

A picture flashed across my mind—an old photograph of Jonathan standing in full uniform, face partially shielded by his hat. And then, just as quickly, I remembered the beautiful woman portrayed in the photograph next to his. Eleanor.

I shook the images of Jonathan and Eleanor from my mind and focused again on Christine. She wasn't like the girls her age in the twenty-first century. Though innocent, she possessed a maturity that made her seem much older than modern-day fourteen year olds. Was it war that caused young people to age so quickly?

"May I see what you're sketching today?" Christine eyed my sketchbook carefully, then gasped as I uncovered the portrait I had been working on earlier. "Oh Eleanor! She's beautiful! Who is it?"

"Nobody in particular. I just sketch what my mind sees."

"She's lovely," Christine smiled, then her face brightened and her eyes widened. "Would you sketch me? And make me look as pretty as her?"

I laughed openly at her honesty as I reached for her chin, turning her face gently from side to side. "I don't know," I teased, "I'm not sure I'm that good."

Christine frowned and I chuckled. "Sweetie, it would be impossible to capture your radiance in one of my silly old sketches."

"Oh, please try, won't you? Father says you could make the most wretched person look handsome when you draw."

I tilted my head slightly and smiled. "Oh, Father said that, did he?" Eleanor's father was a man of rare words. When he spoke, everyone listened. I couldn't imagine him expending effort to placate the whims of one of his children. Still, Christine was painfully honest. Father did not give compliments easily, so for him to make such a comment to Christine was evidence of Eleanor's talents with a sketchpad.

"Please?" Christine pressed. Her pleading gaze made it obvious she wasn't going to relent.

"You'll have to hold perfectly still," I reminded her. I'd tried to sketch her in the past but she could never remain seated in one position long enough for me to get very far.

"I'll be still as a statue, promise." Christine's grin broadened into a triumphant smile.

"Well, we'll see about that," I chuckled. "It will take a while."

I held the charcoal loosely and began to trace the oval contour of Christine's face, marveling at how perfectly symmetrical her delicate features were. Each side of her face was an exact mirror image of the other. She remained frozen for several minutes while I worked on the shape of her eyes. There was something very familiar about them. I searched my memory in an effort to recall images from my life as Beth, but came up empty. I was concentrating on the subtle lift of their outer corners when Christine suddenly jumped up, balancing her weight against my shoulders.

"Look!" she squealed, pointing behind me.

"My, that didn't take long. Distracted already?"

"No, look! It's a traveler!" She leaned forward, as if doing so would help her see more clearly through her squinted eyes.

"Oh! And look!" She bounced up and down, squeezing my shoulder. "I think he's a soldier!"

I gathered my pencils and pad, resting them securely against the log before turning around to spy on Christine's traveler, who was undoubtedly unaware of his eager audience. Although travelers on the estate were common, we rarely ran across a lone soldier. Soldiers tended to travel in groups unless, of course, they were on leave and headed for home. I shielded the sun from my eyes and watched as he came more fully into view.

At first I was sure I was seeing things, that my foolish imagination was playing tricks on me. But seeing him even from a distance struck me with such force that all thoughts of reason disappeared. My unraveled nerves clamored with anticipation as I hoped what I was seeing was real—that Jonathan had finally come to take me home!

To say I wasn't thinking clearly would be a gross understatement. Emotion overcame me when he reached the edge of the clearing and the sun brightened his face. There was no other face like his; even from this distance he was the most beautiful sight I had ever seen. My breath caught when I saw him remove his cap and wipe his forehead with his sleeve. I realized by his movements that he hadn't seen me yet, so I slowly began to move toward him.

That's when I lost my mind completely. I broke into a wild run, attempting to close the distance between us with as much speed as I could manage. I hated the feeling that my muscles were restricted, so without bothering to consider the potential consequences, I bent down and gathered the bottom edges of my skirt and hiked them up far enough to free my legs.

"Eleanor!" a shocked Christine called from behind me. "Eleanor, stop! What's wrong with you?"

I didn't stop. I didn't care. Jonathan was here; nothing else mattered.

"Eleanor!" Christine was pleading now and no doubt struggling to follow me, but I didn't look back.

"Jonathan!" I screamed, quickening my pace. He looked up, suddenly aware of my approach, and braced himself, taking a half step back and dropping whatever it was he held in his hand. A walking stick, perhaps? I wasn't sure and I didn't care. As soon as I reached him, I flung myself into his arms.

"Jonathan!" I sobbed as I pulled myself tightly against him, my lips searching irrationally for his and finally finding them.

It took several moments for me to realize that something was wrong—definitely wrong!

I couldn't quite put my finger on it; maybe he wasn't expecting to find me here, or maybe he was expecting me to be angry that he hadn't come for me nine months earlier as planned. Then it occurred to me that Grace may not have told him I was here as Eleanor. Maybe he was expecting to find me as Beth when he arrived. Oh, how confusing this must be for him. But of course, I could explain all that later.

Then it struck me. It wasn't just his lips that were different, there was more. His smell. His taste. The length of his hair and its lack of shine.

"Oh." A quiet gasp escaped me as I abruptly stepped away from him and stared up at his face for the first time. His eyes revealed total shock, laced mercifully with humor.

"Oh," I repeated in a nearly inaudible whisper.

I turned to the side and found Christine, mouth gaping open, a look of sheer horror in her expression as she shifted her stare between Jonathan and me.

"Christine . . . I . . ."

Her eyes flickered to mine. They held a look of betrayal and disapproval. She paused only briefly before turning on her heel and running in the direction of the house.

"Christine!" I called after her. "Wait! Let me explain!"

Explain what? That I'm just some stranger from the twenty-first century occupying her sister's body? That I've been thrust into the past in an effort to protect me from evil immortals who want to take control of my mind and body? Explain that I mistook this unassuming soldier for the man I love in the twenty-first century? There was no way I could explain this. Not to Christine, not to the bewildered Jonathan who stood before me, and most certainly not to Mrs. Weddington and Eleanor's mother—which was, no doubt, exactly where Christine was headed.

My hand flew to my mouth and I spun around to find a stunned Jonathan watching my every move. I studied his face briefly as the full magnitude of my actions began to slowly creep into my mind and reason returned.

This was not *my* Jonathan.

I was not going home.

And I was in serious trouble.

"Oh!" I muttered against my hand.

Jonathan's mouth twitched slightly, one side hinting at a suppressed smile.

"Miss Hastings?" His voice was smooth, calm, and just as warm and soft as I remembered. That much was the same.

My free hand seemed to reach up of its own volition and press the hand already covering my mouth tightly against my lips, as if to stifle me from further defiling Eleanor's reputation. I wondered briefly if this was a reflex imposed by Eleanor, but there was no possible way for her to erase what I had just done.

"Are you all right?" Jonathan asked.

I shook my head slowly from side to side, not sure if I should run home or just run away. I wondered for a brief second how long it would take to get to Wyoming on foot.

"I'm afraid you caught me at a disadvantage, Miss Hastings, and I admit, slightly off guard," Jonathan said, no longer hiding his amusement. His face broke into a wide, playful grin; it was all I could do not to lose my composure.

"I . . . I'm sorry . . . I didn't . . . I'm so sorry," I finally managed to say as I reached for my skirt and began running toward the house.

"I wasn't prepared," he called after me. I could hear the chuckle in his voice, even without seeing his expression. "Would you give me a little warning next time?"

His choice of words stopped me momentarily. A memory flashed across my mind—the memory of the first time Jonathan had kissed me, a kiss he'd stolen when I wasn't looking. I wondered for a moment if I was mistaken; perhaps this was *my* Jonathan after all and this was his way of giving me a coded message. But reason reasserted itself and I continued to run for the house, afraid to turn around and look at him again. I'd already caused what was sure to be a disastrous scandal for Eleanor's family, perhaps for all of Marensburg.

It was five days before there was any mention of my encounter with Jonathan—five horrendously long, torturous days. I would rather face the strap or the ferocity of Father's reprimand or the disgust in Mother's expression or even the ranting of crazy old Mrs. Weddington (who by now must have reaffirmed her initial suspicions that I was possessed by an evil spirit). But silence? Worse than silence. The family went about their normal routine as if nothing had happened. The only sign of anything different was in Christine's behavior. She didn't ignore me, I could have expected that, but I couldn't handle her complete, utter disinterest in me. She was cordial and ladylike, but not friendly.

The only thing that kept me sane was Sir Charles, the family dog, named affectionately after the Hastings' deceased son. Sir Charles never missed an opportunity to climb into my lap and lick my cheek with his slobbering tongue—a ritual that kept Mrs. Weddington and Eleanor's mother in fits. From the tidbits of information I'd picked up over the past several months, Eleanor's father had discovered Sir Charles down by the river one morning when he was little more than a pup. He'd somehow managed to get himself tangled in some wild blackberry bushes, which was curious because everyone knows that dogs are carnivores. Sir Charles was different; he loved fruit. Apparently, Eleanor was particularly fond of the little guy. I didn't know what kind of dog he was, but he reminded me a little of a Welsh Corgi because of his short legs and long body.

Sometimes, when Sir Charles looked at me, I wondered if he sensed I wasn't really Eleanor.

By the end of the fifth day, I began to question whether Christine had mentioned my unsavory actions to anyone and if the subtle coolness in the air was all my imagination; but that delusion was shattered when Mr. Rollings paid Eleanor's father an unexpected call. A very humble, contrite Jonathan accompanied him—a side of Jonathan I was unfamiliar with.

"Good evening," I heard Mr. Rollings say to Mr. Edwards, the Hastings' butler. "I hope you will forgive the intrusion but we would like a word with Mr. Hastings, please."

Mr. Rollings voice was musical. Poetic. Almost hypnotic.

Edwards' reply was stiffly formal. "Mr. Hastings does not receive callers at this hour. If you'll leave your calling card, I will see that he gets it."

"Thank you for your kindness, Mr. Edwards," Mr. Rollings said politely. I huddled closer to the stair rail, hoping to get a glance at his face before he could leave. "I wonder if you might inquire of Mr. Hastings first. I suspect he may desire an audience with me."

"As you wish," Mr. Edwards replied dutifully. "Please have a seat." He gestured to the tall reception chairs that lined the Hastings' entryway. Jonathan and his father both took a seat, but neither made eye contact with the other.

Mr. Edwards disappeared into the study, then quickly reappeared and directed Mr. Rollings and Jonathan to the drawing room.

That's strange.

Eleanor's father stepped into the hallway and muttered something in Mr. Edward's ear before joining his guests in the drawing room. Mr. Edwards rang the bell signaling for Mrs. Weddington, who appeared moments later. They exchanged words and Mrs. Weddington made her way to the staircase. I hesitated only briefly before heading for my room, but before I could get there Mrs. Weddington found me.

"Your presence is requested in the drawing room." She didn't wait for a response, but paused briefly with her back to me. "Gloves," she ordered.

I looked down at my hands and rolled my eyes. Rules!

I retrieved my lace gloves first, but as I started for the door something stopped me. It was as if my legs would no longer obey my brain's command to move toward the door. I stared blankly at the gloves for several moments and then, in a movement that was not mine, my body glided back to the glove box and I watched Eleanor's hands replace the lace gloves with a pair of sheer white gloves. After a minute, I realized I was holding my breath. I gasped for air, inhaling sharply, and then found myself once again in control of Eleanor's body. I had felt her spirit near a few times, but never had I felt her take over in the way she just had.

Mr. Edwards met me at the door to the drawing room and announced my arrival. Mother was not sitting in her usual spot; instead, she sat next to Father on the couch with her hands folded neatly in her lap, a respectable distance separating them. And of course, she was wearing gloves. An uneasy feeling lodged in the pit of my stomach. I sensed this was bad.

Mr. Rollings occupied the chair closest to the fireplace and Jonathan in the chair opposite. The three men stood at my approach and Mr. Rollings and Jonathan offered a polite bow. Father gestured for me to sit in the chair closest to the couch, which was positioned so that I looked squarely toward Mr. Rollings and Jonathan.

Oh, this was very bad!

Father motioned for Mr. Rollings and Jonathan to sit, and then, as if on cue, Mrs. Weddington entered with a tray of shortbread and tea. Normally, Mrs. Weddington did not tend to such menial duties, but this visit was occurring outside of the normal hours for receiving callers and the staff had already been dismissed for the evening. She poured the tea, handed the guests a cup, and offered them the tray of assorted snacks. Mr. Rollings smiled and thanked her as he reached for a slice of shortbread. Jonathan followed suit. The lingering silence in the room was so thick my cheeks flushed with guilt and shame. I couldn't bear to wait any longer, so I did the unthinkable.

"Father, please, I can exp—"

"Silence Eleanor," Father scolded. His voice was not laced with anger, rather with cool authority.

"Mr. Hastings," Mr. Rollings said, drawing Father's attention away from me. His eyes held a particular fascination for me; they appeared to twinkle in the light, the same way Jonathan's did—not the Jonathan that sat angled across from me now, but the Jonathan in the future. I wondered at what point Jonathan's eyes began their peculiar phenomenon; was it triggered by something significant or was it part of his reclamation?

"I'm sure you have been informed of the unusual events that occurred when my son returned on leave," Mr. Rollings continued. I squirmed in my seat and averted my glance, staring blankly at my hands and fidgeting with my gloves.

"I am aware that an incident occurred, yes." Father was calm, very businesslike.

"My son would like permission to address you regarding the matter."

Father nodded, motioning for Jonathan to speak. Jonathan cleared his throat and shot me a quick glance before squaring his shoulders and facing Eleanor's father.

"Mr. Hastings, I have come to offer my deepest apologies for my behavior the other day. I assume complete responsibility."

I stood without thinking of the consequences. "Jonathan!" I whispered, shocked. Mr. Rollings and Jonathan both stood out of respect. "You don't—"

"Eleanor!" Father shot me a severe warning glare and ordered me to sit down.

I looked at Mr. Rollings and then Jonathan, shaking my head in silent protest. Jonathan met my gaze briefly, but despite the tension of the moment and the serious nature of their visit, I was certain he was stifling the urge to smile.

"Please continue, Mr. Rollings," Father said to Jonathan.

"Thank you, sir. I wish to explain my actions, if I may." Father nodded. Mother sat motionless as a statue, revealing no emotion. "You see, I've been at war for going on two years now. I haven't seen family or friends since I left, not even after being injured at Gettysburg."

I drew in a sharp breath and then quickly covered my mouth with both hands. Jonathan had never mentioned anything about being involved in the Battle of Gettysburg or being injured.

Jonathan ignored my obvious alarm and continued. "Miss Hastings recognized me upon approach and came with her younger sister to offer a hand of hospitality and welcome." He paused, allowing his words to sink in, before continuing. Mother's eyes widened and she reached for Father's hand.

"I was overcome by her gracious welcome and I fear I lost control of my senses. I, uh . . . well, I suppose you know the rest." Jonathan looked down; he was still fumbling with the shortcake, which had crumbled into several pieces by now. He tried to gather the crumbs discretely with his free hand.

"We're here to offer our deepest apologies, and to make the situation right," Jonathan's father added.

Mother twitched in her seat.

"What are you proposing?" Father asked Mr. Rollings.

Mr. Rollings cleared his throat and glanced quickly at Jonathan. Jonathan returned his glance and an awkward silence filled the room. I sensed they were having a conversation—the type that requires no words—and that they had rehearsed the conversation several times before arriving this evening.

"Mr. Rollings," Father's eyes shifted between Jonathan and his father, "perhaps your coming here is a bit . . . premature?"

Jonathan cleared his throat and searched for a spot to set his mangled shortcake. Then he squared his shoulders and turned to face Eleanor's father.

"Mr. Hastings, I am prepared to make Miss Hastings a formal offer," Jonathan finally announced.

Father fidgeted for a second, patted Mother's hand reassuringly, and stood to face Jonathan. He was noticeably shorter than Jonathan, but given his pride and posture it was not apparent.

"Am I correct in assuming you are proposing an offer of marriage?" Father asked.

"Yes, sir, I am requesting your permission to marry Miss Hastings," Jonathan clarified.

My head was swimming with confusion. I'm pretty sure my mouth gaped open as my mind fluttered with disbelief and then shifted back and forth between an excited sort of embarrassment coupled with unexplainable, raging jealousy. The part of me that was Beth wanted to bury my face and run from the room. Fortunately, the part of me that was Eleanor held it together by forcing me to remain calm and poised.

I mentally challenged the propriety of the conversation at hand. In my limited studies of nineteenth century etiquette, it seemed most out of line to propose marriage in such a manner. Shouldn't this have been a private conversation between Jonathan and Eleanor's father?

"Your offer is generous, and I'm sure you are most sincere. Unfortunately, I cannot give you my permission, Mr. Rollings."

Jonathan looked at him quizzically, "Sir?"

Father cleared his throat and offered his hand first to Jonathan's father and then to Jonathan. "Gentlemen, you honor our family with your request. You have been most gracious and noble, Mr. Rollings." He turned back to Jonathan's father. "I won't forget it."

"The offer stands," Mr. Rollings replied.

My eyes flickered rapidly between the three men standing in front of me. They were speaking as though I was not in the room and as though my opinion on the matter was of no consequence.

"I have entered into a previous arrangement on Miss Hastings' behalf," Eleanor's father reported. "I'm afraid she is already spoken for. The announcement will be made once she is properly presented to society. I trust you will receive this information in confidence."

A knot twisted in the pit of my stomach. Jonathan shot me a questioning look. I quickly looked away, unable to meet his reproachful glare.

"Then what may we do to make amends for my son's behavior?" Mr. Rollings asked.

Father looked at Jonathan for several minutes and then offered him his hand. "Let us pretend the incident never occurred. That would be amends enough." Father began walking toward the door and motioned politely for his guests to follow. Mother rose when Mr. Rollings thanked her and I followed her lead. It must have been the right thing to do, because nobody glared at me or told me to sit down.

Mother and I remained in the drawing room while Father escorted Jonathan and his father to the entryway where Mr. Edwards handed them their hats.

"Thank you both for calling this evening. I trust your journey home will be a pleasant one," I heard Father say as they left. It was several moments before he returned to the drawing room.

"Eleanor, I will see you in my study."

I slowly followed him from the room like a chastised puppy.

Mother didn't join us. The study was Father's private sanctuary; we entered only when invited to do so. Father ignored me as he walked to the back of the room and settled behind his desk. He unfolded his spectacles and placed their wire flanges securely around his ears. Then he picked up his quill and dipped it in an ink container. He began scribbling something on a piece of paper and for several minutes he proceeded to behave as though I was not in the room. I began to wonder if I had understood him correctly. He continued writing, dipping his quill, and writing some more. After a long while, my legs began to ache. I started to sit down, but before I could reach the chair, Father cleared his throat in a not-so-subtle reprimand. I immediately stood back at attention and that is how I remained for half an hour. It wasn't until the tears began to roll down my cheeks that he finally spoke, but even then his eyes never left the paper on which he scribbled vigorously.

"Do you consider Christine an honest child?"

His words cut me to the quick. So he knew the truth. He didn't buy Jonathan's version of what happened.

"Yes, sir." My reply was barely audible.

"Pardon me?" This time he did look up, but I almost wished he hadn't. The disappointment in his face was crushing.

"Yes," I said again. "Christine is very honest."

Father stared at me for several moments, then he nodded. "For the next few days, when you are finished with your studies, you will retire to your room and copy from Hosea."

"Yes, sir," I replied meekly. "Any particular part?" I regretted asking the moment the words left my mouth.

Father lowered his spectacles and looked up at me. "All fourteen chapters! Mrs. Weddington will monitor your progress and deliver the completed pages to your mother before you retire each evening."

"Yes, sir." I waited for him to say something more, but he adjusted his glasses and returned to his pattern of dipping and scribbling.

"That will be all," he finally said.

"Yes, sir." I turned and headed for the door.

"Eleanor?" he called after me as I reached for the handle.

"Yes, Father?"

"That boy did you a very kind service tonight—did us all one. You'd be wise to take note."

"Yes, sir." I opened the door to find Mr. Edwards waiting on the other side. He ushered me from the room in silence and closed the door.

Encounter

CHAPTER 3

*I*t wasn't that I minded reading the Bible; after all, my mother had read it faithfully. In fact, she had often been criticized by her colleagues for quoting from it in her writings. She stood by her assertion that the laws of physics could be understood only when one was enlightened by a higher power. But at the rate I was headed, it wouldn't be too long before I had not only read the Bible, but had copied most of its chapters down in writing as well. The last time I could remember having to write as a form of punishment was when my fourth grade teacher made me write, "I promise I will not talk while the teacher is talking," one hundred times. If that wasn't bad enough, when I got home my mother had me repeat the process—just to make sure the message stuck.

I missed my mom. Eleanor's mother was nothing like my mom. I wondered if the two of them would have gotten along had they been born in the same decade. I chuckled to myself as I thought of the two of them together. Eleanor's mother was so proper and had definite opinions about a woman's sense of duty to her community. My mom would have appreciated that about her, but that's likely where the similarities would have ended. While Eleanor's mother rigidly adhered to a strict sense of propriety my mom laughed at protocol, which surprised me knowing how old fashioned she was when it came to me.

A soft tap on my bedroom door interrupted my thoughts.

"Eleanor?" Christine's quiet voice called softly as she inched open my door. "May I come in?"

I hadn't realized how much I'd missed her coming in each evening to say goodnight. Sir Charles followed her into the room and made himself comfortable on the braided rug in front of the fireplace. The flames had long faded, but the embers still glowed with warmth; Sir Charles hadn't rested his head two minutes before he was fast asleep.

"I'm very sorry I got you into trouble," Christine said humbly.

I remained sitting at my vanity—which in light of the amount of writing I had done while seated there might more appropriately be called my desk. I stretched open my arms and received her with a fond embrace.

"It's not your fault, sister," I assured her. "I don't know what came over me the other day."

"I shouldn't have told on you. Will you ever forgive me?" Christine sat on the floor and laid her head in my lap.

I began stroking her hair, the same way my mom used to stroke mine when I was upset or didn't feel well. "It's okay," I reassured her.

We sat that way for several minutes until Christine's weight grew heavy on my legs and I realized she was asleep. I nudged her gently, waking her just enough to move her to my bed, then I crawled in next to her. I lay awake for several minutes trying to make sense of my conflicting feelings about Jonathan. I knew intuitively that my impulsive actions toward him would have an impact on Eleanor and Jonathan's history, but there was no way I could have anticipated just how severe that impact would be.

I was still lost in my thoughts when Sir Charles suddenly raised his head and began to whimper. His eyes were fixed on something in the distance, but when I followed the direction of his gaze there was nothing there. I peered into the darkness, searching for what might have alarmed him, but all was quiet and still. Then, from the corner of my eye, I caught a subtle movement in the mirror that sent chills racing down my spine. When Sir Charles suddenly rose on all fours and let out a single bark, I nearly jumped out of my skin.

"Sir Charles!" I spun around and scolded him. "What's the matter with you?"

Christine made a low grumbling sound and turned over onto her other side.

Sir Charles whimpered and lay back down on the floor, his eyes still staring in the same direction as before. The fur along his back stood erect in a stiff ridge from his head to his tail.

Again I followed his gaze—there was nothing. Reluctantly, I forced myself to turn back around and look into the mirror. After several minutes I finally convinced myself that there was nothing there. Obviously, my canine companion had been dreaming and there was no threat, a belief confirmed by the fact that Sir Charles was again fast asleep and snoring.

When I woke the following morning, both Christine and Sir Charles were gone. No doubt Sir Charles followed Mrs. Weddington out of my room when she came in during the night to move Christine back to her own bed. I always marveled at Mrs. Weddington's uncanny ability to enter and exit a room with so much stealth that her movements often went unnoticed. I also wondered when the woman ever slept!

I spent the next couple of days becoming intimate with the Book of Hosea. Mrs. Weddington had likely warned Christine against making any further late night visits, so I spent my evenings in solitude. I didn't really mind missing out on some of my normal morning duties, but the part I hated most was not being able to spend time at the piano in the afternoons. I suppose I should count my blessings—the punishment could have been worse—but copying pages with quill and ink was tedious work. I'd have given anything for a box of ballpoint pens.

"Miss Eleanor?"

I recognized Miss Dolan's girl-like voice immediately and smiled, grateful for an excuse to avoid the task at hand and give my callused fingers a rest.

"Come in, Lucinda." I scooted away from my desk and secured the lid on my canister of ink. I hadn't gotten very far with my punitive pen this morning; in fact, I had barely penned the heading of the next chapter in Hosea. Father's choices of Old Testament books were undoubtedly supposed to teach me a lesson, but this particular lesson was lost on me. I was obviously missing the point of Hosea and decided that even my mom would have had trouble explaining its intended message.

"Mr. Hastings would like you to dress in your riding clothes and meet him in the stable."

"Riding clothes?" Uh, oh. What riding clothes? Thankfully, I didn't need to ask. Lucinda moved automatically to the wardrobe and began piecing together an outfit for me. I submitted dutifully as she proceeded to help me out of my morning robes and into an outfit that had to weigh twenty pounds and promised to be even more uncomfortable than my calling clothes.

Why does everything have to be so cumbersome in the 1800s, I thought. *What I wouldn't give for an old pair of sweats!*

"Please be still, Miss Eleanor. These laces are rather tricky."

"Did my father happen to mention where we're going?"

"No, but he asked me to inform the mistress that you would not be available for your lessons today, so he must intend to keep you occupied well past midday."

"I wonder what he's up to?"

Lucinda ignored me and pulled strongly at the laces on the bodice of my outfit.

"Ouch! Seriously! I only have one set of ribs. Why do you insist on trying to break them all in one fitting?"

"Now, now, Miss Eleanor," Lucinda grinned, dismissing my protests. "It's not that bad. You used to insist your laces be much tighter than this."

"I'm sure I used to insist on a lot of things," I muttered under my breath.

"Well, be that as it may, there's no need to disappoint your father. You know how he is."

Yes, I thought to myself. *He's a man who enjoys punishing his daughter.*

By the time I arrived at the stables, Eleanor's father had already mounted his horse and held the reins for what I could only assume was my mount. He was ready to go. He gave an expressionless nod to Mr. Godfrey, our stable hand, and gestured for him to help me onto my horse.

This should be interesting, I thought. The most recent memory I had of riding a horse was when I was with Jonathan in the mountains of Wyoming. During our ride a sudden roar of thunder had spooked my horse and he bolted, leaving me flat on my backside. I hadn't been near a horse since—and I'd never ridden sidesaddle, which was apparently the expectation this morning.

Godfrey helped me onto the saddle. It was a much smaller saddle than any I could remember and unless I was imagining it, the horse was much bigger, both in length and height. Father then relinquished the reins to Godfrey who looped them around some gizmo at the front of the saddle and handed them to me. In panic, I looked at Eleanor's father, hoping for some clue as to what I was supposed to do. Before I knew it, he gave his horse a sharp kick, hollered loudly, and we were both off.

At first, I bounced all over the saddle in what could only have been viewed by Godfrey as a pathetic show of inexperience. I reached down and clung to my horse for dear life, figuring it was only a matter of seconds before he sent me flailing helplessly to the ground.

And then something very peculiar happened. Much like the way I had instinctively known which gloves to wear the night Jonathan and his father came to the house, my leg muscles automatically tightened and formed gracefully around the side of the horse and I mechanically leaned forward, relaxing into the animal's gait. In a matter of seconds, I was alongside Eleanor's father. He glanced over at me and for the first time since I had awakened as Eleanor, I saw him smile. His eyes held mine for a brief moment and then without warning, he gave his horse another sharp kick.

"Haw! Haw!" he yelled and his horse flew, kicking up a cloud of dust behind him.

Without a second thought, I snapped my heels into the side of my horse and he broke into a full run.

So, Eleanor, you're a trained equestrian. Figures. Is there anything you can't do? My question was intended to be rhetorical, but somewhere in the back of my mind I could have sworn I heard laughter.

Eleanor's father and I rode for the better part of the morning, taking turns at the lead. I hung on in utter amazement, thankful that Eleanor knew what she was doing. The sheer thrill of going so fast made me remember the afternoon when my cousin Carl had me test the speed of his car by racing down the highway just outside of Andersen, Wyoming. That little escapade had resulted in an embarrassing trip to Andersen's traffic court and a hefty fine; yet here, among the rolling hills of the Hastings' vast estate, there was no highway patrol to stop us. We were free to run without threat of being pulled over, and the ride was exhilarating. I was disappointed when Eleanor's father finally pulled up and signaled for me to do the same.

"It has been a long time, hasn't it?" His voice sounded winded.

"That's certainly one way to put it," I replied. I laughed silently to myself as I thought about what he might say if I told him the truth.

"I'm sorry. I've been so engaged in other responsibilities that I fear I have neglected my duty to you and your sister."

"What do you mean by that?" I watched Eleanor's father for several moments. He hesitated, so I continued. "Christine and I lack for nothing. In what way have you neglected us?"

"I'm not speaking in terms of providing for your material needs." He shook his head. "I'm speaking of something far more important."

"I'm afraid I'm not following."

"Your mother wanted to send you both to a boarding school in France. I'm the one who insisted it was more practical to keep you both home, and I placed your mother in charge of seeing that you both were versed in all the ways of society. I'm afraid that may have been a mistake."

"I don't understand. Why would you say that?" I couldn't imagine being shipped off to school. It's one thing to go away to college, but Christine was young. How could he even think about shipping her oversees to school?

Father shook his head. "After your brothers were both killed, everything changed for me. But your mother wanted things to continue on as they always had. It was as though she refused to admit that your brothers were gone."

I watched Eleanor's father carefully. I had never seen him like this before—so human.

"It wasn't supposed to be this way," Father continued. "Those boys had their whole lives before them. It made me think that perhaps I'd gotten it all wrong."

"Gotten what wrong?" I asked, confused with where this conversation was going.

"Everything, I suppose. Suddenly, the only thing that mattered was keeping us all together. Besides, you had been so ill . . . we were sure we were going to lose you. When you recovered so suddenly, so unexpectedly, I felt as though God in his mercy had given me a second chance to be the father my children deserved. Then when Christopher died . . ." Father's voice cracked, but he quickly composed himself. "After that, there was no way I could bring myself to send you or your sister away. Not then, not ever."

"I had no idea," I said quietly. The words were barely more than a whisper, and I realized it was Eleanor who was speaking, not me.

"I didn't realize, however, that I had placed an unfair expectation on your mother." Father pursed his lips. "You know she blames herself for your behavior with young Mr. Rollings."

"That's absurd," I said incredulously. "That had nothing to do with her at all!"

Father's horse whinnied and started to prance, anxious to continue the run. "Then why? You have always been the pristine example of propriety. What could have possessed you to take total leave of your senses with the likes of Jonathan Rollings? Your mother insists that had you been away at boarding school, the whole incident never would have occurred."

"Father, please. I told you I'm sorry. I don't know what came over me."

"But that's just it, that's not the only incident. Mrs. Weddington is certain you're somehow changed in your mind," he said, tapping his head with his fingers.

He had no idea how right she was; but naturally, I couldn't tell *him* that.

"I know I haven't been *right* since my illness. I've lost much of my memory. I forget even the most basic things, like which fork to use or which gloves to wear. It has nothing to do with Mother or you or boarding school, for heaven's sake."

"But don't you see, your mother is convinced that sending you back to boarding school would somehow help you reclaim your lost memories."

"Father, surely you aren't suggesting you want to send me away now?"

He shook his head and smiled. "No, my dear. What's done is done. Besides, you have a coming-out ball to think about. And of course, let's not forget that soon afterward we will announce your up-coming engagement."

I didn't plan on sticking around for that announcement. Eleanor would have to deal with that one on her own. The only thing I cared about was lying low until Grace came back for me, and if that didn't happen soon, I was going to be forced to act on my own.

"Father, don't you think we should hold off on any announcements until more of my memory comes back?

He smiled a sympathetic smile that although genuine, seemed a little condescending.

"You needn't worry yourself, Eleanor. I have made a solemn oath to your mother to become more involved in your future from here on out. Leave the details to me and I promise you, everything will unfold as it should."

I felt uneasy. I got the ominous feeling that in spite of the compassion he'd exhibited only moments ago, this little outing was intended all along to be nothing more than another opportunity for one of his "one-sided" conversations.

Eleanor's father was very determined and very stubborn, and appar-ently, because of my little "kissing" episode with Jonathan, he had decided to take control of her life. This reality placed me in a rather precarious position. Not only was I trapped in Eleanor's body, I was trapped in her life. And at least for the foreseeable future, I saw no escape.

Father and I continued our ride for the next hour, stopping periodi-cally to give the horses a chance to rest while Father pointed out spe-cific areas of interest in the landscape. He spoke no more of boarding school, propriety, balls, or engagements. Instead, he seemed to focus on reacquainting me with the history of Marensburg. His rhetoric re-minded me of trips my *real* father and I used to take in the twenty-first century. No matter where our family traveled or how much of a hurry we were in, when we came upon a historical marker, my father insisted on stopping and turning our trip into a history lesson. He had a gift for spotting these markers in the middle of nowhere. My mom always teased him about it, but I sensed that deep down it was one of the things that endeared him to her, and she secretly admired him for it.

Eleanor's father was different. He seemed equally apathetic whether pointing out variances in the landscape or discussing the nuances of Marensburg society. I watched him thoughtfully, studying his facial expressions and paying close attention to his choice of words when he described the scenery or shared stories about the local history. By the time the morning sun hit its noon zenith, I had determined he was a man without passion. Perhaps at times he showed some spark of compassion, like earlier when he spoke of losing his sons, but when it came to a passion for life, he came up empty.

Once we completed our ride around the better portion of the Hastings' estate, Father announced he had business to tend to in town, so we began the trek into Marensburg proper. I was obliged to tag along—more out of a fear of getting lost than any desire on my part to extend our impromptu "father-daughter" outing.

Fielding's General Store was the first of several businesses as you entered town via Marensburg Road. The road—and the town for that matter—was named after Kristoff Friedrich Marens in 1794. Fielding's General Store, named after Margaret Fielding, Kristoff's only daughter and the wife of Peter Rodham Fielding, was the main supplier of basic household goods to Marensburg residents. The current Mrs. Fielding ran the store with the help of her two younger sisters, Mrs. Nillson and Mrs. Jensen. All three sisters lost their husbands to fever prior to the war. More tragedy struck the sisters when later, Mrs. Nillson's nineteen-year-old son was reported missing and Mrs. Jensen, the youngest of the three sisters, received news that both of her sons had been killed in the Battle of Gettysburg, along with Eleanor's two brothers.

In spite of the terrible hardships suffered by the three women, they somehow managed to greet their customers with unparalleled hospitality—except for the town's notorious juvenile delinquents who made it a point to pester the sisters relentlessly in hopes of scoring some free candy before being run off. The sisters always acted like the boys were troublesome and unwelcome; but when you looked closely, you could see by the sadness in their eyes that they missed their young sons terribly. I noticed that Eleanor's father seemed to share a special connection with Mrs. Jensen—probably because they both had lost sons in the war.

Today was Saturday and the entire town seemed to be popping with energy. I normally made the trip into town with Eleanor's mother and Mrs. Weddington on weekday mornings when the streets were far less crowded. That way we weren't subjected to the taunting of the "less desirables" of Marensburg, who tended to magically appear in the evenings and on weekends when proper members of society were home with their families or attending church functions. Fortunately, it was still pretty early in the day, so most of the activity in the streets was due to travelers making their connections and hired hands picking up supplies for the coming week.

Eleanor's father and Mrs. Jensen were engaged in a rather jovial conversation as she took her time introducing him to the store's most recent inventory. I took this as an opportunity to meander outside where I could "people watch," a new hobby for me. I say *new* because as Beth, I rarely took the time to really watch other people—unless, of course, they were playing the piano. However, I had discovered that if I paid attention, I could gain a wealth of information about the dos and don'ts of society by just watching others and listening to their conversations. I had gotten so good at it that I dubbed myself the official "society stalker" of Marensburg.

Father finished his business with Mrs. Jensen and found me standing in front of the store watching a frustrated young mother trying to settle an argument over a stick of candy between her two small children. I was amazed by how young she looked; she couldn't have been more than a year or two older than me. It didn't take long to figure out that they were from out of town because they spoke with a thick southern drawl, which probably didn't make them very popular with the local vendors. I couldn't help but feel sorry for them.

"Here," Father said, ignoring the exchange between the mother and her children as he handed me a peppermint stick. His simple gesture surprised me; I did a quick double take to make sure it was indeed Eleanor's father giving me candy. His expression was much softer than normal and he actually seemed to be smiling.

"Thank you," I said as I tucked the stick of candy in my pocket for later.

"I need to head down to the feed store to settle an issue with Mr. Bender. As soon as I've concluded my business there, I'll treat you to some ice cream if you'd like."

Once again, I had to look carefully at Eleanor's father to make sure he was the one speaking to me. I wondered if this was a facade for the townspeople's benefit or if there was some other subversive reason behind his change in demeanor.

"Yes, thank you," I replied, still wary of his motive. I searched inside myself for some hint from Eleanor that something was amiss, but she didn't stir.

I accompanied Eleanor's father to the south end of town on horseback. When we arrived at the feed store, we dismounted and tied our horses to a post. Father gestured for me to take a seat on one of the porch chairs while he went inside to talk with Mr. Bender. I was grateful for the opportunity to get off the horse and rest my legs; but as it turned out, my tight stays made it impossible to sit comfortably for long so I decided to take a short stroll to stretch my aching muscles. I wondered if I would ever walk normally again.

When I turned the corner, I spied a distraught child, one of the children who had been arguing with his mother earlier. He was sitting on the ground with his face buried in his hands. I looked around for any sign of his mother or sister, but they were nowhere to be seen. I wondered how he'd managed to get separated from them so quickly. I approached the crying boy quietly and knelt down in front of him.

"Are you okay?" I asked, noticing his especially dirty knees and hands. On the ground next to him lay a piece of what I ascertained was his portion of the candy stick he and his sister had been arguing over earlier. It was now covered with dirt. He peeked at me through his fingers but said nothing.

"Are you hurt?" I asked again.

The little boy took a sporadic breath and sighed, shaking his head.

"What happened?" I asked, reaching for one of his hands.

He pulled his hand away and raised his head up, revealing two of the most stunning hazel eyes I had ever seen—eyes that for some reason were very familiar. They reminded me of bright crystals, only in a shade all their own.

A string of tears trailed their way through the dirt on his face until he reached up and smeared them with the back of his hand, creating blotches of mud along his tear-stained cheeks. He was both pathetic and beautiful, and I was instantly drawn to him.

"I dropped my candy," he whimpered between sniffles. His rich southern accent melted my heart immediately; I couldn't help but smile.

"Yes, I can see that." My grin widened automatically as I watched his stern expression.

"It's not funny!" he snapped.

"Who's laughing?" I teased.

"You are!" he insisted.

"Am not!" I whined. I was purposely patterning my voice after his, which carried in it the same aggravated tone he had used earlier on his mother.

He glared at me for a moment and then wiped his nose with the back of his hand. His face was a mess.

"Here," I said, reaching into my lapel pocket. I pulled out a small handkerchief and handed it to him. I hadn't even realized the handkerchief was there. He took it willingly and wiped it across his face, which only served to spread the mixture of tears, dirt, and snot along his cheeks.

"Oh my," I said, reaching for the handkerchief. "You are a mess!" I quickly glanced around and spotted some water barrels on the side of the feed store. I stood up and held out my hand. "Come with me and I'll fix you up good as new, okay?"

He thought about it for a moment and then stood up. He looked down at the piece of candy on the ground and kicked it with his shoe. "Stupid candy!"

This time I did laugh. "Come on little guy, let's get you cleaned up."

I led him over to the barrels of water and dipped my handkerchief inside several times before wringing it out and wiping his face. It took several rinses before I was able to get through what had to be several layers of dirt.

"Good grief! How did you get so dirty?"

"Rock hunting," he replied. A proud smile replaced his stern expression.

"Really? Here?" I asked, surprised by the instant sense of pride in his voice.

"I collect rocks everywhere we go," he informed me. I couldn't get over how charming his accent sounded. He was only a small boy, yet when he smiled, his eyes shone with irresistible charm. I wanted to ask him questions just so I could hear him talk and watch his eyes dance.

"I used to have a rock collection. It was pretty cool." I frowned as soon as I said the word, "cool." He looked at me with a confused expression. "That means it was really neat."

He nodded, unimpressed. "Oh."

"No, really. I collected quartz crystals. I had all kinds of them."

His eyes grew big and again I marveled at their bright hazel color. "What kind of rocks are quartz crystals?" he asked innocently.

"Well, actually, they're a type of mineral. Some people believe they have special powers."

"You mean like magic?" His eyes grew even wider. I was making a hit with him.

"Sort of like that," I replied. "They're very special."

"Can I see one?" he asked.

"Well, I don't have any with me right now, but . . . ," I looked around for a piece of granite. I finally found one that contained a good-sized chunk of quartz and dipped it into the water. "Here," I pointed to the glistening pieces of quartz, "you see these shiny stones? These are little pieces of quartz."

"Wow!" he exclaimed. "Those are neat looking. What are these?" he asked, pointing to the other minerals in the granite.

"This one is feldspar, the dark ones are mica."

"Are all the shiny ones quartz?" he asked, his lost candy forgotten for the moment.

"Well, I suppose most of them are, but this is only one tiny sample. Quartz crystals get really big and they come in all kinds of colors. You would love them."

"And they're really magic?" he asked.

I shrugged my shoulders then quickly glanced around out of habit to make sure nobody noticed. "Some people believe they have mystical powers."

"Mystical powers? What are those?"

I chuckled. His innocent curiosity was refreshing. "Mystical powers are sort of like magic. They can help you think more clearly or feel better when you're sick or make you feel happy when you're sad. Some people hang them around their necks so they're protected from bad or scary thoughts."

His eyes grew even larger and his mouth gaped open. "Wow!" he whispered in awe. "I want to get some of those when I get big."

"How old are you?" I asked, leading him over to a bench in front of the feed store. We were good friends now.

"I'm six," he announced. "Well, almost."

"Six is a very good age!" I smiled, and nudged him with my elbow. "I think when you're eight you should be old enough to start collecting quartz crystals." Even at his young age, he could sense by my grin that I was teasing him.

"What's your name?" he asked, returning my smile.

"Beth . . . er . . . I mean Eleanor," I replied quickly correcting myself. "Well, actually, *Miss Hastings* I suppose is more proper. And what shall I call you?"

"I'm not sure I should tell you." His face fell.

"Why not?" I asked, intrigued by his sudden, serious tone.

"Because the people around here won't like it . . . that's what my mother says, anyway. She says it's not safe."

"Oh, I see. That would definitely be a problem. I tell you what, I promise not to tell anyone, okay? And I promise, cross my heart and hope to die, that I will still like you, and I'll make sure you're still safe. Deal?" I held out my hand to him. He studied me for a moment and then reluctantly shook my hand.

"Deal," he replied, but he still didn't volunteer his name. I cleared my throat and tried another angle.

"My full name is Miss Eleanor Louise Hastings. I'm not particularly fond of my middle name, but there's not much I can do about that, right?"

"I guess not." He looked up at me and shook his head. "It's not that bad, though. At least you're not named after a general."

"Wow! A general! Dude, that's awesome!" Again, I cringed at the use of my modern vernacular, but I realized that my new young friend wouldn't know any better, so I relaxed. "Which general are you named after?"

The boy looked around carefully and motioned for me to move

closer. He was so serious for someone so young. He leaned forward and whispered, "He's a Confederate!"

I let out a low gasp and covered my mouth. "Oh, I see!"

"Mama says folks around here wouldn't like that."

I nodded in agreement. "Yes, I can understand why."

"Well, it's not exactly *my* name, just the last part is."

His comment confused me. "So then, what should I call you?"

"I guess you're supposed to call me Theodore." He said his name with such disdain that I started to giggle. "I know, it's awful, isn't it? But my middle name is even worse."

"And what's that?"

"Conrad!"

I couldn't stop myself from laughing out loud. I wanted so much to bend down and squeeze his little cheeks. Oh, how I would have loved having a little brother! An unexpected lump rose in my throat and I immediately thought of Christopher; I realized that Eleanor must miss her brother dearly.

"What's wrong with Conrad?" I asked.

"It's different than everyone else's. People always laugh when they hear it."

"Well, I'm not laughing, and personally, I think Conrad is a fabulous name! In fact, my favorite uncle's name is Conrad, but everyone calls him 'Connor.'" Uncle Connor was also my *only* uncle, but I didn't see the need to share that with my little friend.

"Connor!" He pulled his eyebrows into a tight line and thought for a moment, then he nodded in approval. "Yep, I like that. Can I be Connor too?"

Two things occurred simultaneously: the little boy's full name registered in my mind just as his mother turned the corner with her young daughter in tow.

"Come along, child!" the young mother urged.

I watched the girl pull back on her mother's hand; she wanted to peek in one of the doorways. It took a moment for me to connect the dots. When I finally did, it sent a thrill of anticipation pulsing through my veins and my heart swelled with excitement. There was no doubt about it; she was the spitting image of my new friend.

"Theodore Conrad!" his mother barked. "You get over here this minute!"

My insides burned with disbelief. "Uncle Connor?" I muttered under my breath. My eyes bounced back and forth between the two children. They were unquestionably twins.

Is it even possible? It can't be!

My mind was racing, trying to remember as much as I could about my mother and her twin brother's ancestry. I'd only learned about their true heritage a few months before traveling back to the 1800s. My entire family had managed to keep me in the dark about a lot of things, hoping to protect me from the truth about who I really was—a truth that eventually catapulted me from my life in the twenty-first century to the stage where I was playing out my life as Eleanor Hastings.

I did my best to try to fit the pieces together. Experience had taught me not to jump to conclusions, but the resemblance of these twins to my mother and my uncle was undeniable.

But surely, this has *to be a coincidence, right?* I thought, attempting to convince myself one way or the other.

"Uh, oh," the boy said, "I better go."

"Oh, no." I grabbed his hands quickly and looked into his beautiful hazel eyes. "Please, let me look at you for a moment longer!" He stared up at me with a confused expression and I realized that I probably sounded like a crazy woman. "Oh, you darling little boy! I promise, I love your name. Don't you ever forget that!" I struggled to hide the emotion in my voice.

I stood as his mother approached and tried to catch a closer glimpse of the little girl, but she was hiding behind her mother's skirt.

"I'm very sorry, miss. Has he been a nuisance?"

I stared briefly into the young woman's eyes, but there was nothing familiar about her. I had never met either of my mother's parents while I was growing up. They both passed away long before I was born—or at least that's what I'd been told.

"Oh, no ma'am, not in the least. He has been a delight, and has provided me with such wonderful company while I waited for my father to conclude his affairs. Your little boy is very charming, indeed."

"Pardon me, ma'am. I'm afraid you misunderstand. I'm the nanny."

I felt a sudden disappointment, which dissipated the moment the little girl stepped out from behind her nanny's skirt. She had the exact same sparkling hazel eyes as her twin brother. I immediately dropped to my knees and took her by the hand.

"Oh, my goodness! You have the most beautiful eyes! They remind me so much of my mother's eyes." Emotion swelled inside me and I had to blink several times to fight back the tears forming in the corners of my eyes. "You are so beautiful!" I exclaimed in a hushed reverence that I hoped did not scare the nanny.

Could this be her? Reason prompted me to doubt, but the uncanny likeness was too much for me to ignore.

"Please excuse us, ma'am. We are in a dreadful hurry. I've spent nigh on half an hour searching for the boy, and I'm afraid we're quite late." She grabbed both of the children by the hand and started walking swiftly toward the train station. I couldn't bear to see them go.

"Wait!" I called behind them. I dug into my skirt pocket and retrieved the candy stick that Eleanor's father had given me earlier. I quickly snapped it into two pieces and walked hurriedly toward them.

"Here," I said, handing each of them half of my candy stick. "This will give you something to snack on during your train ride." I looked up at their nanny, "I hope it's okay?"

"I reckon it's fine," she smiled. "Thank you."

"Where are you headed?" I asked.

"North Carolina. I'm afraid we really must be on our way. Thank you again for the candy." She looked down at both children, "Well, have you suddenly forgotten your manners?"

"Thank you, ma'am," they both said in unison.

"Oh, you're very welcome." I smiled and gazed one last time into the matching set of hazel eyes. I couldn't let them leave without knowing for sure. "Your name isn't Hattie, is it?" I asked the little girl.

"No, it's Henrietta," she said shyly. "But I like Hattie better."

I smiled a half smile that I hoped did not reveal my disappointment.

"Come along, children," the nanny said, gathering the two by the hand again. They were all the way across the street when both children turned around and looked at me at the same time. I couldn't shake the feeling that they were in some way related to my mother and Uncle Connor.

"Wait!" I called to them again. I ignored the look of frustration in the nanny's expression. I quickly searched the ground until I found two nice chunks of granite. "Take these with you and add them to your rock collection and some day, when you're older, you will have to travel to the Grand Tetons in Wyoming. You'll find all kinds of beautiful quartz crystals there—the kind that are full of magical powers!"

The two children looked up at me with matching expressions of amazement and wonder.

"Thank you, ma'am," the little girl said as she turned the rock over and over and studied its many minerals.

"What are Grand Tetons?" the boy asked, clearly confused. I thought for a moment and then smiled warmly.

"They are twin mountains, very much alike—just like the two of you."

"We really must go, ma'am. Please pardon us." The nanny was doing her best not to sound rude, but she was obviously growing more and more anxious. I knew I'd worn out my welcome. I stepped back and waved goodbye as they turned once again to leave, but a profound sense of sadness overwhelmed me when they finally disappeared behind the train station.

"Eleanor?"

I turned around and found Eleanor's father standing at the edge of the street in front of the feed store.

"Was that someone we know?" he asked, squinting into the late afternoon sun.

"No, just a little boy who was lost. I gave him and his sister my candy stick."

Father offered a dutiful nod of approval. "Well done," he said.

Even when he was paying me a compliment, he had a way of sounding condescending. I wondered if he did it on purpose.

The outing with Eleanor's father had definitely been interesting. I replayed the encounter with little Conrad and Henrietta over and over in my mind, committing their faces and eyes to memory. I made a solemn oath that when I made it back to the twenty-first century, *if* I made it back, I was going to research the ancestral line of my mother and my Uncle Connor. Twins generally run every other generation, so maybe . . . .

"Something's come up," Father said, interrupting my thoughts. "I've another stop to make before heading home. But first, how about that ice cream I promised you?"

"Is everything okay?" I asked, again puzzled by Father's unusually pleasant demeanor.

"Everything is fine," Father smiled. Now I knew something was up. Eleanor's father rarely smiled—not a sincere smile anyway. Normally, whenever he smiled I got the feeling that he was up to some sort of self-serving scheme. But this smile was genuine, and it made him almost seem likeable.

"And how is Mr. Bender today?" I asked, prodding.

"Who?"

"The feed store. Didn't you say you had to work out some issue with Mr. Bender?"

"Oh that. Yes, of course. Er, he's well, naturally."

I may have been at a disadvantage when it came to wearing the right kind of gloves or distinguishing a fruit spoon from a dessert spoon, but I was savvy enough to know when I was being lied to. "What aren't you telling me, Father? Why the sudden jovial disposition?"

Father seemed to be at a loss for words, but his face revealed something I couldn't have anticipated. He was blushing. An awkward silence followed and I instantly regretted pressing him. "How about that ice cream you mentioned?" I finally asked, changing the subject. Father nodded, and for the next half hour we barely spoke to each other, choosing instead to eat our ice cream in silence.

We were nearly finished when a thunderous commotion from outside startled everyone in the store. Several men sprang from their seats in response to the ruckus when in burst three men, one of whom I recognized as Mr. Gruber from the telegraph station. The other two I had spotted around town on occasion, but they were not among those associated with the Hastings.

"We got 'em!" one of the men announced excitedly as he entered the store. "We got ole Jeb!"

A nervous chorus of audible gasps rang through the store and then everyone began speaking at once, demanding to know "Who got him?" "Where'd they catch him?" "Are they sure it's him?"

"They killed him!" Mr. Gruber replied, responding to the crowd's questions. The two men with Mr. Gruber let out a loud "Whoop!" but others in the crowd were still demanding to know more.

"Father, who are they talking about?" I whispered, not wanting to draw any attention to myself.

Father quickly put a finger to his lips and shook his head. "Shh! Listen."

"Came by way of telegraph just now. Says here he died on Wednesday." Mr. Gruber pointed to a narrow piece of paper he held in his hand.

"Read it!" Several in the crowd demanded.

Mr. Gruber looked down at the telegraphed message and then looked up, surveying the room. He appeared to be taking note of all the women who were present and seemed reluctant to continue. When his eyes reached Eleanor, he did a quick double take and froze.

"Sir?" Mr. Gruber looked questioningly at Eleanor's father, as if asking for his permission to read the telegraph in my presence.

Father placed a reassuring hand over mine and gave Mr. Gruber the go-ahead.

Mr. Gruber read, "General J. E. B. Stuart of Virginia mortally wounded at Yellow Tavern Wednesday the 11th of May. Died 12 May of stomach wound."

For several the moments the room was silent as those present allowed the words to register. I learned only bits and pieces about "Jeb" Stuart when I studied American history in my junior year of high school. I recalled that he was hailed as a sort of "knight" among many in the South. I also recalled that he was noticeably absent during the Battle of Gettysburg and that his absence was likely one of the contributing factors to Lee's defeat in that notorious battle.

Admittedly, I was somewhat puzzled by the animated response that news of his death seemed to evoke in the people who had now gathered tightly around Mr. Gruber, clamoring for more information.

"Look," Mr. Gruber held up the telegraph for the people to see. "That's all it says. We'll have to wait for the rest of the story."

With that, the people began dispersing, each speculating on the details surrounding the infamous general's demise.

As soon as things settled down, I reached over and nudged Father's arm. "Father, forgive me, but I don't understand why everyone is in such an uproar over this news. I mean, Confederate soldiers are killed all the time, aren't they?"

Eleanor's father raised both his eyebrows and gave me an incredulous look as if I had just asked something utterly ridiculous. "Child, General Stuart has been a thorn in Meade's side for some time now. Caused a lot of trouble for the Union, that one. I'm not sad to learn that he's gone." Then he patted my arm as if to reassure me and added, "But this is nothing for you to concern yourself with. You leave these situations to the men and focus on things more suitable for a proper young lady."

"Oh please," I huffed before I could catch myself. Thankfully, Father's good mood hadn't left him, so rather than scold me, he laughed.

Unchaperoned

CHAPTER 4

*I*t was late in the afternoon by the time Father and I returned home from our outing. Mrs. Weddington greeted us at the entrance by the stables.

"The two of you best be getting inside," she said, eyeing Eleanor's father cautiously. "Mrs. Hastings requested the evening meal be served immediately upon your arrival. She's got the entire kitchen staff in a frenzy."

"Humph," Eleanor's father grunted. His cheerful countenance from earlier had disappeared and just like that, things were back to normal.

"Come along Miss Eleanor, Lucinda will help you dress." Mrs. Weddington took me by the arm and led me through the lower entrance up the back stairs to my chambers. It was most unusual for me to use the back stairs, but they provided a direct shot up to the third floor where the bedrooms were located—much quicker than taking the walk around to the front entrance and using the grand staircase. I didn't mind, except for the fact that in the main house, doors and windows remained open to allow for a much appreciated breeze. The back stairs had no ventilation; so in the heat of late afternoon, our trip up three flights of stairs left me both perspiring and out of breath. I made a mental note to speak to Eleanor's father about doing something to resolve the lack of airflow in the servants' quarters.

Mrs. Weddington left me in my chambers where I found Lucinda waiting. She had already drawn my bath and laid out my clothes for dinner. It had taken me several weeks to get used to having someone help me dress, let alone help me with my bath—bathing had always been a private affair in my experience—but as time went on, I decided I didn't mind being pampered in this way. After all, there wasn't much I could do about it, so why not enjoy it?

Eleanor's mother was a stickler when it came to being on time for dinner so I was unable to relax for long during my bath, which was too bad because my muscles ached from riding all morning and the warm water provided some welcome relief. But in minutes, I was once again holding on to the bedpost while Lucinda tightened my corset. I'd always considered turn-of-the-century women in movies lucky to have such tiny waists and dresses that made their figures look so feminine. Ugh! I would gladly give up Eleanor's tiny waist for a pair of comfortable jeans and a tank top. I'd always been amazed by Scarlet O'Hara's eighteen-inch waist in *Gone with the Wind*. Now I understood how she did it—with corsets laced so tightly there was no room for food!

Eleanor's mother was in rare form at dinner. Saturday evenings were generally reserved for invited guests, but tonight there was only the four of us—each dressed in our Saturday evening finest.

"How was your day out?" she asked Father while the servants served the first course of the meal.

"It was uneventful for the most part. We rode the estate, exercised the horses, then rode into town so I could meet with Mr. Bender." Father was unaware of the look that passed between Mother and one of the servants—the one Father referred to as "Johnson." He wasn't one of the regular household servants; he only worked on Saturdays.

"And how about you, Eleanor? Did you enjoy your outing?"

I glanced at Father, confused by the implied insinuation behind Mother's voice.

"I suppose," I answered cautiously.

"Eleanor made some new friends in town," Father chimed in. "Tell your mother how you came upon the Southerners."

Mother put down her fork, her eyes instantly cold.

"Ah, don't fret," Father explained. "She merely helped a little boy who was lost."

Mother relaxed her shoulders a little. "Well, that's noble enough," she commented. "Hopefully you weren't seen by anyone talking to Southerners!"

"Good grief!" I sighed. "Are you kidding me?" The words flew out of my mouth before I could stop them, and I knew immediately I'd put my foot in my mouth—again.

"Eleanor!" It was Christine who reprimanded me this time.

"I apologize, Mother, but he was only a five-year-old boy. Imagine if that had been Christopher; wouldn't you have wanted someone to help him?"

The minute I mentioned Christopher's name the entire room went deathly still—the kind of silence that makes your ears burn and your heart race. Fortunately, Christine jumped in to lighten the mood. She was very intuitive for a girl her age.

"Well, I think it's nice that you helped him, Eleanor. I would have done the same thing in your shoes, Southerner or not."

"Precisely," Father agreed. "And she was even kind enough to offer him and his sister a peppermint stick."

"I see." Mother raised her eyebrows. "I presume this means you stopped into Fielding's?"

Eleanor's father averted his eyes and glanced in my direction. "Yes, for a moment. I promised Eleanor a candy stick after our ride." I stared blankly at him for several seconds, puzzled by his little white lie. His expression seemed to presume that I would not question him on the matter. In spite of his crude treatment of me, I sensed deep down that Eleanor would do anything for her father; although for the life of me, I couldn't figure out why. He was demanding, rude, insensitive, spiteful, controlling . . . and yet, there were moments when he would surprise me, like earlier today, when he actually seemed human and surprisingly likeable.

"Yes, that's right, Mother," I came to Father's defense. I sensed that Eleanor was pleased by that move on my part. "And he also treated me to some ice cream after he finished his business with Mr. Bender. We sort of lost track of time, so Father insisted we hurry home in time for the evening meal."

Wow, that's laying it on a bit thick, I thought to myself, but I didn't care. In the back of my mind, I thought for a brief instant that I could hear a woman's laughter.

"How responsible of him," Mother replied coolly. "And did you find time in your day to pay Mrs. Jensen a visit?"

"You are out of line, my dear!" Father set his fork down and glared at Eleanor's mother. She started to say something else, but he stopped her short. "Silence! I'll not listen to you insult Mrs. Jensen, not in *my* house. Do you understand?"

Christine and I watched this exchange with shocked faces. In the many months I'd been living as Eleanor, I'd never heard them speak to each other in such harsh tones. They had disagreed often, but always there was cordiality between them; this was different, and it definitely raised suspicion in my mind. Father had been noticeably changed after his brief encounter with Mrs. Jensen—and for the better in my opinion. She made him smile, and she made him seem . . . nice, for a change. I couldn't help but speculate as to the depth of their relationship, yet it had all seemed very innocent.

The rest of the evening meal passed in silence, with the exception of a comment here and there about the food or questions about the coming week. Eleanor's mother excused herself early, which was becoming something of a habit with her recently. Eleanor's father didn't seem to mind or care. He retreated to his study shortly after dinner and remained there for most of the evening. He appeared just as Christine and I began to retire for the evening. We had just started up the stairs when he stepped outside his study to wish us both good night.

"Oh, and Eleanor?" he paused, "don't forget you still owe me the book of Hosea."

After everything that had occurred during the day, and particularly during the evening meal, I could not believe he was back on the Hosea kick. Good grief! I wanted to march right up to him and give him a piece of my mind, but Eleanor must have perceived my thoughts because before I could move, she made a brief emergence.

"Yes, Father." Eleanor's sudden appearance in my head was both disturbing and intriguing. She seemed to intervene just enough to keep me out of any *real* trouble.

Not surprisingly, that night I dreamed about my mom and Uncle Connor. It was the same dream I'd had regularly during my first few weeks as Eleanor, but over time its occurrences had become less and less frequent.

The first part of the dream was always hazy. Sometimes I would hear the sound of running water and experience the sensation of falling; but regardless of how the dreams began, I always found myself sitting as a spectator in the secret room located beneath the basement of Uncle Connor's house in Wyoming—the vortex cellar as he liked to call it.

The conversation between Uncle Connor and my mom always led to a heated argument. I couldn't ascertain what they were fighting about, but they were both equally passionate in defending their position. I felt a yearning to reach out to them, to get their attention and convince them to stop arguing. I sensed if they didn't, they would each regret it. Neither of them could have known mom would soon be dead and that all their senseless fighting would be for nothing.

When I awoke the next morning, I felt groggy and stiff and much more tired than normal—which I attributed to my horseback riding adventure with Eleanor's father the previous day. I made a mental note to myself that when I got back to the twenty-first century, I would line my pockets with ibuprofen. That way, if I was ever forced to "travel" to the past again, I would have a ready supply of pain killers with me. I scoffed at the thought.

When I get back to the twenty-first century, there's no way on earth I will ever travel again. Ever!

"Eleanor!" I heard Christine call from downstairs. "What's taking you so long?"

Christine. Always the patient one. As Beth, I would simply yell back for her to hold her horses, but as Eleanor, that would never do. Everything Eleanor did reflected refined discretion, Mrs. Weddington and Eleanor's mother saw to that. Although I was becoming more accustomed to the dictates of society and more confident in my role, I still found many of the rules of etiquette bothersome and tedious. I had learned, however, not to express my thoughts on the subject in front of Eleanor's family. Lucinda had unwittingly reminded me on several occasions that it was "unlike" Eleanor to resist the customs of society. Not wishing to call attention to myself, I vowed to do everything in my power to protect Eleanor's reputation and keep her good name intact.

Unfortunately, Mrs. Weddington still had her suspicions that Eleanor may be under the influence of an unsavory spirit—bewitched by dark magic, even. I'd hoped we were past all that. She pretended to keep her distance from me, all the while taking note of my every move. Sadly, my encounter with Jonathan had pretty much destroyed my chances of convincing her that I was "normal." I'd been extra cautious since then—copying the book of Hosea from the Bible left me little time for anything else—but Mrs. Weddington never passed up an opportunity to remind me that I was not fooling her, not so much by what she said as by what she *didn't* say.

Fortunately, Lucinda seemed sympathetic to my plight. She was only slightly older than Eleanor and hidden behind her soft grey eyes was the secret pain of a young woman who obviously understood what it was like to feel hopeless. I often found myself wondering who the object of her longing was and whether or not she would ever confess the truth to me.

"Eleanor! My goodness! Why aren't you coming?"

I couldn't help but smile at Christine's anxiety. Going to town was something she looked forward to with eager anticipation, especially when Mrs. Weddington had errands to run. That always meant an opportunity for us to peruse the ribbons and fabrics at Fielding's General Store and browse around town without a chaperone—something we both looked forward to (me especially after spending so much time cooped up in my room finishing the Book of Hosea).

"Eleanor?" Christine had given up and come upstairs. She appeared quietly in my doorway.

"I'm sorry for the delay, Christine. Lucinda stepped out and I'm not finished dressing. I'm not sure which gloves I should wear." I gave Christine the most pathetic, damsel in distress look I could manage. It worked, because she took her role as dutiful younger sister quite seriously. Besides, she still felt guilty for telling Mrs. Weddington what happened with Jonathan and me—not because she thought what I did was forgivable, but because it had taken me nearly two weeks to copy the book of Hosea. During those two weeks, Christine could not venture out on the estate without Mrs. Weddington, and Mrs. Weddington abhorred the outdoors.

"Here, wear the lace ones. Then we'll be alike."

I smiled as I pulled on Eleanor's lace gloves. They were made of delicate, finely tatted lace and looked very feminine—although they felt strange if you weren't accustomed to wearing them. I had a continuous urge to pull them off and free my hands, but I knew better. I'd already spent too much time copying verses from the Old Testament.

"Ready?" I asked, reaching for Christine's hand.

"Aren't you forgetting something?"

Oh for the love of Pete, what now? These outings always took a toll on my nerves. I smiled expectantly at Christine, pretending to test her.

Christine shook her head and retrieved my parasol from its stand.

"Honestly, Eleanor. Sometimes I think you've lost your senses."

"Undoubtedly, little sister," I chuckled as I mentally made another note to myself—*remember that exposure to direct sunlight is forbidden among aristocratic society.*

Once you enter Marensburg on Marensburg Road, you walk past a printing shop that's connected to the local newspaper. Further down, the street veers off into several lanes of small homes and a handful of less desirable dwellings where the poor people of the town live and work—if they're lucky enough to work, that is. Directly east of Marensburg Road is Harrison Road. It is lined with small businesses, a family-owned building and loan company, two banks, and a hardware store. Main Street bisects Harrison further down the street. If you turn east on Main, you come to the City Hall and then cross the town square where street vendors ply their wares each day. Beyond the vendors there are three large churches: Presbyterian, Methodist, and Marensburg Community. A short walk from the churches is the town hospital and across from the hospital are the public library, a barbershop, and a park.

If you turn west onto Main Street, you find a string of specialty shops, two hotels, McBride's Candy Store, Newell's Fabric Store, a small bookstore, and the post office. Bender's Feed Store, where I met young Conrad and his twin sister, is located at the south end of Marensburg Road, across from a second hardware store and a large lumber distributor.

There's a smaller general store toward the end of the street, but it only carries a limited inventory of domestic products. Most of its sales come from catalog orders, which can take weeks to arrive depending on the time of year. It does, however, serve cold drinks, so Christine and I made a pact to pay the store a visit when Mrs. Weddington gave us our freedom.

Around the corner from Bender's Feed Store is the train station; Marensburg is a main artery connecting Chambersburg, Bedford, and Harrisburg. The Hastings' estate, along with other wealthy family estates, is located north of the town.

The weather decided to cooperate with us as we made our way south along Marensburg Road. We arrived just in time to see Mrs. Nillson shooing two dirty-faced boys out of her store. She carried a broom, which she promptly planted on the backside of the larger boy. The boys whooped and hollered and then ran noisily down the street. From the opposite direction, three passersby greeted Mrs. Nillson with informal curtsies and polite smiles.

The town seemed to bustle with activity—people coming and going, mothers with their small children in tow, business owners busily setting up for the day—a lot more activity than on a typical Tuesday morning. In front of one building, a group of older men stood engrossed in a heated political debate over whether or not men who provided safe harbor to runaway slaves should be permitted to run for local office. Marensburg had been notorious for its "safe houses" associated with the Underground Railroad, and there was a rising sense of contention between newcomers and families who had lived in Marensburg for years.

But more recently, one couldn't pass through the heart of town without hearing talk of Lincoln's campaign for a second term as President. The election was still six months away and the word on the street was that Pennsylvania would undoubtedly be the state that would sway the election to victory for the incumbent. I didn't pay much attention to all the hype because I already knew the outcome. Regardless, however, I was careful to feign concern for a potential disagreeable outcome on

Election Day, and in doing so, I made a conscious effort to do my part for the good of the cause.

Thankfully, the Hastings women were more involved in domestic concerns today, so we ignored the undercurrents of political angst. Mrs. Weddington accompanied Christine and me toward the shops that ran along the west side of town, and once we arrived we separated, each with our own agenda. I meandered in and out of shops, making my way toward the south end of town. I suppose there was a part of me that wanted to be near the train station—that I might be lucky enough to run into Conrad and Henrietta if I waited there long enough. I knew it was unlikely; they would be in North Carolina by now and grateful to be safely free of northern judgment. Still, there was something very promising in the sound of the train's whistle, and one never knew who they might run into if they hung around long enough. I listened carefully, but was disappointed when I heard nothing. A fleeting thought made me wonder how much a ticket to California might cost and I had to laugh.

"Out with no chaperone?"

I spun around, startled by the unexpected voice, and found myself face to face with Jonathan. I couldn't resist staring at this younger version of the Jonathan I would love so much in the future. The boy who stood in front of me now was definitely rough around the edges, but every bit as handsome as *my* Jonathan.

"Risky, don't you think?" he added when I didn't respond.

When I finally gathered my wits, I glanced around quickly, praying no one else could see him. "What do you want, J . . . Mr. Rollings?" The words sounded sharper than I intended.

"So it's *Mr. Rollings* now, is it? The rules seem to vary where you're concerned. Shall we blame it on the weather? Always a bit fickle this time of year, particularly in Marensburg; wouldn't you agree? Must be something about springtime—"

"Please . . . I can't be seen like this," I interrupted him. As elated as I was to see Jonathan, I wasn't ready for another two weeks of Bible duty.

"Like what, exactly, Miss Hastings?"

"Like this . . . here . . . with you."

"Afraid of what Daddy might say? Or are you afraid people will get the wrong idea about us?"

I studied his face, a face I knew so well and yet not at all. His eyes burned with a fire that I didn't recognize. Anger, perhaps? He watched me study him for several seconds and then the fire softened.

"As a matter of fact, yes!" I said meekly. "I just spent two weeks copying the book of Hosea after we . . . I . . . ." I struggled to find the right words and then gave up. "What do you want, Jonathan?"

"There! You see? That's exactly what I'm talking about."

The sudden rumbling of hoofs in the distance stole Jonathan's attention. He stiffened slightly and watched as several men on horseback sped hurriedly down the center of the road, making no attempt to avoid the people in their way. Passersby quickly darted to the side of the road, allowing them clear passage. Jonathan's eyes followed the speeding horsemen until they were out of sight. He drew in a deep breath and let it out slowly, staring off into the distance long after the dust had settled. I watched him from the corner of my eye, surprised by how agitated he seemed.

I seized the opportunity to change the subject. "There seems to be more of them lately," I commented, gesturing toward the horsemen's path. "Why do you suppose that is?"

Jonathan's eyes remained fixed on the horizon as he answered. "Reckon we can't be too careful with Mosby's Battalion on the loose."

"Mosby?" I searched my limited memory of Civil War history for anyone known by that name and came up empty.

"Mosby's managed to cut off supplies to several of our units. And we can't stop him—seems he's either one step ahead of us or lurking in the shadows somewhere, waiting to make his next move."

"I just can't imagine he'd be someone *that* important or I'd have heard of him." I didn't realize how egocentric I sounded until I heard the words come out of my mouth. There was no way for me to explain to Jonathan that the history books in my high school had condensed a four-year war into a thirty-page abridgement that focused only on key players and battles. I couldn't recall ever reading about someone named Mosby.

Jonathan shook his head. "No, I don't imagine there's much talk of the 'Gray Ghost' among your circles," he muttered.

"Gray Ghost?" I questioned, suddenly intrigued.

Jonathan glanced over his shoulder at me. "That's what people here call him," he chuckled darkly. "He's the leader of Mosby's Rangers. They're mostly just kids from reports I've heard. They disguise themselves as civilians, living among the townsfolk in areas throughout northern Virginia. Lee and Stuart authorized Mosby to organize raids—he strikes quick and he strikes hard. Sneaks in just about anywhere undetected, destroys valuable resources, takes what he wants, and then disappears into the background. Been happening all across northern Virginia— 'lightning strikes' they call 'em—even made his way across our border a time or two. And no one can seem to stop him."

Jonathan continued to stare off into the distance, his mind far away. His frustration was palpable. Without thinking, I reached over and touched his arm. "You're anxious to leave, aren't you?"

Jonathan turned suddenly; his gaze quickly shifted to my hand. He seemed distracted because it took him a moment to respond and when he did, all he could muster was a weak, "Hmm?"

Realizing what I'd done, I moved my hand away and did my best to pretend nothing out of the ordinary had occurred. I started to finish my thought, but apparently, Jonathan wasn't the only one who was distracted. I was having trouble remembering what we were talking about. I ventured a guess, "You know, to get back to your men?"

Jonathan shook his head and turned, again fixing his eyes on the horizon where the horsemen had disappeared. "No," he chewed on his bottom lip for a long moment before adding, "I'm just anxious for this war to end."

I turned, peering in the same direction as Jonathan. "I can only imagine," I finally said. I couldn't help but think about the thousands of lives still to be lost before the southern rebels surrendered.

Jonathan shook his head derisively. "You can't imagine. Nobody can—not unless they've been there. It's such a useless waste of lives."

"The war will end Jonathan, and when it does, you'll see that those lives were not lost in vain."

Jonathan scoffed. "Really?" The biting sarcasm in his voice could not hide the sorrow in his eyes. I longed to take the pain away from him, but I understood all too well that he would yet experience pain even more unbearable than what he was feeling now.

"It will end, Jonathan."

Jonathan glanced down at his feet and dragged his shoe across the loose gravel that paved the road. "There's just so many of them . . . so many." He looked back up at me. "Like your brothers . . . gone. Just like that. And for what?"

I shook my head. I only had a few borrowed memories of Eleanor's older brothers so I couldn't feel the emotions prompted by Jonathan's question, but I knew that deep down, Eleanor did.

"It wasn't all for nothing. I refuse to accept that their deaths were meaningless."

Jonathan shook his head. "Is that what you tell your mother when she cries herself to sleep at night?"

My next words were unexpected—and they were not mine. "We do not discuss their deaths in our home. Mother forbids it."

Jonathan looked at me quizzically and then shrugged. "Well, regardless, it's a terrible loss for both your parents." He paused, watching me carefully, then continued. "I imagine it's especially difficult for your father."

"Why do you say that?" I asked.

"To lose all his sons . . . the heirs to the great Hastings Estate?"

I glared at him coolly. There was an unexplained hostility beneath the surface of his words—a hostility with which I was unfamiliar. I sensed Eleanor's pull to put an end to the conversation; I got the distinct impression that she felt uneasy in Jonathan's presence. I wondered what it was about him that had her so on edge. I decided it was probably because she was afraid of being seen with him—either that or deep down she had a crush on him.

"I really must go, Mr. Rollings."

Just like that, Jonathan's eyes were on fire again, his jaw stiff.

"Please give my regards to your sister," I was saying, when all of a sudden he grabbed me by the arm and hurled me through the side door of a feed barn. Before I could protest, he whipped me around and grabbed me from behind.

"What? Stop!" I demanded.

In a flash, his hand covered my mouth, making it impossible for me to speak. I squirmed to free myself, but his grip only tightened.

"Shh!" The urgency in his tone alarmed me. His hot breath against my ear made it difficult to concentrate. I tried again to wiggle free, startled by his abrupt action.

"Shh!" he whispered, more gently this time. "Your Mrs. Weddington is coming. Be still."

I relaxed slightly and listened expectantly for Mrs. Weddington's footsteps. My mind instantly began planning an excuse for being here, alone with Jonathan. It was bad enough that I had wandered so far on my own, but to be discovered hiding with the boy I had shamelessly thrown myself at just a few short weeks earlier was beyond any reasonable explanation. I reached up and tried to pry Jonathan's hand from my mouth, but that made him hold me even closer.

"Hold on," he whispered, this time sending a shiver from the side of my face all the way down to the tips of my fingers. In a split second, I was in the twenty-first century, pinned beneath the tangled mess that used to be my mother's car. In that flash of a moment, my hand burned with immeasurable pain. The memory was excruciatingly vivid—but it was wrong. Not in the way a dream can feel when something goes wrong and even though you're sleeping, you can change the dream until it feels right. No, this was a memory that should have been mine, but it was very wrong.

My mind snapped back to the feed store. I was aware of the rough dirt floor beneath my feet, the tight squeeze of the corset around my waist, and the chill of Jonathan's breath on my bare shoulder.

This close proximity to Jonathan should have elicited a reaction from Eleanor. Perhaps my own longing to be close to him overpowered her strict need to follow the rules of propriety. Or, perhaps secretly Eleanor was enjoying this.

A moment passed and I became acutely aware of Jonathan's pulse as blood pumped its way through the veins in the hand he held pressed against my lips. He brushed his cheek lightly against mine; was that intentional? I felt a powerful urge to twist my face toward his, to tell him who I really was and to make him love me. I was weighing the consequences of such a move when Jonathan breathed a sigh of relief and slowly released his hand from my mouth.

"Don't do it," he whispered.

Do what? Was he reading my mind? "Do what?" I whispered back.

He brushed his cheek against mine again—this time it was definitely intentional. "Don't marry him."

I stopped breathing long enough for his unexpected words to fully register.

"I . . . uh . . ." I stammered, trying to sort through my thoughts on the spot. But they were a jumbled heap. "I have to go," I finally managed, deciding to ignore his comment. I squirmed half-heartedly beneath his grasp.

"Wait," Jonathan said, pulling me closer. "I don't know what happened the other day. I can't explain it, maybe you can't explain it either, but something happened between us and I've thought of nothing else since then. It's driving me crazy."

Jonathan's words stunned me. Was it possible that he sensed—?

"Eleanor, listen to me."

Instantly, an unexpected explosion of jealousy washed over me and I forced myself free of his hold.

"Don't you call me that!" I exclaimed. I knew the minute I said it he would misunderstand, but I didn't care. I couldn't stand the sound of Eleanor's name on his lips.

Jonathan scoffed and his eyes hardened. "Very well, Miss Hastings." His voice was lathered with contempt. He released me with such disdain that I nearly lost my footing.

"Why don't you tell me what kind of game you're playing, or are you such a tease you don't even know? I'm having trouble keeping up—your rules seem to keep changing."

"There's no game. No rules. At least not the way you mean. It's just not right, you being so familiar with me."

Jonathan scoffed again. "I see. We'll just leave the familiarity to you, right?"

Without hesitation, Eleanor reached up and slapped Jonathan across the face; I know it was Eleanor's doing because the idea of slapping someone was as foreign to me as learning a third-world language. It was definitely not something I would have done as Beth.

Jonathan flinched. He grabbed my arm before I could pull it back and forced me up next to him. I could see the red mark of Eleanor's hand already beginning to swell on his cheek.

"Careful, Miss Hastings," he smirked, "I might just get the wrong idea."

I struggled to wiggle my arm free but Jonathan maintained his iron grasp with ease. After several attempts, I finally gave up. No doubt this would cause Eleanor's delicate arm to bruise.

"What do you want from me, Jonathan?"

He raised his eyebrows. "How very interesting."

"What now?" I made no attempt to hide the fact that I was annoyed.

He shook his head. "You and your one-sided rules. You really are a tease, aren't you?"

Eleanor wanted to strike him again. I admit, I was a little surprised by this new revelation. Eleanor had quite a temper. Thankfully, I was the stronger of the two of us—at least for now. I normally controlled Eleanor's body, except when I made a conscious effort to allow her to take over, like when I didn't know which gloves to wear or what eating utensil to use. When it came to emotions, however, the control didn't work the same way. Eleanor's emotions could surface at any time, and although they didn't overpower my own emotions, it was as if I were experiencing two emotions simultaneously.

I decided it was best for me to leave as quickly as possible, before Eleanor ended up making a real scene. "Goodbye, Mr. Rollings," I said curtly and turned to leave.

"At least tell me why you did it!" Jonathan called after me.

I turned around to face him, careful to maintain a safe distance between us. "Did what?"

"Why did you . . . ," he took a careful look around before stepping closer, closing the distance between us. His eyes searched mine as he lowered his voice. "Why did you kiss me?"

I sucked in some unwanted air and felt the color immediately rise in my cheeks. Jonathan noticed and instantly raised a curious brow. There was no way to explain this one—no way he could possibly understand. I lowered my eyes and shook my head. "I thought you were somebody else," I offered pitifully.

Jonathan nudged my chin with the back of his fingers, forcing me to look at him again.

"Someone named Jonathan?" he asked softly. Although his eyes were gentle and searching, they clearly revealed he knew I was lying. Their intense shade of blue unnerved me; they were the color of the evening sky—rich and mesmerizing. I thought of how many times I had lost myself in his gaze.

"You know, they say when a woman blushes in a man's arms, it leaves a lasting impression."

"Jonathan," I whispered, thinking of the boy I had left behind.

"It was *me* you flew at." Jonathan reached forward and gently brushed the back of his finger against my cheek. "I need to know why? Why trifle with me?"

It took every bit of my resolve to step away from him. "No, Jonathan. It's not like that. I haven't been the same since I got sick. I don't remember things correctly. I say things, do things that I shouldn't. When I saw you, I thought you were . . . that we were . . . ." I shook my head, annoyed that I couldn't find the right words. There was just no way to make him understand without revealing too much.

"That we were what?" His eyes narrowed.

I let out a frustrated sigh. "It doesn't matter, okay? It just doesn't matter."

"I disagree. I think it matters very much. Your kiss," he shook his head, "there was something behind it, something you're not telling me. I mean let's face it, a woman like you doesn't throw herself at someone like me for no reason. What is it you're not telling me?"

"I'm sorry, Jonathan." I took another step backwards. "I'm really very sorry for this whole misunderstanding."

As I turned and began walking away I could feel Jonathan's eyes still fixed on me, but I didn't dare look back until I was safely across the street. Jonathan had stepped forward and was leaning against the post that had concealed us only moments earlier. His arms were folded across his chest and the minute our eyes met, he cocked his head to one side. And there it was. That grin! Jonathan's lopsided grin. I struggled to remain expressionless, to refrain from giving him any further signs of encouragement, but once taken in by that boyish grin of his, I was powerless to resist. And so I did something very unlike Eleanor—I laughed. Jonathan's grin widened as he watched me from across the street. After a moment he looked away, shaking his head.

"Eleanor! There you are! I've been looking everywhere for

you!" Christine's voice stole my attention and I spun around quickly to greet her as she trotted towards me.

"I'm right here," I said innocently.

"Did you already go to the feed barn?"

"I, um," I looked down at my empty hands. "I got distracted."

Christine eyed me curiously, expecting a more detailed explanation. But when I didn't offer one, she gave up and shrugged. "Mrs. Weddington has been looking for you, too."

"Where is she?" I asked, quickly shifting the focus.

"Probably at Newell's Fabric Store. That's where she thought you were going."

"Well then, sister," I offered Christine my arm, "I suppose we'd better make haste and get over there, wouldn't you agree?"

"Did you decide on the ribbon for your gown?"

She was referring to my "coming out" gown, of course, which for some reason was the big buzz in ladies' circles. Plans for the upcoming event had the social elite prattling on about this and that, grateful for any reprieve from talk of war, wounded or missing soldiers, recently-freed slaves from the South, and failed businesses.

"Not yet. I was hoping you would help me," I replied, patting her arm.

Christine straightened her posture and smiled proudly, pleased to share in such an important decision.

An unusual movement in the distance suddenly caught the corner of my eye; but when I turned to look, there was nothing unusual or out of the ordinary—nothing that should have grabbed my attention. It was just a man sitting on his horse, watching me. That in itself was nothing out of the ordinary. Eleanor always attracted men's attention, no matter where she went. But this man was somehow different, and though there was some amount of distance between us, I was certain I knew him.

He tipped his hat in a gentlemanlike fashion and nodded once, confirming my suspicions. Even from a distance, I could see that he was devastatingly handsome.

He gave a quick kick and his horse reared gloriously before taking off at a dead run. I stood motionless, staring intently as the man and his horse disappeared behind a long ribbon of trees.

"What's the matter?" Christine asked, tugging on my arm.

"Who was that man?" I replied, watching for a sign that he might return.

"What man?" Christine's eyes followed mine. She squinted against the bright light of the noonday sun.

"The one that just rode off behind those trees."

Christine shook her head. "I didn't see anybody."

"Funny," I said under my breath. Jonathan's reference to the "Gray Ghost" suddenly flashed through my mind.

"What?"

I shook my head. "The way he looked at me; I'm certain I should know him."

Christine started to giggle and I turned to face her. "What are you laughing at?"

"You," she grinned. "You're always so surprised when men stop and stare at you."

"All right squirt, enough of that. Let's go pick out some ribbon and find old Mrs. Weddington."

With that, we skipped arm in arm to join in the fuss and fury over Eleanor's coming out gown.

Debutante Ball
CHAPTER 5

*A*fter weeks of endless chatter and planning, the day of the Debutante Ball finally arrived. Although I was relieved that all the hype was about to come to an end, I sensed a sadness and regret among the ladies of society. When given the choice, the more refined ladies of Marensburg preferred to focus on the frivolity of a "coming out" celebration over the devastation of the war—a topic that was, at least for the moment, off limits among the upper class women of society.

"Leave all the talk of war to the men," I heard women say repeatedly. "Someone has to tend to the finer details of life, like introducing our girls properly into society. We'll not allow the war to cause us to lose sight of our duties."

I couldn't help but laugh to myself when I thought about how much times had changed. Still, I had to admit, it was hard not to get caught up in all the excitement surrounding the big event. The Debutante Ball had been the subject of many a discussion held in parlors throughout Marensburg, and everyone who was, or hoped to be anyone, found a way to involve themselves in the preparations.

In my life as Beth, the only formal dances I ever attended were my high school Homecoming and Prom. Actually, I doubt you could count

Prom since technically, I wasn't there with a date, I was there as a member of the junior class planning committee. Homecoming was another story. I attended my first Homecoming dance when I was a junior in Carlsbad, California. I went with Adam, my first actual boyfriend, and truth be told, we didn't do that much dancing. High school dances in Southern California could get a little crazy, especially in a school as large as the one I attended. Adam was a senior and we had just gotten back together after one of our many breakups, so that particular evening he was on his best behavior—he could pour on the charm when he wanted to. It had been way too hot to stay on the dance floor because the air conditioning in the gymnasium had stopped working earlier that afternoon, much to the horror of our activities director. The majority of the kids didn't seem to mind, but Adam and I ended up spending the bulk of our night outside where they had set up a karaoke stage. I laughed as I remembered Adam trying to sing.

It was two years later when I went to my next Homecoming dance. Technically, I should have already been in college, but seven months in a coma had put me behind schedule. I attended Homecoming in Andersen with my friend, Darla. Jonathan surprised us both when he showed up unexpectedly and announced that he was there as a chaperone. I chuckled when I remembered how Eric had referred to Jonathan as the "piano pansy."

The Debutante Ball resembled neither a prom nor a homecoming. In fact, I could think of nothing in the twenty-first century to compare it to; at least not from my perspective as the daughter of middle-class parents. I couldn't help but wonder if "coming out" parties still occurred among the upper echelon of modern day America.

May was typically unpredictable in Marensburg, particularly as we neared the end of the month and got closer to June. June temperatures could be quite uncomfortable, but fortunately, Mother Nature decided to cooperate on the afternoon of the Ball. The temperature was mildly warm with a gentle breeze that allowed fresh air to circulate through the open doors and windows of the Hastings mansion, the host house for the Ball. Beginning early in the afternoon, the Debutantes arrived one by one, escorted by their mothers and their maids. Each girl waited in a private room where she would spend the better part of the day reviewing the strict protocols that accompanied such an occasion. These attempts at last minute coaching were redundant. Young ladies of society were trained well ahead of time for their "coming out," with several rehearsals long in advance of the important occasion. Dressmakers and personal seamstresses scurried around, tending to every last detail of their mistress' gowns—each a work of art in itself. Final fittings were made prior to the midday meal, incentive for the girls to eat sparingly. Following our meager meal, we were given strict instructions to lie down and rest.

Nothing about the sequence of events made sense to me, but as soon as the sun began its final slide into the western horizon, everything changed. That's when the real explosion of activity began. Maids and mothers scampered about fussing over this and that, lace flew in every direction, and energy levels hit an all-time high. Corsets were tightened, retightened, and then tightened again—mine to the extent that I was certain my ribs would crack.

"That's too tight!" I squawked. "Land sakes Lucinda, I can't breathe!"

"Sorry, Miss Eleanor. It's the mistress's orders."

"It won't do any of us any good if I faint on my way downstairs," I reasoned.

"Word is, Miss Hamilton's waist measures less than eighteen inches. Your mother will have my head if yours isn't the smallest. Now, hold your breath and suck in your stomach."

I raised my eyes in hopeless submission and braced myself for more torture. Lucinda pulled and tugged until I lost my footing and nearly fell.

"Miss Eleanor!" Lucinda stretched out her arms to help me regain my balance. "That's a seventeen-and-a-half-inch waist if ever I've seen one!" she remarked triumphantly. "There's nobody who can steal your shine." Lucinda shook her head with pride. "Now, let's get you into that dress."

Lucinda led me to my dress, which lay artistically bundled on the bed. She enlisted the help of two other maids, and together the three of them managed to strategically position the dress so that I could step into it with remarkable ease. It required all three of them to fasten what had to be hundreds of tiny hooks and eyes.

Eleanor's dress was in itself a fascinating creation. It was an antique-white silk, richly trimmed with row upon row of alternating forest green velvet and emerald satin ribbons. They ruffled their way along the off-the-shoulder princess sleeves and bodice, which was obviously tailored to advertise Eleanor's feminine figure. Tonight would be the first time the top of her bosom would be on public display for all to view.

Once the final touches were in place, Lucinda summoned Eleanor's mother for final inspection. Mother's face revealed no perceivable expression as she sauntered into the room to survey Lucinda's handiwork. Her eyes traveled up and down the length of the gown and then fixated on Eleanor's waist. Raising one eyebrow, she muttered, "Well, I suppose it will have to do." That was as close to a compliment as I might expect to receive from Eleanor's neurotic mother, but then as a second thought, she added, "I advise you to pass on the hors d'oeuvres tray tonight."

Surely this was the true origins of modern-day eating disorders! I couldn't remember anyone with a waist smaller than twenty-two inches in high school. Even Darla, my closest friend in Wyoming—and the girl with the prettiest shape in school—couldn't boast a waist less than twenty-four inches. If I were to show up in school in the twenty-first century with a seventeen-inch waist, the teachers would hold an intervention and put me in a rehabilitation center for sure.

Mother fluffed my sleeves, pulling them down lower, beyond what should have been considered appropriate, and revealing far more of Eleanor's bosom than even I would have thought proper. I would have to be extremely careful and deliberate with my every movement, or I would quite literally bounce out of my dress. I could only imagine what a scandal that would cause—it would definitely put a unique spin on the phrase, "coming-out party." I started to laugh at the thought, but my corset was too tight. Laughing would definitely result in broken ribs. Somehow, it occurred to me that Eleanor's mother had thought all of this through very carefully. There would be no room for error or lapse in judgment during tonight's gala. Move slowly, stay away from snack trays, and refrain from laughter. If I could have chuckled I would have, for this was the absolute antithesis of a *party* in my mind.

Finally, the moment arrived for me to see for myself what all the fuss of the afternoon had been about. Lucinda and Mother turned me around and walked me over to the grand oval mirror that stood at the far end of the room. My breath stopped as I caught a glimpse of my reflection in the mirror.

"Land sakes!" I whispered in awe. Eleanor's reflection never ceased to take my breath away, but this was unlike anything I had ever seen—unlike anything real. Eleanor was a vision of absolute beauty, the embodiment of perfection. The contrast between her slight waist and full bosom was elegantly underscored by the feminine cut of the dress, in spite of the fact that the low-cut bodice left very little to the imagination.

As proprietor of the host house, it was Father's privilege to welcome the guests before the presentation of the Debutantes began. Each father waited at the bottom of the stairs for his daughter to appear from behind a curtain hung specially at the top of the staircase for this very occasion. When the signal was given, each girl would step out from behind the curtain into full view of the admiring audience. The announcer would then present the name of the Debutante and amidst the "oohs" and "aahs" of the crowd, she would proceed down the stairs to where her father waited to offer her his arm. He would then lead her to the dance floor and wait for the other Debutantes to arrive.

Father made sure I was the last of the five debutantes presented. The crowd, though generous in its applause when each of the other four girls was presented, seemed stunned when I passed through the curtain. I glanced down at Eleanor's father, whose face glowed with pride. I couldn't help but sense that his pride was less about Eleanor and more about him and how it made him feel to escort the most beautiful girl in the room into the ballroom.

As the host, it was customary for Eleanor's father to thank the members of society for their acceptance of the debutantes and welcome those who were there by special invitation—those of social significance. Following the formalities, Eleanor's father escorted me to the center of the ballroom floor for the official beginning of the Ball. As Beth, I could not imagine being on display in such a way, but Eleanor was right at home. Eyes raised, posture perfect, smile appropriately conservative—Eleanor oozed elegance. She knew it, and the gaping crowd knew it. There was no shortage of audible gasps and gawking stares as Father led me in the first dance and paraded me proudly for all of Marensburg society to admire. Part of me felt sorry for the other girls who were, in their own ways, exceptionally beautiful tonight; but all of them paled in comparison to Eleanor Hastings, and I admit, there was a little part of me that relished being thought of as the prettiest girl at the dance.

As custom dictated, each debutante had a dance card with partners carefully pre-assigned. There were openings strategically spaced on the card to allow the girls opportunities to rest or, if they were inclined, to dance if invited to do so. Refusing a pre-arranged dance was not only considered impolite, it could result in social suicide among some; however, a debutant may decline an offer if the offer did not appear on her dance card. Had this been a more traditional Debutante Ball, there would have been a more significant level of concern over propriety; but there was a war going on and eligible men were scarce, so society turned a blind eye to some of the more strict protocols.

Jonathan's name, while generously represented on the other girls' dance cards, was noticeably absent from mine; but that didn't stop our eyes from meeting several times as we danced with other partners. Deep down I felt a twinge of jealousy, for I knew it was Eleanor who held Jonathan's attention tonight, not me—not Beth Arrington. But that didn't stop me from accepting his invitation to dance the first time I sat down to rest.

"Miss Hastings, might I have the pleasure?" His crystal blue eyes unsettled me, as usual. He offered his hand with a polite bow. I felt Eleanor withdraw, but I didn't get the sense it was out of disapproval. Instead, it felt as if she was allowing us some privacy.

I laid my gloved hand in his and stood facing him for a silent moment before he turned to lead me onto the floor. I wished we could remove our gloves so I could feel his skin against mine, but even through the white satin, I recognized his hold. My heart hammered against my chest and I had to avert my eyes to recover.

Jonathan guided me with ease to the far side of the ballroom before turning to face me and placing his free hand on the middle of my back. Our eyes locked as the music began playing a familiar Vienna waltz. Jonathan was uncharacteristically silent; uncharacteristic because the Jonathan of the future was never at a loss for words. Everything in me wanted him to pull me closer. I wanted to touch his face, smell his skin, twist my fingers through the hair at the back of his neck. My eyes traced the contour of his face and rested on his lips. In a flash, I was standing in the music hall at the recreation center across from Andersen High School where I saw Jonathan for the first time. I had been so taken with his performance of Chopin's Etude in E that I'd stopped to listen to him play, unaware that Mr. Laden, the head of the music program, was watching me. I remembered Jonathan's lopsided smile, and how I had fought the urge to reach up and straighten his lips with my finger.

The flash to the future closed and I was once again standing on the ballroom floor, staring at Jonathan's mouth. Without thinking, I let out an involuntary chuckle. I immediately caught myself, but it was too late.

"You're amused," Jonathan said, titling his head slightly.

"Your lips are crooked." The words escaped before my brain could stop them.

Jonathan stopped dancing for a quick second and eyed me curiously. Then he began to laugh. His laugh was not only music to my ears, it was contagious. When I joined in the laughter, Jonathan's eyes lit up. They were deep blue stars, shining just as they did in the future whenever he smiled at me, only without their signature twinkling-like phenomenon. Before I knew it, we were waltzing around the ballroom floor without the slightest care for propriety. To my amazement, my gown managed to hold everything in place, despite the freedom in our movements.

My joy was short-lived however, when the music stopped and my next dance partner stepped in to take Jonathan's place. Lawrence Hamilton was one of Eleanor's many cousins who had vied for her hand, but Eleanor's father had already decided her fate where nuptials were concerned. Her match had been arranged many years prior.

I never had another opportunity to dance with Jonathan, even though there were four additional vacancies on my dance card. Mother whisked me away before the next opening, feigning some need for my assistance with her gown. Father magically appeared for the next opening and asked me to take a turn around the room with him so he could personally present me to a few of the more distinguished guests. Of course, there was no real need for introductions; but this was Father's show, so naturally I indulged him. My aching feet could not stand another dance, so when the last open dance began, I excused myself and headed for one of the balconies for some much needed air and a moment of privacy.

Unlike the large balcony on the third floor which overlooked the south side of the estate and its lush gardens, there were six smaller balconies spaced evenly around the second floor, four of which protruded from the vast ballroom. The other two connected to the library and the sun room, also known as the garden room, depending on the time of year. With only a few rare exceptions, these rooms were strictly reserved for family. I knew the rooms and their respective balconies well; but admittedly, the grand ballroom was my favorite because it was home to the grand piano (which I had come to love almost as much as I loved my piano back in Uncle Connor's basement). The ballroom piano was more elegant and much more powerful than the pianoforte located in the drawing room.

I made my escape to the south corner balcony before the music began. Two younger girls sat on a bench engrossed in a conversation that stopped short when they saw me approach. They quickly vacated the bench and headed back into the ballroom before I had a chance to inquire as to whether they were enjoying the ball. Grateful for the crisp night air, I seated myself on the abandoned bench. Mindful of my tight corset, I carefully bent down to remove my shoes and rub my throbbing feet.

"May I join you?"

I didn't have to look up to recognize who it was; I would have known that angelic voice anywhere.

"Please, sit down," I said, patting the seat next to me. I slid over to make room. Grace smiled graciously and sat down beside me.

"It is a lovely ball, Miss Hastings," she began. "I can't remember ever attending one so exquisite."

"Thank you, Miss Rollings."

"Please, call me Grace," she said politely.

I smiled and nodded. "And you may call me Eleanor."

Almost in unison, we both gazed up at the stars and sighed.

"It's beautiful, isn't it," she breathed.

"Yes," I whispered, "but it's nothing like a Wyoming sky." I paused for a moment and then added, "at least, that's what they tell me."

"I'm afraid I'm not familiar with Wyoming. Is it near here?"

"Heavens no," I responded without thinking. "Wyoming is a big territory out west. Surely you've heard of it?"

Grace looked confused. "I don't recall a territory by that name."

Evidently my knowledge of western expansion was severely lacking, so I determined it might be better if I just let the subject drop.

It was several moments before Grace broke the silence. "Do you know many people who have made the journey west?"

I chuckled softly. "Yes, I suppose I do."

"Well, if your Wyoming sky is lovelier than this, then I hope to travel there myself someday."

I smiled and looked over at her. "I'm sure you will . . . someday. And while you're there, you must find your way to the Grand Tetons." I figured there was no harm giving her a little encouragement.

"What are the Grand Tetons?" she asked, curious.

Again I had to chuckle, for I knew that someday Grace would view the Tetons with as much awe and reverence as I did. "They're part of a great mountain range along the western border of the sta . . . er . . . territory." I couldn't remember when Wyoming officially became a state, but apparently it wasn't even a territory yet. "Some claim the mountains and foothills there have magical powers," I added.

Grace smiled. "Well then, I most certainly must see them."

We sat gazing at the sky again, but after a few moments I learned what was truly on her mind.

"My brother appears to be quite taken with you, Eleanor."

I turned to face her and couldn't help but notice the sparkling moisture in her eyes.

"You don't approve." My comment started as a question, but it dawned on me that I already knew the answer.

"Forgive me, please," she said, shaking her head. "It's just that I feel very protective of my brother. You seem to have caused quite an emotional upheaval in him since he's been home."

"I didn't mean to, honestly. I'm afraid sometimes I take leave of all my senses."

Grace smiled and turned her head to one side. "Oh, dear, I fear perhaps you might be equally smitten."

I could sense Eleanor's life force emerging within me, fighting for a voice.

"I'm sure you must be mistaken. Your brother is an acquaintance, nothing more."

"Yes, of course." Grace lowered her head. "You'll forgive me if I misjudged your feelings for him."

"I am to be married to another." The words surprised me. They were Eleanor's, not mine. Eleanor's life force was so powerful at that moment that I couldn't help but resent her for intruding on my time with Grace.

Grace smiled and nodded. "Yes, the whole town awaits the official announcement." She eyed me carefully for several seconds and then leaned in close. "Eleanor, please do not trifle with my brother's heart. A lady as beautiful and charming as you are is surely not unaware of the impact she has on others. Jonathan is a young man and quite impressionable. He's never been in love before, and I'm afraid he may mistake your friendliness for something more."

The chastisement in Grace's tone was cutting, but her compassion for Jonathan moved me deeply.

"You love your brother very much, don't you?"

Grace smiled. "He's everything to me."

"I can see that," I replied, resting my hand on her arm.

Grace's eyes locked on mine and I had the strange feeling she was keeping something from me. "Be careful Eleanor," she finally said. "I sense your own feelings run deeper than you care to admit." She continued to search my eyes as if she could see right through me.

"Grace," I said, unlocking my eyes from hers, "perhaps in another time, another place, there might have been something—some possibility—but now is not that time. There are rules, obligations."

"Yes, of course." Grace forced a polite smile. "I apologize for speaking so frankly."

"On the contrary, I appreciate your frankness. And I assure you, I have no intention of hurting your brother."

Grace studied my face for several moments before nodding, seemingly satisfied. She compassionately laid her hand on mine and as she did so, I couldn't help but notice she was wearing a very unusual bracelet. I lifted our hands to the light.

"Your bracelet . . ." I said, fascinated.

"Yes?" She smiled proudly and touched it with her free fingers.

"It's so . . ." I couldn't find the right words.

"Peculiar?" she replied, finishing my thought.

"Yes," I agreed. "Peculiar, but also stunning."

Grace smiled again, pleased by the compliment. "It's very dear to me." Her eyes shifted briefly to a faraway place and then back to me.

"What are these markings?" I asked, pointing to an unusual series of asymmetrical shapes that dangled from the entire circumference of the bracelet.

"I'm told they're a modified form of hieroglyphics, but I'm sure that's more myth than reality."

"What do they mean?" I asked, turning her wrist to study the varying shapes.

"They tell the story of a young warrior who fell in love with the daughter of a king. See?" she said, pointing to one of the symbols. "Here he is. You can tell by his bow. The stones near his head show he was a very great warrior and fought in many battles."

"Hmm." I said, inspecting the shape more closely. "What happens in the story?"

About that time the music stopped and small groups began to gather along the balcony.

"Must be the final break," Grace noted.

Then Jonathan appeared holding two beverage glasses. He smiled when he saw Grace, but was clearly surprised to find her sitting next to me.

"Uh oh," Grace whispered. "I'm not going to hear the end of this." She chuckled softly and motioned for Jonathan to join us.

"Ladies?" He greeted us with a polite bow and handed us each a drink, all the while shifting his eyes curiously between Grace and me. "What are you two up to?"

In that split second everything suddenly felt natural, as if the three of us were the same as we'd been in the twenty-first century, sitting around the kitchen table at the Rollings' ranch with no rules forcing a wedge between our families. I was completely at ease and it felt wonderful.

I looked up at Jonathan and smiled. "Your sister was just explaining the story on her bracelet."

"Ah yes. The Egyptian warrior and his fair princess," he smiled knowingly. "Well, go on, don't let me interrupt," he gestured with exaggerated chivalry.

Grace was suddenly very bashful. "Please, don't tease me," she scolded softly. The affection they felt for each other was obvious. "Why don't you tell the story?" Grace suggested with her usual charm.

Jonathan started to protest, but something in Grace's expression made him change his mind. "Okay," he grinned, and his smile nearly stopped my heart. He was so young and so irresistibly handsome. I felt as though I were somehow cheating fate to find myself face to face with a much younger version of the boy I had fallen in love with in the future. He stepped closer and knelt down in front of where Grace and I sat. He reached for Grace's wrist and paused. "May I?" he asked.

"Of course." Grace placed her hand in Jonathan's and he began to slide the bracelet along her wrist, rotating it until it landed in a particular spot.

"The legend goes that the king's daughter knew her father would never consent to her marrying the warrior, for he had plans to form an alliance with a neighboring kingdom. Those plans included the marriage of his daughter to another, even though her heart belonged to the young warrior." Jonathan glanced up at me. "It's the same age-old story told time and again, even in our day." He held my eyes for a slight moment before shifting his attention back to the bracelet.

"The king's daughter came up with a plan which she hoped would convince the king to change his mind. At her request, the king held a huge feast and invited all the noblemen of the surrounding kingdoms to attend. At the beginning of the feast, the king announced a contest wherein the noblemen could compete for the hand of his daughter."

Jonathan grinned and shook his head. Grace placed her finger over his mouth and gave him a playful look of chastisement.

"I'm afraid my brother thinks legends such as this are all very silly." Grace was speaking for my benefit, but she kept her eyes fixed on Jonathan.

Jonathan chuckled and gently moved Grace's finger away from his mouth. "Must you scold me in front of my audience?"

Grace pursed her lips and then gestured for Jonathan to continue.

"This small cluster of jewels represents the noblemen of the surrounding kingdoms." Jonathan pointed to a large red stone surrounded by irregularly cut blue and green crystals, possibly emeralds and sapphires. "The garnet in the center is the young maiden's heart."

"Which one is her warrior?" I asked. I reached over to touch the bracelet and as I did, my fingers brushed against Jonathan's. I pretended not to notice when he didn't slide his hand away from mine, but I was very much aware of the lingering contact as my fingers rested against his. When Jonathan didn't answer my question, I looked up and discovered his eyes were now fixed on me. For a brief moment I forgot everything—who I was, where I was, why I was there. Thankfully, Grace was there to pull us back.

"Go on, Brother, finish the story before the break is over."

I pulled my hand away and turned my focus back to the bracelet, but not before I noticed the concerned look on Grace's face as she watched her brother. Jonathan cleared his throat and continued.

"Naturally, the maiden's warrior fought with great valor and honor. No matter how challenging the quest, he prevailed."

"So he won her hand?" I asked.

"Not quite." Jonathan shook his head. "You see, the king had meant only to humor his daughter, convinced that the young warrior would be no match for the other noblemen. The king did not intend to surrender his daughter's hand to the warrior. Still, he played along—only he upped the stakes."

"What do you mean?"

"He changed the rules. The king told the warrior that the only way he could prove his worthiness was to prove himself in a real battle. It didn't matter that the warrior had already fought valiantly in many battles. So, desperate to prove himself and show his loyalty to the king, the warrior volunteered to serve in the king's army against the brutal, barbaric giants of the east. The king knew that the warrior would never survive on the front line, so he gave his word that upon the warrior's victorious return, he would win the hand of the princess."

"So in a sense, the king was signing the warrior's death warrant," I interjected.

"Precisely," Jonathan agreed.

"Did the princess know what the king was doing?"

"She knew. She begged her warrior not to go. She knew if he went, she would never see him again."

"But he went anyway?" I asked.

"Yes." Jonathan nodded.

"It was a fool's mission," Grace said sadly. I had been so engrossed in the story that I almost forgot Grace was there.

Jonathan pointed to another setting on the bracelet. "These three clear stones represent the maiden's tears."

"So they never saw each other again?" I asked.

Grace picked up the story from here. "The night before he was to leave, the maiden arranged to meet the warrior in secret. She offered herself to him and asked him to run away with her. She was willing to give up all her rights and privileges to be with the man she loved."

"So what did he do?" I asked.

Grace shrugged and tried to smile, but she could not mask the sadness in her eyes. "He was, after all, first and foremost a warrior."

"So, he left her?"

Grace lowered her eyes and nodded.

"He had no choice, really." Jonathan defended the warrior.

Grace gently pulled her wrist away from Jonathan and ran her fingers over the bracelet. "Before he left, he made the princess a promise." Grace's eyes glistened with moisture and she attempted to smile. I had the strange feeling that in some way this story held personal meaning for her.

"What was the promise?" I asked.

"The warrior cut a piece of leather from his laces and tied it around his maiden's wrist, assuring her that he would come for her. Then he said, 'If I cannot come, I will send my love for you to the gods, and they will place my love for you into another soul. When you meet him and he takes you by the hand, you will immediately recognize my love for you, for you shall sense it in his touch, see it in his eyes, and you will know beyond any doubt that my love has returned to you. You cannot stop a love that was meant to last forever.'"

When Grace finished, nobody said a word. Jonathan took both her hands in his and for a moment, he just knelt beside her, waiting until she collected herself.

"It really is just a silly story," she smiled, squeezing Jonathan's hands.

"And one that I'm sure will have a happy ending," Jonathan replied reassuringly. With that, he stood and offered Grace and me an arm. "Now then, shall I escort you ladies back to the dance floor before someone notices that the two prettiest girls are missing?"

"Thank you Mr. Rollings," a deep and unpleasant voice said. The three of us turned in unison to find Eleanor's father standing nearby. I wondered how long he'd been there, and how long he'd been listening.

"Eleanor," he said, stepping forward to offer me his arm. "You mustn't be rude to our guests."

I stood and slid my arm obediently through his. He started forward and then turned back. "Miss Rollings . . . Mr. Rollings." With that, Father offered a polite bow and escorted me back to the dance floor where my next partner would soon greet me.

Announcement
CHAPTER 6

*H*ad the Debutante Ball ended when Eleanor's father found me on the terrace with Jonathan and Grace, I would have happily waltzed upstairs to my room content and satisfied that the evening had been a success. I had danced with Jonathan, despite strategic efforts on Father's part to keep the two of us away from each other. I had also spent time with Grace, and I had a chance to witness firsthand the fondness between brother and sister while still in its youthful innocence. This was more than I could have hoped for from the evening. My only regret was that I had not found out the rest of the story about Grace's bracelet. I wanted so badly to know who gave it to her, and I wanted to know what happened to the warrior and his maiden.

The contentment I felt when I returned with Eleanor's father to the ballroom was short-lived. One look at my dance card reminded me that the evening was far from over. Father delivered me dutifully to my next dance partner and as soon as the music began I was whisked onto the dance floor in a jovial waltz. I didn't recognize the name or the face of my partner, but then that was true of many of the young men present. Mother had successfully managed to "borrow" as many single men as she could from neighboring towns—even as far away as Greencastle and Chambersburg—and although nobody dared say anything, it was no coincidence that most of them were soldiers who found themselves conveniently on some sort of leave during the coming-out season.

It was claimed that many soldiers had been stationed in the surrounding townships as precautionary measures on the part of the Union, to prevent against raids in the southern parts of the state. But regardless of the reason, Eleanor's mother took advantage of the situation. I secretly marveled at the power of old money in Pennsylvania, even in the midst of war. It also didn't hurt that Marensburg was home to one of the largest hospitals in the southern part of the state.

As my partner led me in the waltz, the ballroom quickly flooded with dancers. I was certain there were more people dancing than had been earlier. The room suddenly seemed uncomfortably crowded. It was as though everyone in the town of Marensburg had crammed themselves into the Hastings' ballroom. That wasn't the case, of course, only those who had been properly accepted in society were invited. Still, my nerves were on edge and I had the strangest feeling that the walls were closing in on me. It was a sharp contrast to how I had felt just moments earlier on the terrace with Grace and Jonathan. Voices echoed all around me, laughter grew more intense, and the dance steps quickened until they were noticeably out of sync with the music—yet nobody seemed to notice.

"Beth . . ." a voice whispered from behind me.

I turned suddenly to see where the voice came from, but all I saw was a room full of dancers spinning faster and faster around the ballroom floor.

"Beth . . ." the voice echoed again, only this time I could swear it was followed by a low chuckle. I turned quickly to the other side and glimpsed a dark movement from the corner of my eye. I tried to follow the movement with my eyes, but it disappeared as quickly as it had come.

"Beth . . . ." The voice came from behind me again, and then seemed to cycle around me. *"Beth . . . Beth . . . Beth . . . ."*

Try as I might, I couldn't find the source of the whisper that now pierced me at every turn. Another dark shadow caught the corner of my eye only this time, instead of disappearing, it rose like a thick mist spreading from the ground until it reached the high ceiling of the ballroom. Once there, it began to roll along the ceiling like an ominous cloud just before a thunderstorm. I looked around the room frantically, thinking others saw it too, but the dancers continued to spin and laugh unconcerned.

My dance partner pulled gently against my waist, turning me toward him. I'd forgotten he was there. Perhaps he could explain what was happening. My eyes glanced up to his, then I recoiled in horror as I recognized Bailey's dark image before me. I opened my mouth to scream for help, but the sound caught in the back of my throat, strangling me, until at last it managed to block my airflow. It only took a few seconds for the light to recede, but just before it disappeared, Bailey smiled. Then, in an all too familiar sequence, my world began fading to black.

This time the blackness was different. Instead of shutting down in a state of unconsciousness or escaping to a state of self-hypnotic safety, I was very much aware of everything around me: the clamoring of alarmed voices, the stunned gasps, biting cold air, and the smell of death. Voices echoed in a chorus of concern and I sensed the nearness of the crowd as several guests pressed ever closer. My body began to tingle, starting first with my fingers and toes and then flooding over my entire body. I suddenly felt the weight of my body no longer holding me to the ground. Within seconds, all sense of fear dissipated and I found myself standing in an upright position. When my eyes suddenly flashed open, I was no longer in the Hastings' ballroom; instead, I was floating along the hallways of Andersen High School in Wyoming.

I recognized everything, just as if I had been there only yesterday. I ghosted along, unnoticed by the staff and students who lined the halls. It didn't take long to realize that I had gone backwards in time from the perspective of my life as Beth. By the way the students were dressed, the signs posted along the walls announcing ASB cards for sale, and sign-ups for community service hours, I guessed it was early fall—more specifically, early fall of my senior year. Invisible to the world around me, I was free to roam—to listen in on conversations or simply observe my former classmates.

I quickly figured out that I was in the science corridor—a part of the school I knew particularly well. After discovering that my mother was heavily involved in researching the science of biological immortality, I'd spent a significant amount of time in the physics lab studying anything and everything relating to human cell reconstruction. It was a fascinating endeavor. Although the actual science of biological immortality had not been perfected (and wouldn't be for another twenty years), there were significant advancements in the field, and many groups were willing to go to great expense in order to gain access to the genetic codes. Supposedly, my mother had access to those codes and she was willing to sacrifice her life to keep them from falling into the wrong hands. My intuition told me there was more to her death— something to do with me—but I had no concrete answers. Jonathan and I had been on the brink of putting the pieces together just before the night Eric came to see me at Jonathan's ranch. Eric's death derailed us all and eventually led me to my current plight—trapped in the 1800s in Eleanor's body. My life as Beth Arrington was something I now experienced only in dreams, but there was something different about this particular dream. I had a sense of control this time that I hadn't experienced before, and I liked it.

As I drifted past the darkened classrooms, I caught a glimpse of my reflection in the dual pane windows that lined the labs. At first I thought there was something wrong with my vision—either my eyes were out of focus or having trouble adjusting. The image that should have been a mirror-like reflection of Beth was nothing more than a light shadow of Eleanor. It was like looking at a spirit, only the details appeared vague, almost vapor-like. I stretched my hand toward the window thinking that moving closer would bring my reflection into focus, but nothing changed. I watched in the window's reflection as a group of students passed by. I swung around several times to compare their reflections with mine. Their reflections were normal—absolute mirror images complete down to the smallest detail. I studied my own reflection, troubled that no matter how hard I concentrated, I could not make my image any clearer. After several moments I finally gave up, reminding myself that I was only dreaming.

Even if I was dreaming, it felt so good to be home that I made a conscious effort to stay asleep. Obviously, my mind was working through the confusion of feeling lost in Eleanor's world. I decided that was a perfectly reasonable explanation and that I should relax and enjoy the moment as long as it lasted.

It appeared to be the end of the school day. Friends were congregating outside classroom doors to discuss plans for the football game. A familiar chortle sounded in the distance and I hurried to the end of the hall and turned the corner. Eric was there, leaning against the wall and surrounded by his friends: Tom Stewart, Evan Bradley, and Derrick Miles. Tom and Evan were engaged in a gut-punching contest, each taking punches in the stomach in an attempt to see who could last the longest before finally breaking down and giving in. It all seemed so natural, so real. Eric was mocking them, egging them on. So typically Eric. A sad longing pulled at my heart as I paused to watch the boy who was once my friend. He looked so full of life, so happy and carefree, so very different from the last time I saw him—the night I watched him die.

As I moved closer, the boys continued what they were doing, completely unaware of my presence—or so I thought. At one point, Derrick seemed not only to notice me but somehow managed to look directly at me. His eyes focused briefly on mine and I thought I saw a hint of recognition in them; but then he turned away and rejoined the group.

Evan lost his focus on the game when he spotted someone in the distance and Tom took advantage of the opportunity to sucker punch him. Evan winced, but managed to refrain from doubling over.

"Dude! Nailed him!" Eric laughed, and offered Tom a victorious knuckle bump.

"Destroyed him!" Derrick added.

Evan's face reddened as he managed a defeated chuckle, but his eyes remained steadily fixed on the group of girls walking toward them. Eric followed Evan's stare and laughed heartily when he realized Evan was staring at Darla. Tom and Derrick quickly followed Eric's lead and joined in.

"Dude, forget it!" Tom chided. "It ain't happening. She's Eric's 'has been.'"

"Shut it, Tom!" Eric warned.

"Whoa, snap!" Tom retorted. "No need to be so touchy!"

Eric responded in true "Eric" fashion by slugging Tom in the arm. "Touch that!" Eric said, practically daring Tom to hit him back. He was joking, but I sensed he wouldn't mind if Tom took him up on the offer.

"Cool it," Derrick said, suddenly interrupting the banter. "Avery's watching." Mrs. Avery was the assistant principal. She was only 5'2", but she was tough as nails and had no qualms about benching Andersen's star football players from a game when they broke school rules. The coach had challenged her on a couple of occasions, but she quickly put him in his place. She expected Andersen's athletes to set the standard for model behavior.

Darla, oblivious that Evan was watching her, passed by without giving him a second glance; but she made it a point to look back and make eye contact with Derrick. When she did, she flashed him an inviting smile, which he ignored.

"Looks like you've got some competition," Eric said, nudging Evan in the arm. Evan blushed and shrugged his shoulders. Eric chuckled. I got the feeling that Eric liked Evan and actually felt a little sorry for him.

Just then, Derrick let out a low whistle. "Don't look now, Dude," he said to Eric, "but you've got your own trouble to worry about." Eric and I both turned to where Derrick was looking, and I saw myself, as Beth, walking down the opposite side of the corridor. I was heading in the direction of the recreation center, and I had no clue that four sets of eyes were watching me.

How embarrassing, I thought to myself, *so wrapped up in my own little world.*

Seeing myself as Beth was both exciting and eerie: exciting because it was proof that I existed, that my life as Beth was real; eerie because I was powerless to connect with that image of myself, even though we shared the same mind. I *was* her. I was *so* conflicted—it was so complex.

Tom laughed when he saw me pass by. "Good luck with that one," he said, pleased that Eric was no longer laughing.

"Shut up!" he warned.

"Dude, chill!" Tom backed away. "Why has she got you so weak in the knees? She's not *that* hot."

Well, that was just rude. True, maybe, but rude nonetheless. I was starting to think this dream wasn't such a good idea.

"Seriously? Are you blind, man?" Derrick interjected. "She's totally hot."

What? I stared dumbly at Derrick, waiting for some sort of punch line, but it didn't come. And then Derrick's focus shifted and he looked directly at me again. I gasped so loudly I was sure everyone around me could hear, but there was no reaction. Then Derrick turned his focus back to Eric.

"Seriously hot," Eric muttered under his breath.

Tom shrugged his shoulders. "Whatever."

Evan, who hadn't said a word since Tom sucker-punched him in the gut, suddenly spoke up. "She's cool, Eric." Eric raised a suspicious eyebrow. "No, really. She's different," Evan added.

"Whatever," Tom scoffed, "I'm just sayin', why go for her when he could have Darla any time he wanted?"

"You're a jerk, Stewart," Eric said.

"Oh, yeah. Been there, done that. Right?" Tom sneered.

Eric and Evan both glared at Tom. Evan clinched his fists and reared back, ready to pound Tom. Tom puffed out his chest, daring Evan to hit him, but Derrick and Eric stepped between them.

Save it for tonight's game," Eric said. He smiled as he slapped Evan on the shoulder. "C'mon, let's get out of here."

Evan backed down but his eyes remained fixed on Tom.

Tom laughed nonchalantly and changed the subject. "Dude, did you get a load of Jackson's new running back? What are they thinking?"

With that, the four boys walked off in the direction of the gymnasium. One minute they were ready to kill each other and the next they were cool.

I watched in amazement, shaking my head. What was it with guys?

As fascinated as I was by this glimpse into the male psyche (which was thick with testosterone), this was *my* dream, and I couldn't resist the impulse to follow my other self, who by now had turned down another hallway and was out of sight. I knew just where to go. Eric had mentioned there was a football game tonight, and that meant it was Friday. I was on my way to meet Jonathan before the game. My heart raced at the thought. As soon as I pictured the practice room in my mind, I was there.

I floated to the back of the room and waited. A few moments later, I watched myself enter and sit down at the piano. I felt so detached that I couldn't help but think of myself in the third person. My life as Beth seemed so far away, so distant. I watched her raise her hands to the keyboard, and caught a glimpse of her deformed hand—my hand. Fingers bent, twisted inward into a near fist, with only the thumb and index finger visible from where I hovered.

Was it possible I had forgotten—even for a moment? My injured hand? The accident? A sudden wave of panic rushed through me. How could I let those memories fade?

Beth began playing Beethoven's Moonlight Sonata, slowly at first, then faster as she picked up the tempo and gained confidence. I floated behind her, wanting to get as close as possible—wanting to *be* her again. I was so entranced by the melody that I almost didn't hear Jonathan approach. When I looked around, he was standing in the doorway, watching. He stood frozen for several moments, mesmerized by the music—or was it by her? When he leaned against the door jam and smiled, my heart sank.

Oh Jonathan! I thought to myself. *I miss you so much.* This was *my* Jonathan!

Another wave of panic washed over me as I considered the possibility that I may never be with him again. I was instantly jealous of the girl at the piano. If only I had the ability of an Intruder! If only I could—

"Eleanor?" a voice called from the distance. I spun around, looking for the source. I felt something cold on my forehead as I watched Jonathan move closer to Beth. I couldn't hear what they were saying, but Beth looked confused and was pointing to her shoulder.

"Here, get hold of her legs. Let's get her to the sofa."

"Poor dear!" another voice said quietly.

"What happened?" a familiar voice asked.

Jonathan and Beth faded from my view.

No! Not yet! I just got here! I cried silently.

"Most likely it's heat exhaustion. Bring me more cool rags."

I sensed a scurry of movement around me as I gradually became aware of my surroundings. Eleanor's mother was close and doing her best to keep everyone else away.

"She's fine. She just needs some water and a cool cloth. Why, it's shamefully hot in here." Eleanor's mother began fanning herself, as if she too might faint from the heat.

It was Grace who brought the glass of water.

"Thank you, Miss Rollings," Mother said somewhat curtly.

"May I bring her a plate—"

"That won't be necessary," Mother interrupted, dismissing Grace as if she were one of the servants.

"Mother," I managed to prop myself up. "Please don't be rude to Grace."

There were several audible gasps and I quickly realized I had made yet another mistake. Grace quickly came to my rescue.

"Forgive me," Grace said to Eleanor's mother, but loud enough for those around her to hear. "Miss Eleanor and I have become such fond friends that I insisted she call me Grace."

"Yes, of course, Miss Rollings," Eleanor's mother quickly replied with an appreciative nod. Grace's timing and finesse were perfect, as usual, and she managed to deflect the attention from the fact that I had just accused Eleanor's mother of being rude. Heaven forbid!

"I'm sorry, Mother," I said. I was still trying to catch my breath and piece together what had happened. "I'm not quite myself yet." I managed to feign a ladylike laugh. "I don't know what came over me." Somehow, my attempt at social prowess paled in comparison to Grace's. Deep down, I could sense Eleanor grimacing at my awkwardness.

Eleanor's father, who had been standing quietly on the sidelines, suddenly spoke up. "Please everyone, she's quite all right. Please carry on!" He gestured with his arms for the guests to continue dancing and motioned to the musicians to start playing. Within a few minutes everything was back to normal. The guests quickly paired off on the dance floor and the evening picked up where it left off as if nothing had happened. I glanced around the room looking first for Jonathan, but he was nowhere in sight, and then for Bailey, who, although he was nowhere to be seen, I sensed was looming nearby.

"Eleanor?" Father offered me his arm. "Let's you and I sit this one out. Agreed?"

I took a deep breath, wishing I could take a pair of scissors to my corset. "Yes, Father. Thank you."

Father helped me to my feet and led me from the ballroom to the small sitting room at the end of the hall. He motioned for me to have a seat on the plush burgundy sofa situated near the center of the room. Father settled himself directly across from me in an ornate brown leather chair that creaked with his weight.

"What happened in there?" he asked, eyebrows raised.

His question confused me. "What do you mean?"

"You were fine when I escorted you from the terrace." He cocked his head to one side as if somehow the terrace and my apparent fainting on the dance floor were linked.

"I don't know what came over me. One minute I was dancing and then the room started to spin. I guess I got overheated."

"Unlikely." Father muttered.

"I'm sorry? What's that supposed to mean?" I asked.

"Nothing. It no longer matters; you're obviously fine now."

A gentle rapping on the door interrupted our conversation.

"Enter," Eleanor's father responded. The door opened slowly and Miss Dolan stepped into the room.

"Pardon my intrusion, Mr. Hastings. Mrs. Hastings sent me to check on Miss Eleanor."

"It's good you're here," Father said with genuine relief. "Please prepare Eleanor to rejoin us promptly."

"Excuse my asking, Mr. Hastings, but do you mean to say Miss Eleanor is returning to the ball?"

"Yes, of course she is."

Miss Dolan looked perplexed. "Sir?"

"You heard me, Miss Dolan. Have Miss Hastings ready promptly. There is to be an announcement this evening and my daughter will want to be at her best."

"Yes, of course, sir," Miss Dolan said quietly.

Father left the two of us alone and Miss Dolan immediately began fussing over me. I was too preoccupied to really pay attention; I was still searching my mind for some explanation of what had happened. Perhaps seeing Bailey was all just part of my dream. That had to be it, right? If not, then perhaps exhaustion had caused me to imagine seeing him. I preferred either explanation to the alternative.

Mother joined us several minutes later, no doubt to make sure I was fit to return to the evening's festivities. Had times been more normal, she would have insisted I retire to my bed and the evening would have come to an abrupt end; but the war had changed many things, including the frequency of events as formal and spectacular as a Debutant Ball. There would not be another event of this magnitude for some time, particularly with so many of the young men soon returning to their companies.

There was another knock on the door and Father entered the room. "Are you ready?" he asked, offering me his arm.

"Father, I'm really rather tired. Must I return to the ball?"

Father stared at me for several seconds—I could sense the wheels turning in his mind. "My dear, surely you would not rob your mother of this night. She has spoken of nothing else for months, not to mention all her planning. It would cause her no small degree of embarrassment among the ladies of Marensburg society. You must see the truth in that."

I did. There was no denying that Eleanor's mother would be devastated were Eleanor to bow out of the ball early. "Yes, of course, Father. You're right." I weaved my arm through his and together we made our way back to the dance floor. Eleanor's mother approached as we entered through one of the side doors. I detected a subtle frown of disapproval as she surveyed my waistline. Seriously, this woman was nuts! Miss Dolan had only loosened my corset enough to allow air to actually reach my diaphragm. I never realized how much I enjoyed deep breathing until tonight. If I ever made it back to the present, I vowed to wear nothing but loose fitting T-shirts for the rest of my life.

The first four dances upon my return were uneventful. My partners were polite and charming and each danced with effortless, although unimpressive, precision. The surprise came with partner number five. I had scarcely turned to thank my previous partner when I sensed something unusual happening—unusual because the occurrence was emanating from Eleanor's life presence. A fiery sensation warmed my heart and for some unexplainable reason, my pulse began to race. A few seconds later, when partner number five arrived to claim his dance, I began to figure out why.

"Miss Eleanor?" Partner number five spoke with a voice as smooth as velvet. Eleanor turned and gracefully offered him her hand

"Captain," Eleanor spoke softly, acknowledging her partner. It was as if I were having an out of body experience. Eleanor's life force had suddenly surfaced with unnerving authority and presence.

Partner number five smiled and raised Eleanor's hand to his lips.

Though I sensed a slight blush rising in my cheeks, Eleanor managed to remain composed and poised. Partner number five lifted his deep brown eyes to meet hers and gently brushed his thumb across the tops of her lightly bent fingers, causing Eleanor's heart rate to quicken. His eyes were almost the same shade of brown as mine—although it had been more than a year since I'd looked into a mirror and seen my own eyes. Partner number five's eyes would definitely qualify as "deer" eyes, and I got the strangest feeling that if I allowed myself to look into them too long I, too, would be hypnotized by them.

All this happened in a matter of seconds, but it felt as if we were moving in slow motion; and although I was still present, I was clearly nothing more than a spectator. Eleanor's life force had not only emerged, it had taken over and now dominated my every movement. I was powerless to act on my own, which probably should have freaked me out; but instead of feeling threatened by her suddenly powerful presence, I was intrigued.

As Eleanor and partner number five danced, they did so with a splendor and gracefulness surpassing anything I had experienced to date in my role as Eleanor. It quickly became apparent that there was a history between the two of them—no doubt a secret one. They seemed to embrace each other with their eyes, and despite the fact that they exchanged no words throughout the duration of the dance, there was a familiarity between them that told me they were more than mere acquaintances. Nobody in the room seemed to pay any attention to the two dancers who were utterly lost in each other's gaze—not like they did when Jonathan and I danced. When Jonathan and I danced, it felt as if every eye in the room focused on us.

The music ended and partner number five escorted Eleanor to her mother's side, as protocol dictated. He offered a polite bow to Eleanor's mother and gave Eleanor's hand a lingering yet subtle squeeze before finally releasing her and turning away. She watched him disappear into the crowd and then, just as suddenly as it had emerged, Eleanor's life force retreated to its previous hiding place somewhere deep inside me.

Partner number six approached, but before he could offer me his arm there was an unexpected rumbling on the other side of the dance floor, close to where the musicians were playing. Every eye in the room followed the sound. Eleanor's father was standing on the steps that led from the ballroom to the main entrance hall. He raised his glass high in the air and summoned everyone's attention.

"Ladies and gentlemen, distinguished guests, honored friends and dignitaries. Mrs. Hastings and I have a very special announcement to make this evening—one that has long been anticipated by many in our company and one which, I must confess, is shamefully overdue."

He paused, allowing the guests to converse amongst themselves, each nodding as if they knew what was coming next. Father was enjoying his moment in the spotlight as he looked toward the main entrance and gestured with his glass.

"Colonel Hamilton, would you please join me?"

Several audible gasps swept throughout the room as the tall, handsome colonel entered the ballroom. He handed his hat and cape to one of the servants and made his way through the parting crowd to join Eleanor's father on the steps. He was dressed in a formal Union Officer's uniform, complete with navy jacket, red sash, and gold braided trim, which inspired melting sighs from many of the women in the room.

It took a moment, but I was certain I had seen him somewhere before; then it dawned on me. I had only seen him once, from a distance, but I was sure he was the man who had tipped his hat to me the day I ran into Jonathan in town. At the time, it appeared that the man on the horse was devastatingly handsome, and I must admit I was correct in that assumption. In fact, one quick glance into his crystal blue eyes nearly made my knees wobble.

Eleanor's father greeted Colonel Hamilton warmly and then turned his attention back to the onlooking crowd.

"Normally," Father began, "this would not be the most appropriate setting for an announcement of such an intimate nature, but times are changing, and circumstances sometimes dictate that we adjust according to the times."

There were several understanding nods in the crowd, accompanied by a few low mutterings of "Hear, hear!"

A rush of panic launched itself in the pit of my stomach and I began quickly searching the sea of guests for Jonathan. He was standing toward the back of the room watching Eleanor's father intently. Grace stood at Jonathan's side, her eyes fixed on her brother. A little off to the left, near the exit to the far balcony, stood partner number five. He too, was watching Eleanor's father intently.

Eleanor's father continued. "It is with profound pleasure that Mrs. Hastings and I announce the engagement of our daughter, Miss Eleanor Hastings, to Colonel William Carlton Hamilton."

The ballroom immediately exploded with applause, and suddenly every eye in the room turned toward me. Partner number five, whose expression indicated that he knew this announcement was coming, raised his glass and offered me a knowing nod. My eyes shifted to where Jonathan stood. His eyes met mine and held them for what felt like several pained seconds before he turned away and made his way to the exit and out the door. Grace followed him.

There was nothing I could do. Everything was happening too quickly, and before I could think of an appropriate way to react, Father and Colonel Hamilton were standing in front of me.

"Eleanor," Father addressed me, but spoke loud enough for the entire room to hear. "I believe the rest of your dance partners will understand that you are otherwise engaged for the remainder of the ball."

I stared at Father, too stunned to respond. His use of the word "engaged" hung in the air like thick vapor, nearly causing me to choke on my own breath.

"Miss Hastings," Colonel Hamilton offered me his arm. I stared dumbly at his outstretch arm for a long moment, paralyzed, still processing Father's surprise announcement. Eleanor's father cleared his throat and reaching for my hand, carefully placed it on Colonel Hamilton's arm. The colonel smiled politely and led me to the center of the ballroom floor.

Colonel Hamilton was every bit as attractive up close as he was from a distance, particularly for a man his age. He appeared to be somewhere in his late twenties or perhaps even his early thirties. He had a mature face, clean-shaven, which was unusual among so many of the men of the day, particularly soldiers. His hair was neatly groomed and his eyes were impossible to ignore—they were a crystal-clear shade of blue that had the appearance of blue diamonds, and they shined when he smiled. He looked, smelled, and carried himself as someone who oozed money and charisma, though not in a deliberate or obnoxious way.

As Beth, I couldn't help but feel intimidated by Colonel Hamilton;

but Eleanor, who seemed to perceive my awkwardness, was quite comfortable in his presence. Physically speaking, they were equals—in fact, he was the first man I'd seen who could stand next to Eleanor and hold his own when it came to beauty—even including Jonathan, who, though he could steal my breath away with a simple smile, lacked the refinement and polish of his much older rival.

Colonel Hamilton turned to face me as the music began playing. He slid his hand onto the small of my back and raised his other hand, pausing for me to place mine on his before beginning to dance. The guests looked on with anticipation, eager to watch the newly engaged couple in their first official dance together. The colonel's eyes rested patiently on mine as he waited for me to take his hand. Anticipating my reluctance, he reached down and gently took my hand in his, and then led me in the waltz. I followed. What else could I do?

"Surprised?" he asked, as he released my back and spun me into a carefully executed twirl before pulling me next to his side where he continued the waltz in perfect time. He was obviously an experienced dancer and very easy to follow.

"Nothing you do ever surprises me, *Colonel* Hamilton."

The words came unexpectedly, and I realized that they came from Eleanor, not me. I sensed she was doing her best to help me, and I was thankful not to be left on my own with Colonel Hamilton.

"I must apologize for the dramatic entrance," he said. His voice was kind and sincere. "I'm afraid your father preferred not to wait for a more traditional announcement."

"Nothing my father does surprises me, either," I replied—again with Eleanor's help. "Congratulations on your new title, Colonel Hamilton. I'm confident it is well-deserved."

"Thank you. Your faith in me is most appreciated. But don't you think it's time you called me William?"

"How long will you be on leave this time?" Eleanor asked, ignoring his invitation to call him by his first name.

Colonel Hamilton nudged me into another spin, this time ending up on the opposite side with our arms crossing each other's body. His proximity to me was unsettling. I was sure I heard several "oohs" from the adoring crowd. Maybe it was my imagination.

"I'm only here for one night, regrettably. I must return in the morning immediately after breakfast."

"And where will your next assignment take you?"

"I won't know until my orders arrive at dawn."

Eleanor nodded. "I presume you will be staying with us?" she asked matter-of-factly.

"Yes. Your father was gracious enough to extend an invitation. As usual, it is my pleasure."

Eleanor and Colonel Hamilton were cousins on her mother's side, although I wasn't exactly sure how distant they were. A copy of the family tree was written on the pages of the family Bible; I made a mental note to study it more carefully.

We took a short break after our third dance. Colonel Hamilton deposited me at Mother's side while he went to get the three of us a cold drink. A few minutes later, one of the servants approached me. He was holding a silver tray in his hand and sitting on top of the tray was a folded piece of parchment paper addressed to "Miss Hastings." I waited for Mother to retrieve the note, but she shook her head and deferred to me.

"No, my dear. You are out now. You may retrieve your own messages."

A thought flitted through my mind when she said the words, "retrieve your own messages." I couldn't help but think of my e-mail account. How many messages must there be by now? Part of me smiled and wanted to chuckle—the other part of me wanted to cry.

I picked up the letter and unfolded it. The message simply read, "Stick to the plan, it won't be much longer now."

I quickly folded the note and looked around the room.

"Who gave you this note?" I inquired of the servant.

"I beg your pardon, Miss Hastings. The gentleman said that you would know who it was from." I looked around the room again, searching for a sign, a subtle look or hint from someone that would let me know who had written the note, but there was nothing.

"What did he look like?"

"Forgive me, ma'am. He had his coat and hat on and delivered the note to me as he was leaving. I didn't ask his name."

My heart fell. It wasn't from Jonathan or the servant would have mentioned Grace.

"Thank you," I said, dismissing him.

"Eleanor?" Mother tugged lightly on my arm. "Is everything okay? You look distressed."

I forced a smile and shook my head. "I'm fine, Mother."

"What does the note say?" she pressed.

"Just someone offering Colonel Hamilton and me their congratulations." The lie came quickly and easily.

"Excellent," Mother said smiling. "You must share it with Colonel Hamilton."

I struggled to remain calm. "Yes, of course." I replied.

Where's a trash can when you need one? I thought to myself.

I excused myself quickly and headed after the servant who had delivered the note. I caught up to him just as he was about to head downstairs.

"Please destroy this for me at once," I ordered, handing him the note. "Please," I added more softly, hoping not to sound demanding or disrespectful.

"As you wish, Miss Eleanor." The servant smiled politely and took the note from me. I breathed a deep sigh of relief and slowly made my way back to where Mother and Colonel Hamilton waited. Colonel Hamilton smiled as I approached and offered me a glass of punch, which I accepted graciously. After a few sips, I searched for a place to set my glass down. Colonel Hamilton took it from me and summoned one of the servants to take both of our glasses away.

"Shall we?" he asked, offering his arm.

Together, we stepped back to the dance floor and fell into sync with the other dancers. Eleanor's life force weakened as the evening continued, leaving me to make small talk with my newly betrothed stranger. Eleanor's father joined us just prior to the final dance and assured us that the marriage would take place very soon as he saw no reason to delay it any longer. Colonel Hamilton, or William as he insisted I call him, seemed to appreciate Father's eagerness to hold the wedding as quickly as possible. My head was spinning with fear and confusion. How was I going to get myself out of this one? Time was running out for both Eleanor and me. If I didn't figure out something quick, we would both end up married to a man that neither of us loved.

The ball ended somewhere between 2:00 a.m. and 3:00 a.m. I fell into bed exhausted the moment Miss Dolan removed my corset; I didn't allow her to take my hair down, insisting that it wait until morning.

I lay flat on my back, staring at the dimly lit ceiling of my bedroom. The candle next to my bed was just about to its last flicker, and it seemed to fight vehemently to stay alight.

I did my best to sum up my current situation.

Eleanor and I were both engaged to marry a man approximately ten years our senior who, though pleasant enough and undeniably handsome, neither of us loved. I was in love with Jonathan, who had no idea that the girl he loved was not Eleanor but actually Beth Arrington, a girl from the future whom he would not meet for another hundred and fifty years. Eleanor, I suspected, was in love with the mysterious gentleman who I only knew as partner number five. And let's not forget the appearance of Bailey earlier this evening. It would figure that the only person who knows who I really am is the one person who wants to destroy me. How could my situation possibly be worse?

Father's Surprise
CHAPTER 7

*I*t was well past noon when Lucinda finally woke me the next day by bringing me a tray full of fresh fruit and biscuits. She set the tray down on a small side table near the window and reached up to grab hold of the heavy rope used to tie back the terrace curtains. The sun was bright and high in the sky, with all the promise of another lovely spring afternoon.

I thought about my home in Andersen, Wyoming. By now, Andersen would have seen the last of its cold weather and spring would be well on its way to ushering in the hot, dry months of summer. Andersen was different from Marensburg in that sense. Marensburg's summers were typically ten degrees cooler than Andersen's, but because of the humidity, Marensburg was practically unbearable at times.

Growing up in Carlsbad, California, we didn't experience much variance in the weather. I remember hearing my parents talk about missing the four seasons, but as far as I was concerned the two things that determined the seasons in Carlsbad were school and tourists. Living in Andersen had been my first exposure to significant shifts in temperature, but it wasn't until I'd lived nearly a year in Marensburg that I fully grasped what my parents had meant when they talked about experiencing all four seasons.

"Your mother is most displeased this morning," Lucinda stated as she began the tedious process of removing the pins from my hair.

"So what else is new?" I remarked. By now, Lucinda had become accustomed to my sense of sarcasm, and I even caught her joining in from time to time when no one else was around.

"Oh, she's in a bit of a fit to be sure."

I smiled at Lucinda's serious expression. "What has Mother in such a tizzy this time?"

"Well, it seems your Colonel Hamilton had to be on his way. She insisted that he say a proper good-bye to you, but he was not inclined to wait. He refused to let me fetch you before he left, saying something about his wait being over in a couple of weeks and that I should allow you to sleep all day long if that's what you desired." Lucinda blushed slightly. "I tell you Miss Eleanor, the colonel has a way about him. Set a girl's heart a flutter if she's not careful."

I chuckled. "Yes, I suspect he has that effect on many women."

"Oh, yes ma'am. That's a clear fact." Lucinda removed the last of my hair pins and began brushing my hair. "Why, he even had Mrs. Weddington fanning herself this morning. Caused quite the stir, that one."

"I'm sorry I missed that."

"The two of you looked mighty handsome dancing together last night." Lucinda caught my eye in the mirror. "Not such a bad match if you ask me," she nodded.

"Really? And what would you know of matches?" My words came out cooler than I intended, and I instantly regretted them when I saw Lucinda's altered expression.

"I mean no disrespect, Miss Eleanor. I'm just saying if you can't be with the one you love, well—"

"Then love the one you're with, is that it?" I remarked, quoting a popular song from the twentieth century. Lucinda paused a moment and then frowned. I wondered if perhaps she had been referring to her own situation.

"Is there someone special in your life, Lucinda?" I wondered why it had never occurred to me to ask her about her life before. I suddenly felt very selfish and self-centered.

"I don't expect it matters much, Miss Eleanor."

I turned around to face her. "Oh, but it does matter. Of course it does. Who is he?"

Lucinda smiled a half smile and motioned for me to turn back around so she could continue fussing with my hair. I wasn't about to be put off that easily.

"Is he from around here?" What was I saying? Of course he was. Where else would she have met someone? "I mean, how long have you, er, been—"

"Miss Eleanor, please. Might we change the subject?" Lucinda looked away and I was certain she was fighting back tears. I decided not to press the issue further, but I knew my curiosity would eventually get the better of me and I would have to know more.

Lucinda finished my hair and went to the wardrobe to retrieve my clothes. I was surprised when she brought out a set of riding clothes. They were similar to the ones I had worn when I rode with Father, only they appeared to be for warmer weather.

"I'm going riding?"

"Yes, Mr. Hastings requested you join him this afternoon. Says he has a surprise for you."

I could only imagine. "Wasn't his surprise announcement at the Ball last night enough?"

"I couldn't rightly say. He ordered Mr. Godfrey to prepare the horses shortly after Colonel Hamilton departed. He told Mrs. Hastings not to wait on the two of you for the afternoon meal."

Wonderful. Another outing with Eleanor's father. Apparently, he had meant it when he told me during our last ride that he intended to be more involved in my life.

"That man desperately needs to find a hobby!" I muttered under my breath.

"Come, now. As I recall, you had a very nice time on your last ride with Mr. Hastings."

"Oh, sure," I thought of young Conrad and Henrietta and smiled. "But as you might also recall, I couldn't sit down for a week after spending all afternoon on horseback."

Lucinda laughed. "You have the same complaint every spring. By midsummer you'll be outriding the best of them, including your father."

Eleanor's father spoke very little during our afternoon ride, pausing only briefly here and there to identify a particular type of tree or bush or to point out the boundaries to neighboring estates. There was no question about it—the Hastings' estate was enormous. I followed Eleanor's father as he cut through a grove of trees and headed down a narrow path toward a river. I wondered if it was the same river that ran along the back of the house, but I didn't dare ask for fear of sounding foolish. There seemed to be rivers and creeks running all through the Hastings' property.

The horses clopped along the bank of the river, crunching sticks and stones in the mud and leaving irregular patterns in the path behind us. We followed the river upstream, dodging periodic sprays of water carried by sudden gusts of wind that seem to whirl out of nowhere and then disappear. I closed my eyes, listening carefully as I concentrated on isolating the sound of the wind in the trees from the sounds of the running water.

At last I spotted a small cottage nestled among the trees about a hundred yards beyond a bend in the river. The quaint building was surrounded on three sides by large oaks, their branches forming a protective canopy above it. If you didn't approach the tiny cottage from the front, you would never know it was there.

Father dismounted and led his horse to the water for a drink. I joined him.

"It's beautiful here," I said, fishing. Had he brought Eleanor here before?

Father nodded. "It is." He gazed at the rippling water for a moment and then added, "But that's not why I brought you here. Come."

He led me up a crooked path to the entrance of the cottage. The building was very crude, very small, and very un-Hastings-like. It was obvious the moment we entered that nobody had been inside for a while. The ripe odor of musty wood and mildew struck me with intense force. Even after opening the windows and allowing fresh air into the room, it was several minutes before I could breathe normally. That's all it was, really, an oversized room with a little sitting room toward the back. There were a couple of wood chairs stuffed in one corner near a small table, and along the front wall near two large windows was a long table that reminded me of my grandfather's old workbench.

Page after page of sketches were scattered everywhere in no particular order. They were fantastic renderings, mostly of detailed landscapes. There were literally dozens of them, and they were quite impressive. I picked up several and studied them carefully before noticing the three easels that sat on the opposite side of the room, near another large window.

A studio. Whose?

"This is incredible!" I whispered. "It's like something from a storybook."

Eleanor's father eyed me quizzically for a moment before pulling out a chair and offering me a place to sit.

"I think it's about time for us to have a talk."

"Who did all these?" I asked, ignoring his comment and holding up a handful of sketches.

He crossed the floor to where I stood and reached out his hand for the sketches. He laid them on the table and gestured again for me to take a seat.

"Did you? Are these—?"

"Mine?"

I nodded.

"Yes."

I stifled a gasp . . . "I had no idea," I said so quietly it was almost a whisper.

So, Eleanor inherited her talent for sketching from her father.

"Father, these are great. I mean, they're really good."

"So?"

"What do you mean, 'so?'" I looked at him, confused. "You obviously have a gift."

"Bah!" he scoffed. "It's a passing fancy, Eleanor. The workings of a foolish man."

"Don't say that Father, I—"

"Yes child," he interrupted. "I know you share the same foolish fancy. That's why I brought you here."

"Does Mother know?"

"About this place?"

I nodded.

"She knows there's a cottage here. She knows I come here to be alone. She never asks what I do while I'm here, and I do not discuss it with her. I expect you to respect that as well."

I nodded again. I was having trouble piecing together why he had decided to share this with me. So he and Eleanor had a similar knack for sketching—so what? Why all the secrecy?

Eleanor's father glanced around the room and then pulled the other chair from its spot in the corner and placed it directly in front of me. He removed his cap and wiped his forehead with his sleeve before tossing the cap on the table and taking a seat.

"What have you learned in your studies of our family heritage?" he asked.

"Pardon me?"

He waited several seconds before continuing. "Do you understand the significance of the arrangement I have made for you?"

"I'm not sure I follow," I replied hesitantly.

"Eleanor, the future of our family rests with you; surely you must know that."

I shook my head from side to side. I had no idea what he was trying to say . . . no idea why he had brought me here . . . no idea why his sketches were a secret. Father watched me carefully in silence. After several moments, he took a deep breath and sighed.

"What?" I asked, half annoyed and half perplexed.

He stood and shuffled over to the corner of the room where a group of paintings sat neatly stacked on a small three-legged stool. One by one, he picked up each painting and laid it carefully on the floor. Each picture revealed a new view of the same landscape, chronicling the four seasons. As he unveiled the last painting, he motioned for me to move closer.

At first I thought it was a portrait of Eleanor, but the face that stared at me from under the brim of a delicately placed hat was not Eleanor's— not exactly—yet the resemblance was unmistakable. The woman in the portrait was fair-skinned. Ebony curls framed her oval face and were such a contrast to her emerald eyes that I had trouble deciding on which to focus. The striking green eyes won the tug of war in the end. They were exact replicas of Eleanor's eyes.

"Who is she?" I whispered.

Father stood at my side, admiring the portrait. I could feel his eyes shift from the painting to me and back to the painting.

"The resemblance *is* remarkable, isn't it?" His casual tone confirmed that he was not surprised by what he saw. "You definitely have her eyes."

"Who is she?" I asked again.

"This, Eleanor, is Veronica—my sister."

"Your sister?" I asked, confused. I searched my memory—Eleanor's memory—for any sign of recognition, but found none.

"You wouldn't remember her, of course. She died shortly after you were born."

I looked up at Father to see the resemblance in his face, then turned back to the portrait to continue my study of Veronica's features. "What was she like?"

Father chuckled. "In many ways, she was a lot like you."

"How so?"

Eleanor's father raised his hand toward his sister's face, brushing her curls with the back of his fingers.

"She lit up a room the moment she entered; she couldn't help it. Her eyes glowed in any light—the same way yours do; people could not help but notice her. Sometimes, whole conversations came to an abrupt halt simply because she smiled."

"That's not me, Father," I said humbly.

He grinned. "My dear, you underestimate the effect you have on people . . . particularly men."

Deep inside, my jealousy alarm buzzed.

"And when she was angry, everybody knew it! Her eyes could burn a hole straight through you. And her jaw, right here . . ." he dragged his forefinger and thumb along her jaw line, "would clinch tight as a vice, and you knew you were in trouble."

He smiled, as if recalling a fond memory. "You get that same look sometimes. I saw it last night at your coming-out ball, just after I announced your engagement to William and dismissed the remainder of your dance partners."

I searched my mind trying to figure out what he was referring to, but came up empty—except for—hmmm.

"How did Veronica die?" I asked, deciding it was safer to change the subject.

Father eyed me for several seconds before deciding to respond. "Doctors said it was consumption."

"You sound skeptical."

"I never agreed with their findings," he explained.

"You have a different theory?"

Father hesitated for a moment and then shrugged. "Well, if you ask me, I'd say she died of a broken heart."

I reached for Father's arm, stunned to hear him, of all people, speak of broken hearts. He placed his hand on top of mine and turned to look at me. His eyes were sad.

"What happened?" I asked, squeezing his arm.

"I'm afraid hers is a most unfortunate story, Eleanor." He motioned toward the tiny sitting area tucked beyond a narrow archway at the far end of the cottage. An over-stuffed armchair framed one side of a flat stone fireplace and an oddly shaped sofa that curved inward on the ends flanked the other side. Though I had never seen a piece of furniture styled in this fashion before, it suited the quaint charm of the room. Further enhancing the décor, a modest picture window captured a poetic view of the vast, green scenery that wrapped itself around the cottage.

"The Hastings," Father began, "have a somewhat . . . peculiar reputation among folks in these parts, and with good reason. My grandfather was well known for his lack of convention when it came to how he handled his affairs—personal and business. One thing you'll discover in life is that when you own enough land, you are inadvertently granted the power to make your own rules. My grandfather was what you might call . . . creative."

"It seems to me that we follow the same rules as the rest of society," I stated. "The people of Marensburg practically treat us like town royalty."

Father wrinkled his nose and walked to the window. He peered through the glass as though searching for something.

"Perhaps that's true now. I owe a great deal of that to your mother. She's the reason the Hastings' name has come to mean so much to folks around here."

The quizzical expression on my face made him chuckle quietly.

"My dear, there's a great deal you don't know about our family. Suffice it to say that the Hastings were not always revered as model pillars of society. The Hamilton's," Father paused for a moment and then laughed. "Well, the Hamilton's are a much finer breed than most. Good blood, if you know what I mean."

I was confused. "Father, why are you telling me all this? Why here? Why now?"

Father sat down and rested his chin on his clasped hands. "You see, Eleanor, Grandfather Hastings—he'd be your great, grandfather, had no sons. He had five daughters, which meant, technically speaking, he had no legal heirs. To perpetuate his family name and ensure that Hastings land remained in the hands of blood descendants, he made provisions in his will wherein strict guidelines were set forth regarding the marriages of his daughters. He expected each of his daughters to choose a husband from among their first cousins on the Hastings side. In turn, the husbands were required to sign an agreement that the land would never be sold."

"That doesn't seem like such a big deal . . ." I interjected, my twenty-first century language surfacing. Father narrowed his eyes, but chose to ignore my crude language.

"That's not all. He also made them agree to divide their inheritance equally among their children, with no respect to birthrights. That, of course, was simply unheard of."

"But they all agreed?"

Father snorted. "Here's where it gets interesting. Two of my aunts fell in love—and I use that term with skepticism—with wealthy plantation owners from North Carolina. They willingly forfeited their claims to any portion of their birthright. My mother, along with my other two aunts, vied for the attentions of their cousins, only one of which had the right last name."

"Grandpa Hastings?" I took a shot in the dark.

Father nodded. "He married your grandmother."

"And the other two sisters got nothing?"

He chuckled, "I wouldn't say that. They both married well-to-do cousins, but neither could legally own a section of Hastings land. My mother felt the arrangement was unfair to her sisters, so she made a promise to arrange marriages between her children and their children and as a wedding gift, she would allot the newlyweds a section of the Hastings estate."

I was beginning to feel dizzy, not to mention that I was still disturbed by the thought of first cousins marrying. Regardless, her gesture seemed noble.

"She sounds like a generous woman."

Father scoffed. "Don't be fooled, Eleanor. My mother was a very calculating and shrewd woman. She never did anything without a reason." Father fidgeted in his seat. "But in your grandmother's case, fate had other plans."

"How so?" I asked. I dared not let him know what I was thinking at that moment—that he had obviously inherited his mother's personality along with her land.

"Well, as fate had it, my two brothers were both killed during the war with Mexico, leaving only my sister and me. Mother arranged both our marriages, but at the last minute, Veronica," Father gestured toward the painting of his sister, "did the unthinkable. She refused her arranged match and ran off with the lowest society had to offer."

"I don't understand. Did she marry a convict or something?"

Father chuckled darkly. "Worse. She married an Irishman."

I couldn't hold back the urge to laugh.

"Oh, it was anything but funny to my mother and father. They were both devastated. When Veronica left, they never saw her again—by their own choice."

"Is that why you think she died of a broken heart?"

Father let out a sarcastic laugh and shook his head. "Most certainly not. Veronica understood the price she would pay for her defiance—and she never regretted her decision."

"Then why do you claim she died of a broken heart?"

"Because she never got over the death of her husband."

"He died?"

"Yes. Another casualty of the war with Mexico. The fool actually thought playing the war hero would somehow elevate him in his mother-in-law's eyes."

"So even though he was killed, Veronica wasn't allowed to come home?"

Father swallowed hard. I could tell this was a sensitive subject for him. "No. As far as they were concerned they had lost two sons and a daughter in that war. I was the only child that remained, and I was bound by duty to marry my arranged partner."

"Mother?"

Father nodded. "And a Hamilton, don't forget."

"Did you love her?"

"Not in the way you mean, no. She was family. We saw each other a handful of times growing up, but there was no special bond between us."

"Yet you married her anyway."

"Yes, Eleanor. It was the right thing to do."

Several moments of silence passed before either of us spoke. I was certain Father had a reason for sharing this story with me. He was leading up to something, and the heavy feeling in my stomach was growing heavier by the moment.

"Do you love her now?" I finally asked, afraid I already knew the answer.

Father fidgeted for a moment and then chose his words carefully. "There are many forms of love, Eleanor. Your mother and I are fair companions. That's what matters."

"Fair companions?" I asked incredulously.

"Yes, just as you and William will be."

There it was, the purpose behind Father's conversation. I turned away from him, searching my mind for an opportunity to change the subject. But Eleanor's father wasn't about to let me off that easily.

"You think I haven't noticed? That I don't know what's happening?" Father's voice was stern and commanding.

I tried brushing him off. "I don't know what you're talking about," I replied innocently, but he ignored me.

"What I can't figure out is how it could have happened . . . *when* it could have happened."

"Father, I'm afraid you're speaking in riddles. What has happened?"

His eyes narrowed. "Let me spell it out for you. I want you to explain to me just how it is that you have come to think you are in love with this young Mr. Rollings?"

"Father, please!" I squirmed, looking for a way to escape, but I was cornered. "I can't have this conversation with you."

"You can and you will," he stated flatly. He paused before continuing. "It's not like the two of you have ever spent any significant time together. To the best of my knowledge, you have never given him the time of day. When he went off to join the Union Army, you didn't weep for him. There were no inquiries, no letters, no tokens shared between you. I cannot for the life of me think of any occasion where you showed the least interest in him. That is, until the day you shamelessly threw yourself at him."

I stared at Father, stunned. Up until this moment, the thought had never occurred to me that Eleanor and Jonathan might have been indifferent to one another. "Well, this certainly changes things," I muttered under my breath. Father heard me and immediately jumped to an erroneous conclusion.

"This changes nothing!" he barked as he took a deep breath. "The matter has been settled. You and William will be married immediately. I have already instructed your mother to begin making the preparations."

Father's unwavering resolve stunned me but not before my own stubbornness surfaced. "No, Father!" I said, determined to stand my ground.

He raised his eyebrows and his face turned crimson. "You will do what is expected of you!" he said angrily.

"I don't love him!" I snapped.

"Love? You think marriage has anything to do with love? You think any of this . . ." he threw his arms in the air as if to encompass his estate with the gesture, ". . . is about love?"

"It has everything to do with love!" I argued.

"You naïve child!" Father shook his head disdainfully. "Marriage among our kind has never been about love. It has always been—and always will be—about duty. It's about honoring those who sacrificed everything to make us who we are today. It's about taking your obligations and responsibilities to your family—*to your family name, even*—seriously! It's about perpetuating the very legacy of your birthright!"

I could sense the cold, bitter taste of anger on my tongue. "You mean it's about money!" I glared at Eleanor's father. "Money, wealth, your precious land, and your precious power among those you consider the elite!"

"How dare you!" Father bellowed, raising his hand. He was poised to strike, but stopped short. "How dare you!" he said again, quieter this time, but with a cold chill of accusation in his tone. I sensed I had crossed a very critical line.

"Father, please," I tried to reason. "Of course all that is important, but how can you possibly understand how I feel? You've never been in love—you admitted it yourself. You refer to you and Mother as 'fair companions.' I want more than that. I want to marry someone I love desperately. Don't you want that for me, too?"

"And you think marrying young Mr. Rollings is the solution, do you? A mere boy?" Father eyed me with an expression that almost appeared to be one of pity, but his question caught me off guard. Here I was, having a conversation with a man I hardly knew—a man who held my immediate future in his hands—about marrying a man I would not technically meet for more than 150 years.

But then, why not? Why not marry Jonathan now? We already loved each other in the future; didn't it make sense that we would love each other now as well? Why shouldn't we rewrite our history? What did we have to lose? In fact, wouldn't marrying Jonathan now keep him from making the serious, costly mistakes that would cause his family to suffer for so long? Why not live our lives together now? Why wait for a future that, at least for me, may never come?

"Well?" Father was still waiting for me to respond. No doubt he expected I would come to my senses. Little did he realize that I could be just as stubborn as he was.

"Yes, Father. I want to marry Jonathan. That's my answer."

"I forbid it!" he hollered.

"I love him."

Father scoffed loudly. "Enough! I'll hear no more of this from you. You will marry William and that is final!"

"So," I said with deliberate sarcasm, "this is why you brought me here. You, who have never known love yourself, are determined to sentence me to a loveless marriage for a lifetime."

Father growled. "Just as stubborn as your mother!" His muttering was so low I wasn't sure I heard him correctly.

"My mother?"

"It doesn't matter." He shook his head and stared at the floor. After several moments, he sighed. "I didn't bring you here to argue."

"Then why did you bring me here?" I asked, confused by the sudden change in his demeanor. When he finally raised his eyes from the floor, they held an unusual sense of sadness in them.

"Follow me," he said quietly.

Annabelle

CHAPTER 8

I followed Eleanor's father into the front room of the cottage and over to the far corner where an easel stood with its back to us. By its position in the room, it seemed to hold a particular place of honor among the other furnishings in the cottage. Father walked slowly around to the front of the painting until he stood face to face with its subject. I watched as his expression transformed from guarded and determined to something I had never seen in him before, and for a brief moment, his face was practically unrecognizable. He smiled pensively as he admired the painting. I got the feeling that he'd done this many times.

"This . . ." he gestured toward the canvas but his eyes remained fixed on the subject of the painting, "this is why I brought you here."

Compelled by the expectation in his voice, I moved around the easel and stood by his side for a moment before I turned to view the painting. The moment I did so, memories from the twenty-first century flashed forcefully through my mind. One minute I was standing in a cottage in the 1800s looking at a painting on an easel; the next minute I was transported to the guest room of the Rollings' ranch in Wyoming. The two paintings were identical, except that the one in the cottage was fresh and vibrant whereas the painting in the Rollings' guest room had faded over the span of 150 years and had acquired an antique quality. My heart tightened as my eyes worked through each detail of both paintings, my mind shifting in involuntarily leaps from past to present while I compared the likeness of each image. There was no doubt in my mind that they were the same painting. I felt my knees weaken as I tried to piece together just how this exact painting could end up on the wall in Jonathan's guest room more than a century from now.

Still speechless, I stepped closer to the painting and reached toward the delicate face that stared back at me. I traced the contour of her cheek and ran my finger lightly over her eyes as they peered up at me from beneath the brim of her hat. Her smile was subtle, her face wistful, youthful. Yet more compelling was the gentle longing in her eyes—hers were the eyes of a woman in love.

"Who is she?" I whispered.

"This," Father said with reverence, "is Annabelle."

I searched my memory, tattered as it was, but I could not recall any mention of an "Annabelle" in the family conversations that took place in the Hastings' home. I waited for several moments, hoping that Eleanor might surface—that she might give me some clue as to who Annabelle was—but all I sensed from her was confusion.

"I'm sorry, Father. I don't recognize her. Is she one of our distant relations?"

Father chuckled softly. "No."

"I don't understand. Who is she?"

"I met her when I was in Texas." Father studied my reaction and then motioned for me to sit down. "You had better take a seat, Eleanor."

I made myself as comfortable as I could on a three-legged stool, annoyed that Father couldn't have moved the painting into the room with the comfortable couch. I smiled inwardly when I realized those were Eleanor's thoughts, not mine.

"As I mentioned earlier, my brothers—your uncles—served alongside me in the war with Mexico."

I nodded. "Yes, and that's where they were both killed, right?"

"Yes." Father closed his eyes and paused before continuing. "Like them, I, too, was wounded and left for dead. But I was lucky. A passing soldier took notice of me and dragged me out of harm's way. He left me with enough provisions to survive until a group of volunteers came to gather the wounded men. From there, I was taken to an enemy camp across the river where my wounds were treated. I'm sure as the laws of battle go, I was to be treated only until strong enough to undergo interrogation."

"You never mentioned . . ." Father raised his hand to cut me off.

"Please, allow me to finish. This isn't easy for me."

"Of course. I'm sorry."

"One of the nurses there took me into her care, and although she only spoke fragments of broken English, I could sense she wanted to help me. Eventually, she arranged for me to escape to a mission just north of the river."

"And she is the woman in the portrait?"

Father shook his head. "No. I'm not sure what happened to the woman who helped me escape, although I heard rumors that she was reassigned, which could mean anything."

"I'm not following. If she's not the woman in the painting, then who is . . ."

"I'm getting there." Father took a deep breath and wiped the back of his hand across his forehead. "While I was at the mission, there was a nurse. She was young, and," Father's eyes met mine, "she was beautiful."

"Annabelle."

Father nodded. "Annabelle."

"So, what happened?"

Father shrugged and smiled half-heartedly, as though he were embarrassed. "I fell in love." He shook his head. "No, *we* fell in love." The sadness in his eyes revealed more than he probably planned for me to see, but he continued anyway. "She was unlike anyone I had ever met. She was so alive , , , so full of dreams! There was never any pretense with her. And there were no rules—no elitist protocol to stifle her spirit." Father shook his head. "But she was good, you know? I mean she was good inside and out."

I nodded in understanding and immediately thought of Jonathan.

"I wanted to share everything life could possibly have to offer with her." Father backed away from the portrait, reaching behind him for the back of the stool that he obviously knew was there. He sat down and rested his aging chin on his folded hands. His eyes remained focused on the portrait of Annabelle. I wondered how often he had sat in that very seat, pining for what might have been.

I hated to interrupt his thoughts, but I had to know. "Why didn't you marry her?"

Father took a deep breath and sighed heavily. "Believe me, I wanted to. I would have married her without hesitation, but I had a responsibility to the family. My sister, for all intents and purposes, was lost to us forever. My brothers were dead. I alone bore the burden of honoring the wishes of the family trust and carrying on the Hastings' legacy."

"And you couldn't do that if you married Annabelle?"

Father scoffed. "No!" The defiance in his tone led me to believe the decision was never his to make.

"That's so unfair," I stated.

"Perhaps, but that's how it was then." Father looked squarely into my eyes. "And that's how it is now. That's the way it will always be."

"Not always," I mumbled.

"What's that?"

"Nothing." I waited before continuing. "I don't get it," I finally said.

"Get what?"

"Why wasn't Annabelle good enough? Why couldn't you marry her?"

Father pursed his lips and released another frustrated sigh. He reached up and pinched the bridge of his nose between his thumb and forefinger and then began massaging the area between his eyes. "Isn't it obvious?" He cut his eyes toward mine. "Annabelle didn't share the Hastings' blood. Remember, my mother made a promise to her sisters—a promise that due to the death of my two brothers and the insolence of my sister, she had not been able to keep. But even if she hadn't made that promise, she never would have given me her blessing."

"Why not?"

Father looked down and pursed his lips. "Because Annabelle was Spanish and a Catholic and—" He paused.

"And?" I prodded.

"And she was poor." He shook his head. "We never had a chance."

"Well, that's just lame!" I blurted without thinking.

"I beg your pardon? What is this language coming from you?" Father's eyes grew cold and angry. I lowered my head, ashamed of my outburst. It was so hard to remember the rules, let alone obey them.

"Forgive me, Father. It's just that, it seems so wrong that you couldn't marry the woman you loved."

"That's how it is, Eleanor. That's what I'm trying to make you understand. The sooner you resign yourself to this, the better off you'll be. William is a good man—an honorable man. He'll be a decent husband and father." Father grabbed a blanket, carefully unfolded it, and draped it over the painting. For some reason, this simple gesture frightened me. "We are Hastings!" He said proudly. "We always do what is expected of us." His piercing eyes burned into mine. "Always!" He stood, signaling that the conversation was now over.

I sat speechless as I watched him walk across the room and grab his hat from the table near the door.

"We should head back before your mother begins to worry." Father's assumption that the topic was no longer up for discussion annoyed me.

"Does she know?"

Father stopped, but didn't turn around.

"Well? Does she?" I insisted.

"Yes."

With that, he stepped out the door and walked down the dirt path toward the river's edge where our horses waited. I followed quietly behind him. He took hold of the lead to his horse and reached up to pat the side of its head. I followed him out and caught my horse's lead in my hand.

"Eleanor," he said without turning around.

"Yes?"

"You are permitted to come here whenever you like—on your own."

This was a startling announcement. Suspicious, I waited for him to finish his thought.

"Here . . ." he gestured around him with his arm but kept his eyes fixed on his horse, "you may dream of your Mr. Rollings, or whomever you choose to fancy in the future, as often as you like, and here you may wish for what might have been. But . . ." he turned slowly and fastened his determined gaze on me; I had never before seen this degree of stubborn resolve in his expression, "you will marry William and you will take your rightful place as the mistress of the Hastings' estate and you will bear William's children. You will fill his home with children! Do I make myself clear?"

I began to cry. "I can't do it, Father! I can't marry a man I don't love! Why would you force me into an arrangement that will make me miserable?"

"It-is-your-duty! You owe it to your family! You owe it to *my* legacy!" Father raised his voice to make his point. "*That* is how you will honor your brothers who died fighting to protect the life you are privileged to live. You and William will produce the heirs that your brothers were robbed of producing. Hastings' blood will flood your children's veins. I will die before I will revoke my arrangement with William and his family and allow you to pollute your legacy by marrying an outsider."

Father's face burned with contempt. He was so angry that he spat his words, his nostrils flaring with each syllable. His dictatorial stance shocked and sickened me. I had never been in the presence of someone with so much pent up anger. He was glorious and terrifying all at once. I opened my mouth to continue my protest, but Eleanor surfaced suddenly and restrained me from responding.

"We will talk no more of this," he said, motioning toward the cottage. "Any of it!"

With that, Eleanor's father mounted his horse and immediately began plodding his way along the river's edge, back the way we had come. He never looked back. He assumed I would simply follow behind in blind obedience. Hah!

Tears streamed down the sides of my face. I hadn't realized how emotional I had become. My body started to shake as I stood dazed, watching Eleanor's father disappear from view. I dropped to my knees, still squeezing my horse's lead in my hands. I cried openly for the better part of fifteen minutes. I wanted to go home to Andersen, Wyoming. Worse than that, I wanted to die; for I would rather die than resign myself to a life spent as a baby-making machine with a man I would never love—living a life with no purpose other than to produce precious heirs for Eleanor's family bloodline.

This is not my birthright! I thought to myself. *I was born to do something important with my life.*

"This is not my legacy!" I screamed into the air. I searched the sky, angry with a God that if he existed at all, was cruel enough to leave me alone with no way to get home. "Why?" I yelled. "What am I supposed to do?" I waited, foolishly expecting God to answer. Then I chuckled darkly to myself.

You fool! There's nobody listening to you! I dropped my gaze and stared at the ground, my tears creating dusty ringlets as they fell in the dirt. I was clutching the lead in my hand so tightly that my knuckles had turned white and were beginning to tingle. I pried my fingers open, revealing a bright red line across the palm of my hand.

No gloves. Great!

"Thanks for nothing!" I said sarcastically to the sky. Just in case there was a God, I wanted him to know I was pissed!

Realizing I must have left my gloves in the cottage, I stood up and stomped my feet in frustration. As I huffed in exasperation and headed back toward the cottage, it occurred to me that I was throwing a childish tantrum.

Just as I was preparing to open the door, a sudden bolt of lightning flashed around me; it was immediately followed by an equally impressive explosion of thunder. A quick survey of the sky confirmed what I already knew—there were no clouds.

I knew I wasn't alone the moment I stepped through the narrow doorway leading into the cottage. The very atmosphere of the room was notably altered. Instead of musty air and stale wood, the room smelled fresh, new, like . . . I searched for the right word in my mind, but I was afraid to hope. And yet the scent was unmistakable.

One glance into the tiny sitting room confirmed what I dared to hope. Although she stood facing the window and I couldn't see her face, I knew immediately who it was; nobody brought dignity and elegance to a room the way she did. *Not even the perfect Miss Eleanor,* I sneered bitingly to myself.

I stepped softly across the floor, afraid if I made too much noise she might disappear. Besides, if this was another one of my dreams, I most definitely did not want to wake myself up.

As I approached, she turned around slowly. The expression on her face told me that she was expecting me; only instead of anticipated joy, her face reflected anguish.

"Hello Beth," she said softly. Her lips twitched as she forced a smile. The sound of my name nearly cut all circulation from my legs. I reached for the back of a chair to steady myself. My relief at seeing her overshadowed any doubts planted by her reluctant smile and I ran to her, throwing my arms around her neck.

"Oh, Grace!" I cried. "I can't believe you're actually here!"

"Beth, there isn't much time." She stepped away from me and held my hands in hers. She looked down, seemingly sidetracked by the fact that I was not wearing gloves. Then she traced the contour of my left hand and smiled. "Are you playing the piano?"

I looked down and bit my lips together. I had been living in Eleanor's body for so long I had taken the use of my left hand for granted. Returning to the present with Grace would mean losing the mobility in my fingers again. Instead of being graceful and delicate, my fingers would be bent and deformed. Useless. None of that mattered, though. Grace had come, and that meant I was finally going home.

"I'm sorry, Beth," Grace apologized. "It's just that I know how much you love to play."

"It's all right," I shrugged. "I've always known it was temporary."

Grace seemed to brush off my comment, something very uncharacteristic of her.

"Grace? What's wrong?" I felt my pulse quicken.

"Beth, listen to me. I don't have much time. In a moment, Eleanor's father will realize you aren't following him and he'll turn around. I can't be here when he arrives."

"Oh, yes, of course," I replied. I started to reach for her arms, prepared to clasp them as I had when Grace and I traveled from the present to where I was currently trapped. But before I could do so, she stepped away from me.

"No, Beth. You don't understand."

"Understand what? Just tell me what to do and I'll do it."

"It's not that simple."

"What's not?" I searched her eyes, hoping to see some hint of what she was trying to say, but what I read in her expression was that something was wrong—something was dreadfully wrong. "Grace, what's wrong? Is it Jonathan? Is he okay?"

"He's fine, Beth. Jonathan is fine."

"Thank goodness," I said, relieved. "What is it then? Is it Carl? Uncle Connor"

"No," she said quickly, shaking her head. "Nothing like that. They're all fine."

"Then what?" I asked, confused. "Why aren't we leaving?"

"I can't take you back Beth."

I stared at her in disbelief. "What did you say?"

"Beth," she reached for my arm, "listen carefully. Something has happened—something that has altered the future. Somehow, you have gotten on the wrong course."

"But," I struggled to make sense of what she was saying. "I haven't done anything." I was starting to panic. "Grace, please. Take me with you. I'm sure we can figure out how to fix things when we get back to Jonathan."

"Eleanor!" Eleanor's father called in the distance.

Grace and I both jumped. Grace moved swiftly to the edge of the window.

"Beth, Eleanor's father will be here any minute."

"Grace, you have to take me with you! Please!"

"I can't Beth."

"But why? You promised you'd come back for me!"

"I know I did, and I meant it. You have to believe that."

"Then why?"

"Because, Beth," Grace looked squarely into my eyes, "in the current present, you no longer exist."

"What? That's impossible!"

"Eleanor!" Father was getting closer.

"Grace! Tell me what's going on?"

"Beth, you disappeared the night your mother died. Jonathan wasn't there to save you." Grace spoke in rapid-fire sentences. "A time paradox has created a sort of ripple in our timeline. It has to be fixed."

"Eleanor!" Father's voice grew louder and more distinct.

"Grace, please!" I begged.

"Beth, you have to correct the paradox or you'll be stuck here indefinitely."

"But how? I don't know how to do that! What am I supposed to do?"

"Eleanor!" Father's voice was full of urgency and panic.

"Jonathan has to find out about—"

A bright flash of lightening interrupted Grace before she finished her sentence. A million thoughts swept through my mind in a split second, and then the crackling booms of thunder began.

"I have to go Beth. I'm sorry."

"Grace, please! Don't leave me here!" I was on the verge of hysterics. I could hear Father's footsteps crunching against the pebblestone pathway. I knew it was only a matter of seconds before he would come through the door and Grace would be gone. "I don't know what to do!" I screamed. The next round of thunder shook the small cottage and a bright flash of light filled the entire room, blinding me. Father pounded on the cottage door.

"Eleanor! Open this door!" he ordered.

I stood paralyzed. "Please don't leave me, Grace!" I sobbed.

I started to reach for her, and then one last bolt of lightning snapped and filled the room with brilliant light. When the light disappeared Grace was gone and in the fading light I thought I heard her say, "I promise I'll help you."

Desperation was quickly giving way to nausea. A low rumble drowned Father's yelling while the light faded and the door flung open violently and fell to the floor. I shrieked, feeling my failing senses slipping away as Father rushed into the room. I clutched the side of the chair, trembling uncontrollably while I watched Father's frantic eyes search the room until they landed on me. When I tried to speak my legs folded beneath me and I crumpled into a helpless heap on the dusty stone floor.

"Eleanor! What's happened?" Father stooped down next to me and wrapped his arms around me. "Are you all right?"

"I'm sorry," I sobbed, burying my face against his arm.

"Why didn't you follow me? I thought you were right behind me!"

"Lightning," I managed through my tears.

"Lightning?" Father patted my back protectively. "Since when are you afraid of a little lightning?"

"I wanted so much to go home!" I was crying uncontrollably now.

"Shh. Shh. There, there. I'll take you home." Father wrapped his arm around my shoulder and drew me close to him. "I know you are upset right now. It's only natural. In time, you will grow to love William. And you're going to be a wonderful mother."

I sobbed even harder. He had no clue. Nothing was all right. Nothing about my situation was natural.

"Father, you don't understand."

"I think I do. The doctor warned us that you might be prone to occasional fits of confusion that could lead to hysteria. There's nothing wrong with you. Everything will be fine, you'll see. You just need a few days to get used to the idea."

It was hopeless. There was nothing left for me to say. Father had won this round. I stood up and attempted to compose myself.

"That's my girl," Father gave an approving nod. I resisted the urge to roll my eyes.

"I lost my gloves," I sniffled. Father looked down and began to chuckle.

"Well, my dear, it appears you found them."

I glanced down at my hands and was surprised to discover I was already wearing my gloves. I stared dumbfounded at my gloved hands for several moments. Was I losing my mind?

Father wouldn't permit me to ride back on my own. Instead, he helped me onto his horse and climbed on behind me. As we made our way along the bank of the river and across the Hastings Estate, my mind again recalled the day Jonathan and I had gone riding together in the mountains of Wyoming. I needed to keep remembering—to replay every detail as often as possible; otherwise, I feared that all my memories as Beth would become nothing more than fading dreams.

A stray tear found its way down my cheek. Nothing in Eleanor's world mattered. All I wanted was to go home, to go back to Jonathan, back to my family. I wanted to reclaim my life. Eleanor's birthright and the Hastings' legacy were not my burdens to bear. I was Elizabeth Anne Arrington. I had my own birthright to claim—and my own legacy to leave behind.

I replayed Grace's words over and over in my mind. A time paradox had created a ripple in the timeline, creating an alternate time line where I no longer existed because Jonathan wasn't there the night of the accident to save me. Grace had said I needed to fix the paradox, but how was I supposed to fix it when I didn't know what caused it? When I saw Grace at the cottage I was certain my wait was over, that I was finally going home. Why did I let her leave? I kicked myself for not grabbing on to her and refusing to let go. I would've been home by now, right? What had Grace meant when she said I no longer existed? Had I died in the car crash? If so, why didn't Grace say it that way? Why say that I no longer existed?

I racked my brain repeatedly trying to make sense of Grace's visit. I found some comfort in knowing that she had come—that she knew how and where to find me and hadn't forgotten me. If she made contact once, then she'd be back, right?

I pondered Grace's words again; they kept haunting me. Why wasn't Jonathan there the night of the accident to save me? I couldn't piece together a connection between what was happening now in the 1800s and what had happened the night of my accident.

That night, instead of sleeping, I sat down and scribbled as much as I could remember about Jonathan's life prior to meeting me in the twenty-first century. Jonathan had only given me bits and pieces, but Grace had filled in many of the blanks the night she came to see me at Uncle Connor's house. I bulleted every detail that came to mind and then read through the list repeatedly looking for a connection.

Jonathan never told me who had assigned him to watch me. He had implied that it was just another assignment, like many others he'd been given. According to Jonathan, he had seen something special in me the night of my piano recital, and his fascination with whatever he'd seen was part of what led him to intervene in my life. But none of that explained how he could have known a car accident would occur. How was it that he had happened to be there? And who was there with him? I couldn't believe I'd never asked him about the other person who was there.

I looked down at my scribbled notes and began reading through them again when a loud popping sound startled Sir Charles and he started to whimper.

"Silly pooch," I muttered, pushing my chair away from the desk. I walked over and began to stoke the fire. "It's just the fireplace. No need to whine." I reached down and patted the top of Sir Charles's head. "Silly pooch," I said again.

I poked at the remaining logs until they crumbled into a pile of glowing embers. I knelt down beside the fire and as soon as I did, Sir Charles wormed his way onto my lap. I stared blankly at the warm glow of the embers while stroking Sir Charles' ears. My eyelids grew heavy, and before I knew it both Sir Charles and I were fast asleep.

"Do you, Jonathan Stanford Rollings, take this woman to be your lawfully wedded wife? Dost thou promise to love and cherish her, and to cleave unto her from this day forward, so help you God?"

"I do," Jonathan said, smiling. He squeezed my hand and winked. He was dressed in white, and it took me a moment to figure out where we were.

"And do you, Elizabeth Anne Arrington, take this man to be your lawfully wedded husband? Dost thou promise to love and honor him, and to cleave unto none else from this day forward, so help you God?"

There was a long pause as I searched for my voice. I looked over at the officiator but he didn't acknowledge me, he just continued to stare forward. I followed his gaze to the guests who had gathered for the occasion. Sitting in the audience were several people that I didn't know. I searched for my family—for my dad, Uncle Connor, Marci, Carl, anyone familiar, but no one from my family was there. The guests were watching with glazed-over expressions, waiting for me to respond to the officiator. I looked up at Jonathan, who was still smiling and waiting for my answer.

Something was wrong.

A commotion from the back of the room caught Jonathan's attention, and he turned away from me to see what was happening. The immediate change in his expression caused my blood to curdle. I turned my head and there, standing in the doorway at the back of the room, stood Eleanor.

I gasped, woke up, and the scene disappeared. Sir Charles raised his head and tried to lick my face.

"Stop that, you mutt!" I said reproachfully. My heart was still pounding and it took me several minutes to settle my nerves and convince myself that I'd only been dreaming.

I looked up toward Heaven. "What are you trying to tell me?" I whispered into the dark. "What's the connection?" I listened foolishly for an answer, then chided myself for being such an idiot.

I stretched out on the floor and found a comfortable position where I could feel the warm embrace of heat emanating from the orange embers in the fireplace. It must have been somewhere between 2:00 and 3:00 in the morning, which meant it wouldn't be too much longer before Lucinda would sneak into my room to put fresh logs on the fire. How she managed to do that night after night without waking me remained a mystery.

I was drifting back to sleep when I heard a strange grinding noise coming from somewhere near the fireplace. I instantly sat up and fixed my gaze on the faintly glowing embers, trying to discern exactly where the noise was coming from, but after what felt like a very long minute, I relaxed my tense muscles and gave up. Just as I turned away, a gust of cold air swept past me and scattered the embers, putting them completely out. The room instantly turned dark except for a thin sliver of light that crept through a crack between the curtains. After a few moments of silence, the grinding sound returned. I leaned forward to listen more intently. It seemed as though the odd noise was coming from *inside* the fireplace. I stood and quickly made my way to the vanity to retrieve my oil lamp, determined to find the source of the strange noise. I set the lamp near the hearth and began to feel my way around the inner walls of the fireplace when I noticed something wedged between two stones at the far side of the chimney wall. I reached in and pulled out a folded piece of parchment. It was singed around the edges, but otherwise miraculously undamaged.

I backed away from the fireplace opening—my gown covered with soot and ashes—and held the folded paper close to the lantern. Carefully, I opened it and read:

Dearest Love,

I haven't much time, but could not manage another moment without telling you how eager I am to see you again. I can only hope that your feelings for me have not waned during these past weeks, nor will they in the coming months. My company moves out before sunrise and I've no way of determining when I might find occasion to write to you again, at least not for some time. Know that I carry the memory of you with me, and were it not for recalling our last meeting, I am certain I could not have survived these past weeks. I have not forgotten our plans, nor the promise I made to you. I will come for you soon. Then we will be free of this place and this war forever. Till then, stick to the plan, my love, and always remember that my heart rests with you.

For the longest time, I just sat there staring at the letter. I read it again, and then again, each time stunned by the words on the page. "Stick to the plan?" Those were the same words written on the note I had received at the Ball. I cursed myself for not keeping that note so I could compare the handwriting, but given the anxious pounding in my chest, I knew both were written by the same person.

Curiosity getting the best of me, I grabbed my lantern and crawled into the large fireplace. I searched every crevice, pulling and tugging on the stone bricks, but there was nothing out of place. No loose stones or hidden grooves. I was about to give up when I banged my head against a protruding stone high on the fireplace wall. I reached up and discovered a small gap between the protruding stone and the brick just above it. Twisting onto my back, I was able to reach up and slide my hand into the tiny opening—just far enough to pull out three more folded sheets of paper and a pressed flower.

It took a minute for me to maneuver my way out of the fireplace. I didn't care that I was now covered head to toe with soot—although I would have to figure out some clever way of explaining the mess to Mrs. Weddington and Lucinda in the morning. Eager to know what Eleanor had been hiding so carefully, I quickly unfolded each letter and scanned the contents. I wasn't sure of the order as only one of them included a date, but there was no doubt they were all written by the same person.

Two of the letters couldn't really qualify as letters; they were requests for Eleanor to meet somewhere after the family had gone to bed. The pressed flower resembled an orchid, but it was too tattered for me to know for sure. The third letter was dated January 28, 1863—approximately six months before I entered Eleanor's body. It read:

Dear Eleanor,

How long shall I endure this silence from you? I dare to admit that I find myself hoping that it is some calamity that keeps you from writing, for I cannot bear the thought that your silence is by any choice of your own. As luck has it, I shall pass through Marensburg next month, weather permitting. It has been exceptionally cold these past few weeks and unexpected snowstorms have slowed our efforts to a large degree. We are all growing anxious as small bits of news reach us about the battles directly south and east of our township. By now you will have heard news of the latest, that J.E.B. Stuart and his men raided Chambersburg. It's said they destroyed the railroad and made off with horses and guns. Thankfully, they failed in their attempt to burn the railroad bridge at Conococheague. We are all grateful for that, but rumor has it that Lee plans to occupy the town and push north upwards to Harrisburg.

You can imagine there are right now plans to prevent Lee from obtaining his objectives. I am confident given our strength and numbers that there won't be a breach anywhere near Marensburg, and in that I find comfort.

On a pleasant note, you'll be pleased to know that I ran into Miles but two days ago. I confess he looked tired, but he assured me that he was well. Knowing of my propensity to write home frequently, he asked if I would send his love *to your family in my next letter. Of course, he couldn't know that I would be writing directly to you. He indicated that he has not had word of your older brother Charles in some time, but when he saw him last he was faring well. I hope these words bring you some peace; I only regret that you cannot share them with your family so that they might be comforted as well.*

My darling, it remains in me to come for you when the time is right, if you will still have me. Though I know you claim our love to be nothing more than childish folly, I assure you I have every intention of proving you wrong, however foolish that may seem to you. Take care, love. And please write soon so that I may no longer suffer the suspense of your silence.

When I reached the end of the letter, my heart twisted in a gut-wrenching knot. It was signed, "All my love, J."

Could it be? The thought was more than I could stand. But who else could "J" be if not Jonathan? And yet there was a familiarity in these letters that definitely did not fit the relationship between Eleanor and Jonathan, unless I was missing something, or unless Eleanor was hiding more from me than I realized. Then again, if not Jonathan, then who? It obviously wasn't William.

My thoughts went to partner number five from the Ball. No matter how hard I tried, I could not recall the name on my dance card. But then, most of the guests were strangers to me, so their names wouldn't have meant anything to me anyway.

"Blast it all!" I whispered.

I let out a deep yawn and rested my head on Sir Charles. He squirmed for a brief moment, but quickly relaxed. Before long we were both fast asleep.

When I awoke the next morning I was in my bed. I turned quickly toward the fireplace. Sir Charles was gone. No doubt Lucinda had put him outside to take care of his morning business and sure enough, the fire was burning brightly like normal. I didn't bother to wonder how I'd ended up in my bed in clean linens with no sign of my soiled gown in sight. I'd figured out some time ago that between Lucinda and Mrs. Weddington, nothing was impossible.

I panicked as I suddenly recalled what I'd been doing before falling asleep on the floor. I threw off my blankets and went straight to my vanity. To my horror, there was no sign of the letters anywhere. I searched through every drawer and shelf in the room—I even tried to reach into the fireplace; but the flames made it impossible for me to get anywhere near the small ledge high on the fireplace wall. Then I looked down at the flames and paused—was that a small piece of parchment curled up beneath one of the burning logs?

Meeting

C H A P T E R   9

I kept a low profile for the next few days. I didn't dare ask Lucinda or Mrs. Weddington about the missing letters. I only prayed that whichever one of them had found them had not mentioned them to Eleanor's mother or father. Neither hinted at having burned them, but there was no other explanation. I had no alternative but to act as if nothing had happened.

There was another problem, one that I hadn't anticipated. Ever since finding the letters in the fireplace, Eleanor's life force had been gaining strength. She was surfacing more frequently. And if that wasn't cause enough for concern, there was something else—something alarming that contradicted everything I had previously believed about Eleanor. She may have been intrigued by Jonathan, perhaps even attracted to him to some degree, but she was not in love with him—not the way I was. I suspected that Jonathan might be right, Eleanor was fickle. There had definitely been something between her and her mysterious "partner number five" from the night of the Ball. The tension between them was obvious. Then there was her totally unexpected, weak-kneed response to William when he whisked her onto the dance floor. (Although truth be known, those might have been *my* knees knocking.) As for Eleanor, I was having a difficult time keeping up with her, let alone getting a true read on her emotions. Especially now, with the unanswered question of who had written the letters she'd hidden in the fireplace. But one thing was certain, Eleanor had her own agenda—and it didn't include me.

While I struggled to keep Eleanor's life force at bay so I could focus on devising a plan of my own (a plan that included getting out of marrying William and convincing Jonathan that we belonged together), Eleanor's mother and Mrs. Weddington immersed themselves in the arrangements for Eleanor's wedding. They fought over the arrangements constantly; but I paid little attention to their bickering because in the end, all Eleanor's mother needed to do was say the word and that would be the end of it. She was, after all, mistress of the house. Still, it was abundantly clear that she enjoyed the ritual of the banter. Eleanor's father had issued a firm directive that the event would be small and simple. I soon learned, however, that small and simple meant something very different to Eleanor's father than it did to her mother.

None of that mattered. I was *not* going to marry William, and that was that! Whatever the consequences, I would find a way to postpone the nuptials. However, I wasn't in a hurry to draw unnecessary attention to myself. I realized that with Eleanor's mother and Mrs. Weddington so involved in the wedding plans, I had a welcome dose of free time on my hands—which was exactly what I needed in order to figure out what I was going to do about Jonathan, and how I was going to fix the rift that had somehow occurred in the timeline.

Instead of spending my coveted "alone" time at the piano, which was what I normally would have done, I spent it at the cottage. I worked quickly and methodically to capture as many of my memories from Wyoming as possible and put them down on paper. Eleanor's neurotic father may have destroyed my journal, but this time I would tell my story another way. Instead of putting my memories in writing—where Eleanor's father might find them again and haul me off to the insane asylum—I would tell my story in pictures.

My plan was moving along just fine until I overheard Grace in a conversation with Mrs. Madison following the weekly meeting of the Poetry Club. It crossed my mind that Mrs. Madison had a bit of a history in Marensburg. As I recalled, it all had to do with the rules of visiting etiquette.

Paying calls was a tradition among most levels of society in 1864 Pennsylvania; but among the elite it was more than just tradition, it was a duty performed with precision. When you visited someone at their home, you handed the butler a calling card. The mistress of the house was then obliged to return the visit within a given number of days. Every society lady had specific times set aside as her *at home* time, which meant she was available to receive callers. It was all very formal and structured. Whenever a family of renown or financial stature moved into town, the gentlemen of the town would pay a call on the man of the house and welcome the family to the community. If there was a perceived advantage to be gained, the newcomers would be invited to dine with the visitors' families.

Once properly introduced, the women would then take over. If the newcomer made an error in judgment at this point, it not only reflected poorly on her but could negatively impact her entire family. This is where Mrs. Madison made her mistake. Apparently a Mrs. James Albert Rutherford paid Mrs. Madison a call and left her calling card. When two weeks passed without a return visit from Mrs. Madison, Mrs. Rutherford took steps to have the Madisons blackballed among Marensburg's more prominent citizens. Fortunately for the Madisons, they were extremely wealthy; that seemed to buy Mrs. Madison a healthy dose of forgiveness among Marensburg's upper crust because even though the Madison's fortune was considered "new money," it came in very handy during the city's fundraising efforts to help support the war effort in the North. (I couldn't help thinking that if Mrs. Madison had owned a smart phone, her whole ordeal might have been avoided.)

Anyway, Mrs. Madison was inquiring about Grace's brother. Apparently, she was expecting a visit from her niece soon and wanted to invite the Rollings family to dine with her family in hopes of introducing her niece to Jonathan. I had always liked Mrs. Madison, even defended her when others in Marensburg society had temporarily shunned her, but when I heard her speaking of introducing Jonathan to her niece, it was all I could do to remain civil.

"I'm sure I speak for my entire family when I say we'd be delighted to dine with you," Grace said in her perfectly polished manner. Even Grace was starting to annoy me.

"Wonderful!" Mrs. Madison replied. "I'll tell the cook to plan for four extra plates on Sunday."

"I'm afraid you'll have to make it for three. My brother has received his orders and must depart before sunup that morning."

"Then might I impose on you to join us for an afternoon picnic on Saturday?"

"I must make some inquiries first, but I'll send you word quickly," Grace replied.

"Oh, I do hope we can arrange it. I'm quite certain your brother would find my niece most agreeable."

With that, Mrs. Madison and Grace said their goodbyes and Mrs. Madison departed. I knew it was irrational, but I couldn't help feeling betrayed. Grace was supposed to be in my corner, wasn't she? I knew the answer to that; the only corner Grace was in was Jonathan's.

With Jonathan set to leave on Sunday, I needed to act quickly. I wasn't sure how to approach her, but Grace was the only chance I had of seeing Jonathan before he left. If she couldn't convince him to meet me, then all my hopes of fixing the paradox would be dashed.

"Grace, might I have a moment of your time?" I asked when she was finally alone.

"Yes, of course," Grace smiled angelically. "How are the plans coming along for your wedding?"

Grace's question cut me to the quick. This wasn't going to be easy.

"I couldn't really say, for sure. Mother is in charge and sees no reason to involve me in the details."

Grace eyed me curiously. "Well, I'm sure as the day draws nearer, that will change."

"Grace, I'm afraid I have a most unusual favor to ask of you. It involves your brother."

My abruptness shocked Grace. "Jonathan?" She looked confused.

"Yes," I replied.

"I'm afraid I don't understand."

I reached for Grace's arm. "Would you please indulge me with a moment of privacy?"

Grace agreed, and for the better part of half an hour I did my best to convince her, in spite of her several protests, to relay a message to Jonathan. In the end, all I could do was beg Grace to trust me. She assured me she would give Jonathan the message, but she let me know that if he asked her opinion, she would advise him against meeting me.

"That's the best I can do," Grace said.

"Thank you, Grace. I won't forget your kindness."

Grace shook her head. "No need to thank me, Eleanor. But do me a favor in return."

"Yes, of course. Anything," I responded.

Grace took my hand in hers and looked me squarely in the eyes. "Let this be the end of it. Deal?"

There was no wavering in Grace's expression, and I sensed I had overstepped my bounds in our friendship. I hoped she would find it in her heart to forgive me.

"Deal."

Saturday arrived before I knew it. I left earlier than necessary, which seemed to raise a suspicious brow or two at the Hastings' estate. I didn't care. Today was my last chance to try and do something about mending the ripple in the timeline. It never entered my mind that Jonathan might not show for I knew his curiosity would get the best of him, in spite of any prompting on Grace's part to dissuade him. I purposely set our meeting for noonday in hopes of sabotaging Mrs. Madison's attempt to play matchmaker between Jonathan and her niece, who I already decided I would never like.

I recognized Jonathan in the distance as he approached on horseback. I'd been watching for him through the window of the cottage all morning hoping he might arrive earlier than summoned, but he didn't. He was right on time. The sun was nearly straight up and captured his every move, and even though his hat shaded his face, there was no mistaking it was him. I could easily identify him from a mile away. As I watched him drawing closer, I could so readily picture in my mind exactly how he looked the first time he came to Uncle Connor's house to pick me up. I remembered the baseball cap he wore and how every time I saw him with it on he reminded me of a little kid.

Once again, I recalled sitting next to him on the bank of the river separating the upper and lower Palisades lakes. He was so relaxed as he sat back and drank in the splendor of the afternoon—mesmerized by how the sound of the slowly flowing river united harmoniously with the wind as it breezed through the surrounding trees. Jonathan loved the outdoors and he loved the mountains.

That was the day I told him about my accident. That was the day he kissed me on the cheek. And that was the day I saw his peculiar blood and suspected there was something "special" about him. It seemed like a lifetime ago. I chuckled to myself as I recalled falling off my horse and how the rain caused us both to end up soaked and muddy. I hadn't realized it at the time—nor would I have admitted it if I had—but I was already in love with him. How could I not be?

My mind abruptly returned to the 1800s as Jonathan arrived at the cottage, tethered his horse, and made his way up the stone path to the door. In a moment of unexpected panic, I turned away from the entrance. My nerves had me so rattled I couldn't bear to face him just yet. I knew if I did, my longing for him would override any hope of rational behavior on my part. He knocked lightly and when I didn't respond, I heard him enter.

"Hello," I said without turning around.

"I half expected you not to be here," he responded. I could sense frustration in his words. I guess I deserved that.

"I shouldn't be," I replied, shaking my head slightly. "If my father finds out I met you here—"

"Yes, I know. We've been through this before. And yet, here we are." Was that sarcasm I detected in his tone? Jonathan took a couple of steps toward me.

"Please don't," I said quietly, my back still to him.

"Eleanor," Jonathan stepped closer. I didn't attempt to move away from him. I couldn't. I sensed him moving closer until I could hear his labored breath directly behind me. He reached up and touched my hair, sliding it away from my neck. I leaned slightly, inviting him closer still. The nearness of him, the burn of his touch, was more than I could take. Months of emotion swelled to the surface. At that moment, I no longer cared that he thought I was Eleanor, that it was *her* name he had spoken. I loved the boy standing behind me. I loved him just as I loved the boy I'd left behind in the basement of Uncle Connor's house so long ago. I missed him. I needed him. And I didn't care that being with him now could jeopardize our future—that it might somehow further alter the course of history and rip a gaping hole in the timeline I was trying to reset. I was too weak to resist him any longer, and although Eleanor's life force fought for control and tried to stop me before it was too late, she was no match for the power of my desire to be with him— right here, right now!

"Jonathan," I whispered.

He immediately wrapped his arms around me from behind and pressed his face against my hair. His breathing shifted as I leaned into his embrace, allowing his lips to search until they found my bared neck. When I didn't resist, he pulled me closer to him, turned me around, and pressed his lips against mine.

His kiss was awkward; he was not the relaxed, confident Jonathan of the future. It occurred to me that this was very likely a new experience for him. The day I ambushed him on the road may very well have been his first kiss ever. That possibility made me deliriously happy.

Jonathan's lips were hesitant, something that endeared him to me. I wanted nothing more than to lose myself in him completely, to never stop kissing him, but Eleanor battled against me until finally I broke his kiss and turned away. Jonathan relaxed his hold on me, but he didn't let go.

"I'm sorry," he said, flustered and out of breath. "I know I'm out of line."

I raised my eyes to his and instantly realized that he seemed taller than I remembered. It dawned on me that Eleanor was shorter than I was—probably by two or three inches. I read the confusion in Jonathan's expression and chuckled softly to myself.

"Perhaps we could walk?" I offered.

Jonathan nodded but he didn't move, his arms still locked around me. I started to laugh.

"What's wrong? You're laughing at me?"

He was clueless. "Well, we can't very well walk if you won't release me," I teased.

Jonathan's cheeks blushed bright red and he backed away. "Right." He cleared his throat. "Of course."

We hiked down to the river and began following its path upstream. I was grateful for the opportunity to spend time alone with him, real time. I wanted to learn everything I could about him, about his family, so I did what Beth does best—I began asking questions. Jonathan talked openly and freely about his mother and father, mainly his mom's cooking, which for some reason took me by surprise. He had rarely mentioned either of his parents in all the time we were together in the twenty-first century, except during the holidays. I recalled how much he enjoyed Grace's cooking and decided she must have gotten that from their mother.

"Did you know my mom makes the best pumpkin hotcakes in the state of Pennsylvania? Perhaps even the world!" He eyed me playfully.

"Ah, the infamous pumpkin pancakes," I said under my breath.

"You've heard about them?"

I laughed. "Not exactly, but they sound like something I'd like."

"Trust me, you would."

"Tell me about Grace," I said.

"What do you want to know?"

"I don't know. Anything. Everything. She's so amazing."

"Yes, very." It was easy to identify the pride in Jonathan's smile. "She the most remarkable woman I've ever known."

"The two of you obviously care for each other very much."

"Yes, we've been through a lot together. Our whole family has."

"Really? How so?" I couldn't recall Jonathan or Grace ever mentioning hardships, at least not until after Eleanor's disappearance.

"Well, I suppose with the war and all, just about everyone has faced some sort of loss or trial, so I guess we're no different than other families."

Little did Jonathan realize that I knew just how "different" his family really was from other families. I couldn't help but wonder if he knew their secret yet.

"To be honest," Jonathan continued, "I worry about Grace."

"Worry? Why?" I asked.

Jonathan shook his head. "I can't say exactly. Grace is . . . let's just say . . . different."

"In what way?" Could he be referring to her being a traveler?

Jonathan shrugged, scratching his chin. "That's just it; I don't know. When we were kids, she laughed all the time. She was optimistic, happy, outgoing, but in the past two years, she has become rather melancholy, pensive maybe, and noticeably more quiet. She was never shy when she was young, but ever since our—" Jonathan stopped abruptly. "Well, you've seen her. You know what I mean. She's shy beyond reason."

I thought of the reclusive Grace of the future. I had always assumed her shyness and reclusiveness were the result of her lost love.

"Could it have anything to do with her . . ." I hesitated, not knowing what to call him, "the one who gave her the bracelet?"

Jonathan forced a sad smile and shrugged. "Possibly, I suppose that's one explanation. I know she misses him something fierce. Still . . ." he looked away and shook his head, "I know there's more to it than that."

"Like what?"

He picked up a smooth stone and held it in his palm. He stared at the stone for several moments and then sighed before tossing it into the river. "I can't talk about it," he said finally. When I questioned him with my eyes, he added, "Maybe it's this war. It seems to have changed us all."

I had an uneasy feeling Jonathan was keeping something from me—something he wanted to tell me, but for some reason couldn't.

"It's almost over," I said before thinking.

Jonathan looked at me questioningly for a second and then scratched his head. "We're all hoping for that, aren't we?" He stared at me for a moment and then turned back to face the river. He picked up another stone and tossed it sidearm into the water. He watched as it skipped across the surface.

"And after it ends, then what?" he asked, his eyes fixed on the spot where the stone sank. I studied his profile, trying to follow his train of thought.

"Then Grace's soldier can come home. They can marry, and everything will be back to normal." I was lying. I knew that Grace's soldier would never come home. Somehow, I suspected that Jonathan knew it too.

"And what, they'll live happily ever after? Is that what you think?" Jonathan raised a disapproving eyebrow as he turned to look at me.

"Actually, I—"

"Exactly."

"Why are you so certain that he won't come back for her?" I asked.

Jonathan scoffed and shook his head, but he didn't respond.

"Well?" I pressed. "Do you know something?"

Jonathan turned away and kicked at the ground.

"Jonathan?" I tugged on his arm. He put his hand over mine and turned to look at me. He studied my eyes thoughtfully and then managed a semi-smile.

"If he loved her as much as he claims—as much as she believes he does—then he would have found a way to come back before now." Jonathan paused, then added, "I know *I* would have."

"Is that fair, though? What if it's beyond his control?"

Jonathan shook his head. "That's what I'm afraid of. If he truly loved her he would have somehow managed to see her—or at least contact her. That he hasn't for so long tells me the worst has happened."

I was puzzled. The Grace of the future told me that her engagement came to a halt as a result of Jonathan's unfortunate antics. Grace never mentioned the possibility that her soldier had died. "When was his last contact with her?" I asked, trying to piece the facts together.

"It's nearly been three years now, Eleanor." Jonathan stared deep into my eyes. "Don't you see?"

Actually, at that moment all I "saw" was Jonathan's deep blue eyes boring into mine. Their crystal-like luster was just as hypnotic now as they would be more than a hundred fifty years from now—only then, they would twinkle when he looked at me. I shook my head, releasing his gaze.

"He's never coming back," Jonathan lamented, "and Grace will never accept that fact."

Sadly, I knew he was right, and it explained to some degree what would eventually become Grace's gradual withdrawal from society.

Jonathan continued. "So many suitors would have asked for her hand—so many *did* ask. Some of them would have been excellent choices. Honorable husbands, strong fathers, but Grace," Jonathan shook his head.

"Grace is loyal," I finished his thought.

"*Fiercely* loyal," Jonathan corrected me. He turned around and muttered something quietly that I wasn't supposed to hear, but it sounded like, "It's in her blood."

We continued our walk along the river's path in silence, my arm tucked inside Jonathan's. The rocky, unforgiving ground made it difficult for me to maneuver easily without relying on Jonathan's steady support.

If only I had a decent pair of tennis shoes! I thought to myself. Still, I had to admit that I appreciated any excuse to be close to Jonathan.

The afternoon sun began its gradual decline in the western sky and I knew I'd been gone far too long. I was sure to catch some choice words coupled with a lengthy lecture upon my return. I didn't fret too much, though. After all, Father had given me permission to visit the cottage whenever I pleased—although I doubt his permission included Jonathan. Or did it?

Hmm . . . I wonder if he meant—

"Eleanor?" Jonathan squeezed my arm.

"I'm sorry?" I shook the thought from my head. "Did you say something?"

Jonathan looked confused for a moment and then grinned. "Nothing important."

His smile dazzled me. How could I possibly say goodbye to him again? Yet what choice was there? Tomorrow, Jonathan would return to his unit in the middle of heaven knows where, and a few days after, William would arrive for the wedding. Short of running away, I had yet to work out a reasonable solution for getting out of the marriage—let alone getting back to my life in Wyoming. Grace's story of Eleanor and Jonathan never mentioned Eleanor actually getting married, only that she was engaged to a man she didn't love.

"Jonathan?"

"Yes?"

"Do you believe in fate?"

Jonathan thought for a moment, then shook his head.

"No."

His reply surprised me. "So you think things happen by chance?" I asked, searching his eyes.

"I didn't say that. I believe things happen for a reason, but I don't think our decisions are predetermined."

"Isn't that sort of a contradiction?"

"No, not necessarily," he replied. "Oftentimes it feels like we have no choice in our decisions; but in reality, there's always a choice."

"But you have to leave tomorrow," I challenged. "Is that your choice?"

"It may not appear to be on the surface, but on a deeper level, yes. It's my choice."

"That makes no sense to me," I said, frustrated because he wasn't saying what I wanted to hear.

"Sometimes we sacrifice our right to make choices in order to accomplish a greater good. I'd like to think that makes us noble."

I smiled a half-smile. Little did Jonathan know that for years he would fight an internal battle over this very principle.

"But in the end," I reasoned, "isn't it all up to fate? Something or someone somewhere decides we are part of a bigger plan, and we have little say in the matter."

Jonathan eyed me skeptically. "I think you're confused, Eleanor. I presume you're speaking about your father forcing his will on you?"

I stared blankly at Jonathan for a second. He was completely missing my point. I was so frustrated that I didn't think before blurting out, "Damn it, Jonathan! Pay attention!"

Jonathan's jaw dropped. He took a step backward and stood gaping at me, stunned. My hands flew to my mouth. *Oh crap!* I thought. *I'm such an idiot!* Where was Eleanor when I needed her?

"I am so sorry, Jonathan." I lowered my head in shame as I struggled to recover what dignity I could.

Jonathan was still staring at me in disbelief. Then he pressed his lips together and I realized he was doing his best not to laugh. His eyes shone with mischief, and I would have given anything to know what he was thinking at that very moment. After several seconds, he cleared his throat.

"No need to apologize," he said generously. "I believe you have my complete attention now." I detected the slightest hint of a smile behind his words and when I looked more intently at him, I realized his eyes were twinkling. It was the first time I had seen his eyes dance since my arrival in the past.

"Well?" he pressed, obviously wanting to comprehend what had caused me to cuss at him.

"Nothing," I said, embarrassed. "It just sounds silly now."

Jonathan stepped closer to me and reached for my hand. "What sounds silly?"

I shook my head. "I mean, when something is meant to be, then fate will find a way to make it happen. I have to believe that's true." Jonathan didn't respond right away so I continued. "I just meant, if two people are supposed to be together then they will be, right?"

Jonathan slid his hand along my arm and squeezed gently. "It doesn't always work like that, Eleanor. When you want something badly enough, you go after it; you don't leave it up to fate."

Jonathan's thoughtful gaze unnerved me.

"You make it sound so easy," I said weakly.

Jonathan brushed the back of his fingers along the side of my cheek. "Not easy," he shook his head. "But is the alternative any easier?"

I closed my eyes and focused on his touch, sighing. "I want to go home," I whispered, thinking of Wyoming.

Jonathan took a deep breath and backed away. My eyes flew open once I realized what I had said.

"Yes, of course," he began. "I guess I—"

"No," I interrupted him. "I didn't mean it like that." I pressed my fingers against my temples. "I mean, I . . ." I studied Jonathan's eyes for a moment. I wanted so desperately to tell him the truth. "Jonathan, do you believe in time travel?"

Jonathan's face was suddenly very serious. "I'm sorry?" he said, watching me carefully.

"What if you could travel through time?" No harm throwing the idea out there, right?

Jonathan laughed nervously. "Have you been reading novels, Eleanor?"

I cleared my throat. "Um . . ." I couldn't tell if he was sincerely confused or if he was dodging my question, so I decided to tread lightly. "If you could travel through time, where would you go?"

Jonathan raised an eyebrow. "Eleanor, where is this coming from?"

"Please," I urged him, "humor me."

Jonathan took a deep breath and turned away. "All right, I suppose I would travel to the future."

"Why?"

He shrugged his shoulders. "I guess I'd like to know how things turn out. I'd like to see my children, grandchildren, you know, that sort of thing."

I hadn't expected that answer. The Jonathan I knew never mentioned being a father. I never realized he thought of himself in that role. Did I really know so little about him?

Frustrated, I found a felled log nearby and plopped down on it, burying my face in my hands. My hands smelled of the outdoors and I realized I wasn't wearing my gloves. I tried to recall when I had removed them and decided it must have been back at the cottage. *What is it with me and gloves?* I thought, dejected.

"Eleanor, what's going on?" Jonathan sat down next to me. "What is troubling you so?"

I shook my face against my hands.

"Tell me," he pleaded. He pulled my hands away from my face and nudged my chin with his finger, forcing me to look at him. "Tell me," he repeated softly.

"It doesn't matter, Jonathan. None of this matters. Tomorrow you will leave and in less than two weeks, I will become Mrs. William Hamilton. We're fooling ourselves if we think anything is going to change."

Jonathan moved his hand away from my chin, but his eyes remained steadily fixed on mine. "I see."

"What do you see? Tell me," I insisted.

"Do you *want* things to change?" he asked.

I sighed. I was speaking in riddles again. But if I told him the whole truth he would think I was crazy, or mad. Then again, the Jonathan of the future believed me when I told him about the night of my accident. But that was faulty logic. Of course he believed me—he'd been there.

Jonathan shook his head and suddenly stood. Evidently he'd mistaken my silence for some form of rejection.

"It's not what you think," I said quickly.

"Really?" Sarcasm colored his tone. "Enlighten me."

"I don't belong here," I said stubbornly. "This place. This time. This family. I don't belong to any of this."

Jonathan's eyes shifted from side to side as he struggled to make sense of what I was saying, but how could he possibly make sense of it all without having all the pieces of the puzzle?

"And where exactly is it that you *do* belong?" Jonathan's generosity had reached its limit. He was clearly frustrated.

I closed my eyes and thought of home. I thought of Wyoming, Uncle Connor's house, my piano, my disfigured hand, and Jonathan. "I belong in Wyoming near the foothills of the Teton Mountain Range with my baby grand piano, my eccentric uncle, my insane cousin . . ." I paused for effect, "and you."

Jonathan didn't respond. After several moments I opened my eyes. Jonathan had turned away from me.

"Jonathan?"

"What?" He stood, making circles in the dirt with the toe of his boot. I watched curiously.

"Did you hear what I said?"

"I heard."

"And?"

He used his heel to draw a large "X" over his circle. "And what?" His angry eyes pierced mine.

"You're upset." I stated the obvious.

"You're going to marry him, aren't you? That what you've been trying to tell me with all these riddles, isn't it? There's no hope for us because you're going through with your father's wishes." Jonathan's eyes sparkled with emotion.

I stepped toward him and put my hand on the side of his face. "I'm trying to tell you that it's out of our hands."

As I spoke the words, I realized I was admitting defeat.

In a stiff, formal gesture Jonathan offered me his arm, which I reluctantly accepted. "Well then, Miss Hastings, I had better get the bride-to-be home, hadn't I?"

"Jonathan," I let go of his arm. "Don't be like this."

Jonathan cut his eyes to the spot on his arm where my hand had been and shrugged his shoulders. "It's just as well. You've got a wedding to prepare for—and I've got a war to fight."

Jonathan and I started back to the cottage in silence. As we walked, I glanced at him out of the corner of my eye. His face held no expression and his eyes were fixed on the narrow path. I studied the soft wave of his hair beneath his hat. I longed to reach up and run my fingers through it. I longed for many things. How could I make him understand how much I loved him, but that our time to be together wouldn't happen for another century and a half? How could I ask him to wait for me?

I was running out of options. Tomorrow, Jonathan would be gone, and he would leave convinced that I was going to marry William. I had to figure out some way to give him hope, to convince him that there was a reason for him to come back for me. That's the way it was supposed to happen, right? Grace had told me the *whole* story, right? I concentrated hard, trying to recall exactly what Grace had said when she came to Uncle Connor's house to tell me about Jonathan's past. Little by little, bits and pieces of the conversation came back to me.

"The fear of Eleanor acquiescing to her father's wishes drove Jonathan crazy. Not knowing what was happening became such a distraction that Jonathan requested temporary leave, but leave was denied. The anguish he experienced following his separation from Eleanor would have killed any mortal."

"He returned for her, but their reunion was short-lived. They planned to go away, but then she disappeared. Jonathan went crazy."

"Jonathan refused to accept that she was gone. He was convinced that the Lebas had somehow intervened."

"I suspect they would do almost anything to preserve a pure bloodline."

Somehow, through some series of events unbeknownst to me, Jonathan and Eleanor had gotten off their natural course. Something had happened to trigger a shift in their timelines so that nothing was playing out exactly as it should. The only way to nudge Jonathan back on course was to make sure he had a reason to return for Eleanor.

Give Jonathan a reason to hope.

The words rang in my head with distinct clarity. Grace never actually said that Eleanor did not marry William; she only said that Jonathan *feared* she would. What I needed to do was give Jonathan a reason to return for me.

I had to think fast. I had to let Jonathan know that I loved him—no, not that I loved him, for I had discovered that "love" alone was not the basis for most decisions made in the 1800s, at least not in Marensburg. I had to make Jonathan believe that he *needed* to come back for me, and that the need was so urgent he'd risk his reputation and standing in the army to do so.

We reached the tiny cottage and without a word, Jonathan turned toward his horse which was grazing on a patch of wild flowers nestled among some raised tree roots.

"Jonathan," I called after him.

He stopped, but didn't respond. I perceived that as permission to continue.

"There's something I'd like to show you."

Jonathan turned around and cocked his head to one side. His jaw was firmly set. He closed his eyes and shook his head.

"Eleanor, please, just let me go." His harsh expression masked his pain.

"I promise it will only take a minute."

Jonathan looked to one side and let out an aggravated sigh. He kicked at the ground and then walked toward me. He reminded me of a stubborn horse. When he was close enough, I reached for his hand. I felt Eleanor's presence as she started to protest. She must have sensed what I had in mind. I ignored her influence and pushed her away in my mind. My time with Jonathan was running short and I was determined to let him know just how deeply my feelings for him ran before I risked losing him, now and forever.

I led him through the entrance of the cottage and over to the far side of the room where the easel stood. Father's paintings were still stacked in rows against the wall. Jonathan said nothing as his eyes surveyed the room. I stopped at the long table that spanned the entire length of the window and began sifting through my most recent sketches. Finally, I found what I was looking for.

"Here," I said, handing a stack of sketches to Jonathan.

Jonathan pursed his lips as he flipped through the drawings.

"They're good, of course," he said matter-of-factly, and handed them back to me. I looked down at the sketches and placed my hand on top of his, pushing them toward him again.

"Look carefully at them." I looked up into his puzzled eyes. "Please," I whispered.

Jonathan took the drawings from me and I motioned for him to sit down. I grabbed a nearby stool and sat directly in front of him. I searched his face for any signs of recognition as he studied each of the sketches. I don't know what I was hoping to observe in his expression, but whatever it was, I didn't find it.

Several minutes passed while Jonathan studied the drawings. He scratched the side of his head and looked up at me questioningly. "I'm not sure I understand. I mean, they're all good. They're really good, but are they supposed to mean something to me?"

"No," I smiled. "Not yet."

Jonathan thumbed through the drawings again. "Where is this place?" he asked.

"Wyoming."

Jonathan shook his head. "Never heard of it," he stated matter-of-factly. He got up and set the pictures on the table, then pointed to one of them. "This one," he said, pointing to a sketch of a large ranch home tucked neatly among the foothills of the Tetons. The twin Teton peaks stood like watch towers in the background. "I think this one is my favorite."

My smile broadened. "Yes, that's one of my favorites too."

"Your drawings make it seem like you've been there."

"I suppose you could say I've been there many times—in my dreams."

Jonathan smiled a half-smile. "These mountain peaks," he pointed to the Tetons, "they're unlike any I've seen."

I nodded. "Yes. They're unique to Wyoming."

"And where *is* this Wyoming you keep talking about?"

"It's out west. I'm not surprised you're not familiar with it, but I promise, one day you'll know it well."

Jonathan eyed me curiously and then scratched his head. "Well, they're beautiful drawings; you obviously have a gift, but I still don't see what they have to do with me."

"Let me try to explain. When I envision the two of us . . . you and I," I turned and faced him, "this is where I see us. Together. Far away from here . . . from all of this." I looked around the room. "No family obligations. No war. No society dictating the rules we live by."

"Eleanor," Jonathan took my hands in his. "You're talking in riddles again." His eyes pleaded with mine for answers—answers that I couldn't give him completely. But one thing was certain, I could not bear to be this close to him for one minute longer without telling him everything.

"Jonathan, I love you. I have loved you for a very long time. I—"

Before I could say more, he folded his arms around me and pressed his lips against mine. I melted into his embrace, determined to kiss him for as long as he wanted me.

This time there was no awkward hesitancy in his kiss, no second-guessing himself. There was a determination in his lips that not only caught me off guard but made my knees buckle, causing me to lose my footing slightly. Jonathan tightened his hold on me as we stumbled against the table, sending its contents tumbling to the ground. Neither of us paid attention to the drawings that now lay scattered in disarray at our feet.

I wrapped my arms around Jonathan's neck, partly for support, but mostly because I could no longer keep the depth of my feelings a secret from him; nor could I think of one good reason why I should.

After what seemed like a very long time, and yet not long enough, Jonathan pulled away slightly and looked into my eyes.

"Come away with me," he smiled. "Today . . . tonight . . . tomorrow . . . just say when. We'll leave all this behind us and find that place you dream about called Wyoming." He made a gesture toward the scattered drawings on the floor.

"Jonathan, I—"

"Marry me, Eleanor!"

"Jonathan, wait. We need to think this through. You're leaving—"

He put his finger to my lips and grinned. His smiled melted me, and I couldn't think of any reason to say "no." Why not go with him? What did I have to lose? Why not kick fate in the teeth and write our own destiny? We could build a new history together and rewrite our future. Maybe I couldn't find my way back to the twenty-first century, but dang it all, Jonathan and I could still be together now. Wasn't that enough?

"At least promise me you'll think about it," he urged. The fact that I didn't respond right away seemed to encourage him. "Say you will, Eleanor. Just say it."

Words escaped me. Eleanor's influence fought again to bring me to my senses, but once again she was no match for the elation I felt at the thought of being in Jonathan's arms for the rest of my life.

I sensed a final, desperate plea from Eleanor. She was sad, of that I was certain, but then she retreated, disappearing into some dark corner of my mind. Eleanor was crying. A sudden wave of sadness washed over me as I thought of her.

There was no way for me to live my dream without robbing Eleanor of hers.

I lowered my arms and stepped away to reestablish my bearings. I needed to think. I bent down and slowly began gathering the sketches from the floor. Jonathan knelt beside me to help. He picked up the drawing of the ranch.

"Just think about it. Us. Here." He pointed to the Tetons. "Away from this bloody war and death, living our lives together. Why the hell not?"

I watched his eyes, so full of anticipation and determination, yet so full of the innocence and naivety of his youth. But my Jonathan of the future had eyes that reflected wisdom and experience; and though they often danced with mischief (in a way that was far from innocent), they also showed hints of sadness and regret. If I ran away with him now, would that spare his family the shame and disgrace of his desertion, or would it make their future even more complicated?

How I wished I could talk to somebody. I needed advice, but I needed it from somebody who understood all that was potentially at stake.

Who could I possibly turn to?

Intervention

CHAPTER 10

*A*s if fate were purposely sabotaging the moment, the sound of a horse's hooves in the distance interrupted my thoughts. Jonathan inclined his head to the side and listened. He relaxed as the sounds of the unexpected intruder grew louder.

"Don't worry, it's only Grace," he said reassuringly as he steadied my shaking hands.

I listened intently for a moment, concentrating, trying to hear what Jonathan was hearing.

"How can you possibly know that?" I finally asked.

Jonathan smiled proudly. "I would recognize the sound of her horse's gait from a mile away. You can't miss it."

I listened again and pretended I heard it too.

"Oh, no!" A thought suddenly occurred to me. "I can just imagine what Grace will think when she sees us like this—and this mess!" Jonathan gave my hands a gentle squeeze and helped me to my feet. We began quickly putting the room back in order. Jonathan collected my sketches and arranged them neatly on the table, all except for one.

"Whoa, what's this?" He held up a rough depiction of two people sitting at a piano. It was a crude likeness of Jonathan and me—or rather

Jonathan and Beth—as if observing them from behind as they sat together at the piano. I had drawn it from memory. It was a copy of the picture Jonathan had painted for me at Christmas. It depicted the two of us sitting at the piano with my disfigured hand lying on top of his. I recalled thinking at the time that he had perfectly captured the memory of the afternoon he taught me to play Eleanor's Theme.

Jonathan looked closely at the sketch. "I like this, the idea of it. It's . . ." he paused, searching for the right word, "sensual."

I nodded and managed a half smile. "Well, it's not finished."

Jonathan set the drawing on the pile with the others and picked up another. "May I have this?" He held up the drawing of the Rollings' ranch. When I hesitated, he quickly apologized. "I'm sorry, that was presumptuous of me."

"No," I said, placing my hand over his as he set the picture down with the others. "I would very much like for you to have it." The sight of my hand on his reminded me of the drawing we had looked at a moment ago. I gathered by Jonathan's reaction that he'd made a similar connection.

Gradually, our surroundings began to transform; it was as though the chemistry between our two hands somehow catapulted me forward in time—to modern-day Wyoming. I found myself seated next to Jonathan at the piano in the practice room at the Community Recreation Center, and for a brief moment, I relived the memory of that afternoon as I watched Beth play Eleanor's Theme with Jonathan.

I floated through the room and hovered behind Beth, just as I had done when I'd fainted at the Debutante ball and found myself roaming through the halls of Andersen High School. A rush of jealously consumed me as I watched Beth and Jonathan's hands play as one, and I couldn't help but feel both angry and sad at the same time. It was as though Beth and I were separate souls, leading separate lives. Reason told me this wasn't the case, that this scene was coming from my memories as Beth; but I couldn't shake the feeling of angst knowing she was there with *my* Jonathan. It made no sense, but the resentment I felt was palpable.

My eyes fixated on Beth's disabled hand resting on top of Jonathan's. I once viewed that hand with revulsion, but it seemed different now. Even in its deformed state, it was beautiful. Beautifully imperfect. A profound sense of loneliness came over me as I considered the possibility that my life as Beth might be over forever.

I longed to make contact with the girl at the piano who was living *my* life. I was desperate to reach out to her—to connect—to unite. I wanted my life back!

Grace's delicate knock at the door snatched me back to reality and the scene of Beth and Jonathan at the piano faded. Jonathan had been watching me, puzzled. I moved my hand away from his as Grace knocked louder, this time more urgently. Jonathan let her in.

"I'm sorry," she stammered, out of breath. "Eleanor! Your father! He's coming!" Grace flashed her anxious eyes toward Jonathan. "Go, Jonathan! Quickly!"

Grace didn't need to say more. Jonathan shot me a quick glance, as if he were waiting for me to say something. There was no way I could muster up the courage to face Eleanor's father with Jonathan present. It's not that I cared if he was angry with me, that was pretty much status quo with us these days, but I worried about what he might do to Jonathan. It occurred to me that Eleanor's father might kill him.

"Jonathan, please! Hurry!" Grace pleaded with her brother.

Jonathan stared at me for a moment longer, then nodded and headed for the door. I followed him outside and watched him swing agilely onto his horse. He pulled back on the reins and turned his horse around for a final look in my direction. His horse pranced anxiously, as if it sensed impending danger. I couldn't bear the thought of Jonathan leaving because I had no way of knowing when or how I might see him again. My heart ached at the thought of being away from him. His horse reared again and Jonathan turned to go.

"Wait!" I yelled after him.

"No!" Grace called out to Jonathan from behind me. "Jonathan hurry!" Then she grabbed hold of my arm. "Eleanor, please," she lowered her voice, "please let him go!"

The anguish in Grace's eyes crumbled any last minute impulse I might have felt to run after Jonathan and climb onto the horse with him. I sighed, crippled by my compassion for Grace. I turned back to Jonathan and held his eyes. I had no parting words for him except for one.

"Wyoming!" I mouthed the word silently, but slowly enough that

Jonathan could read my lips. He tipped his hat and gave me a knowing smile. He held up the folded drawing in his hand and nodded. Then with a quick kick on his horse's side, he was off. I watched him ride away until he disappeared from view.

"Eleanor," Grace called from behind me. "Come inside, quickly."

I turned to face her, surprised by her sense of urgency.

"Your father will be here any minute. He mustn't find you out here or he'll *know*."

I followed Grace back into the cottage, but I couldn't shake the image of Jonathan riding away. Grace did a quick survey of the room before gathering several charcoals and a sketchpad from the table near where Jonathan and I had stood only moments earlier. I rested my fingers against my mouth and tried to recapture the feeling of Jonathan's lips on mine. Grace ignored me for the moment and scurried around the room, busily trying to create an appropriate setting before Eleanor's father arrived.

"Here," she said, handing me the sketchpad and charcoal. "Sit down and start drawing!"

I looked blankly at the pad of paper and shook my head. "What am I supposed to draw?"

Grace looked around quickly and then pulled a small stool up close to me. "Draw me," she said, positioning herself daintily on the stool.

I glanced down at the paper, not exactly sure where to begin. Up until now, I had only sketched landscapes or images from my memories as Beth. I looked up and studied Grace's features. Then, as if I were no longer in control of my hands, I began sketching. The automaticity in my movements surprised me, and I realized Eleanor had taken control.

"Turn your head slightly to the right," I said, checking the light source as it captured her eyes. "Chin down, just a little." My hand worked frantically, but my eyes never left Grace. Although only a brief time passed before we heard the approaching horse, I had made significant progress in the drawing.

Eleanor's father didn't bother to knock. He bolted through the door, then stopped abruptly. His rapid breathing and shocked expression told me he had expected to find me here with Jonathan. I was instantly relieved and grateful that Grace had arrived when she did.

"Father?" I asked innocently. "What is it? Is something wrong?"

Father's eyes shifted repeatedly from Grace to me, and then he looked around the room—probably searching for signs that Jonathan had been there. Thanks to Grace's quick thinking, Eleanor's father found nothing out of order. He cleared his throat and removed his hat.

"Uh, I've come to escort you back to the house. It's nearly dusk. You shouldn't be out alone—neither of you should be." I didn't miss the contrived concern in his tone, but I played along.

"Thank you, Father."

"I'm afraid this is my fault, Mr. Hastings," Graced chimed in before I could continue. "I saw Miss Eleanor's drawings and I begged her to do a sketch of me." She lowered her head. "I fear my vanity has robbed me of my good judgment. You see, I hoped to send a likeness of me to my fiancé, who, as I'm sure you know, is away fighting in the war. Please, forgive me for detaining Miss Eleanor. I know she has far more pressing matters to engage her time."

It took every ounce of my self-control to keep from outwardly marveling at Grace's poise. Father stood silent for a moment, then little by little his expression softened.

"I beg your pardon, Miss Rollings. Please allow us to accompany you home." Father's tone was more curt than friendly, but at least he appeared calm.

"Thank you. That is very generous of you." Grace stood and smiled graciously. Then she held out her hand to me. "Shall we?"

I took her hand in mine and mouthed a silent, *Thank you.*

As Eleanor's family sat around the dining table that evening, there was no mention of the cottage. Father handed me the bowl of yams and picked up a plate of string beans. He had given the servants the night off, so we served ourselves. I normally enjoyed these meals the best; they reminded me of home, of dinners with my mom and dad as a child, and it was one of the rare times when Eleanor's family behaved in a less formal way.

Initiating the conversation, Father said, "I hadn't realized you and Grace had become so friendly."

"It has only been in the past couple of months, ever since I began attending the poetry club," I replied.

"Yes," Mother interjected, "but attending poetry readings hardly accounts for your sudden intimacy. How is it the two of you have come to know each other well enough for you to refer to her by her first name?"

I took a moment to replace the spoon in the yam bowl and pass it down to Christine, who was listening with unusual enthusiasm for someone her age.

"Well, Grace is . . . I mean, Miss Rollings is . . ." I cleared my throat, stalling, hoping the right words would come to me.

"I think what Eleanor is trying to say," Christine cut in, "is that both she and Miss Rollings are to be married, so they have something special in common."

A rock launched itself into the pit of my stomach. Christine was right, of course. In the thrill of my time with Jonathan earlier this afternoon, I had put any thoughts of Eleanor's engagement to William out of my mind. The wedding was just around the corner, less than two weeks away.

"And they're both engaged to soldiers," Christine added enthusiastically.

Father grunted under his breath. "I doubt that's all they share."

"Christine is right, Father," I continued, hoping to nudge the focus of the conversation in another direction. "Grace's fiancé has been away for three years now. She misses him terribly."

"Three years is a long time," Mother commented. "It doesn't sound as though *her* marriage will take place any time soon. Besides, I've heard no mention of any plans, and we must agree that much can change in three years."

"Oh Mother, if you could have heard her speak of him the night of the ball you wouldn't say that. She's determined to marry him the moment he returns."

"Is that what the two of you were talking about when I found you on the balcony together?" Father asked.

"That's exactly what we were talking about. Miss Rollings is one of the lucky ones."

"How so?" Father asked.

I gave Father a knowing look that bordered on defiance. "*She* is engaged to a man she loves with all her heart."

Father set his fork down and folded his fingers together. He returned my gaze with equal defiance and added a sarcastic smile. "Well then, we wish her our best, don't we?"

"If you ask me, Eleanor is the lucky one," Christine remarked innocently.

"Me? Why?"

"Isn't it obvious? You're marrying a colonel!" Christine's eyes were wide with naïve envy.

"And a handsome colonel at that," Mother acknowledged. She placed her hand on Christine's arm and gave it a gentle squeeze.

"And let's not forget that he's also rich." Bitterness buttered my tongue. "Isn't that the most important part?"

"He's also good blood," Father inserted, dismissing my comment. "Let us never forget that."

"Yes," Mother smiled at Christine. "William is all these things, and more. Eleanor is a very lucky young woman."

"Won't be long, Mother," Father said proudly, "and our home will be full of the pitter-patter of young ones who carry the Hastings' blood." Father cut his eyes at me, almost daring me to object. I scooted my plate away from me and started to get up.

"Sit down, Eleanor," Father ordered. "You are not yet excused from dinner."

"I'm no longer hungry, Father," I said coldly.

"Now hush you two," Mother said, trying to soften the tension between Father and me. "Let's focus first on the wedding, and then there can be talk of children."

My patience had finally hit its limit.

"Stop it!" I threw my napkin on the table. "All of you! This is not going to happen, do you get that? There isn't going to be a wedding, are we clear? No wedding—and most certainly NO babies!"

A frightening silence suffused the room. Nobody moved or made a sound. Christine's mouth fell open as she gaped at me in shock. Mother and Father stared blankly at each other. A silent communication passed between them that caused the hairs on the back of my neck to stand at attention. I instantly regretted my outburst, but it was too late to take back the words, nor would I have recanted if given the opportunity. I wondered what my punishment would be this time. Copying all sixty-six chapters of Isaiah perhaps? Or would Eleanor's father be more creative this time? Maybe he would have the servants take me down to the woodshed and teach me a proper lesson! I didn't care. The simple fact remained—I was not going to marry Colonel William Hamilton, and I certainly was not going to fill the house with his babies!

"Eleanor, dear, you are obviously very tired." Mother spoke with controlled coolness. "Perhaps it's best if you retire early tonight."

That was Mother's way of sending me to my room.

"Whatever!" I replied in the most belligerent twenty-first century teenage attitude I could muster.

Father stood and slammed his fist on the table. The dishes rattled and a thick splotch of gravy flew into the air, landing in splatters on Mother's favorite table cloth.

"I'll have no more of this defiance in my house!" he bellowed. His face burned bright red with anger, the veins bulging in his forehead and neck. "You will leave this room at once!" he ordered.

Well, that was fine with me. That would give me a chance to figure out exactly how and when I would make my escape. I was so "over" the hypocrisy of the Hastings family.

I retreated to my "chamber" and immediately started to undress. I worked frantically to undo the snaps and hooks and ties that kept me from relaxing my posture. I was so sick of dressing in layers! I needed to breathe. I piled layer after layer of clothing onto the floor until at last I was free, stripped down to my undergarments. I reached down and pulled at the elastic band at my knees, yanking at it until the elastic finally snapped. I repeated this on the other side, and then proceeded to tear the elastic completely off. I didn't stop there. I tore around the material until eventually all that remained was a crude version of modern-day cutoffs.

There. That's more like it!

I couldn't do much about the bodice; my breasts would have to remain hostage until I changed into my nightgown. I vowed that when I got back to the twenty-first century, I would wear loose T-shirts and go braless for at least a month—maybe even a year!

I surveyed the pile of clothing on the floor and decided it was a grotesque waste of material. I kicked the pile across the floor, leaving the remnants strewn between where I stood and the fireplace on the far side of the room. When I decided I was finished with my rampage, I sat down at the vanity and started on my hair. It was probably a fortunate thing that I didn't own a pair of scissors. In my present state of mind, I might have given Eleanor a more artistic hairstyle. I laughed out loud at the thought of the beautiful Eleanor Hastings with a spiky Mohawk. Then I pursed my lips and sputtered a colorful cuss word. *Knowing Eleanor, she'd probably even make* that *look good!*

Instead of butchering Eleanor's luscious locks, I removed the clips and let her hair fall. She truly was a beautiful woman. Perfect. I rested my elbows on the table and put my face in my hands and let out an exaggerated sigh of resignation.

Are you quite finished with your tantrum?

I sat up straight, checking the room behind me. I knew there was nobody else in the room, but I'd heard the words just as clearly as though I had said them myself. I listened, but heard nothing.

"Great! Now I'm losing my mind," I said into the mirror.

The eerie sound of a woman's laugh came from somewhere behind me, and again I snapped my head around to see who was there.

"Who's there?" I called out. "Show yourself!"

Again, I heard laughter coming from behind me. I whirled back around to the mirror. For a split instant I thought I saw something move in the mirror's reflection. I looked more closely, but saw nothing out of place.

A light rapping at the door startled me and I jumped.

"Eleanor?" Christine's tiny voice called from the other side of the door. "May I come in?"

I opened the door, forgetting I had stripped down to barely anything. Christine's eyes flew open wide at the sight of me; she nearly dropped the tray she was carrying.

"Mother insisted you have some tea to help calm your nerves so you can sleep." Christine did her best to avert her eyes as she handed a tray that held an empty teacup and a steaming pot of tea. There were two biscuits sitting on a small plate beside the teacup.

I took the tray from Christine and forced a smile. "Thank you."

"Eleanor, are you sure you're all right?" Christine asked cautiously. Her eyes spied the scattered clothes that now carpeted the wooden floor.

"I'm fine," I assured her, but she didn't seem convinced. "Really, Christine, I'm okay. I'm so sorry for my outburst at the table. I don't know what came over me. I'm sure Mother is right; I just need some rest." I was lying, and it seemed to me I was doing a good job at it because I nearly had myself convinced that I was fine.

Christine smiled. "Is there anything else I can get you?"

"No, sister. Please thank Mother for the tea."

"Goodnight, Eleanor," Christine said as she backed away from the door.

"Goodnight," I replied. I nudged the door shut with my knee and carried the tray to the table beside my bed. I poured some of the tea into the cup and began sipping it. It felt warm and smooth on the way down and as soon as it reached my stomach I realized I was hungry. I wished I had waited to have my outburst until after I'd eaten.

The next thing I knew, it was morning.

Sunlight peeked through my curtain panels. A low fire blazed in the fireplace and the clothes that had covered the floor were gone. A tray of fresh bread and jelly, along with a boiled egg and a fresh pot of tea, had replaced the tray from the night before. I sat up and noticed I was dressed in my nightgown, yet I had no memory of changing my clothes or going to bed.

What the heck?

I slid out of bed and put on the robe that hung across the back of my vanity chair. I ran the brush through my hair and clipped the sides back into a loose twist, then walked over to the window and opened the curtains, allowing the sunlight to flood the room. I opened the windows and soaked in the fresh scent of the morning air. It was a beautiful, warm day and I decided it was the perfect morning for breakfast on my terrace where I could eat in peace and enjoy the view of the gardens. I went back for the breakfast tray and noticed another tray sitting on my vanity. It held my morning messages. There were several notes: some in envelopes sealed with wax, others simply folded and addressed to me. Most of them were probably thank you notes which were still trickling in from the night of the debutante ball. I, of course, was expected to reply to each note—which made no sense to me. Who replies to a thank you note?

I carried the tray of letters along with the tray of food out to the terrace and began shuffling through them as I drank my tea. It was just as I supposed, note after note thanking my family for hosting the ball, with their compliments to the musicians, dance card coordinators, etc. Blah blah blah. I set the letters aside and spread some jam onto a slice of bread. One thing I did like about living in the 1800s was the homemade jams and jellies. It was like eating fresh fruit picked right from the tree. I couldn't recall anything as tasty in the present—except, perhaps, Marci's pies.

One of the sealed notes caught my eye. It was written on a piece of parchment that was a shade darker than the others. I wiped my jelly knife against a piece of bread and then used it to break the seal on the note. The message read:

It won't be long now. Until then, remember that you carry my heart with you wherever you go. Don't lose faith. I promise you won't have to bear the ordeal any longer than necessary.

Yours faithfully and forever,

James

I reread the note several times, studying it carefully. I recognized the handwriting. It was the same as the writing in the note that a servant had delivered to me the night of the ball—the note I later asked him to destroy. And it matched the handwriting in the letters I'd found in the fireplace.

"So," I whispered to Eleanor, "your mysterious suitor has a name after all."

Eleanor's spirit stirred. I sensed she wanted to tell me something.

"Okay, Eleanor. I'm listening," I said aloud. I closed my eyes and waited, but no words came.

After a moment, I folded the note and laid it on the table. I read the remaining letters and finished my breakfast while enjoying the tranquil morning breeze. By noon, the air would be still, and would remain so until the sun's decent in the west; then the wind would kick up again. The pattern was very predictable.

The sound of keys rattling caught my attention, and within seconds Lucinda appeared at the terrace door.

"Are you finished, Miss Eleanor?"

"Yes, thank you."

She retrieved the tray and started for the door. "I'll return in a moment to help you dress. Will you be wanting your bath this morning?"

"No, thank you. I want to get a head start on responding to my messages before making my calls."

"As you wish." She started for the door again but then stopped short. Reaching into her apron pocket she said, "I almost forgot. Mrs. Hastings asked me to give this to you." She pulled out another folded note and started to hand it to me.

"Just leave it on my vanity . . . I'll read it later."

"Mrs. Hastings asked me to be sure I handed it directly to you."

I pursed my lips and took the note from Lucinda, who then excused herself and shut the door. Then I heard the sound of keys rattling again, and I realized she had locked the door. I raced over and quickly tried turning the handle, but it didn't budge. I shook the handle and pounded my fist on the door.

"Lucinda! Open this door!" I ordered. There was no reply. "Lucinda! Open the door, now!" I shouted. Again, there was no reply. I continued pounding on the door until my fists began to ache, but there was no response from the other side.

I lowered my fists and realized I was still holding the note she had delivered. I quickly opened it and read its contents.

Darling,

It pains me to see you so troubled with fatigue and burdened with the enormous responsibilities that accompany the preparations for a wedding. Therefore, I feel it necessary to intervene on your behalf. Rest assured that all brides experience anxiety and doubts prior to their wedding day. Do not be dismayed. This will all be over soon, and then you will be free to begin your new role as the mistress of the Hastings' Estate. I have carried the responsibility for more than a quarter of a century, and now that honor will be yours. To help you regain your strength and prepare you for your big day and your new life as mistress of the estate, your father and I feel it necessary to relieve you of all social and family obligations until after the wedding. We trust that by doing so, you will be quite rested and back to your normal self in no time.

With all my love,

Mother

So—this was my punishment for last night. I was to be held prisoner in my bedroom until the wedding. Evidently, I had underestimated Eleanor's father and his ability to think creatively when it came to discipline. I would gladly copy every page of the Old Testament over this form of cruelty.

I ran to the terrace and searched for any possible way down, but Eleanor's bedroom was situated on the third floor of the grand house— floors with very high ceilings. There was no perceivable hope of escaping without taking a suicidal leap over the terrace wall. I would have to figure out some other way to get Eleanor's parents to allow me out of my room, even if that meant having a change of heart—or in other words, lying.

I spent the next several days in solitary confinement. Mr. Edwards accompanied Lucinda each morning as she arrived to tend to my morning rituals. He waited outside the door just in case I tried to bolt, and reminded Lucinda with each visit that she was not to tarry any longer than necessary. She came three times a day to dress me, bring me my food rations, and deliver my messages. Except for her brief visits, I had no contact with anyone.

A week had passed, and I realized that each minute I spent locked away in my room brought me a minute closer to my wedding. Only seven days remained before I would be forced to walk down the aisle and agree to love, honor, and obey Colonel Hamilton "until death do us part."

We'll see about that! I thought repeatedly to myself. *You can hog-tie me and carry me down the aisle, but you cannot force me to speak vows that I do not intend to keep.*

My mind was made up, my resolve firm. There would be a horrible scandal when I openly defied my father in front of the entire family and embarrassed all the honored guests who would no doubt be present for the big wedding event, but I was willing to risk that and more in order to make my point.

That was at the end of day seven.

On day eight, I began to second-guess myself. I started asking all sorts of "what if" questions, and by the end of the day, I'd managed to work myself into a panic. I pictured a public stoning, or worse, confinement in a loony bin, neither of which would surprise me. I was beginning to believe that nothing was off limits where Eleanor's father was concerned. He was rigidly determined to prove to me, the family, his associates, and in fine, to all the members of Marensburg society, that he was master of his household and could control his defiant daughter. I recalled the story he told me about his sister, Veronica, and how the family shunned her for refusing to do what was expected of her. Now she was dead. I suddenly felt a deep sense of empathy with her.

I began playing several scenarios in my mind. What if I went through with the marriage, but then refused to be a proper wife to William? Was he enough of a gentleman to respect my wishes, or would he force my hand? I could always run away after the fact, but where would I go? I couldn't run to Jonathan; he'd never entangle himself with a married woman. Doing so would surely bring the greatest possible shame to his family. The only possible chance I had of running to Jonathan for safety was if I did so before the wedding.

Maybe I had this all wrong. Maybe the real Eleanor *did* marry William. Maybe that's why Jonathan left his men and went AWOL. Maybe coming home to discover Eleanor had gone through with the wedding would explain why Grace had said their reunion was bittersweet. Maybe this wasn't about me. Maybe it was never about me. Maybe marrying William was Eleanor's fate, and I was the one standing in the way.

The resolve that seemed so firm only yesterday now began to waver.

On day nine of my solitary confinement, Eleanor's father paid me a visit.

"How do you feel?" he asked when he entered my prison cell.

I had rehearsed this conversation many times in my head, certain that I had worked out the exact words I needed to say in order to give the appearance of acquiescing to Father's will without actually doing so. Therefore, there was no reasonable explanation for my response.

"How the hell do you think I feel?" I cringed the instant the words flew out of my mouth.

You idiot! What is the matter with you? I scolded myself.

Father turned away and started walking back to the door.

"Wait!" I called after him. The desperation in my voice surprised me. Eleanor's father stopped, but didn't turn around. He stood silent, waiting for me to speak.

"I'm sorry, Father. Please don't go." My resolve had all but crumbled, but the pleading words I uttered were Eleanor's, not mine. Her life force had surfaced without warning, and she desperately wanted her father's forgiveness. She *needed* it.

Eleanor approached her father and pulled gently on his arm. "Please don't leave me," she begged. "I'll go crazy if I have to stay in here alone any longer." A single tear slid down the side of Eleanor's face. I caught it with the back of my hand. Eleanor was on the verge of hysterics; it was up to me to hold her emotions in check. In her present state of mind, she might very likely promise her father anything. I concentrated all my internal strength on usurping her will with mine.

Eleanor's father turned to face me. "All right," he said as he patted my hand. "Perhaps you are ready for a turn around the grounds?"

The thought of actually getting out of my room, even for a short time, elated me. "Oh yes!" I cried. "I would like that very much!"

Father smiled and took my hand in his. "That is what I was hoping to hear," he said softly. "Come, I have a surprise waiting for you."

Alternatives
CHAPTER 11

I followed Eleanor's father down the long flight of stairs, bypassing the second story and going directly to the ground floor. I should have guessed what that meant. Father led me to the drawing room where I found Colonel Hamilton waiting patiently near the piano. He removed his hat the moment I entered the room.

"Good morning, Miss Hastings," he said with a polite bow.

"Colonel Hamilton." I acknowledged him with equal cordiality; after all, I was so relieved to finally be out of my chambers I'd have been cordial to a rebel soldier.

Eleanor's father gestured for Colonel Hamilton to step forward. "Let us dismiss with formalities. William is practically family," Father shot me a meaningful glance, "and in a very short time the two of you will enter into your nuptials. I see no reason why you should not address each other by your Christian names."

"Much obliged, sir," the colonel nodded. He was still holding his hat in his hands.

"Eleanor?" Father said, waiting for me to respond in kind.

"Yes, of course Father, as you wish." It required a great deal of self-control to keep from rolling my eyes and shaking my head.

"William has been granted a few days leave to prepare for the wedding. He has graciously agreed to honor us as our guest until then." Father eyed me expectantly.

"Welcome . . . William," I said, offering him my hand. The simple gesture had become so automatic that I no longer wondered if the act was Eleanor's doing.

Addressing William by his first name felt awkward because in the twenty-first century, my father was a military man, and he insisted on addressing officers by their title out of respect for their position. Then again, he hadn't been engaged to marry one of them.

"Eleanor," William blushed slightly as he took my hand in his and raised it to his lips.

"Ahem." Eleanor's father cleared his throat. "I'm sure the two of you would appreciate some time to visit, so if you'll excuse me, I have business to attend to in my study. Edwards is available should either of you need anything."

Father turned to leave, acknowledging William with a bow.

I watched, dumbfounded, as Eleanor's father exited the room, leaving William and me alone—unchaperoned.

Now what?

I turned to face William. His clear blue eyes were hard to ignore, and I could tell by looking at them that he had something on his mind. I motioned for him to take a seat.

"Actually," he hesitated, "I wonder if you might join me for a walk."

I hadn't been outside of the house for a week. I probably would have agreed to walk to Canada and back if he had asked me, so I readily accepted his invitation.

"Where to?" William asked when we were finally outdoors. I felt a compelling temptation to run, not that I had anywhere to go, but I wanted to take advantage of my sudden freedom, regardless of how short-lived it may prove to be.

"Perhaps we could walk down to the river," I suggested, testing him. The river was a significant distance from the house—and certainly beyond eye and earshot of Mr. Edwards.

"You prefer the river to the gardens?" William asked, surprised.

"Oh yes, most definitely." I didn't really like the river better than the gardens, but I was determined to make the colonel as uncomfortable as I was. "Do you disapprove?"

William studied me for a brief moment, his pleasant smile revealing no hint of discomfort. "Not at all. It's just that as I recall, you have a particular fondness for gardens." William raised an eyebrow suggesting a subtle hidden meaning behind his statement. I quickly searched for any clue of a suppressed memory, but found none.

"The gardens are lovely, of course," I tried to sound nonchalant—I made a mental note to press Lucinda for information later, "but I've had my heart set on a walk along the river for some time now."

"All right then, shall we?" William tipped his hat and offered me his arm, which I readily accepted. I hesitated only briefly when I laced my fingers around his bicep. It was as hard as stone, and I couldn't help but look down to make sure it was real. I noticed a sly look of satisfaction in his smile, and it made me question for a moment if men in the 1800s were as obsessed with their muscles as men in the twenty-first century were. I chuckled silently to myself as I thought of Eric—he was always so proud of his biceps, and he made it a point to show them off as often as he could. I somehow doubted Colonel Hamilton possessed the same need for attention that Eric did. There was a sense of humility about William that reminded me of my father.

We followed the pathway that wound around the side of the estate and then crossed to the wooded trail that led to the river. It was a particularly warm morning and the air was heavy with the humidity of spring. It didn't take long before I felt a layer of perspiration form at the base of my neck. Soon, Eleanor's hair would begin to wind into loose curls—the kind that girls in the future would spend a ton of money and time trying to duplicate.

What I wouldn't give for a ponytail holder right now! I thought to myself as I fought the urge to wipe away the sweat with my arm—something I'd learned the hard way was an absolute "no-no"!

When we finally reached the river, I was grateful for the cool breeze it generated. The water was deep where we were, so the river moved more steadily and peacefully than it did at the shallower portion that flowed near the cottage. It reminded me of the Colorado River, and I couldn't help but recall the time Uncle Connor, Carl, Nick, and my family had decided to tie a bunch of large inner tubes together and float for miles down the river. I was only about ten years old and had a huge crush on my cousin Carl, who teased me relentlessly. He had me convinced that day that they were going to sneak me into Mexico so they could sell me to a family that was looking to adopt a girl of its own. I was pretty sure he was kidding, but I made it a point to stay close to my father, just in case.

"Do you remember the day you nearly drowned down there?"

William's question brought me back to the present. He smiled as he gestured toward a spot near the river's bend.

"I what?"

"Surely you haven't forgotten that," he chuckled. "I'll never forget how angry you were when I finally pulled you from the water. Your scowl was full of vengeance and determination! It was enough to frighten the meanest rebel soldier."

I stood watching William as he recalled the memory with apparent fondness. I searched my mind for any hint of recollection.

"I don't remember anything like that," I finally said, frustrated that he seemed to have the upper hand by knowing more about Eleanor than I did.

"You can't be serious," he remarked. "Surely you remember giving Miles a healthy dose of disapproval—after all, it was *his* fault."

That was the first time I'd heard anyone speak of Miles. No one in Eleanor's family shared stories about her deceased brothers. It upset her mother too much, so any mention of them was off limits.

William flinched as soon as he realized what he'd said and quickly apologized. "I'm sorry. How thoughtless of me."

I shook my head. "Please, don't apologize. It has been so long since I've heard any of my brothers' names mentioned aloud. If you ask me, it's criminal to pretend as if they never existed."

A stunned William raised his eyebrows in surprise.

"I mean no disrespect to Mother," I explained. "It's just that in my opinion, we should honor them and keep their memory alive by remembering them often in our conversations."

"Nevertheless, it was careless of me." He nudged a small rock with the toe of his shoe, flipping it over several times before launching it skillfully into the water with his foot.

"I really don't mind," I assured him. "Were the two of you good friends?" I considered this as appropriate a topic as any for small talk, and truth be told, I was genuinely interested in hearing more stories.

William looked puzzled. "You honestly don't remember, do you?" He studied my expression for several moments. "Wow. That must be very difficult for you—and frustrating. Do you remember *anything* from before your illness?"

I forced a sad smile. "It's pretty much hit and miss. I'm afraid my memories seem to have a mind of their own."

"Pardon?"

I chuckled quietly to myself. "I can be going through a typical day, and then a memory will come to me out of the blue. It's like I hear a voice inside my head telling me something I should know—such as where I keep my hairbrush, which gloves I'm supposed to wear before dusk, who the president of the United States is—you know, the kinds of details you would normally take for granted. Even then, when the memories come, it's as though it's someone else's memory, not mine." I looked over at William, who was watching me with obvious interest. "I'm probably not making any sense at all, am I?"

"Yes, actually you are. I'm fascinated, but at the same time I regret that it puts me at an unfortunate disadvantage."

"How so?" I asked.

William flashed a sheepish grin that made him look years younger than he was. "You used to have a mash for me; I was sort of counting on you remembering that."

"I beg your pardon?" It was frustrating that I could still be caught by 1800s words and this one sounded suspiciously personal.

"Please forgive me, Eleanor, I meant no disrespect," said William, apparently caught off guard. "I thought perhaps you might remember your young . . . infatuation."

William's unexpected moment of awkwardness did nothing to calm a sudden uneasiness forming in the pit of my stomach—the kind of feeling you get when there is an awkward silence and it's your turn to speak but you have no idea what to say. On the other hand, I couldn't resist the desire to find out more.

"I had a crush on you?" I felt the blush rise in my cheeks the moment the words came out. I sensed that Eleanor had hoped I wouldn't pursue this topic.

William chuckled. "A 'crush . . . .' A bit odd, but I suppose you could say it that way. Believe it or not, once upon a time you were . . . how should I put this . . . quite enamored with me."

I couldn't help but laugh out loud.

"Careful now. You're going to hurt my feelings," William teased. "You might even bruise my over-active ego."

I laughed harder. "You know, I'm actually relieved that I lost my memory."

William let out a hearty laugh, but then his expression suddenly grew serious. "I imagine this is most unsettling."

"What is?"

"The realization that you are about to marry a man you have no memory of ever knowing."

William's directness threw me off balance. I had been enjoying our conversation up to this point, but the mention of marriage instantly sobered me and nearly made me sick to my stomach.

"I have no intentions of getting married," I assured him.

"Yes, your father mentioned you were somewhat reluctant to marry."

"That's certainly putting it mildly."

"May I ask why? I mean, why now, after all these years, are you so adamantly opposed to our engagement?"

The subtle insinuation in William's question surprised me. "Do you mean to imply that I felt differently at one time?"

"Obviously I would not presume to speak for you, Eleanor, but yes, I'm fairly confident that you looked upon the match favorably at one time." William seemed to be remembering something that he was choosing not to share with me. "Besides," he added, "the decision was made a long time ago." He sounded sincerely perplexed. "Why do you question it now?"

"Why shouldn't I?"

"Because it's not your place to question."

"Not my place?" I almost shouted. "How can you say that? We're talking about the rest of our lives—*my* life! I'm not supposed to have a say in who I spend my life with?"

"Perhaps we should go back to the house. I've obviously upset you."

"No!" I insisted. "I deserve an answer. You aren't in love with me, and I'm not in love with you, so why in heaven's name would we get married?"

William took a deep breath and backed away. "I'm afraid this is a conversation you should have with your father. I hope you'll forgive me for causing you distress. Please, let me escort you back to the house."

I knew what that meant—more time spent as a prisoner confined to my room. No, thank you! I needed to make him understand how wrong this was.

"Let's not go back yet, please. I'm sorry I'm being so difficult; I'm just trying to wrap my head around all this."

William pulled his eyebrows into a tight line and reached up to rub the side of his neck, which was suddenly patterned with splotches of red. My father's neck used to do the same thing when he was nervous or really frustrated.

"I'm afraid I don't understand," he said, obviously confused. It took me a second to realize that I'd used a modern-day expression he would be unfamiliar with. I decided to approach it from another angle.

"William, have you ever loved a woman?"

He looked puzzled. "Why would you ask such a question?" I could tell by the intonation in his voice that he was annoyed.

"Just humor me."

"I am learned in the ways of women, yes."

"Oh, for the love of St. Peter, that's not what I'm asking. I want to know if you have ever been *in love*?"

"Sure. Hasn't everybody?" He shifted his weight nervously, but his eyes never left mine. He still seemed annoyed, but behind the annoyance I sensed there was something else.

"Then you know what it's like to want to spend your life with somebody, right?"

"Eleanor, you're talking like a child. You're too naïve yet to understand that marriage among our kind isn't about falling in love. Why, people fall in and out of love all the time."

"How can you say that? You know that's not true."

"It is absolutely true. I fell in love with Martha McNulty in second grade when she shared her candy stick with me. In fifth grade, it was Ingrid Johnson. I put a toad in her book pack, and instead of screaming and telling the teacher, she winked at me and laughed. Then she kissed the toad and pretended it turned into a handsome prince. Then there was Hazel Ringstead, she—"

"Aarrgghh! Oh my gosh! Are you always this annoying?"

William laughed, and even though I was extremely irritated, I couldn't help but laugh too. I couldn't tell if he was purposely trying to give me a hard time or if he was serious.

"I'm simply trying to make a point, Eleanor. Marriages among people like us are built on the solid foundations of family bloodlines, duty, and mutual understanding and respect— values that last, or that stand the true tests of time. This is the way it has always been for our kind. Marriages based on less are subject to the whims and fleeting fancies of emotional instability. Only commoners would condone such a union—and half of them are either destitute or miserable."

I stared at William, dumbfounded. He wasn't pulling my leg at all; he was actually sincere. What's more, there was something in his logic that almost sounded reasonable. I had to shake my head and silently remind myself that I disagreed emphatically with him, but I couldn't come up with a solid argument to refute him. I wanted to tell him about my mom and dad. They loved each other with all their hearts—they would have done anything for each other—and they were neither destitute nor miserable. Quite the contrary in fact.

William's diamond blue eyes searched my expression for signs of understanding or acceptance. "I've upset you again, haven't I?" he asked quietly.

"I need to sit down," I conceded. "Do you mind if we talk about something else?"

"Does this mean you're willing to give me a chance?" William flashed me a hopeful grin. For a split second, he reminded me of Carl.

Great. I'm engaged to my cousin. Way to go!

William seemed content with my lack of response and began searching for a place for me to sit down. "There you go," he said, pointing to a smooth, fallen log. "That should do." He helped me over to the log and held my elbow steady while I seated myself.

"Now then, what should we talk about?"

"Tell me about the war," I replied, hoping to direct the conversation away from marriage.

William bent down and picked up a handful of stones. "I expect there's not much to say on that topic. I'm sure you know all that's fitting to know."

"What's that supposed to mean?" I asked, trying very hard not to take offense by the implication in his words.

William looked confused. "Don't you receive regular updates in the town newspaper and through telegraphs?"

"Yes, of course. But they seem to leave out the details. I want to hear about what goes on behind the scenes."

William fixed his eyes on mine. He studied my expression carefully before shaking his head. "Eleanor, what happens out there . . ." he gestured by nodding his head to one side, "behind the scenes as you say, is something no one should ever read about in the papers. You can't imagine the horrors," he paused briefly, "nor should you ever have to."

My knee-jerk reaction was to accuse William of being sexist, but something told me his remarks weren't only meant for women. I'd seen copies of old photos in books, photos of soldiers who died at Antietam and Gettysburg; but somehow it never registered in my mind just how horrific those scenes must have been in real life. Maybe that was partly due to the graphic violence depicted in so many modern movies I'd seen. It was eerie to consider for a moment that any one of the soldiers in those photographs could have been Charles or Miles—or any of the boys from Marensburg who'd lost their life in those battles. I couldn't bear to dwell on the topic a moment longer, so I shifted gears.

"What do you know about Mosby and his rangers?" I asked.

William's eyebrows raised in astonishment. "Well now, you are full of surprises, aren't you?"

"Don't tease me, William. I'm curious, that's all."

William flashed me a wide grin and chuckled, "You mean, the 'Gray Ghost'? Or the 'Phantom' as some refer to him."

"Yes, that's the one. Is he really as stealthy and clever as they say?"

"Eleanor, where do you hear such tales? You make him sound almost heroic. Do you have any idea the damage he's caused?"

"I . . . I only meant . . . I mean . . ." I took a deep breath and let out a frustrated sigh. "I'm sorry, William. That's certainly not how I meant it. I'm just curious, that's all. I only heard of him recently."

William watched me for a moment and then nodded, apparently satisfied. He turned to face the river and began tossing the stones he'd been holding one-by-one into the air. He pressed his lips together and watched as they arched and then fell into the water. He appeared to be aiming for a particular spot, and smiled in approval when he finally hit it. I got the distinct impression that any further prodding on my part about war or Mosby's Rangers was unwelcome.

Without realizing I was doing it, I found myself studying William's profile as he continued to throw the stones high into the air. His profile was beautiful—I couldn't think of another word for it. He tossed his last rock into the air and watched it hit the water. He must have been unhappy with the landing, because he let out a low grunt of disgust and bent down to gather another handful of stones. He started to throw the first rock into the air, but stopped midway and turned to face me.

"I promise that I'll be good to you, Eleanor." He paused and held my gaze. "Always." He studied my stunned expression for a second and then continued. "I'll care for you, and I'll do all in my power to make you happy if you'll let me . . . and," he hesitated briefly, "you have my solemn promise that you will never have cause to doubt my loyalty to you."

"William, I . . ." my words caught in my throat. He definitely knew how to ambush a conversation. I wondered if they taught that in "colonel" school.

William shook his head. "You don't need to say anything. I know this marriage isn't what you want right now, but if you will just give it a chance, maybe we'll get lucky and discover some day that we love each other after all." He paused again and a serious look of concern crossed his face. "I mean, you're not completely repulsed by me, are you?"

I couldn't help but laugh to myself. His looks were certainly not the problem; he was definitely Eleanor's equal in that respect. In fact, I had to fight to keep from blushing. William seemed to have a knack for throwing me off guard. I had to be careful because I didn't want to encourage him, but I didn't want to hurt his feelings, either.

"You are a silly man!" I chuckled nervously. "Go back to throwing your rocks." Try as I might, I couldn't stop the blush from rising in my cheeks.

William raised an eyebrow and studied me for several seconds before breaking into a satisfied grin. "Yes ma'am," he replied, saluting me with a tip of his hat. With that, he began chucking his handful of stones one by one into the water in rapid succession, this time targeting a large tree root near the far side of the river. I stared in awe as I watched each stone hit the exact same spot with precise accuracy. I glanced over at William and by the smug grin on his face I could tell he was obviously pleased with himself. He cut his eyes at me and then let out a deep sigh. He searched the ground for a moment, turning over several stones with his shoe, finally deciding on one. Using the toe of his shoe, he wedged his foot under the rock, which was approximately the size of a baseball. He looked at the root he had used as a target earlier and shifting his focus between the rock and the root, pulled back his leg carefully and launched the rock across the river, hitting the target square center.

"Impressive," I remarked.

William's face lit up and he breathed a sigh of relief. "Finally! I was beginning to run out of tricks."

The remainder of the day passed quickly. Too quickly. William and I strolled along the path by the river, pausing each time he found a new target to either throw or launch stones at with his foot. There was a childlike innocence in William that made him appear much younger than he was, but when he looked at me his eyes betrayed that innocence, revealing years of experience. He seemed to possess a sense of patience that separated him from the boys who were closer to Eleanor's age. I enjoyed his company. Perhaps that was because I preferred it to being locked away in my bedroom. Eleanor's father had certainly stacked the deck in William's favor, but a pleasant outing wasn't going to change my mind about marrying someone I didn't love, and it wasn't going to make me stop loving Jonathan. It was high time Eleanor's father understood that once and for all.

It was after dinner before I found an opportunity to speak to Eleanor's father alone. Christine had challenged William to a match of checkers, and Mother had excused herself, retiring to bed early because of a sudden—no doubt convenient—splitting headache.

"Father, might I have a word with you?" I asked quietly once Christine and William's first game of checkers was safely underway.

"Yes, of course. Go on," he gestured for me to sit in the chair across from his in the drawing room.

"Actually," I glanced quickly around the room, "I was hoping perhaps I could speak to you in private."

Father's skeptical eyes studied mine for several moments before he excused us and led me to his study. He turned to face me as soon as he shut the door. "Well," he said impatiently, "what is it that requires such privacy?"

"It's about the wedding," I began. "There's something you need to know."

Father raised his eyebrows. "I'm listening," he said.

"I know you plan to force me to marry William, but I need to make something perfectly clear." Father's eyes turned cold. He waited for me to continue. "You can lock me away, you can disinherit me, threaten to disown me, you can even bring in hired hands to drag me down the aisle, but when Reverend Pat asks me if I promise to love, honor, and obey my husband until death do us part, I will not say the words, 'I do.' That's one thing you cannot force me to do. I am not going to make that vow to a man I don't love, no matter what."

Father didn't say a word. He just stared coldly at me for a long moment.

"Well?" I finally asked, demanding a reaction from him.

"Are you quite finished with your little *announcement*?" he asked. He was too calm. I suddenly felt very uncomfortable.

"Yes . . . I suppose that's all I wanted to say."

Father turned back toward the door. "We'd better rejoin our guest. We wouldn't want to be rude, would we?"

I had just played my trump card, and Eleanor's father seemed totally unaffected by it.

"Father? Do you understand what I just said?" I wondered if he could sense the sudden uneasiness in my voice.

"Yes, of course," he answered. "Thank you for making your position clear."

He opened the door and stood aside, waiting for me to follow him. When I hesitated, he motioned with his arm for me to exit the room. "Come along, Eleanor. I'm sure the others have noticed our absence by now."

I took a deep breath and walked to the door. As I passed Father, he took me by the arm and led me back into the drawing room where Christine and William were still engaged in their game of checkers. William had a perplexed look on his face that indicated he was falling behind. I wasn't surprised. Christine had an unusual gift when it came to checkers. Such a seemingly simple game, but with her it was like doing higher-level mathematics. She was always five or six steps ahead of her opponent.

Once seated, Father dropped his bombshell.

"Oh. I forgot to mention something," he said nonchalantly. He was speaking directly to me, but spoke loud enough for everyone in the room to hear. "Your friend's brother, young Mr. Rollings, received orders for a new assignment earlier this week. He's been transferred to General Meade's Unit, set to join Grant in an assault on Petersburg. Shocking news for his family, in light of recent events. Remind me to send his father and mother a letter sharing our concern for their son."

Father's announcement caught me completely by surprise. I had to sit down. I quickly began searching my memories of the future for any recollection of this happening, but my conversations with Grace about Jonathan's military service only mentioned him being transferred to another unit, not fighting somewhere on the front line. This wasn't right. I may have had no background knowledge of Mosby and his rangers or Chambersburg or raids occurring in southern Pennsylvania, but Petersburg was a name I recognized at once. It was a major campaign, and if my memory was accurate, it involved the capture of a large number of Union soldiers—not to mention a high number of casualties.

"Our Mr. Rollings is a strong lad, just the kind of brave young man we need leading the fight on the battlefront. General Lee is pressing down hard, and it looks like a Confederate victory is underway. You've got to admire the courage of brave soldiers like Mr. Rollings, don't you agree, William?" Father raised his voice slightly to make sure William heard everything he was saying. He paused; the tension in the room was palpable. I could tell that William was uncomfortable.

"Yes, sir," he replied. His eyes shifted back and forth between me and Eleanor's father. He was obviously confused, and seemed to detect the subtle sarcasm in Father's tone. "I'm sure Captain Rollings will lead his men in a valiant effort on behalf of the Union," he added hesitantly.

No. This isn't right at all. Jonathan is too young for this. A captain? When did that happen? Jonathan is only seventeen. It will be two more years before his body goes through the process of reclamation. That means . . . .

A sudden chill ran through my blood causing my entire body to tremble. William was watching my reaction with some interest.

"Father, no!" I cried. "He can't. He's too young. This isn't what's supposed to happen!" The emotion in my voice made William sit up and move forward slightly, as if ready to come to my aid; but Eleanor's father was quick to respond first.

"Now, now, dear," Father said. His feigned concern angered me. "I know how much you care for his sister. You mustn't let on that you are worried about her brother. She will surely need to draw from your strength, should the young captain . . . well, should the worst happen."

"Father, stop! Don't you say those words to me!" I was on the verge of hysterics. This was all wrong. Perhaps this was what Grace was trying to tell me when she appeared in the cottage—that Jonathan wasn't there to save me the night of my accident because he'd died a hundred and fifty years earlier. *Oh no, dear Lord, No!*

Eleanor's father continued, "Of course, we will all pray that our young captain remains safe, but this *is* war, after all. The lives of many young men have already been sacrificed in honor of our country. Why, I think we must regard Captain Rollings in the highest esteem for his willingness to knowingly put himself in danger in order to serve the Union."

"Father, please! You have to stop this! Please!" There was no sense trying to stop the tears that now streamed in steady lines down the sides of my face.

"Eleanor, your concern for your friend's brother is most admirable, but surely there is nothing to be done. The orders were sent almost a week ago."

William suddenly stood. "Pardon me, sir, perhaps I may be of some assistance."

"Well, I don't know," Father said nonchalantly. "What can be done? To my knowledge, our young Mr. Rollings has already received his orders."

"I am well acquainted with Major General Meade. I can arrange to send a replacement for Captain Rollings and request he be reassigned to a local unit."

I reacted without thinking. "William, could you?"

"Now Eleanor, I'm sure the colonel has enough on his plate. It would be impolite to impose on him just now. Perhaps after your nuptials . . . ."

Father's subtle grin may have fooled William, but I recognized the obvious triumph behind his eyes immediately. So this was his plan, was it? My freedom for Jonathan's safety. I hadn't realized that Eleanor's father was willing to stoop so low in order to get what he wanted. A memory flashed through my mind—Christmas day at the Rollings' ranch in what seemed like another lifetime. A possessed Eric had arrived unexpectedly, prepared to kill Jonathan and take me for himself. Bailey had been behind Eric's scheme, playing on Eric's confusion and emotions. Bailey had forced me to agree to give myself to him in return for sparing Jonathan's life. Fortunately, his plan was interrupted by Eric's final act of bravery on my behalf. Essentially, this was no different; only instead of forcing me to give myself to someone for a night, Father was condemning me to a life sentence.

"Father, this is blackmail," I said coldly.

"I'm afraid I don't understand," William interjected. I could tell by the sincerity in his eyes that he was an innocent participant in this conversation and not privy to Father's scheme.

"Nonsense!" Eleanor's father chuckled. "Pay her no mind, Colonel Hamilton. As soon as the two of you are settled, then yes, please do whatever you can to bring Mr. Rollings back safely to his sister. She is a very dear friend to Eleanor, and I know she would be grateful to have her brother closer to home."

"Consider it done," William said, shaking Father's hand. "I will prepare a letter as soon as Eleanor and I arrive in Greensburg."

Jonathan's safety for my freedom. Father's cards were on the table and there was nothing I could do to stack the deck in my favor. However, despite my conviction to stand my ground, one reality played repeatedly in my mind—if Jonathan were to die in the war, I could never return to my life as Beth.

"I'm sure I speak on behalf of the entire Rollings family when I say we appreciate your kindness, Colonel Hamilton." Father offered William a polite bow. "And now, I believe it's time we retire for the evening, wouldn't you agree?"

"Yes, of course." William returned Father's gesture and turned to me. "Mr. Hastings, would it be possible for Miss Eleanor and I to have a moment before we say goodnight?"

"Certainly. I see no harm in a few moments of privacy, but don't be too long. I'll be across the hall in my study. Eleanor, you'll come in to say goodnight before you go up."

"I'll escort her to you myself," William said dutifully.

Father and Christine vacated the drawing room leaving me alone with William. William gestured for me to have a seat on the sofa and sat down beside me, taking both my hands in his.

"This Mr. Rollings, I take it he's someone special to you?"

William's directness surprised me. It was equally unusual and refreshing.

"Yes," I admitted quietly.

William squeezed my hands gently. "Then I promise to do everything in my power to ensure his safety."

I searched William's eyes for any hint of an ulterior motive, but found none. "Do you mean that? Really?"

"I'll draft a letter tonight and see to it that it's delivered with haste."

"Oh William, thank you," I said, relieved.

William smiled and gently stroked the side of my cheek with the back of his hand. "I told you, I will devote my life to making you happy." He bent forward and I stiffened. I was certain he was going to kiss me, but instead he put his lips against my ear and whispered, "I promise."

William raised my hand to his lips and said goodnight after depositing me to Father's study. It had been an exceedingly long day and I was looking forward to going to my room—even though the threat of being locked in my chambers lurked in the back of my mind. I didn't care. I needed to be alone where I could think.

"Father, I would like to go to my room. Please, I'm very tired."

"Yes, I suppose you must be. No doubt it has been an eventful day for you. I'm glad you were able to spend time with William. I hope you enjoyed your day with him."

"We had a pleasant day, yes."

"He's a good man, Eleanor. Solid. Honest. You are a fortunate young woman."

I was in no mood for Father's games. He had shown his true colors and I now knew where I stood. Any previous wavering on my part regarding his character was now permanently squelched by his actions, not only tonight but for the whole past week

"Goodnight, Father." I turned toward the door.

"Eleanor," Father stepped in front of me and grabbed my arm. "You do understand the stakes here, right?" I stared at him, a cold anger pulsing through my veins. "You will say 'I do' or I will make sure your precious Jonathan never returns to Marensburg. Do I make myself clear?"

"I hate you," I growled. "I will never forgive you for this."

"I don't recall asking for your forgiveness you silly child. Besides, some day you will thank me for having the sense to direct your life appropriately. Now, do we understand each other? You concentrate all your efforts on marrying William this Saturday and having his children, and William and I will see to it that your boy soldier comes back alive. I'm sure he'll appreciate getting on with his own life once he sees that you are happily married."

"Are you quite finished, Father?"

"I'm still waiting for your response." Father added more pressure to his already firm grip on my arm. "There are no other alternatives. Have I made myself clear?"

"Perfectly."

"There. Was that so difficult?" Father smiled and bent down to kiss me on my forehead. "Now then, off to bed with you. You have a wedding to prepare for; you're going to need your rest."

Arrangement
CHAPTER 12

The smell of aged wood and floor wax alerted me that I was in a familiar place. There was a distinct odor common among old university concert halls, and it was an odor I would recognize anywhere. I sauntered silently along a narrow hallway lined with doors. Instinctively, I knew that the hallway led to several rows of heavy stage curtains. At the end of the hallway, a young girl knelt on the floor with her forehead pressed against the cool wall. Her fists were curled tightly against her stomach as she concentrated on not throwing up. She was dressed in a simple, flowing gown. Her auburn hair was arranged in a loose twist that hung halfway down her back and was tied at the end with a green satin ribbon.

I recognized the dress and hair immediately, and the moment I saw her I knew exactly where I was—the Performing Arts Center at the University of California Santa Barbara in California. The girl was me—Beth Arrington. It was the day of the piano competition; the day I had won the full-ride scholarship to the Berklee College of Music in Boston. I had forgotten how nervous I'd been.

I watched as Beth stood and tapped her fists firmly against the wall three times—a ritual that had begun several years prior when my father had convinced me that tapping the wall would bring good luck during my recitals. I smiled and watched with eager anticipation as she exited the long hallway and made her way through the dark curtains and onto the stage. The audience offered a polite round of applause. She acknowledged them, then took her seat at the shiny black Steinway piano.

A rush of envy flowed through me as I watched her. This was *my* recital! *I* should be the one sitting at the piano—and yet logically I knew that it *was* me.

I followed, hovering behind. My eyes panned the audience and rested on the spot where my parents were seated. Torn between my desire to be close to my mom and dad and my desire to be at the piano, I floated gracefully into the audience for a moment in order to have a closer look. My parents suddenly seemed so young. Perhaps that was because I was comparing them to Eleanor's parents, or perhaps I had just never paid close attention to their ages before.

The room grew quiet, the lights dimmed, all except for the spotlight which rested on the center of the stage. All eyes were on Beth at the piano. I longed so much to be her—to be the one about to play. The longing I felt must have possessed energy of its own, because the moment she raised her hands to the keys, I found myself not only next to her, but with her. It was as if my spirit rested directly upon her—and through her.

I took a deep breath, elated to feel whole again. An upward glance into the back of the audience revealed what I already knew—Jonathan was there. I hadn't met him yet as Beth, but Jonathan had informed me later that this was the first time he'd seen me, when the Lebas assigned him to observe me. He was standing toward the far corner of the auditorium. I smiled at him, but he didn't appear to notice, even though his eyes were fixated on me—or rather, on Beth. Was it possible to be jealous of yourself?

Beth began playing the first measures of the Bach Prelude, and instantly my hands were her hands. It was as if two sets of hands played as one—perfectly synchronized and flawless. I focused on channeling all of my energy into Beth's hands, and from her hands to the piano keys. It felt so good to play as Beth again. Don't get me wrong, Eleanor was very accomplished. She was obviously gifted at playing the piano, and

I was grateful for every opportunity to sit at the piano in the Hastings' home and lose myself in the music. Doing so had helped to keep me sane during the past several months. This was different, though. This was me connecting with that part of myself that I had left behind nearly a year ago, when I left Uncle Connor's basement with Grace and traveled to the 1800s.

Of course, I had no idea at the time that traveling meant I would give up being Beth Arrington and become Eleanor Hastings. That hadn't been part of the package—at least, not that I was aware of.

Together, Beth and I played through Bach effortlessly and then moved directly into Beethoven's Sonata Pathetique. I threw myself into the opening measures with as much passion as I could. I was so grateful to share this with her. I knew the connection I had made with her was temporary, and therefore I played as though every note might be my last.

Once we finished all three movements of the Pathetique, we settled into Chopin's Nocturne No. 2 in E flat. All too soon, it was over. We sat silently, together, our fingers still resting on the keys as the last vibrations of the piano strings faded into the distance. Moments later, the audience exploded into a loud roar of applause. Beth stood to take her bow, leaving my spirit still sitting at the piano. I glanced up at Jonathan. He hadn't moved; he was still standing in the same place, and his eyes were still fixed on Beth. The fact that he didn't know I was there made me sad.

It was time for me to leave, but when I tried to move, I couldn't free myself from the piano bench. It didn't make any sense—I should have been able to float silently into the background and disappear. I tried willing myself to leave, but I was paralyzed.

The judges stood to acknowledge Beth's flawless performance, and she acknowledged them with a gracious bow. She then turned toward her parents, both of whom appeared to be crying. This was their moment. I was the uninvited intruder, and I couldn't even bow out gracefully and exit the stage; all I could do was sit by and watch her living the life that had once been mine.

I turned away, unable to bear more. I knew in a few moments she would disappear behind the curtains and return again when the winner of the competition was announced. I wanted to scream, to cause some sort of disturbance, something, anything that might release me and allow me to leave, but I was trapped at the piano. I tried to strike the keys, but no matter how earnestly I focused, my fingers only floated through them. I was a ghost.

A low laugh drew my attention away from the piano and toward the heavy black curtains. It took a moment for my eyes to make out the shadowy figure of a man against the dark patina, but there was no mistaking his eyes—two yellow spheres that revealed no light. Although he was too far away for me to discern his features clearly, I knew immediately it was Bailey; I would recognize his disparaging sneer anywhere.

I tried in vain to squirm free of the piano bench and this pleased Bailey, who continued to taunt me from the folds of the curtains.

"Relax, my fellow Intruder," he gibed with feigned sincerity.

My eyes quickly skirted the room, but nobody seemed to hear him.

"I'm not interested in you, at least not at the moment."

I searched the faces in the audience again.

"They can't hear us, you foolish child." Bailey nearly spit the words as he said them.

"Why are you here, Bailey?" I asked.

"Oh, good. I prefer to skip the part where you pretend you're someone you're not. It's much better this way."

"Get out of here," I demanded.

"It's like I said, I'm not here for you; but while we're asking questions, isn't it a bit risky for you to leave Eleanor's body . . . eh . . . unattended?"

"What are you talking about?"

"Oh, my. Could it be you don't know?" The confusion on my face pleased him; his mocking smirk was apparent, even among his shadowy features. "Oh, I see. You truly haven't a clue."

"What's your point?" I insisted. I was losing my patience and this delighted Bailey even more.

He shook his head reproachfully. "I'll put this simply. You can't be in two places at once, not even in your mind. Therefore, you must ask yourself who needs protecting more . . . her . . ." he pointed toward Beth, "or the person whose body you've stolen?"

"Stolen! I haven't stolen any—"

Bailey's condemning scoff interrupted me. "You've taken over a body that does not belong to you. Is that not true? That makes *you* the Intruder here."

"But, I didn't . . . I mean, it's not like that," I stammered.

Bailey's attention shifted away from me and back to the front of the stage. I turned, following his gaze, and watched as Beth came from behind the curtain to receive her recognition as the winner of the competition. A cold chill crept through me as I sensed Bailey's movement behind me. I turned in time to see him gliding across the front of the curtains, trying to get closer to Beth. He closed his eyes and his shadowy figure dissipated into a dark mist which oozed toward the front of the stage where Beth was standing. The pungent odor of death filled the room as the mist moved closer; all my senses began to recoil.

"No!" I screamed. "NO!" In the flash of an instant, I flew from the piano and positioned myself between Beth and the black vapor that was gravitating toward her. I spread my arms wide and focused on holding back the impending darkness. As the shadow came closer, I concentrated more fervently. As I did so, light began to emanate from my arms and legs, creating an impenetrable barrier separating Beth from the black shadow. I held firm my position with only one thought in mind—keep the darkness away from Beth.

The dark shadow screeched a howling protest as it came in contact with the light and quickly receded. It tried several times to break through, but each time it got close the light repelled the shadow, sending it backwards in a rolling mist. After several attempts, the black mist began to shrink away and then rose from the ground, forming itself into the shape of a man. A few seconds later, the yellow eyes returned.

"Well done, child," Bailey mused. "Impressive even." He studied me for a moment, then added, "Until we meet again . . . Beth." His eyes traced the shape of Eleanor's body and he smiled. "Or do you prefer I call you Eleanor?"

I glared at him, too angry and too drained to respond.

He chuckled, obviously pleased with himself, and then retreated, disappearing into the black backdrop of the curtains. I waited until I was confident he was gone and then collapsed onto the stage floor.

"Eleanor," a voice whispered in my ear. I was too tired to reply, so I batted the voice away with my arm.

"Eleanor, wake up!" The whisper was more intense this time. "Hurry!"

When I opened my eyes, I was lying in Eleanor's bed. Lucinda pushed gently on my shoulder. "Please, hurry! There isn't much time!"

"Lucinda?" I said, squinting against the brightness of the candle she held.

"Yes!" she sighed impatiently. "Get up, please!"

"All right!" I swung my legs over the side of the bed and sat up. "What in the world is the matter?"

"It's the captain, he's waiting for you down by the stables. You must hurry before we get caught."

The urgency in Lucinda's voice was surprise enough, but the implication of her words startled me. "Captain?" I couldn't keep from yawning as Lucinda worked in frantic silence to put my robe on me.

"No need to pretend, I've known about Captain Herman for some time."

I was at a loss for words. Was it possible that Eleanor had another secret that I didn't know about—another secret she'd managed to keep hidden these many months?

What now Eleanor? I thought to myself. *What else have you been hiding from me?*

"Please hurry!" Two voices spoke at the same time. One of them was Lucinda's; the other came from inside my head. A sudden surge of energy announced Eleanor's strengthening presence, and rather than fight it I relaxed my mind and allowed her to take control. I was very curious to find out more about the mysterious Captain Herman who had evaded me for all this time. Eleanor had been very careful to keep her thoughts of him hidden from me.

Lucinda led us hurriedly down the back stairs, tiptoeing past the servants' quarters, down through the lower level entrance and beyond the main entrance to the stables. The night air was thick with vapor, and for a brief second I thought about the dark mist that had tried to reach Beth earlier in my dream. I chuckled nervously to myself, surprised by how real the dream had seemed. Eleanor paid no attention to my overactive imagination.

As soon as we turned the corner toward the side entrance of the stable, Eleanor broke into a run.

"James!" she squealed as she flung herself into the arms of partner number five.

Ah, so my suspicions were accurate. Partner number five and the elusive "James" from the hidden letters were the same person after all— Captain James Herman.

"Eleanor!" James folded his arms around Eleanor's waist and pulled her to him. "It's true then. You haven't forgotten me. I'm so sorry I couldn't arrange to see you sooner."

Whoa! Hold on a second here. I'm not okay with this! My inward protest went unacknowledged and within seconds I found myself lip-locked with this complete stranger. His hold on me was so strong that I found it impossible to push myself away—but then I was fighting against the combined wills of both James *and* Eleanor.

Two against one. That's not fair!

I finally mustered enough willpower to pull away slightly and catch my breath.

Beth, please. Leave us alone. Eleanor's plea came through loud and clear in my head.

"What?" I said aloud.

James grinned, and reached up to brush a stray lock of hair away from my cheek. "I said I'm sorry I couldn't arrange to meet you earlier." He bent down and kissed Eleanor again.

Leave us alone, Eleanor whispered again in my mind. She wrapped her arms tightly around his neck and gave herself completely to his kiss. Once more, I had to fight her to pull away.

"I can't do this," I voiced into the air as soon as there was an opportunity to speak.

"Do what?" James backed away slightly. He looked perplexed.

Beth, please—leave!

"This isn't right," I said, responding to both of them equally. I needed a moment to gather my wits and figure out what was happening—and what I should do about it. I had sensed some kind of connection between them at the ball, but the level of passion that Eleanor felt for this man surprised me. This was a complication I hadn't planned on.

"Forgive me," James replied. He released his hold on me and took a couple of steps backward. "I've just missed you so much!"

It had to have been a good year since the two of them were together.

Good grief! I said inwardly. *You're only seventeen, and already at least three men that I know of are in love with you. That's a bit embarrassing, don't you think?*

I was teasing, but Eleanor seemed hurt by my insinuation and I felt her life force weaken as she retreated back to her hiding place in my mind, leaving me alone to deal with partner number five.

Oh, come on! I scolded her. *I was only kidding.*

James had taken my lack of a vocal response as a silent reprimand. "I truly am sorry." He reached out and took Eleanor's hand in his. "Things have taken some unexpected turns, and I couldn't sneak away any sooner."

Eleanor started to respond, but James put his finger against her lips. "Shh! There isn't time for further explanation, Now listen carefully," he said in a hushed tone. "This wedding is complicating our situation a little, but the plan is still on."

"What are you talking about?" I shook my head, wondering why all the cloak and dagger.

"Nothing has changed, not really." He was trying to reassure Eleanor, but it almost sounded as though he were trying to reassure himself as well. I was clueless regarding their so-called plan, so nothing he said resonated with me.

"How can you say that? *Everything* has changed, James. I'm to be married in three more days. How do you propose to stop that?"

"I don't," he said matter-of-factly.

"You what?"

"We can't stop the wedding, Eleanor, but you can stop the marriage." He winked and gave my hand a gentle squeeze.

"What are you saying?" There was no masking the aggravation in my tone.

"I know it's not ideal, but we can still move forward with our plan to be together."

I shook my head in frustration. "You're not making any sense."

"Don't you see? It will actually make things easier for us. After you're married, nobody will suspect anything. Your father will relax his hold on you and that will free us up to be together."

I couldn't believe what I was hearing. Eleanor suddenly resurfaced, and I could tell she was equally appalled.

"I don't mean it like it sounds," James quickly equivocated. "I mean, we can finally leave Marensburg, together. We'll go where nobody knows either of us, just as we've always planned. Nobody needs to know that you were ever married. We can even have it annulled if you want. I'm sure we can find someone to help us. Either way, we'll be able to start *our* life together."

"Do you realize what you're saying?"

"Yes," James replied, squeezing my hand again. "And do you think it pleases me to think of you being with *him*, even for a short time?" He motioned toward the house with his shoulder where an unsuspecting William was fast asleep. I wondered how James knew that William was a guest of ours.

"I can't stand the idea of you and him together, but he'll be called away soon and we'll be free to leave this place. Nobody will suspect—"

"No, James!" I interrupted him. "I won't do that to William."

James raised a suspicious brow. "William, is it? How cozy."

"He's my cousin, James. He's a kind man and I'll not hurt him that way." I couldn't tell which of us was protesting more—Eleanor or me. I'd only spent a little time with William, but I found myself secretly rooting for him over this James character, although I couldn't explain why; Eleanor was obviously deeply infatuated with James.

"Then that's it? We just throw away all our dreams because your cousin is a nice man?" James complained, his tone almost cross.

Eleanor's heart sank. "I don't know, James. I'm too confused to know what to do."

James searched Eleanor's eyes and then sighed. "Don't worry love," he reached for Eleanor and pulled her toward him, "we'll figure something out. I promise."

"Oh, James," Eleanor whimpered and buried her face against his chest. "I can't bear this anymore."

Oh, please! I chided her in my mind. *Aren't you being a bit dramatic?* My unsolicited rebuke didn't help matters; it only made Eleanor cry harder.

"There, there," James consoled. "Everything will be okay. You'll see. We just have to be patient a little longer."

A soft rapping at the stable door reminded all three of us that Lucinda was still waiting outside, and she'd probably heard everything that was said.

"Pardon me, Captain Herman," Lucinda said quietly, "but I should be getting Miss Eleanor back to her room before the servants begin to awaken."

"Yes, of course," James replied. "Thank you, Lucinda."

With that, James prepared to leave. But before doing so, he bent down and kissed me hard on the mouth. Eleanor melted into his kiss and clung tightly to his neck, unwilling to let him go. When I'd had all I could stomach of their passion, I pulled away and made my escape with Lucinda back to the house and up the servants' staircase.

Once safely back in my bed, I began to sort through the conversation between James and Eleanor. Clearly, they'd had a secret relationship long before I came onto the scene—childhood sweethearts perhaps? She couldn't have been more than sixteen when she saw him last, which would indicate their relationship began when they were both very young. Did Eleanor's mother and father know about it? I'd never heard either of them mention James before, and yet he'd been invited to the Debutante Ball, so he had to be somebody of reputable upbringing. He apparently cared for Eleanor or he wouldn't be willing to risk losing everything in order for them to be together. Heck, he even loved her enough to allow her to marry another man if that was the price they were required to pay in order for their plan to work: albeit a pretty strange kind of love if you ask me—bordering on the absurd.

That's the part of their conversation I couldn't wrap my head around. When a man loves a woman, he can't bear the thought of her being with someone else—regardless of how short-term. If James really loved Eleanor, it would drive him crazy to picture her and William living together as man and wife, even if only for one night, let alone weeks or months. The Jonathan of the twenty-first century went AWOL in the 1800s, sacrificing his family name and honor, because the very thought of Eleanor married to another man drove him to a point far beyond reasonable distraction. I buried my head in my pillow. No, I was not at all sold on this Captain James Herman.

Eleanor? I searched my mind for any sign that Eleanor might be listening in on my thoughts. *I don't know about this James fellow.* I paused, listening, then added, *Be careful.* There was a long silence—which I assumed meant that Eleanor had gone, but then I heard her voice as distinctly as though she were standing next to me in the room.

He loves me. That's all you need to know, she stated.

I sighed heavily. I remembered having discussions with my mother about my first love, Adam. We argued continuously about him, and I defended him relentlessly. It wasn't until I fell in love with Jonathan that I began to understand all those lectures my mother gave me about boys. I was too stubborn to listen while my mother was alive. Eleanor seemed to have a very similar stubborn streak regarding her feelings for James. And although I couldn't put my finger on it, James did not strike me as someone who had Eleanor's best interest in mind.

Well, if you want my advice, you should just marry Colonel Hamilton and forget about James.

You *marry Colonel Hamilton*, I heard Eleanor respond. Then she laughed, and the sound of her laughter rang throughout the room, echoing off the bedroom walls.

Very funny, I replied. This was the first time Eleanor and I had carried on an actual conversation, which confirmed my suspicion that her life force was gaining strength daily. I couldn't ignore the implications of what that might mean.

There was a long pause before Eleanor spoke again. This time her voice was not audible.

Why didn't you run away with Jonathan when you had the chance?

I thought carefully before answering her.

I was trying to do the right thing.

Yes, Eleanor responded quickly, *and now we are both going to lose the men we love.*

I had no rebuttal for Eleanor's argument. Jonathan was gone, sent to the front line and doomed to remain there until I sealed the deal with William. I had failed to put events back into their proper order on my twenty-first century timeline. Once married to William, Jonathan would have no reason to come back for me; but at least he would survive the war and reach the age of his reclamation. And if fate was kind, maybe someday our paths might cross again—in another time and another place. If I was fortunate enough for that to happen, I vowed I would never leave his side again. That was all I could hope for.

Breakfast was served on the terrace of the garden room. Eleanor's parents had just finished eating when I made my entrance. Christine had long since finished and was scampering about in the garden collecting flowers for the wedding. She and Mother planned to spend the morning creating arrangements and garlands to decorate the parlor, which was where the ceremony was to take place. Mrs. Weddington was no doubt downstairs in the kitchen coordinating the last minute details with the rest of the staff. My job was to be at Lucinda's beck and call as she finished my dress, and then to spend the remainder of the day "resting."

"A young bride needs her rest," Father reminded me as he folded his napkin and laid it next to his plate. "William is a strong, healthy man who has waited patiently for several years to claim his bride. I'll not deliver you to him in a state of exhaustion." Eleanor's father had a way of lacing his comments with innuendos that made me feel self-conscious—to the point of nausea. He acted as if I were a piece of property he wanted polished and shined before selling it at auction. I wondered if he did that on purpose, and if so, what could he possibly hope to accomplish? Was this just another way for him to show off?

My eyes felt like heavy weights in the bright morning sun and I was pretty sure that the dark circles beneath them were going to be a permanent discoloration. It had been too long since I'd had a restful night's sleep, and with the wedding so close I didn't see that changing any time soon. I sensed Eleanor's presence was near, but she was quiet.

If anyone out there in the twenty-first century cares, this would be a great time for you to come back for me! I screamed the words in my mind, but I knew it was in vain.

"Miss Eleanor?" Lucinda came out on the terrace with a tray filled with a variety of breads and fruit marmalades. "You have a caller waiting for you in the drawing room."

"A caller at this early hour?"

"Shall I tell her you are indisposed?"

"That won't be necessary." William, who had followed Lucinda into the garden room, answered on my behalf. "I'm confident Miss Eleanor would enjoy a visit with Mrs. Rollings."

I stood at once. William's eyes met mine and he gave me a subtle smile that suggested he knew something I didn't.

"Good morning, Eleanor," he said, inclining his head slightly. He was dressed casually and seemed much more relaxed and confident than he had during the previous day.

"Grace is here?" I asked, ignoring William's pleasantries.

"No, Miss Eleanor," Lucinda replied. "*Mrs.* Rollings has come to pay you a call."

"Mrs. Rollings?" My gaze shifted back and forth between Lucinda and William. "*Mrs.* Rollings!" I said again, unable to believe what I was hearing. William and Lucinda both nodded in the affirmative.

"Shall I escort you?" William offered.

"No." I smoothed my skirt and fidgeted with my hair. I had not been prepared to receive callers this morning. "Thank you, William. I can manage."

William smiled and nodded. "Very well, then. Shall I wait for you?" he asked, I assumed regarding breakfast.

"No, please. Go ahead." I motioned toward the service buffet that was now lined with an array of morning fruits, spreads, bread, and hard-boiled eggs.

Lucinda accompanied me downstairs to the drawing room where I found Mrs. Rollings sitting alone. She had removed her gloves and was holding them in her lap. She stood the moment I entered the room.

"Miss Hastings." She greeted me with a polite curtsy.

I returned the gesture and motioned for her to sit down. "This is such a lovely surprise Mrs. Rollings. I'm honored." I had seen Mrs. Rollings before but never up close like this, and I had never had the chance to speak with her privately.

"It is I who am honored," she smiled, and her deep blue eyes sparkled, exactly the same way Jonathan's would in the twenty-first century. He definitely had his mother's eyes. "I hope you won't think me rude if I speak frankly." She lowered her gaze for a moment and began twisting her hands together nervously.

"Of course not, Mrs. Rollings. Please, feel free to speak as candidly as you like."

"Thank you, Miss Hastings," she nodded.

"Please call me Eleanor," I replied.

Jonathan's mother ignored my invitation. "It's my understanding that you'll soon marry Colonel Hamilton," she began.

I squirmed uncomfortably in my seat. "I suppose the entire town has heard by now." I had to avert my eyes from hers. I felt as though I had betrayed her by not fighting harder to be with Jonathan.

"It's wonderful news." She placed her hand on top of mine. "Congratulations."

"Thank you, Mrs. Rollings. I . . . I don't quite know what to say. It's all happening so fast. I never expected it to . . . I mean for this to—"

"Sometimes that's the best way," she smiled, "when things are out of our hands."

"I suppose," I responded. "But I . . . eh . . . Jonathan and I, we . . ." I was frustrated that I was having so much difficulty putting words together.

"No need to explain, dear," she patted my hand. "He's the reason I've come this morning."

"Is he okay?" I asked, suddenly nervous.

"He will be, thanks to you. I understand you have asked Colonel Hamilton for a favor on behalf of our family." My mind raced with questions—how could she possibly know about Father and William's agreement?

I started to speak, but she stopped me. "Please, let me finish. I was so overcome with emotion when Mr. Rollings gave me the news that I rushed over in haste this morning, forgetting that I must be intruding on your privacy. Please accept my apology, and my very sincerest gratitude for your kindness."

Evidently Eleanor's father hadn't lost a moment's time before exploiting William's generosity. "Mrs. Rollings, you have nothing to apologize for." I squeezed her hand reassuringly. "I would do anything for your family. Jonathan and Grace mean the world to me."

"Your kindness is most generous. If there is ever anything we can do for you, please do not hesitate to call on us. We're deeply indebted to you."

"Oh, Mrs. Rollings!" Tears formed in the corners of my eyes. "There's so much I wish I could say to you."

"I'm afraid I've taken enough of your time this morning. May I have permission to call on you again, after the customary time for new brides to settle into marriage?"

"You may call anytime you please. And Grace as well. I would like so much to visit with her. Would you tell her that for me, please?"

"Yes, of course." Jonathan's mother stood and held out her hands to me. Her simple gesture reminded me so much of Grace. Grace always held her hands out to me whenever she greeted me. "I really must be going."

I placed my hands in hers and gave them a gentle squeeze. "Thank you so much for coming. I hope we see each other again very soon."

I walked Jonathan's mother to the entrance hall where Mr. Edwards met her and escorted her to the door. I watched her leave, and a thread of hope began to weave its way into my thoughts as I repeated her words in my mind.

If there is ever anything we can do for you, please do not hesitate to call on us. We're deeply indebted to you.

Perhaps this was finally the key to my ticket home.

Wedding Day
CHAPTER 13

*"S*hall we?"

William offered me his arm and led me down the grand staircase and out to the garden. The flowers were in full bloom, as was typical for this time of year, and that meant an over-abundance of insects. The humidity didn't help matters. When I wasn't batting away flies, mosquitoes, or a hundred other flying pests, I was fanning myself to keep sweat from dripping down my neck. The fact that Eleanor's hair was a thick mass of black curls only made perspiration patrol more challenging. In the morning hours the sun wasn't as hot, but there was little or no breeze so it felt like an oven outside unless you stayed in the shade. During late afternoon a cool wind from the northeast would breeze through the estate, making the higher temperatures much more tolerable. But that's when the brigade of flying, jumping, and creeping pests seemed to swarm in mass, and every one of them seemed to be on the same mission—to drink Eleanor's blood. Mrs. Weddington kept a ready supply of a topical ointment on hand that the locals swore by when it came to repelling the little blood-suckers, but for some reason it didn't seem to bother them where I was concerned.

After twenty minutes of strolling along one of the garden paths,

I'd already had enough of the morning insects. The little buggers were smart. They came out with the early morning sun, napped during the hottest part of the day, and then, when the sun began its decline in the west and the heat abated, were ready to party again.

"You know, they don't have bugs like this in Wyoming," I said, batting at a swarm of gnats that had formed an attraction with the silk flowers that adorned my hat.

"Pardon me?" His confused expression suggested that just like Jonathan and Grace, William had never heard of Wyoming.

I let out a deep sigh. "It's a territory out west." I really did need to study my geographical timelines more carefully.

William turned to face me and began picking gnats out of my hat. "And what's so special about this Wyoming that there are no bugs?"

I shrugged my shoulders and pressed my lips together. William chuckled at my obvious frustration with insects.

"You really think it's much better somewhere else?"

"A lot better!" I said too quickly. "Have you ever heard anyone from California complain about bug problems?"

William laughed heartily. "And just what do you propose to know about California?"

"You'd be surprised," I remarked.

William eyed me with curious amusement. "Yes, I'm sure I would be." He finished rearranging my hat and then added, "I think you'll discover that no matter where you go, there is always something to complain about. The challenge is to overlook those things that are disagreeable about a place and focus on what it has to offer instead." He bent down and picked a cluster of bluebells and handed them to me. "Take these for example. You would likely never see bluebells in the dry place you call Wyoming. They prefer wooded areas, just like here, and they symbolize constancy and gratitude, which is something we all could use a little more of—especially now when so many lives are in turmoil."

Oh my gosh. I'd forgotten I was speaking to a colonel. He was right, of course. Here I was complaining about bugs and a few gnats that had decided to eat my hat for breakfast, and there were still thousands of men facing the horrors of war. Jonathan was one of them! When had I become so self-centered?

"You're right, William. How very selfish of me."

"It's not my intent to chastise you, Eleanor, just to offer another perspective."

I shook my head. "No, you are right to chastise me. I'm afraid I haven't been thinking of anyone but myself."

"Don't be so hard on yourself. It seems to me that a very grateful mother left here only yesterday. Is she not beholden to you because you have placed such a high priority on her son's safety?"

I stared at William, unable to respond. He forced a smile as his eyes searched mine. I made no attempt to hide what he saw in my expression—he needed to see how much I loved Jonathan. Perhaps then he would understand why I was so against marrying him.

"You made the right choice, Eleanor." William seemed to be reading my thoughts. "You would have lost this fight with your father, no matter what. At least this way you lose knowing that you acted out of concern for someone else. There's nothing selfish about that."

"It's more than just concern, William." I looked him squarely in the eyes. "I love him."

William took a deep breath and let it out slowly. "I suspected as much."

"I'm sorry. I don't mean to be cruel," I reached for William's hand, "but you need to understand how I feel."

William raised my hand and pressed his lips gently against the back of my fingers. "Thank you for your honesty." He stepped back and offered me his arm. "Now then, let's get you away from the bugs."

I stared at William for several moments before finally taking his arm. I didn't know what to think of him. He seemed perfectly at ease with the idea of marrying someone who didn't love him. He deserved much better. He was so agreeable and so handsome, and he possessed a sort of wisdom and patience that made him very interesting.

You should love him, Eleanor, I said in my mind; I didn't care whether or not she was listening.

By noonday, William and I found ourselves wading in a shallow portion of the river. It had required some coaxing to convince him that I had no problem exposing my bare feet and ankles in front of him. In fact, the cool water felt so refreshing that before I knew it, I had hiked my dress up to my knees and started running along the riverbank, splashing in and out of the water as though I hadn't a care in the world.

William watched from the sidelines as he stood on the sandy bank holding his shoes and stockings. He looked so proper and out of place that it made me laugh. Without considering the potential consequences, I ran toward him and kicked water in his direction. I must have had reasonably good aim, because I managed to spray him with a nice trail of water from his toes clear up to his chest. He didn't flinch. He just raised his eyebrows and nodded slowly. Then he tossed his shoes aside and started running after me. I screamed, hiked my skirt up as far as I could manage, and started running. It didn't take him very long to catch up—he was a colonel, after all.

Apparently, I had overestimated William's sense of chivalry because as soon as he was close enough, he began heaving water in my direction so quickly that I couldn't retaliate. All I could do was laugh while I tried to dodge his aim. In no time, I was soaked from head to toe, which in the twenty-first century wouldn't have been that big a deal, but I was certain the wet T-shirt look was a big "no-no" in the 1800s. I wondered which Old Testament book Eleanor's father would assign me this time.

I decided if I was going to get into trouble I might as well make it worthwhile, so rather than trying to avoid getting any wetter I threw all caution aside and focused on making sure William was as wet as I was. The competition didn't last long, however, because William had backed me so far into the river that I lost my footing and fell in. He immediately dove in after me, most likely to make sure I was okay; but I was laughing so hard I couldn't tell for sure.

The strength of the current took me a little by surprise; it was deceiving because from the bank, the water appeared to moving much slower than it was. If William hadn't grabbed me, I might not have regained my footing. We were standing only waist-deep in the water, but he made sure my feet were firmly planted before easing his hold on me. I stared up at him, once again keenly aware of his impressive stature. His eyes held mine briefly and then drifted downward. He seemed to freeze in place as his eyes quickly traced the outline of Eleanor's breasts. There was no concealing them, even through three layers of clothing. I stood there for an awkward moment before folding my arms across my chest—not only to shield myself from William's gaze, but because I suddenly realized I was shivering.

William began to unbutton his shirt. I backed away nervously and made a swift beeline for the shore. William got there before me and quickly offered me his hand, which at first I refused. But the weight of my wet clothes was dragging me down; I needed the extra support to get back onto the bank.

Once safely on dry ground, the afternoon wind swirled around us. My knees, hands, and teeth were shaking uncontrollably. William chuckled and finished unbuttoning his shirt, which he then used to wrap around my shoulders. It wasn't exactly dry, but it helped. The sight of his muscular chest further warmed a spot deep inside me. Once again I couldn't tell if the reaction was mine or Eleanor's.

"We'd better get you back to the house and get you dry," he commented while trying to keep a straight face. "Your mother is going to tan my hide when she sees you!"

I started to argue but he was right about one thing, Eleanor's mother was not going to be pleased.

We made our way back to the pathway leading up to the side of the Hastings' house. I caught our reflection in the large windows of the drawing room—I was a mess. My hair was wet and tangled, my skirt was stained with mud, and I was wrapped in a man's shirt. Even Eleanor couldn't make this look good. William, on the other hand, was a different story. As I watched him stealthily in the window's reflection—wet pants, bare feet, and no shirt, I couldn't find anything in his appearance to criticize.

Not bad, Colonel Hamilton. Not bad.

Before we reached the main entrance, Christine came bounding around the corner out of breath. She stopped short when she saw us, but whatever she had on her mind must have taken precedence over our unseemly appearance. William and I glanced briefly at each other before turning back to Christine.

"Colonel Hamilton, come quickly! I've been looking all over for you!"

"What is it?" he asked, suddenly serious.

Christine shook her head. "I don't know, but there's a man here to see you and he won't leave until he talks to you directly."

We quickly followed Christine into the house and were met by Mr. Edwards, Mrs. Weddington, Lucinda, and Eleanor's mother. Each stood gaping at us in disbelief, but surprisingly, nobody said anything about our appearance. Mother directed Lucinda to draw me a warm bath and sent Mrs. Weddington for some dry towels. Mrs. Weddington returned quickly with the towels and held one out to me as I removed William's shirt and gave it back to him.

"William," Eleanor's father appeared in the entrance hall. "There's a Major Lawrence waiting for you in the drawing room." Father eyed William curiously and then motioned for him to join his guest. Once William disappeared into the drawing room, Father turned his attention back to me. His raised eyebrow told me he had jumped to an erroneous conclusion.

"Looks as though you two have been enjoying yourselves."

"Father!" I started to protest, but Mother chimed in before I could finish.

"Best you get yourself upstairs; your bath will be ready. The last thing you need is to catch a chill just before the wedding."

"I'm afraid the wedding will have to wait," William announced as he returned with Major Lawrence.

"What's this?" Eleanor's father did not sound pleased.

"I've received new orders. I must leave tonight. My regiment has been ordered to join the 38th Infantry in the eastern division. I'm afraid it could be months before I return."

"Oh, no!" Mother complained. "Can't they give you just one more day?"

"I have my orders. The General has arranged for an escort to arrive here tonight at half past eight."

I couldn't believe my ears. A wave of relief washed over me and I had to struggle to keep from showing it in my face.

Eleanor's father folded his arms, then started to rub his chin between his thumb and forefinger. This was always a bad sign—it meant he was concocting something. He cut his eyes over at me and watched my reaction. Then he turned back to the group.

"We'll have the wedding today!" he announced. Everyone stared at him. "Mother?"

Eleanor's mother looked stunned. She gaped at her husband for a moment before finally responding, "I suppose we have no other choice, do we?" She turned quickly to Mrs. Weddington, "What do you think?"

"I'll inform the staff immediately," Mrs. Weddington replied.

"Excellent," Father exclaimed. "I'll make the arrangements with Reverend Pat." He stepped beside William and reached out to shake his hand. "My boy, looks like the wedding won't have to wait after all."

William looked at me sympathetically while Eleanor's father shook his hand. "Sir," William said quietly to Father, "I'm afraid it won't be much of a wedding day for Miss Hastings, what with me leaving tonight. Surely it would be more agreeable to her if we waited?"

"Nonsense!" Eleanor's mother interrupted. "We'll have the ceremony today, just as soon as Reverend Pat arrives. There will be plenty of time for celebrating once you return."

"It's settled," Father agreed. "Now then, there's much to do to get ready." He signaled for everyone to get to their assigned tasks.

"First things first," Mrs. Weddington stated. "Let's get this child upstairs and turn her into a proper bride."

The rest of the afternoon passed in a blur. As soon as I finished my bath, Lucinda and Eleanor's mother helped me into my dress for a final fitting. Lucinda did her best to convince Mother that an eighteen-inch waist would suffice, whereas Mother was still insistent on smaller.

"Remember what happened the night of the ball?" Lucinda reminded her. "We don't want to risk another episode like that, do we?"

"I suppose not," Mother agreed. "We can't take any chances with this wedding. Colonel Hamilton must leave here a married man."

"Then it's settled," Lucinda remarked. Mother marked the areas along the bodice where she wanted Lucinda to add more lace. "A bride's bodice should enhance her natural features, don't you agree?"

"Yes, but it's the train that people remember, and if I don't get started I won't be able to add the satin roses you requested." Lucinda did her best to sound patient, but I sensed she was worried about finishing on time. I might as well have not even been there; nobody was asking my opinion on anything—not the dress, the size of my waistline, how my hair should be fixed, or any other detail. Then again, there was no secret that this was a shotgun wedding, at least as far as I was concerned; only the gun wasn't aimed at the groom, it was aimed at me.

When Lucinda left to put the finishing touches on my dress, Mother insisted that I lie down and take a nap. "You'll want to look fresh when your father gives you away," she commented.

"Gives me away? Don't you mean 'sells' me?" I scoffed.

Eleanor's mother gave me a stern look. "You'd be wise to hold your tongue, Eleanor, and remember that the life you lead—that all of us lead—requires sacrifice."

"Well, I never asked to be part of this life," I snapped. "This isn't the life I want!"

"You're young. You don't know anything about life!" she reprimanded me. "Do you honestly believe you're the first bride to feel this way? You are so naïve!"

"I don't care about other brides; I care about this bride!" I pointed to myself. "And I'm not too naïve to understand that nobody should be forced to marry one man when they're clearly in love with another!"

"Love!" Eleanor's mother said the word with contempt. "You throw that word around as if it were a credible argument. Thank goodness decisions as critical as marriage are still left for those who possess the wisdom to make them."

"Argh!" I bellowed. "You people drive me crazy! You are all hypocrites and bigots!"

Eleanor's mother wasted no time with words. She planted her open hand across my cheek, slapping my face sideways with such tremendous force that it nearly threw me off balance. My face burned as though it had been lit on fire with a thousand tiny sharp needles. I buried my face in my hands and winced in pain.

"How dare you use such language with me! If it weren't for your father's coddling and interference, I'd have taken a whip to you a long time ago! I've a good mind to do so now if it weren't for William discovering your insolence."

I was still holding my face, astounded by the depth and degree of Mother's anger; and I sensed that Eleanor, who had been hovering near, was equally stunned. I had never been struck before, and although it infuriated me to the point that I wanted to strike back, my will crumbled and I began to cry. Once the tears started to flow, there was no stopping them. The floodgates were open, and months of fear, frustration, and intense longing for home washed over me in violent heaves. I dropped to the floor, buried my face on the side of the bed, and sobbed. Eleanor's mother sat in a chair behind me and looked on in silence.

When I finally reached the point that all my energy was spent and there were no more tears to shed, Eleanor's mother stood and cleared her throat.

"Now then, we'll have no more of this. Understood?"

I no longer had the strength to protest. I knew I was trapped and I got the distinct impression that Eleanor had given up—she had been forced into submission and was willing to accept her lot, leaving me powerless to fight any further. Besides, fighting was moot because Eleanor's father held the final trump card. He held Jonathan's safety in his grasp, and there was no way for me to change the stakes without going through with the wedding. I was at least thankful that William was leaving tonight so that our time together as husband and wife would be limited to one evening. As soon as I knew Jonathan was safe, I would pay his family a visit and rules or no rules, I would tell them everything. They were my only chance of ever returning to my life as Beth, and I was putting all my hopes on them.

Eleanor's mother helped me onto the bed, loosened my corset, and brushed the hair away from my tear-stained cheeks. "You rest now," she said, patting my arm gently. "You'll discover soon enough that this is all for the best. You're too inexperienced and too distraught right now to see clearly, but in time you'll come to understand that it's very common for all brides to have these apprehensions. When you feel the first inklings of life growing inside you, you'll forget all this foolish talk about 'love' and you'll begin to comprehend the true nature of what love is. Love is not a free gift, Eleanor, it comes through sacrifice, responsibility, and at times, great pain."

I didn't respond. I let her words bounce off me without rebuttal. I saw no point in debating the issue further. Eleanor's father and mother held firm to the old-fashioned views about marriage and love that most of their society valued, and these values wouldn't change for several decades. I thought about Eleanor's Aunt Veronica. She was a woman far ahead of her times, willing to risk everything for love—and she paid a hefty price for it.

Eleanor's mother finally left me alone to drift off to sleep in private. I dreamed about home—about Carl and Uncle Connor, about Wyoming and the Grand Tetons. I dreamed about playing the piano, openly and freely, without having to think about whether or not a composition was published in the right era or whether or not it would be accepted as "proper" among members of society. And I dreamed about Jonathan, about his twinkling eyes, his infectious laugh, and how he held me so tightly sometimes I couldn't discern where my body ended and his began.

My dreams of Jonathan were so vivid and so real that I cried when Lucinda woke me. It was time for Eleanor to marry William. I had to think of it in that vein or I couldn't bear it. William was marrying Eleanor Hastings, not Beth Arrington. I was a trespasser here—an uninvited guest. I was an Intruder, just as Bailey had said.

Eleanor, I said in my mind. There was no response. *Eleanor!* I concentrated harder, still nothing. *Damn it, Eleanor I can't do this alone!* I paused, waiting, hoping. *Please, Eleanor. I need you.*

I'm here, Eleanor's weak voice sounded in the back of my mind. *I'm here.*

Somehow, I knew that if Eleanor stayed with me, I could get through this.

Lucinda brushed my hair and began twisting it and pinning it into loose curls that hung delicately from the top of my head down the center of my back. I watched her in the mirror, amazed by how quickly she transformed Eleanor's mass of thick hair into an elegant array of curls that accentuated her cheekbones and drew attention to her emerald eyes. Intuitively, I knew that William would be pleased. Lucinda added a slight blush to my cheeks—nothing like a blushing bride, right? Then she dabbed lavender oil on my neck and along the top of my bosom.

Mother joined us when it was time for me to get dressed. Together, she and Lucinda helped me into the dress and began fussing over how beautiful I was. The wedding dress was gorgeous; there was no denying that. It was simple and elegant, and it showed off Eleanor's feminine curves in such a way that no twenty-first century model could match.

Mother and Lucinda took a step back and admired their work.

"You are beautiful!" Mother said, nodding. "The very image of your mother," she added under her breath.

I thought her comment quite strange. It wasn't like her to refer to herself in the third person. "What do you mean by that?" I asked.

Eleanor's mother shook her head and smiled. "Oh, there's no time for such silliness right now. Here . . ." she reached over and retrieved a gold box from the vanity. Inside was a string of pearls with diamond clasps. The iridescent glow of the pearls told me they were genuine. "These were your grandmother's. I promised her I would give them to you on your wedding day. They're yours now."

"Oh, my!" Lucinda gasped. "They're stunning!" She reached into the box and held the pearls up to the light. The diamond clasps sparkled, catching the late afternoon sun and casting glittering patterns of dancing light all around the room. The pearls were no less impressive. They glowed.

Lucinda carefully placed the string of pearls around my neck and clasped them together, letting them fall against my bare breasts.

Mother turned me toward the standing mirror in the corner of the room.

"Hmm," she said, shaking her head. "Let's see . . ." She took hold of my sleeves and slid them off my shoulders and down the sides of my arms. "That's much better."

"But Mrs. Hastings, it's too early for bare shoulders," Lucinda remarked.

"Nonsense, Lucinda," Mother brushed off her comment. "This is considered an evening wedding, regardless of where the sun is presently. Why, if we waited until dark, it would be too late. Besides, it's fitting for a bride to enhance her assets on her wedding day. It makes the groom that much more grateful."

I wanted to puke. Even on my wedding day I was being treated like a piece of property.

Eleanor's mother played around with the sleeves a moment longer and ended up pulling them down a little further, making sure the full roundness of my breasts were exposed. At least this time I wasn't expected to dance. Or was I? I had no idea what to expect. I sincerely hoped the evening didn't involve dancing. Eleanor's ball gown had managed to hold everything in place—it was built for dancing—but this was a wedding dress, and I feared the slightest jolt in the wrong direction would make me the first topless bride of the 1800s.

There was a knock at the door, followed by Father's voice. "She's ready," Mother announced. Eleanor's father entered the room and stopped short when he saw me.

"My dear, you're a vision!" he stated. "You look like an angel!"

"Doesn't she?" Mother agreed.

"Lucinda, you've outdone yourself this time." Eleanor's father nodded. "She couldn't be lovelier."

"Thank you, sir." Lucinda gave him a slight curtsy, her smile full of pride.

"Mother, it's time for you to take your place. Reverend Pat is ready." Father motioned for Eleanor's mother to leave. Lucinda followed her out the door, leaving Father and me alone.

"I know we sprung this wedding on you rather quickly, Eleanor, but the situation being what it is, there was really no choice. I am sorry that you won't have a proper period of time to adjust to being a wife before William leaves, but that will work itself out in due time, I promise."

"Let's just get on with this Father, shall we? I really don't feel up to another lecture right now."

Eleanor's father raised his eyebrow at me and chuckled. "Very well then, shall we?" He offered me his arm, which I dutifully accepted, and we began the long march down the two flights of stairs to the parlor where William, Reverend Pat, Christine, Mother, and a handful of guests were waiting.

Contrary to everything I might have imagined about a nineteenth century wedding among the wealthy elite, the wedding was bare bones simple. There was no music. No wedding march. No fanfare. Eleanor's father and I simply walked down the stairs as if we were going to attend a garden party. When we reached the bottom of the last flight of stairs and turned toward the front parlor, my stomach began churning the same way it had whenever I was about to go onstage for a piano recital. I wanted to double over and grab hold of something. In a few seconds, it would be too late to turn around—too late to run. I closed my eyes tightly and began breathing deeply. Eleanor's father paused briefly, giving me a moment to catch my breath. I said a silent prayer.

Oh God, please help me get through this. Please keep Jonathan safe, and please . . . please find a way for us to be together some day.

Then in a last minute plea I begged Eleanor for forgiveness.

I am so sorry, Eleanor. I have to make sure that Jonathan is safe—there's nothing more I can do. Please don't hate me.

Eleanor's father patted the top of my arm with his free hand. "Today you make me very proud, Eleanor, very proud indeed. This is a day I have dreamed of ever since you came into our family."

Father's choice of words confused me and I thought for a moment I must not have heard him correctly. I didn't have a chance to question him, though, for as soon as we turned into the parlor entrance, all eyes in the room shifted to me. There were several low, audible gasps as Eleanor's father escorted me to William's side.

William was dressed in his formal Union uniform. He looked similar to how he did the evening of the ball; only somehow, in this setting he appeared even more impressive. His piercing blue eyes watched my every move as he waited patiently for Father to give him my hand.

Reverend Pat began the ceremony immediately.

"We are gathered here today in the face of this company to join together Colonel William Carlton Hamilton and Eleanor Louise Hastings in holy matrimony, which is an honorable and solemn estate and therefore not to be entered into unadvisedly or lightly, but reverently and soberly. Into this estate, these two persons now come to be joined. If anyone can show just cause why they may not be lawfully joined together, let them speak now or forever hold their peace."

Reverend Pat paused only briefly before continuing. In my mind, I changed Reverend Pat's words, substituting Jonathan's name in place of William's.

"Who gives this woman to be married to this man?" Reverend Pat asked, in accordance with tradition.

"I do," Eleanor's father stated. At that point, Eleanor's father took my hand and placed it on William's. He then took a few steps back to stand next to his wife.

Reverend Pat turned to William and continued.

"William Carlton Hamilton, wilt thou have this woman to be thy wedded wife, to live together after God's ordinance in the holy estate of matrimony? Wilt thou love her, comfort her, honor, and keep her in sickness and in health; and, forsaking all others, cleave thee only unto her, so long as ye both shall live?"

"I will," William answered. This took me by surprise. I had been expecting the traditional, "I do."

Now it was my turn. Reverend Pat turned to me and asked a similar question.

"Eleanor, wilt thou have this man to be thy lawfully wedded Husband, to live together after God's ordinance in the holy estate of Matrimony? Wilt thou obey him and serve him, love, honor, and keep him in sickness and in health; and, forsaking all others, cleave thee only unto him, so long as ye both shall live?"

I wanted to die! More accurately, I wanted to somehow cease to exist. Was that the order of things? I was to obey first, then serve? "Love" came in third? How was this right? How was it fair?

A low murmur passed through the room as everyone waited for my response. I searched William's eyes, pleading silently for him to do the heroic thing and free me from making a promise I knew I couldn't keep. Instead, he simply squeezed my hand gently and smiled.

I can't do this, I said to myself. *I just can't do this to him, or to me.*

I turned to Reverend Pat, prepared to accept the consequences for what I was about to do, knowing full well that Eleanor's father and mother would never forgive me for defying them in front of their family and friends; but when I opened my mouth to speak, I choked on the words. A surge of energy swelled from within me, and before I could stop her, Eleanor uttered the words that everyone in the room was waiting to hear.

"I will."

William's smiled widened, and without hesitation Reverend Pat finished the ceremony by having William and Eleanor repeat their vows.

Colonel Hamilton, please repeat after me, "I, William, take thee Eleanor, to be my wedded wife, to have and to hold from this day forward, for better or worse, for richer or poorer, in sickness and in health, to love and to cherish till death us do part; and thereto, I pledge thee my troth."

Likewise, Eleanor repeated her vows.

"I Eleanor, take thee William, to be my lawfully wedded husband, to have and to hold from this day forward, for better or worse, for richer or poorer, in sickness and in health, to love, honor, and obey, till death us do part; and thereto I pledge thee my troth."

It hadn't occurred to me prior to this that there would be a ring, so I was shocked when Revered Pat asked William to place a ring on my finger.

William slid a delicate gold band on my ring finger and repeated after Reverend Pat, "With this ring I thee wed, with my body I thee worship, and with all my worldly goods, I thee endow; in the Name of the Father, and of the Son, and of the Holy Ghost, Amen."

Then came Reverend Pat's final announcement.

"William and Eleanor, by the powers so vested in me by the State of Pennsylvania and by Almighty God, on this day, the 16th of June, in the year of our Lord one thousand eight hundred and sixty-four, I now pronounce you husband and wife. William, you may now kiss your bride."

William took both my hands in his and leaned forward until his face was only inches from mine. He hesitated briefly while his eyes searched mine—as though he were asking for my permission. I couldn't move. I was there, fully aware of everything that was happening, but Eleanor's life force exuded such a surprising presence and power that my own energy began to disengage, forcing me to relinquish control to Eleanor.

Before I knew it, William's lips met mine. His kiss was polite and unassuming, but as he moved his lips gently against mine, an unexpected feeling of warmth flowed through Eleanor's body, causing me to tremble slightly at the knees. William backed away and grinned. Instantly, the room exploded into a round of applause, followed by several congratulatory hugs and well-wishes.

A string quartet began playing quietly in the background as the family and guests made their way into the dining room for a formal sit-down dinner. William and Eleanor were the guests of honor, naturally, and therefore sat in the seats closest to the center of the long table.

One-by-one, each course of the meal was served beginning promptly at five o'clock. Wine flowed freely and liberally as guests took turns offering their toasts to the bride and groom, beginning first with Eleanor's father, who muttered something about filling the estate with children.

Normally, when the Hastings held formal dinners they were lengthy affairs, spread out over the course of several hours. This time, however, there seemed to be a sense of urgency since William's escort was due to arrive at half past eight. Eleanor's father seemed particularly obsessed with the time spent on each course of the meal. At precisely seven o'clock,

Eleanor's father excused William and I from the festivities in order for us to "properly" prepare for William's eminent departure.

Apparently, during the ceremony Mr. Edwards and Mrs. Weddington had transformed the guest room into a bridal suite—complete with champagne, trays of finger foods, fresh satin linens, and luxurious robes.

The moment I saw the room, I wanted to faint. Eleanor's life force had conveniently regressed back to its weakened state, leaving me to deal with William on my own.

Eleanor, I called frantically. *You can't do this! You can't leave me alone with your husband.*

Options

CHAPTER 14

*E*leanor was gone. She didn't respond to my internal pleas, and when I searched deep within me for any sign of her presence or energy there was nothing. Her life force, which I could normally sense even in its weakest state, seemed to have disappeared without a trace. She was hiding, but I didn't know if she was hiding from me or from William. Perhaps she was hiding from both of us.

William poured us each some champagne and handed me a glass. Then he raised his glass in a toast.

"To you," he clicked his glass against mine and chuckled. "You've had a hell of a day, wouldn't you say?"

I looked at my glass of champagne. I wondered how much I would have to drink in order to forget the fact that I was now "legally and lawfully" married to Colonel William Carlton Hamilton. I swallowed a quick swig of the champagne and winced the moment it reached the back of my throat. It felt like my entire insides had burst into flames. I did my best to mask the fact that the champagne not only burned all the way down, but had also set my gag reflex into overdrive. William seemed amused by the sour expression on my face.

"Whoa, take it easy," he chuckled. "You're supposed to sip this."

I held my hand up to silence him, and without worrying about the consequences I swallowed the remainder of the champagne in my glass. Again, my gag reflex kicked in and I had to cover my mouth with my free hand in order to hide the fact that the champagne tasted downright horrid. I held my glass out to William, indicating that I wanted more. He gave me a questioning look as he poured another drink, which I then quickly gulped. William watched my reaction with interest.

"You don't need to do this, Eleanor," he smiled sympathetically and shook his head.

"Do what?" I replied. My voice was barely audible because of the burning sensation in my throat.

He reached for my glass and set it down on the table. "There's no need for you to be so nervous."

I cleared my throat and twisted my hands into a tense ball. "William, I'm going to need a lot more of that," I pointed to the bottle of champagne, "if you expect me to—"

William rested his finger against my mouth. "Relax," he said calmly. He shook his head again and smiled. "We don't have a lot of time before I have to leave." He reached down and took my hand. "Come here. We should probably have a little talk."

Talking was good—I could do that.

William glanced quickly around the room; I assumed he was looking for a place to sit down. He apparently decided against the matching set of chairs because we ended up seated on the side of the bed. My heart began to pound anxiously.

"I'm really going to need that bottle of champagne, William." I started to get up, but he pulled me back.

"Would you sit down, please?" He turned toward me and cupped his hands over mine. I could feel his blood pulsing against my wrists. "We're man and wife now and that isn't going to change, but that doesn't mean I'm not without empathy or regard for your feelings." He paused briefly to let his words register and then continued. "I realize things happened rather unexpectedly today, and you're going to need some time to . . . adjust to all this, and to your new role."

"Time isn't going to 'adjust' how I feel, William. I don't want to hurt you, but we both know I love someone else."

William squeezed my hands gently. "I hope, for your sake, you'll choose to forget him."

"For *my* sake?"

"We're married, Eleanor, and as I've said already, I will do everything in my power to make you happy—but I have no intention of sharing you."

I thought about the absurdity of his comment. I wondered what he'd do if knew he was already sharing me and that he'd gotten far more than he bargained for when he married Eleanor—he now had me to deal with as well. I also wondered what he'd do if he knew that Jonathan wasn't his only rival. Somewhere out there, lurking in the shadows, James was waiting for William to take his leave, and as soon as William was safely out of the way, James planned to convince Eleanor to run away with him.

Oh William, I thought to myself as I studied his expression. *You have no clue, do you?*

An unexpected wave of compassion washed over me as Eleanor's energy suddenly emerged and began to vie for control. She must have perceived my thoughts because all of a sudden, just as it had during the ceremony, her life force took over, forcing my own energy into the background.

William seemed to sense that something had changed. He must have erroneously interpreted my silence for submission because his breathing shifted and he leaned forward. I knew he was about to kiss me, and although *my* instinct was to pull away, Eleanor stopped me from doing so. I had no choice but to close my eyes and brace myself.

William's kiss was tender at first, but after a moment he pulled back slightly. My eyes opened slowly and met his gaze. His blue eyes seemed to look right through me and into that part of my soul where Eleanor existed. I felt something stir inside me, and before I knew it, William's lips were on mine again—only this time his kiss was more fervent and he pulled me closer to him.

Eleanor! I called in my mind. *Eleanor! Stop this!*

William pulled away and shook his head. "I'm sorry," he said quietly. Although I knew it was impossible, I had the craziest feeling that he had somehow heard me.

"What is it?" Eleanor asked him. He took a deep breath and squeezed my hand.

"I said I would give you time to adjust, and I'll not go back on my word." He raised his hand and brushed the back of his fingers along the side of my face. Eleanor closed her eyes and concentrated on the tingling sensation of his touch. I was powerless to move or speak.

"No! Damn it!" William stood abruptly and backed away from me. "I won't take advantage of the situation, not when I suspect champagne has weakened your senses."

Admittedly, I did feel a little light-headed, but I couldn't tell if that was a result of the champagne or the fact that Eleanor's energy was so strong. Either way, my head was in a bit of a whirl and I had the sudden urge to giggle.

"Sure, you laugh now, but I imagine you won't be laughing later when the champagne wears off." William pursed his lips into a tight line. He bent down, placed his hands on the tops of my arms, and using very little effort, lifted me to my feet. "Now, how do we get you out of this thing?" He made a funny face and gestured at my dress.

"Excuse me?" I snickered. It was definitely the champagne.

"I can't very well leave you up here like this, can I? It might raise some suspicion if Lucinda discovers you here, still dressed in your wedding clothes, don't you agree?"

"Good thinking, Colonel Hamilton." I couldn't stop giggling.

William turned me around and began releasing the hooks along the back of my gown. Once he finished unhooking me, he steadied me and helped me step free of my dress. Then he went to work on loosening my corset. I didn't bother to protest it felt so good to be able to take a deep breath and relax, but the moment I did, the room began to take on a sort of foggy glow, and all I wanted to do was lie down.

Wow, no wonder they give brides champagne on their wedding night. My thoughts made me giggle all the more.

William grabbed my robe from the foot of the bed and wrapped me in it. Then he reached behind me and began removing the pins and clips from my hair so my black curls could hang freely. He twisted his fingers through my hair and positioned the curls so they cascaded down my back and along my shoulders.

"You're so beautiful, Eleanor," he breathed as he continued to slowly arrange my hair with his fingers.

My insides started to feel a bit funny—sort of anxious and nauseas at the same time. "William," I said, interrupting his train of thought. "I'm afraid I may need to lie down for a moment. All of a sudden I'm not feeling so well."

"I figured as much," he chuckled as he helped me onto the bed and fluffed the pillows for me. He made sure I was comfortable before taking a seat beside me. He studied my eyes carefully.

"What?" I asked, suddenly self-conscious.

"I was seventeen when our parents arranged our marriage, did you know that?"

I shook my head.

"I was young and ignorant and I thought, 'I'm not marrying a little girl!' You were only six or seven at the time, but it was already apparent to everyone who met you that you were destined to be unusually beautiful. Yet at the same time—if I may be so bold—you were a bit spoiled. It wasn't your fault; your brothers doted on you constantly. As the years passed, I watched you grow up—from a distance, of course—and I remember thinking, 'That girl is going to break a lot of hearts!' I was the chosen one who had won your hand, but I knew that was only half the battle. Somewhere along the line, it became paramount to me that I win both your hand *and* your heart."

William looked down and flashed a shy grin. "When you were finally old enough for me to try, the war broke out and I was sent away. I knew there were others competing for your affections and that you even fancied one or two of them, but you were still young so I didn't pay it much mind. Then you took ill." William's expression grew anxious. "I don't know how much they've told you about your illness, but it came on rather suddenly and lingered for many months. Your father was devastated. Then he lost Charles and Miles in the war, and when he thought he was going to lose you, too, he was inconsolable. He brought in every expert in the field of medicine, desperate for one of them to give him a reason to hope."

William paused, his thoughts on the past.

"I didn't know," I replied.

"When the doctors had done all they could, your father finally resigned himself to the fact that your death was imminent and he released me from our agreement, freeing me to choose someone else to marry."

He looked up at me and brushed his fingers along my arm. My eyelids were beginning to feel heavy, but William's story held me spellbound—I wanted to hear more. Eleanor was equally interested in what he was saying.

"But then I got well, and that's why you had to honor the original agreement," I said, filling in the blanks for him.

William looked disappointed. "No, that's not how it was. Not at all."

"Then why? I mean, what happened?"

"You'll think I'm crazy." He shook his head slightly and looked away.

"Why would I think that?"

William shrugged his shoulders and smiled a half smile. "I started to pray."

"You what?" This time it was Eleanor who responded.

"I know it sounds rather foolish. After all, I'm a logical man. Everyone else had come to terms with the doctor's diagnosis. They were just waiting for you to slip silently away some night, and that would be the end; but I couldn't just sit idle and wait for you to die. So I started to pray. Don't get me wrong, I'm a Christian man, born and raised, but praying was something we normally only did at church or at our evening meals."

"You prayed for her?" I whispered in awe. The words had escaped before I could think about what I was saying. I caught my mistake instantly.

"I prayed for *you*," William clarified.

I was so touched by his simple declaration that emotion swelled in my throat, making it difficult to swallow.

William took a deep breath and continued. "You see, somewhere along the line, during all those years while I was watching you grow up, I realized I had fallen in love with you. I didn't want to be released from our agreement, nor did I want to marry someone else. I wanted you to live, and I wanted to win your heart. Nothing else seemed to matter to me. So, I prayed morning and night that God would spare your life and allow you to get well." William paused briefly. "And he did."

I didn't know what to say. William was *in love* with Eleanor. This wasn't just some prearranged marriage that he'd been forced into against his will. William had married the love of his life.

I don't belong here, I thought to myself.

A profound sense of regret flooded my soul. I had said those words to myself a hundred times—a thousand times—during the past several months, but never had I meant them more than I did right now. This was Eleanor's story, not mine. Bailey had accused me of "stealing" Eleanor's body, and regardless of the circumstances that might have led up to it, that's exactly what I'd done. Like the "Gray Ghost," I'd come in undetected and had lived among Eleanor's family as one of them, all the while plotting to take whatever steps necessary in order to get what I wanted.

Bailey was right; I was an Intruder.

"Well, like I said, it sounds crazy." William patted my arm and started to get up.

"Don't go," Eleanor whispered.

Ah ha! I said to her in my mind. *You see it too, don't you?* Eleanor didn't respond, but I knew she was listening. *William loves you! James has nothing on this guy!*

There was a brief silence before Eleanor responded.

Maybe.

"I'm afraid I don't have a choice, Eleanor. They'll be waiting for me downstairs." He stood and straightened his uniform. "You stay here and rest. Nobody will expect you to come down until tomorrow." He glanced around the room and smiled apologetically. "I'm sorry this wasn't exactly a wedding night to remember, but as soon as I return I promise to take you wherever you want to go and give you a proper honeymoon."

Eleanor reached out to William and he took her hand. "Thank you," Eleanor smiled. Her energy receded and within a few seconds she was gone.

William bent down and kissed me tenderly on the forehead and then brushed his lips against mine. "Write to me when you can," he requested.

"I will," I promised. "And William?"

"Yes?"

"It was a lovely wedding night. Thank you."

William placed his hat on his head and adjusted it slightly. Then he tipped it in my direction and grinned. I watched his dazzling eyes dance beneath the brim of his hat and at that moment, the sight of him took my breath away. There stood Colonel William Carlton Hamilton in all his glory—an officer indeed—and every whit a gentleman.

Another thought occurred to me just as he opened the door and started to leave. "One more thing," I said quickly.

"Yes, ma'am," he replied as he turned to face me.

"Be safe." My heart ached at the thought of anything happening to him.

His grin widened and he tipped his hat to me again. "Yes, ma'am."

William closed the door behind him and I listened as his footsteps faded down the hall. I wondered if Eleanor's mother and father and their guests would still be waiting for him downstairs. If so, I hoped it wouldn't be too awkward for him. I was very content to remain safely behind closed doors, away from curious speculations.

I lay in bed for a long time thinking about William's story and how difficult it must have been for him to hold back earlier. He could have persisted and nobody would have faulted him, but he had chosen compassion over his own desires.

You are a lucky girl, Eleanor Louise Hastings, I commented in my mind. *Don't let this man get away.*

Eleanor didn't respond.

You know I'm right, I added.

I continued to lay there alone with my thoughts. Eleanor, if she was present, wasn't speaking to me. She belonged with William; I knew that. I sensed it with every fiber of my being. What could I do to convince her to forget her stubborn fantasies about running away with James? I knew in my heart that if Eleanor would give William a chance, she would fall in love with him and the two of them would be happy. Somehow, I needed to make her see that James wasn't the man for her and that to leave William for him would be the biggest mistake of her life.

How do you convince a stubborn seventeen-year-old girl that she's wrong about someone? I had to chuckle to myself because immediately the memory of Adam popped into my mind. My mom had tried everything in her power to make me see Adam for the jerk he was, but I wouldn't listen. Instead, I accused my mom of being old-fashioned and sticking her nose in where it didn't belong.

I laughed. "Eleanor, you can accuse me of many things, but you can never accuse me of being old-fashioned!" I burst into laughter and buried my face in my pillow. "Oh my gosh! When did I suddenly become the one to give unsolicited advice?"

I lay there plotting, scheming in my mind how I might deal with their situation when I realized Eleanor was probably already listening to my thoughts about James anyway, so I gave up. Instead, I turned my focus back to my own plight. I gave thanks in my heart that William had not forced me to be untrue to Jonathan tonight; but I knew my thanks would be short-lived because William would only be gone for a few months, and when he returned he would expect me to welcome him into my bed.

If I was going to be with Jonathan I would need to act soon, and that meant I would need to stop waiting around for someone to come for me and take me home. It was time for me to take the initiative and do something. My reasoning was simple. I belonged with Jonathan—it no longer mattered to me if that meant in the twenty-first century or the 1800s. Listening to William's story had convinced me of that. One way or another, I needed to find my way back to Jonathan *before* William returned.

There were only two options churning in my mind—return to the twenty-first century and resume my life as Beth Arrington or run away, find Jonathan, and convince him to flee to Wyoming with a married woman. I took a long, deep breath and released a hopeless sigh. Neither of those options seemed very likely. The first depended on Jonathan's mother actually believing my story; the other presumed that Jonathan would be willing to ignore his sense of right and wrong and cast aside his morals. I couldn't ask him to do that.

There was a third option, and though the idea was disturbing, it seemed to be the most realistic scenario. I would continue to live the rest of my life as an intruder in Eleanor's body. When she grew old and died, perhaps then my spirit would be free to find its own way back home. That scenario, though the most logical, was also the most disconcerting and the least palatable.

Ugh! I pressed my fists against my temples. *There has to be a better way to get back where I belong!*

Frustrated, I threw back the sheets and climbed out of bed. I wandered around the room, and pretended to take an interest in details—such as the swan carvings on the bedposts at the foot of the bed and the silk, purple thread used to monogram the letter "H" on William's white robe which lay undisturbed across the foot of what was presumably "his" side of the bed. I meandered across the floor, the bottom of my robe dragging along the floor behind me. I pulled aside the heavy curtains and peeked out the window. Night had fallen. Somewhere, not too far from here, William rode with his escort to join his men. Somewhere else, much further away, Jonathan was camped near the front line.

I searched my memory for any additional information I could access about the Civil War, hoping to piece together some sort of timeline. The Battle of Gettysburg was usually the first thing that came to mind. My family had visited the Gettysburg Military Park during one of our family vacations when I was in grade school (I use the term "vacation" loosely, because having been raised by a military father and a scientist mother meant that our vacations were actually more like field trips). My father had insisted on a historical tour of the east coast one summer while he was stationed in North Carolina. While touring, I'd learned that Gettysburg was a major turning point in the war. It was also the battle with the greatest number of casualties. It occurred in July of 1863—a date I would never forget because that's when I arrived in the 1800s, just two weeks after the bloody battle had claimed the lives of Eleanor's brothers, along with thousands of others.

I could remember such battles as Harpers Ferry, Antietam, Fredericksburg, and Petersburg, but my recollections of dates was far too vague to help me much. In the beginning, there was Fort Sumter and Bull Run. I'm embarrassed to admit that the only reason I remember those two names is from a movie I watched once. I shook my head, disgusted at how utterly ignorant I was when it came to American history.

Fortunately for me, none of those dates mattered at the moment. What I needed to know most was what was happening right now, and where Jonathan and William would be in relation to the front lines. It was highly doubtful that General Meade would have received William's letter by now, so I had to assume that Jonathan was somewhere between here and Petersburg. But Petersburg was a nine month siege that involved months of trench warfare, and even though the campaign would result in a Union victory and put Lee in his final retreat, there would be tens of thousands of lives lost, with both sides experiencing high numbers of casualties. The thought of Jonathan being in the trenches there was more than I could bear to imagine.

The Union won, I reminded myself repeatedly. *Lee will surrender next April and the war will be over. Jonathan and William will be safe, right? I had to hold on to that hope because the alternative was inconceivable.*

An ominous sense of foreboding suddenly flooded my mind. I couldn't shake the feeling that something dreadful was about to happen, or worse, had already happened.

Jonathan! A distant voice cried out in my head. His name echoed repeatedly in my mind. The sound seemed to be coming from several directions at once. A moving shadow passed over the ground along the side of the Hastings' estate and then disappeared. I opened the curtains a little wider and peered into the night, trying to discern what might have created it. Was it an animal, or perhaps a large cloud passing in front of the moon? I waited, watching in the distance for any signs of movement; but everything was silent and still. Too still.

The temperature in the room dropped drastically, causing my breathing to deepen. As I exhaled, my breath formed a foggy mist on the window. I reached up to wipe away the moist film and as I did, a large figure suddenly passed in front of me on the other side of the window. I jumped back, letting go of the curtains and nearly losing my balance. My heart pounded furiously as my blood pulsed its way through my veins, fighting for oxygen.

After several seconds, the temperature in the room returned to normal, and so did my heart rate. I debated leaving, but that meant going downstairs where I risked running into Eleanor's mother or father. Surely I was more rational than that!

I took several deep breaths and chided myself for over-reacting. *Think logically, Beth*, I said in my mind. *You're supposed to be a scientist's daughter, remember?*

I began searching for logical explanations for what had just occurred. Obviously, the temperature outside was much cooler than I realized—that's certainly plausible when there's so much humidity in the air. By opening the curtains, I must have allowed some of the cool air into the room. That would explain the sudden temperature drop. And as far as the figure outside the window—that had to be my eyes playing tricks on me. After all, I'd had two full glasses of champagne earlier. That's enough to mess with anyone's mind—especially someone who'd never had it before.

I crawled back into the bed, grateful to hear the faint sound of voices coming from downstairs. The men's voices were closer than the women's voices, which told me Eleanor's father had invited his guests to join him in the billiard room. That meant the party was just getting started for the men. If I listened carefully, I could make out the cackles of women's laughter from the first floor. No doubt the ladies had begun a bridge match in the drawing room. Christine would be in bed by now. Her bedroom was located in the opposite wing from the guest room I was occupying, but knowing she was near calmed me.

Comforted by the low rumblings of familiar sounds, I snuggled down into the sheets and resumed my earlier thoughts. I needed to make certain that my priorities were straight, beginning with Jonathan. William had arranged to reassign Jonathan to ensure that he would be out of harm's way, so I convinced myself that at least for now, I could let go of my concern for his safety.

Up until now, I'd been thinking emotionally, guided by my feelings rather than logic. It was time for me to set my emotions aside and approach my situation scientifically; that meant thinking beyond the realm of reason. I considered my three possible options, mulling them over repeatedly in my mind and contemplating the potential consequences of each. No matter how many times I analyzed the details or manipulated the variables, the outcomes were the same.

I had to be missing something. If I had traveled from the twenty-first century to the 1800s, there had to be a way to reverse the process. I took a deep breath and yawned. I promised myself that one way or another, I would figure out a way to spend my life with the man I loved.

I was moments away from sleep when I heard a whisper in my mind. *There is a fourth option, Beth.*

The voice startled me. I knew instantly that it hadn't come from Eleanor.

No! I shook my head against my pillow in protest. *Not Bailey! That can never be an option!*

The next morning I awoke with a terrible headache. When Lucinda drew back the curtains to let in the light, I buried my face in my hands and groaned.

"Oh, Lucinda!" I exclaimed. "I feel horrible!"

"It's the champagne, Miss Eleanor. Or . . ." she stopped suddenly, "or should I call you Mrs. Hamilton now?"

"Ugh! Please Lucinda! Don't ask me stupid questions!"

"My, my," she mused. "We are grumpy today, aren't we?" She threw back my covers and did a double take at the sheets. She raised her eyebrows but didn't comment. "Did you sleep well?"

"I said, *no* questions!"

"All right. Come along then, up with you." Lucinda pulled on my arm. "I've already drawn your bath."

"What? Why so early? We haven't even had breakfast yet," I complained, although the thought of eating made me feel nauseas.

"Early!" Lucinda scoffed. "It's half past eleven! You slept right through breakfast."

"What? How is that possible?" I started doing the math in my head. If William left at eight-thirty and I stayed awake for another hour or possibly two, that meant I had slept for— "Thirteen hours?" I gasped.

"I reckon that's about right," Lucinda confirmed.

"Why didn't you wake me?" I complained.

"Your father insisted you needed to rest, what with the wedding and all."

"Oh, that," I sighed. Of course, Eleanor's father would have assumed that William had taken full advantage of his marital rights as a husband.

Grrrrr. Eleanor! Your father creeps me out sometimes!

"Come on, now. Let's get you ready for the day. You are, technically, the mistress of the house now, and we have a lot to do!"

"Mother is still the mistress," I reminded Lucinda. "That hasn't changed yet."

"It will soon enough," she insisted. "In the meantime, we must order your new calling cards, write your letters, and decide on suitable chambers for you and Colonel Hamilton."

"Whoa! Hold everything! William won't be back for months. We have plenty of time for all of that."

"Details like that take time," Lucinda corrected me. "I've never been a mistress's maid before, but Mrs. Weddington says there are a lot of responsibilities. I don't want to disappoint anyone."

I smiled. Lucinda had been Eleanor's maid ever since Eleanor returned from school. It had never occurred to me that by marrying William and becoming the next mistress of the Hastings' estate, Lucinda's position would change. This was a promotion for her.

"Yes, yes," I humored her. "Then I suppose we'd best get busy."

I knew facing Eleanor's father would be awkward. He would no doubt be watching my abdomen in coming months—expecting that already there would be a grandchild on the way. He would flip if he knew what really happened last night. I certainly didn't plan on breaking the news that my marriage was still unconsummated. Knowing Eleanor's father, he would devise some strategy to get William and I together, even if it meant shipping me off to the battlefront. The man was certifiable!

As it turned out, I had nothing to worry about because Eleanor's father and mother had left together to make calls, and they weren't expected to return until time for the evening meal. This pleased me immensely because it meant I was free to roam the estate and do whatever I wanted. I ate a quick snack and drank plenty of water, which made my head feel much better.

As soon as I finished going over the details of the day with Lucinda, I marched upstairs to the ballroom and threw off the large sheet that covered the grand piano. It was a rare opportunity when I was able to sit at this instrument and play freely, so I spent the better part of the next three hours revisiting my favorite compositions—starting with Chopin's Etude in E.

I closed my eyes and let visions of Jonathan and I together stream through my mind, beginning with the first time we met in the hallway of the Andersen Community Recreation Center. That was the first time I'd heard him play the piano. I pictured every memory of us together, every time we sat next to each other to play a duet, every time he told me he loved me, and every time his smile and his twinkling eyes stole my breath away.

I opened my eyes and stared at Eleanor's hands. Her long, slender fingers were flawless—the envy of most pianists, and they opened gracefully like delicate fans spanning well beyond an octave, which was unusual given that Eleanor was so petite. Her hands made playing the piano appear effortless to onlookers—another envy of most pianists.

I saved "Eleanor's Theme" for last. I never tired of its simple melody or of playing around with different variations of the theme. When I added the bridge—the missing link in Jonathan's version—the music suddenly began to take on a life of its own. I closed my eyes and allowed Eleanor to share control of our hands, and together we played the piece in its entirety.

When we finished and the last tones of the final chord faded into the distance, a thought struck me with such perfect clarity that I couldn't believe I hadn't figured it out sooner.

Eleanor was not the composer of her theme—*I* was.

Epiphany
CHAPTER 15

To say that I endured the week that followed with difficulty would be a gross understatement. It was as if I were dreaming, and no matter how hard I tried, I couldn't make myself wake up. Instead, I switched back and forth between spectator and player, frustrated that I couldn't just stick to one or the other.

As I sat at the large desk in Father's study, I contemplated the seriousness of my plight. The house was unusually quiet this morning, and the repetitive rhythm of the large mahogany Grandfather clock that stood neatly tucked into a niche in the hallway was a constant reminder that time passed in an unwavering push forward, without regard for the consternation left in its wake. The clock—grand and regal by any standard—seemed insignificant among the grandeur of the furnishings that lined the ornate entry hall. Yet ever since the night of the wedding, the demanding tone of its chimes echoed repeatedly the message that time was my enemy.

The daunting reality of my situation was unfathomable; it *had* been since that first glimpse in the mirror when I discovered I had taken possession of Eleanor's body. At the time, the idea had intrigued me— Eleanor was, after all, exceptionally beautiful—but my curiosity and infatuation with living Eleanor's life had since lost its appeal and had evolved into a growing source of panic which if I wasn't careful, would soon be bordering on hysteria.

"Pardon the interruption, Mrs. Hamilton." Mr. Edward's deep, guttural voice broke my concentration. I looked up without responding. "What time shall I tell Wilson to have your carriage ready in the morning?"

I stared blankly at Mr. Edwards for several seconds, searching my memory for some recollection of why I might require a carriage in the morning.

"Mrs. Hamilton?" Mr. Edwards stifled a slight inclination to smile. "Shall I tell him the usual time?"

"Yes, of course. That would be fine." I had no idea what the usual time was, but I was confident that Lucinda could enlighten me before I retired for the evening.

"Very well, then. Will you be requiring anything else this evening?"

"No. Thank you, Mr. Edwards. That will be all."

Mr. Edwards offered a slight bow and thanked me as he exited the room. I picked up the stack of stationary that lay neatly placed on the corner of the desk and ran my fingers over the raised embossed "H" at the top of the page. It was becoming more and more difficult to maintain a clear sense of who I was. I feared that it wouldn't be long before I lost my identity altogether. I sometimes wondered if I already had, but just refused to admit it to myself. Eleanor's life force, once frail and virtually unperceivable, was now ever looming, waiting to reclaim control at the first sign of weakness on my part.

To further complicate matters, while I battled to maintain dominance, I couldn't escape the fact that I was now married. I'd been powerless to stop the wedding and part of me wondered if that had something to do with Eleanor's emerging presence. After all, as Mrs. Weddington repeatedly reminded me, Eleanor was heir to one of the grandest estates in all of southern Pennsylvania. Despite her secret feelings for James, I couldn't help but wonder if the prospect of being William's wife (and hence presiding as mistress of the Hastings' estate) was too tempting a prospect for her to ignore. Regardless, I knew something Eleanor could not know. The war would end in just under a year, and both William and James would be home to collect their prize.

Had things gone as planned, I would have developed into my simultaneous roles as Mrs. William Hamilton and the new mistress of the Hastings' estate slowly—over time—while allegedly awaiting William's return from his recent assignment. As fate would have it, however, the transition came sooner than anyone could have anticipated. Shortly after the wedding, Eleanor's father took ill unexpectedly. Dr. Richardson, who had been the family's doctor for several years, did not seem hopeful that his recovery would be a quick one. As a result, Eleanor's mother, who had survived the fever as a child, abandoned all of her normal responsibilities to assume the role of dutiful nursemaid. Thereafter, she spent the majority of her time in Father's bedchambers tending to his needs.

By the end of the first week of his illness, Father's condition had worsened so much that Eleanor's mother flatly refused to come downstairs at all. She even insisted on taking all her meals in the sitting room adjacent to Father's bedroom. This left Christine and me to manage on our own. Mr. Edwards and Mrs. Weddington made noble efforts to ensure that the numerous affairs of the household continued to run seamlessly and function normally—and they did so with remarkable efficiency. Both acquiesced to me as the decision-maker, but it was clear to the entire staff that neither Mr. Edwards nor Mrs. Weddington required my advice on any matter; they merely wished to afford me the courtesy and respect of my new position. It quickly became apparent to me by their inadvertent musings that I knew very little about running an estate. It didn't take long for me to develop a genuine appreciation and respect for Eleanor's mother, not having realized the details she attended to on a daily basis.

I started to blow out the candle that sat next to a heavy paperweight at the top of the desk, but paused to watch the dancing flame flicker back and forth in the soft evening breeze flowing through the study window. I placed my hand alongside the flame, blocking the movement of air, and watched as the flame instantly transformed into a tall sleek stream that stretched toward the ceiling. I stared, mesmerized, as the thin glow of light disappeared into the darkness of the high ceiling. I couldn't help but liken its journey to that of my own.

Mother's unexpected knock startled me.

"Eleanor? What are you still doing up? Why, you haven't even changed into your night clothes yet."

"Good evening, Mother." I ignored her subtle reprimand. "How's Father?"

"I'm afraid he's much worse," she replied. "He wants to speak to you."

"Now?" I asked.

Mother released a dark chuckle. "Yes, but I insisted that he wait until morning. He needs to rest right now. You see, he's quite delirious and doesn't know what he's saying."

"Of course," I nodded. I studied Eleanor's mother carefully for a moment. She looked so tired. This was the first time I had seen her this way. The sunken frown lines around her mouth made her look much older than she was, and the dark circles around her eyes bore a sharp contrast to her ivory complexion, almost making her appear ghost-like. The shadows cast by the candlelight didn't help.

"Perhaps tomorrow, after your calls. Perhaps by then . , ." Mother's words trailed off to a weak whisper; I couldn't help but sense that she hoped Father would change his mind about seeing me before then.

"I'll come straight away," I said.

Eleanor's mother took a deep breath and started to teeter as though she might fall, but she caught herself on the back of a chair .

"Mother!" I stood and steadied her. "You aren't well; you need to rest. I'll call for Mrs. Weddington and have her help you to your room. I can stay with Father tonight."

"No!" Mother said sharply. "No," she repeated in a softer tone, "that won't be necessary Eleanor. I'm fine. I can manage."

Eleanor's mother was not one to argue with when she put her foot down, so I let it go. But I still couldn't shake the feeling that she didn't want Father to talk to me.

When Eleanor's father first became ill, I didn't think there was any-thing odd about mother insisting she stay at his bedside. I thought it was sweet—a side of Eleanor's mother that I only saw in rare glimpses. Lately, however, she seemed determined, to the point of obsession, to keep Christine and me away from him, and I was determined to find out why.

In spite of her protests and weak efforts to bat my hands away, I man-aged to help Mother back upstairs and called for Mrs. Weddington to make sure she got some rest during the night. Mother may not listen to me, but I'd learned that if there was one person in the household more stubborn than Eleanor's mother, it was Mrs. Weddington. In spite of her many objections, Mother finally relented and agreed to rest, but only after insisting that Mrs. Weddington be the only one with Father in her absence. She made it abundantly clear that neither Christine nor I be permitted to see Father unless she was present. Mother's obvious angst concerned me, but I saw no point in arguing with her until she was calm and could speak rationally.

Once mother was asleep, I tiptoed down the hall to Father's room and quietly opened the door. Mrs. Weddington instantly rose to her feet and blocked my way into the bedchamber where Father lay motionless.

"It's no use, Mrs. Hamilton," Mrs. Weddington said in a low voice. "The fever's got him. He won't even recognize you."

"That may be so, but he asked for me, and I'm here."

"It's really best not to disturb him when he's resting comfortably. I'll call for you tomorrow when he's awake."

"I appreciate your concern, of course. I promise only to stay for a moment."

"Miss Eleanor, your mother gave me specific orders not to let anyone disturb his sleep. I must insist that you come back in the morning."

I was just about to relent and let her have her way when all of sudden Eleanor's life force emerged with such strength I nearly stumbled.

"I might remind you, Mrs. Weddington, that it's 'Mrs. Hamilton' now. And while I commend you for your loyalty to my mother, I must also remind you that she is no longer the mistress of this estate—*I am.*"

Mrs. Weddington's mouth flew open and she took a step backwards. "Well, I never!" she exclaimed. "You would disregard your own mother's wishes?"

"What I do or don't do is none of your concern. I'm confident that Colonel Hamilton would agree; but if you'd like, we can bring the matter up with him once he returns. Until then, I must insist you remember your place in this household."

Whoa Eleanor! Where'd that come from? I said in my mind. Eleanor's unexpected display of authority even made *me* want to take a back seat and mind my own business. It occurred to me that maybe I'd misjudged Eleanor all these months, mistaking her feminine elegance for weakness. But standing there in front of Mrs. Weddington (who suddenly looked more frail than frightening), I saw a side of Eleanor that I had no idea existed.

Mrs. Weddington stepped aside and allowed me to pass. I paused, waiting for her to comment, but she remained silent.

"That will be all, Mrs. Weddington," Eleanor said.

"Mrs. Hamilton?" she replied, as though she had misunderstood.

"That will be all for now. I'll ring for you when I'm finished sitting with Father."

Mrs. Weddington shifted her stunned gaze between me and Eleanor's father several times.

"Mrs. Weddington . . ." Eleanor motioned to the door, "please leave us alone now."

Mrs. Weddington hesitated a moment, but finally gave a defiant bow and left the room. Eleanor turned and sat in the chair next to her father's bed. He was almost unrecognizable—so pale and pathetic—nothing like the man who had ruled with an iron fist only weeks earlier. But even in his weakened state, I felt no compassion for him. Eleanor on the other hand, despite the despicable treatment she had received from him, was full of emotion.

"Oh Father," she whispered, taking his limp hand in hers. "You mustn't leave us—not now—not like this."

It was all I could do to keep my thoughts to myself. This was, after all, Eleanor's father, and no matter how ruthless and stubborn he had been, Eleanor carried a soft spot for him. I did my best to stay in the background and allow Eleanor to take complete control.

"Eleanor," Father's weak voice croaked as he called to her.

"I'm here Father. What is it?"

"Your mother—" He coughed several times and gasped for air. Eleanor grabbed a wet cloth from the nightstand and patted his forehead gently.

"Mother's resting for a moment. Do you want me to get her?"

Father continued to cough but shook his head no. Eleanor continued to pat his head and tried to quiet him. He made a feeble attempt to speak, but it only made the coughing worse.

"Don't try to talk, Father. Just rest."

He shook his head from side to side, obviously anxious to communicate, but he couldn't get the words out. He managed to lift his hand and point to the desk on the opposite side of the room.

Eleanor looked in the direction he was pointing. "What is it, Father?"

A single tear spilled from his eye as he struggled to get the words out. "There's a . . . letter . . . ." His voice trailed off and he dropped his hand.

"You want me to read the letter to you?" Eleanor asked, trying to understand.

Father let out another stream of coughs. There was no question about it, he had pneumonia. His eyes shut for a moment and he shook his head. When he spoke again his voice was barely more than a whisper.

"It's for you."

As soon as he uttered the words, his body relaxed and he slowly fell into a deep sleep. Eleanor continued to pat his forehead until she was certain he was as comfortable as possible, then she rested her face against his hand and cried.

Several minutes passed before I realized Eleanor's life force had once again retreated. I left the bedside of her dying father and went straight to his bureau to find the letter he had mentioned. I searched the drawers thoroughly, but couldn't find it. I was about to give up when a quiet voice whispered, "Look behind the drawer." I chuckled to myself, convinced that I'd watched too many murder mysteries on television in the twenty-first century; but sure enough, when I pulled out the top drawer, I found a letter tucked behind it addressed to Eleanor.

Dear Eleanor,

If you are reading this, then I have either died or will be dead soon, as I made a solemn promise to your mother that I would keep this secret from you until my dying breath. You asked me if I loved your mother, and the truth is I loved her with all my heart, though never in the way you meant; for you see, my sister Veronica is your real mother.

My free hand flew to my mouth as Eleanor let out an audible gasp. I continued reading:

*O had secretly hoped that when O showed you her por-
trait, you would recognize her - that somewhere deep inside,
her memory was still alive in you. O will die knowing that in
keeping a promise to my wife, O failed to honor the memory
of my beloved sister. Your mother never wanted you to know
about Veronica, and it would break her heart to find out that
O've told you now. But how can O go to my grave with this
secret on my conscience?*

I stopped reading for a moment to allow the words to sink in. Father's revelation didn't surprise me as much as it did Eleanor. Eleanor
had apparently missed the fact that her father and mother had let a
couple of clues slip during the past few weeks. I suppose that being a
third party and not emotionally invested in the family made it easier for
me to pick up on the signs. Eleanor would no doubt need time to sort
everything out in her mind, but as far as I was concerned, this was great
news for truth be told, I wasn't particularly fond of either of Eleanor's
parents. Still, my heart went out to Eleanor.

*O'm afraid O must pass the burden of this secret on to
you, Eleanor. O beg you to indulge the final wish of your
dying father and never reveal what you have learned.
     You are so like her, Eleanor. Veronica was a vision of
beauty and adored by everyone. You claim that O know
nothing of love and matters of the heart. O share with
you now that my heart has been broken twice in my lifetime; once with the death of my sister, and again when O
turned my back on the only woman O ever really loved. Of
O'd possessed half the courage my sister had, O would
have taken you and run away with Annabelle when O had
the chance. But Veronica had been denied her birthright,
and she died poor and destitute. O vowed to her that her*

daughter would want for nothing, that you would inherit what was rightfully yours - Veronica's portion of the Hastings' estate. And so my darling, beautiful Eleanor, in your marrying William I can die knowing that despite whatever sins I may have committed in this life, I have given my sister back her birthright. I hope that someday you will find it in your heart to forgive me, but if not, I will at least know that you are married to a man who will cherish and love you forever.

May God's grace forever shine on you.

Father

My heart was heavy as I folded Father's letter and placed it in my pocket. I would likely never forgive him for the cruel way he treated me, but learning the truth about Veronica shed new light on why he was so set on Eleanor marrying William. I hated to admit it, but he might have gotten that part right.

Eleanor was understandably in a fit of emotion. And who could blame her; after all, she had just learned that her mother wasn't really her mother—and that meant her father wasn't her real father, either. I got the feeling that in spite of his despicable treatment of her recently, Eleanor loved her father very much and felt betrayed that he would keep the truth about Veronica a secret from her all these years.

For the next hour or so I sat in silence, pondering over the implications of Father's letter to Eleanor and wondering what, if anything, should be done about it. I took one last look at Eleanor's father before ringing for Mrs. Weddington.

Eleanor's father didn't make it through the night. I had gone upstairs to bring Mother and Mrs. Weddington a tray of tea and breakfast fruits, and had decided that regardless of her inevitable protests, I was going to sit with Father again this morning. I perceived that Eleanor needed to be alone with him, to make her peace with everything he'd done. But as I approached his door, I could hear the faint sounds of Mother crying. I didn't bother to knock. When I entered his room, I discovered Mother sprawled across Father's cold and lifeless body and Mrs. Weddington kneeling at the side of the bed, doing her best to console her.

That afternoon, Mrs. Weddington placed a wreath on the door and ordered the servants to bring in sprays of fresh flowers in preparation for Father's services. It all happened very quickly. Guests dropped by to share their condolences and Father's business associates came one by one, hat in hand, to pay their respects. Father Patrick delivered a moving graveside eulogy and those in attendance at the service took turns dropping flowers into his grave before the servants began covering his lowered casket with dirt.

The entire household was in mourning. The master of the Hastings' estate was gone, and no one seemed to take his death harder than Eleanor and her mother. Mrs. Hastings couldn't come to grips with the realization that her husband was really dead. His life had ended so abruptly—after all, in her mind he was just sick. People got sick all the time, but they didn't die. She just couldn't make sense of it.

During the next several days, Eleanor's life force retreated to a place so deep inside me that it seemed as though she had disappeared altogether. She was, no doubt, deeply saddened by the sudden loss of her father, and severely shocked by the knowledge of her true identity. I, on the other hand, felt nothing. Actually, that's not exactly true; I did feel something—relief and anger. I knew it was morally wrong for me to feel this way and that it revealed a coldness in my character that I never knew existed, but I couldn't help it. I was relieved that he was gone, and I was angry that he hadn't gone sooner. I mean, if the stubborn and demanding fool was going to die, why not die before forcing me to marry William against my will? The irony of his timing seemed more than a mere coincidence. (I knew I was being selfish, but maintaining my anger allowed me to hide the fact that his motives might have been nobler than I cared to admit.)

The somber mood that overshadowed the household was depressing. I hadn't realized what an impact Eleanor's father had on the day-to-day business of keeping the estate alive with purpose and energy. I had always assumed Eleanor's mother was the driving force, but with Father gone, she had all but shut down, both emotionally and physically. She had never struck me as particularly loving toward Eleanor's father, so her reaction to his death surprised me. She was distraught, so lost in her grief that she no longer functioned normally. She was a mere shadow of her former self, content to pass her days in solitude. Mrs. Weddington attempted to assure me it would pass, that Mother was in mourning but would soon be her old self again. Yet I sensed we both knew otherwise. After all, Mother was no longer the mistress of the estate; she was now essentially a guest in someone else's home. The loss of status deflated her, and regardless of Mrs. Weddington's insistence to the contrary, I did not see Eleanor's mother recovering anytime soon—if ever.

In adjusting to the added demands now placed on me, my personal leisure time dwindled to the point that it was virtually nonexistent. My schedule quickly morphed into one typical of the mistress of an estate. When I wasn't signing papers; writing letters; responding to invitations; or approving flower arrangements, menus, and china selections; I was overseeing Christine's schooling and finishing lessons. This meant coordinating with her tutors and monitoring her progress on a regular basis. Additionally, as protocol deemed appropriate, I assumed the social obligation of making calls on behalf of both Eleanor's mother and myself as the new Mrs. Hamilton—a name to which I was not adjusting gracefully. Nor did I possess any desire to do so. This obligation included volunteering at Marenburg's hospital once a week and working with the heads of local charities to provide food, clothing, and medical supplies to the poor. It also included visiting the families of our servants to bring them baskets of food and small luxuries such as sugar and certain varieties of herbs and spices that were not only difficult to find during the war, but also very expensive. During my designated "at home" time, I received callers, several of whom brought gifts to celebrate my marriage to William and left invitations for us to dine with them upon the colonel's return.

The days passed quickly, and no matter how much I accomplished, there was always more to be done. I marveled at how Eleanor's mother had managed to make running the estate look so easy, and I wasn't involved in half the charity work she normally performed. Mrs. Weddington continually reassured me that I would make my own way and find my own sense of balance in time, but her reassurances seemed to contain subtle hints of disapproval and skepticism. I knew I was not measuring up to the stature of her former mistress. I didn't worry about it too much, because I didn't intend to remain the mistress of the Hastings' estate for long.

In spite of all the added demands placed on me, I remained preoccupied with my own agenda. The problem was finding the necessary time to act on it, for with so much requiring my attention, it was difficult to carve out the time I needed to formulate a reasonable plan for reclaiming my life as Beth Arrington and finding my way back to Jonathan.

The death of Eleanor's father further complicated matters because three weeks after Father's death, I received a letter from William.

Dearest Eleanor,

I hope you will forgive me for not writing sooner, but I received the shocking news of your father's death just this morning. It grieves me so that you have had to bear the sadness of your loss in my absence. I wish so that I had been there to offer you my comfort. I suspect by now you have had the entire burden of handling the affairs of the estate placed dauntingly upon your shoulders, and you without the support of your husband to guide you. I do not wish to place any degree of importance on myself, for I know you to be capable of handling any task required, yet I know that if I were there I could help to ease the transition.

After some negotiating on my part, I have convinced Major General Meade to grant his blessing in affording me a short leave so that I can be there to assist you. This was no small feat as the Confederacy has claimed victory at Petersburg and every able unit is on alert. Our men are entrenched throughout the surrounding areas, cutting off supplies to Lee and blocking railway lines wherever possible. I tell you this not to cause you worry or concern, but to indulge your curiosity regarding details. I hope that the news of my coming is welcome and that my presence may be a source of comfort for you. It will take a few days for me to make the required arrangements, but I promise I won't delay any more than necessary. Until then.

Your devoted husband,

William

P.S. Please pray for our men who find themselves in harm's way. Sometimes it seems the very jaws of hell are looming nearer. I long for the relief of your embrace.

William

    Whatever anxiety I had experienced up to now quadrupled when I read William's letter. His intent and desire to be by Eleanor's side during what he understood to be a heart-breaking and difficult time for her was sweet and genuine. He obviously longed to be a husband to her. Yet knowing he was coming home made my situation even more urgent. William would expect me to fully receive him into my bed where he could provide me with the full measure of a husband's comfort; and in fairness to him, he had every right, legally and morally, to expect that of me. His devotion touched me, and I could sense that Eleanor was equally moved by his desire to be by her side. But I also perceived a sense of guilt emitting from her life force—a guilt which I did not fully comprehend.

    Regardless of sentiment, I was out of time. William's arrival would thwart my plans and make it impossible for me to move forward with my intention to find Jonathan. The simple truth was, I was married. By now, Jonathan would have given up on the idea of us ever being together. Even if I could find him, there was no guarantee he would even talk to me. Why should he?

I scolded myself repeatedly for not acting sooner, for waiting all these months for someone to come for me or for something to happen that would put me back in control of my life. Instead of taking charge of the situation when I had time on my hands and to spare, I'd spent day after day feeling sorry for myself and pining away at the cottage, making sketches of the past and dreaming of what should have been.

I had been foolish and I knew it. So tonight, I wouldn't dream about what might have been or what should have been. Tonight, I would do something that I should have done months ago—I would take charge of my future.

As I lay in my oversized four-poster bed, cradled in the luxury of crisp white linen, I considered carefully the details of three potentially viable plans, mulling over the possible outcome of each. With the promise of William's imminent return, Eleanor's life force was back. Perhaps she sensed that he could fill the void left by her father's death. Whatever the reason, she was returning with a vengeance.

Intuitively, I sensed a shift was underway and I knew that time was running out for me. I could not fool myself into remaining a passive player, hoping for some magical moment when all was well again in my timeline and the Grace of the future would come for me. Grace was obviously playing by the rules, but I was out of time, and therefore the "rules" were moot as far as I was concerned. I no longer cared about alternate timelines or changing history. If I couldn't get back to the twenty-first century on my original timeline, then I would enter it on another; I'd deal with the repercussions once I got there. I needed to find Jonathan—to find him and tell him everything—and then hope he would allow me to stay with him until his reclamation was complete. Jonathan was a traveler, after all, or at least he would become such after his reclamation. Surely, once he heard the whole story, once he learned how much he and I would love each other in the future, he would move heaven and earth to take me home, regardless of the rules.

My eyes grew heavy as I contemplated every aspect of my plan, searching for holes in my logic, but I could find no flaws—at least, none that bore any major significance.

When I could no longer fight against the increasing weight of my eyelids, I relented and closed my eyes. Within minutes, my mind and body settled into a peaceful state of rest. It felt so good to let go and allow my spirit the freedom to wander. I drifted aimlessly through time, revisiting memories—a moment here, and a moment there—with no particular rhyme or reason guiding my course. I watched myself as Beth walking hand in hand with Jonathan at the duck pond adjacent to the recreation center in Andersen, and then I observed from a distance as we rode bikes along the trail to the waterfalls. I had been so amazed by the beauty of the falls that day that I'd failed to notice Jonathan watching my every move. When a gentle wave of wind blew my hair to the side, his eyes traced the contour of my neck. In what appeared to be a completely natural reflex, he raised his hand and started to stroke my hair with the back of his fingers while I wasn't looking; but when I moved suddenly, he changed his mind and instead reached up and straightened his baseball cap—the cap that had quickly become my favorite. He drew in a nervous breath and blew it out slowly. When I finally turned to face him, he was perfectly composed. Then, in the blink of an eye, we were sitting next to each other at the grand piano in Jonathan's house, battling each other with impromptu renditions of "Three Blind Mice." I longed to linger, to relive these lost moments from my life as Beth, but the images only held briefly before dissolving from view and transforming into another scene.

An unexplained impulse urged me to shift directions, and obeying the impulse I saw myself in the distance as Eleanor, sitting next to Jonathan by the river on our last day together, before he rode away to rejoin his unit. The memory wasn't exact for we appeared more relaxed with each other than we had been on that day, and Jonathan seemed happier than I remembered. I was compelled to look more closely, and as I did, I was able to discern two distinct images in the body of the person sitting next to Jonathan. Not surprisingly, one was Eleanor's image and the other was mine. It was like watching two versions of the same movie with one reel superimposed over the other. Eleanor's image was the more distinct of the two; this made me uneasy until the image of me as Beth laid her head on Jonathan's shoulder and he smiled.

Without warning, a strong rush of wind whisked me away from the trio at the river's edge, and I found myself flying rapidly through the densely wooded area adjacent to the river's winding course. The wind forced its way through the thick clusters of trees, clearing a path directly in front of me and enticing me to follow in its wake. The pleasing odors of mature pine needles and crisp running water permeated the air around me, inviting me to pause and take note of my surroundings; but a persistent push from behind urged me forward.

I recognized the bend in the river immediately, but the surrounding trees and shrubs were different, smaller. I heard the shrill scream of a child and watched as a younger version of Eleanor bobbed up and down, arms flailing frantically in the pool of deep water near the river's bend. She was in a panic until an equally younger version of William dove in and pulled her to safety. Two other boys stood at the bank of the river watching intently, one of whom wore a triumphant grin on his face. I knew instinctively that the two boys were Eleanor's older brothers. A profound sense of sadness flooded over me as I observed them. They were so young, so strong looking, and so full of life. William was clearly the eldest of the three by at least five or six years. By my estimation, Eleanor was only six or seven years old, which meant William was probably seventeen or eighteen. That might explain my reaction at the sight of him, for he was wickedly handsome, and judging by the muscles rippling beneath the wet shirt that clung indecently to his form as he climbed out of the river, he was enviously solid.

A new gust of air rose suddenly and ignoring my silent pleas to tarry, it hoisted me upward and carried me speedily away. After traveling some distance, the wind gradually began to fade until it finally released its hold on me and left me hovering, suspended, over the very same bend in the river where I had been just moments earlier—only the landscape was more mature and I was alone.

I waited with anticipation for a new scene to materialize when without warning, the sky suddenly turned black and the air around me began to stir, slowly at first, and then more rapidly. Pockets of energy began to explode in front of me and with each eruption of energy, the air gained momentum, forming itself into a spinning whirlwind that steadily increased in energy and speed until the river was forced upward into a tornado-like spiral.

I stared in awe at the watery vortex as the giant funnel twisted and bent back and forth, altering the natural flow of the river. It was like watching Poseidon's finger churning the river with all the force he could muster. Then something truly magical happened. Bright beams of color began emanating from the core of the funnel, casting brilliant hues of purple, green, and blue in every direction. The vibrant patterns of light mesmerized me. I was acutely aware that this was a dream, and because of that I found it peculiar that I should perceive such vivid colors, for I knew subconsciously that experts considered dreaming in color scientifically impossible. It mystified me. It was a phenomenon I couldn't remember ever experiencing before. I hoped the memory of it wouldn't fade the moment I awakened.

I was contemplating this when all of a sudden the funnel began to swell. It brightened to an intense, vibrant yellow, causing everything within its water-sprayed trajectory to glow. The water beneath where I hovered instantly became alive with energy, gravitating toward the beckoning call of the vortex. Streams of visible energy began flowing from directly beneath me toward the center of the spinning water and then began to gather in the funnel's core, gaining height and strength with every rotation. The energy gradually increased until it enveloped the entire vortex and gyrated at the very tip of the funnel's core. It was a remarkable sight. I suddenly felt strong and powerful—so powerful it frightened me.

I watched the phenomenon with amazement, noting how the rising sheets of water provided a perfect backdrop for the blazing beams of light. When the vortex could no longer contain the light, the center of the water funnel burst into thousands of tiny water droplets, each glowing an intense shade of yellow. I studied the flaming beads and watched as they began to pair themselves off into sets of two. I gasped the moment I realized I was suddenly surrounded by hundreds of sets of glowing yellow eyes—eyes that were watching me.

My initial instinct was to run, but then it struck me that these were not like Bailey's threatening yellow eyes. Bailey's eyes were flat and lifeless, exuding no true light. They hinted at something artificial—merely mimicking light when surrounded by darkness. His eyes made me recoil. But these beautiful glowing eyes had the opposite effect. They made me feel safe and protected, as if a hundred guardians were watching over me and forming a protective shield around me.

The eyes moved closer, gathering around me until I was completely encompassed in their light. The sensation of movement alerted me that I was being lifted away from where I hovered, and within seconds I found myself at the very top of the vortex—which by now had mushroomed out as if preparing to receive me. The surrounding yellow eyes deposited me at the mouth of the mushroom and then gathered into one impressive stream of light directly above me. In the flash of a second, the beam of light shot downward and pushed me into the heart of the vortex.

The next thing I knew I was underwater, completely submerged and heading straight toward the bottom of the river. I wanted to fight against the forces both pushing and pulling me downward, but I somehow understood that such a fight would be in vain. Instead, I closed my eyes and submitted to the powerful pull of the light. Within moments, the sensation of being pulled down disappeared and was replaced by a force equally as powerful. It lifted me upward through the water. In a matter of seconds, I broke through the surface and before I could gather my wits and catch my breath, I felt the security of dry land beneath my feet.

When at last I opened my eyes, I found myself standing on the bank of the river separating the upper and lower Palisades in Wyoming.

Birds tweeted with excitement in the surrounding fir trees and the flowing water playfully danced along its winding course. The sudden roar of a plane caught me by surprise. My heart thrilled at the sight of its jet trail forming a line that divided the blue sky in half. Off to the side and a little further away, I saw an airplane disappear into a bed of puffy white clouds. I waited with enthusiasm for it to reappear on the other side, and I smiled when it did.

Then, just as it had earlier, a rush of wind lifted me off the ground and began carrying me from place to place. The places I visited were familiar but the memories were not, for they were not *my* memories.

A scene opened in front of me. I was in the great room at Jonathan's ranch. Jonathan was seated next to Grace at their grand piano. She was playing a Hayden Sonata. I was taken aback by the sight of her— graceful as always, and truly angelic as her fingers floated over the keys. I had never heard her play before, and I paused for a moment to consider why that was. Jonathan sat with his eyes closed, listening intently to every note.

"There!" he said suddenly. "Right there. Did you hear it?"

Grace shook her head and smiled. "No. I still don't have a clue what it is you're hearing. Are you sure you aren't just entertaining yourself at my expense?"

"As tempting as that might be, no. There's a flaw in the publisher's edition of this sonata. The trills are too . . ." he searched for the right word, "happy."

I chuckled, but quickly caught myself when he suddenly raised his eyes and looked in my direction. He shifted his glance around the room and then turned back to the music.

"You think it should sound more like this?" Grace played the segment with the trills again, this time a half step lower. Jonathan listened and then shook his head.

"Closer, but it's still not right."

"How about you run along and find someone else to torment, okay?" Grace pushed on Jonathan's arm as if she were trying to shove him away from her. Jonathan grabbed her by the wrist and started jabbing her gently in the ribs with his free hand.

"Knock it off, you idiot," Grace said between chuckles, but Jonathan persisted until Grace had finally had enough. "Go away!" she said sternly. "Go find someone to tutor, will you? You're driving us crazy around here."

I was enjoying the playful banter between brother and sister when the scene suddenly faded from view and I found myself transported to the recreation center across from the high school in Andersen. I was in the corner of the practice room where Jonathan was playing Chopin's Etude in E. His eyes were closed as he soared through the climax of the piece and on to its peaceful resolution. He tilted his head slightly and leaned forward as the last tones of the final chord faded. There was a commotion outside the door and Jonathan turned around and quickly rose to his feet.

I knew exactly what was coming next.

Jonathan exited the room and joined Mr. Laden, Darla, and me—as Beth—in the hallway. I eavesdropped on the conversation between Mr.

Laden, Beth, and Jonathan, mouthing the words as they spoke. This was a conversation I had replayed repeatedly in my mind for the first few weeks after meeting Jonathan. I watched from a distance as the color in Beth's cheeks brightened with a subtle blush which, judging by his grin, Mr. Laden seemed to notice.

When Beth and Darla turned and headed for the door, I naturally assumed I would follow them. But for whatever reason, I remained with Jonathan and Mr. Laden. Both men watched the door close as the girls exited.

"There, my friend, goes one of life's cruel ironies," Mr. Laden said, shaking his head sadly.

Jonathan raised an eyebrow. "Indeed."

Mr. Laden gave Jonathan a strange look. "You know who she is?"

Jonathan caught himself and shrugged. "She's obviously someone important if *you* know her."

"Indeed," Mr. Laden nodded. "Elizabeth Arrington was one of the most talented pianists of the decade."

"Was?" Jonathan asked.

"Yes . . . until a tragic car accident about a year and a half ago damaged her hand. She lay in a coma for months—finally pulled out of it a not too long ago—but the damage to her tendons and nerves was too far gone. For a while, there was a rumor spreading through the guild that they would have to amputate. Fortunately, it didn't come to that."

Jonathan took in Mr. Laden's story with interest, which made me smile. Jonathan already knew this.

All part of his façade, I chuckled to myself.

"She will play again," Jonathan uttered under his breath. Mr. Laden heard him and shook his head.

"No," he said with finality. "It was a miracle they could save her hand at all, but . . ." he paused, "she'll never play again. That's the tragic irony of it all. To think, a god-given talent like hers, gone."

"Hmm," Jonathan replied.

The scene suddenly closed and Jonathan and Mr. Laden were gone. A split second later, I found myself sitting as an invisible passenger in Jonathan's car as he headed toward Jackson. He was on the phone, but I wasn't sure who he was talking to.

"Okay, it's done," Jonathan said into his phone. There was a brief pause and then, "No. Nothing from either direction." There was another short pause. "It's too late for that. I'm well past caring about their opinions." This time there was a much longer silence as Jonathan listened with growing irritability. Then finally, "Your job is to observe, that's it." A short pause, and then, "I'd advise against it."

The scene dissolved and once more, I was carried away in a surge of wind. I found myself at the ranch again. This time, Jonathan was seated at the piano and playing Eleanor's Theme. I recognized the simple melody immediately. Grace glided down the stairs and entered the room, stepping quietly until she stood beside Jonathan at the piano.

"I haven't heard you play that in a very long time," she said softly.

Jonathan ignored her and continued playing.

"Jonathan?" Grace pressed.

Jonathan nodded. "She's here, Grace."

"Jonathan, please!"

"Nope. I promise you, it's her." Jonathan gestured toward the piano with his chin.

"I thought you came to terms with this years ago!"

"It's not like that, Grace." Jonathan stopped playing and turned towards his sister. "This is different. She's here."

Grace took a deep breath and sighed. "Oh Jonathan, please don't do this."

"It's okay," he smiled. "I know what you're afraid of, but you're wrong. She's here." Jonathan reached for Grace's hand and placed it on his chest over his heart. "She's here," he said pressing his hand over hers.

Grace stared at Jonathan for a moment and then smiled a half smile and nodded. "Jonathan, you can't know."

Jonathan got up and walked out of the room, leaving Grace behind at the piano. He went down the hallway to his bedroom and made his way to the Victorian chest in the corner of the room. He glanced briefly at the pair of old framed photographs that sat on top of the chest and then opened the drawer and began fumbling through the contents until he found what he was looking for. He first pulled out a sketch of the ranch. The paper had yellowed and the drawing had faded over the years, but I still recognized it. It was the same sketch I'd given him at the cottage the afternoon before he left to join his regiment. He set the drawing aside and dug deeper into the drawer before pulling out a set of aged parchment papers, rolled up and tied with a red ribbon. He carefully untied the ribbon and unrolled the papers, smoothing them against the top of the dresser, revealing the original score to Eleanor's Theme. He smiled, and then setting the parchment aside, reached one more time into his drawer and pulled out another sheet of yellowed sketch paper—this one smaller than the last.

Jonathan marched back into the great room and found Grace still standing next to the piano.

"This . . ." he said handing Grace the sketch. "This is how I know."

Grace reached for the sketch. I floated behind her and looked over her shoulder at the drawing. I gasped when I saw the picture of two hands one perfect and flawless, the other twisted and bent, almost into a fist. I recognized them instantly—they were both mine. But I couldn't explain how Jonathan had come to have a sketch of them in his possession. There was a caption at the bottom of the sketch, but it was written in an old-style font and I couldn't make out the words before the scene began to fade into nothingness.

I reached outward as if I might somehow bring it back, but my efforts were fruitless. Within moments, the familiar sound of rushing wind returned and I was whisked away. This time, when the wind ceased there was no new scene, only the familiar sound of wood crackling softly in the background and the sense that I was again cradled in the comfort of crisp linens. When I opened my eyes, everything was just as I expected. I was back in the 1800s, lying in the bed that now belonged to William and Eleanor.

I threw back my covers and reached for the lantern that sat on top of the side table. I turned up the flame and made my way up to Eleanor's former bedroom. The room hadn't been occupied since the wedding weeks earlier. A wave of panic washed over me until I felt the reassurance that nothing had been disturbed since I'd vacated the room.

I set my lantern on the vanity and began quietly rummaging through the drawers, sifting through their contents until at last I found what I was looking for. In the confusion and excitement of Eleanor's seemingly miraculous recovery, and following the wake of Christopher's untimely death, I had stored them away and forgotten about them. As I held the several sheets of rolled parchment paper in my hand, Grace's words to me my first night here struck with sudden clarity.

"Find Jonathan and give him this."

I was confused as to what she meant that night; her request was in complete opposition to the original warning that I not interfere or interact with anyone in Jonathan's sphere of influence. At the time, the admonition was moot. I had expected to come when Jonathan was a small child, and I expected to come as Elizabeth Arrington—someone he would neither know nor remember. Therefore, there was very little chance of us having any interaction with each other. I never expected my journey to the past would require taking over someone else's body—and not just anyone's body, but the one person most likely to influence and potentially alter Jonathan's life path. Those critical details had not been part of the proposal, and I suppose if they had been brought to light ahead of time, Jonathan would never have agreed to Grace's plan. As close as Jonathan and Grace were, I couldn't help but wonder how it was that she managed to hide the risky details of her plan from him. Why would she keep something this important from the person she loved more than anyone in the world? These were questions that had plagued my mind often during the last several months, particularly after realizing I wouldn't be going home anytime soon.

Initially, once I recovered from the shock of discovering that my spirit now inhabited Eleanor's body, I had concluded that Grace's "plan" was for me to fulfill some role in bringing Eleanor back to health. It made sense at the time because Grace had shared with me that my traveling was part of a bigger plan—that nothing was happening by accident. I had presumed upon learning that Eleanor had been near death only moments prior to my arrival that my role here was to somehow unite my life force with hers until she was strong enough to cope on her own. Two weeks had seemed a fair amount of time for this to occur, and then I would be on my way back to the twenty-first century.

But of course, that's not what happened.

Carefully, I untied the crimson string that held the rolled pages together and smoothed out the sheets of parchment. They were blank, just as I remembered. I pressed the pages against the top of the vanity and stared at them for several minutes before beginning to cry. Through my tears, I located my quill and ink container and quickly went to work. It took the remainder of the night and into the wee hours of the morning, before I finished penning the original score to Eleanor's Theme.

Hope

CHAPTER 16

*A*s a result of Eleanor's father's death and becoming accustomed to my new position of responsibility on the estate, it became necessary that I postpone my planned visit to Jonathan's mother beyond the respectable time of mourning and the adjustment period for a new bride. This necessity put me on edge, and that edginess increased significantly with the arrival of two particular posts—one from Mr. and Mrs. Thomas Stanford Rollings and the other from Miss Grace Rollings. The letter from Jonathan's parents was brief and formal, congratulating the colonel and me on our recent marriage and wishing us both a long and bounteous life together. They also extended their sincerest condolences and apologized for not writing sooner to convey their sympathy. Apparently they had been "traveling." There was no mention of Jonathan, nor any word of his reassignment.

Grace's letter was a little less formal, but distressing nonetheless. It read:

My dearest Mrs. Hamilton,

I wish to express my deepest sympathy at the loss of

your father. You no doubt miss him terribly and have suffered a tremendously grievous loss. I know how devastating it is to lose someone close to you. Please know that your family is ever in my prayers.

On a happier note, I was surprised to learn of your recent marriage. I know I am not the first to congratulate you, but I want you to know that I wish you and your husband every happiness together. I do hope you will allow me to call on you, and it goes without saying that you are most welcome here at any time.

My mother spoke of her visit with you prior to your wedding. I wish to bestow upon you my very deepest gratitude and appreciation for the colonel's hand in securing my brother's transfer and promotion to Captain. He is young for such a lofty title, but I have every confidence that he will serve in the position honorably. Please extend my personal thanks to your husband for his kindness and generosity and note that we are, and forever will be, in your debt.

Yours faithfully,

Grace

I read and reread both letters several times, hoping to find some message hidden between the lines; but try as I might, I found none. By the sounds of it, Jonathan's family had only recently learned of my wedding, but it wouldn't be long before the news reached Jonathan, if it hadn't already, and this filled me with unbearable anxiety and regret. I desperately wanted Jonathan to understand why I had married William, but I knew deep down that there was nothing I could say or do that would matter at this point. Jonathan would learn of my marriage, and regardless of his feelings for me, that would be the end of us. Unless I could somehow let him know that the marriage had not been consummated, that I did not love William, Jonathan would have no reason to return for me. And that meant that the future would be forever altered. I had to risk sending a message to Jonathan. I needed to act quickly, and my only hope of doing so without raising eyebrows or speculation was to somehow convince Grace to once again intervene on my behalf, an act that if she were caught, would put her own reputation at risk.

The following Thursday, I arranged to visit Jonathan's mother during her "at home" time. Although both Mrs. Weddington and Lucinda protested, I insisted on traveling unchaperoned. Lucinda was extremely loyal and devoted to me, so I knew she wouldn't say anything, but Mrs. Weddington was another story. She was deeply dedicated to the Hastings' estate, but regardless of the fact that I was now the mistress of the estate, I couldn't help but sense that her loyalties still lay with Eleanor's mother rather than with me. I didn't blame her though, I appreciated the depth of her affection—in fact, I was counting on it.

I arrived at the Rollings' home around half past ten, just in time for Mrs. Rollings' morning "at home" tea. She received me with all the warmth and affection customary of the day, and immediately made me feel at ease in her home. She was so different from Eleanor's mother.

"I'm so pleased that you've come, Mrs. Hamilton," she greeted me.

I'd had a difficult time getting used to being called "Eleanor" when I arrived in the 1800s so many months ago, but I would never get used to being called "Mrs. Hamilton."

Jonathan's mother was wearing a silk lavender dress trimmed with black satin ribbons and pearls along the bodice and sleeves. Her dress was a little before its time in that it scooped downward at the waistline in both the front and back. It wasn't over-stated, quite the contrary. It was simple and modest, but at the same time very elegant and expensive looking. I hadn't noticed any of the women in Marensburg wearing a similar fashion.

"Would you prefer to sit inside or out in the garden?" Mrs. Rollings continued. "The roses have recently bloomed, so it's really quite lovely out there."

"The garden would be perfect," I assured her.

She led me through the sitting room and past their dining hall toward the back of the house. The Rollings' home was significantly smaller than the Hastings' estate, yet it was tastefully decorated in a style that suggested they were wealthier than people may have surmised.

The garden was intimate and free flowing, alive with color and variety—a sharp contrast to the grandeur of the Hastings' gardens which were manicured to resemble the formal gardens of English royalty.

I was determined to communicate the real purpose for my visit, but I didn't know where to begin. I decided to open with the usual small talk.

"Please tell me who made your dress," I began. Fashion was normally a safe topic with women. "It's so different from any I've seen. Did you design it yourself?"

"Oh, good gracious, no!" she laughed. "I am far from accomplished in the areas of design. I'm afraid I must confess my husband surprised me with this dress after returning from one of his many travels."

I raised an eyebrow when she used the word "travels." "How very generous of Mr. Rollings," I suggested.

"Oh yes, indeed. Mr. Rollings is most certainly in the habit of spoiling me, I'm afraid." She suddenly blushed. "Oh, nothing like the way I'm sure your father spoiled your mother—or the way Mr. Hamilton will spoil you—but Mr. Rollings is exceedingly thoughtful of me when he's away on business."

"Does he travel often?" I asked.

"I'm afraid he does. Even more so since the war."

"I see," I replied.

"Permit me to change the subject, Mrs. Hamilton. I would much prefer to hear about you and your family. How is your mother? I regret that I haven't seen her since our return from New York. It must be so difficult for her to cope with the loss of your father. For you, as well, I'm sure."

"Yes, of course, thank you. We all thought he would recover; we were stunned when his condition took a turn for the worse. Thank you for inquiring after Mother. I'll let her know you asked about her."

"I would appreciate it if you would." Mrs. Rollings picked up a pitcher of tea and a small cup. "May I?" she asked.

"Yes, thank you," I replied. She handed me the cup and then poured one for herself.

"Now then," she said once she was settled, "how is Colonel Hamilton? Do you hear from him often?"

I started to take a sip of my tea, but instead set the cup down. "Colonel Hamilton is fine. In fact, I've only recently received word that he'll be home soon on leave."

"Oh, I'm delighted to hear that. You must be anxious to see him. It's my understanding that he was rushed away soon after your ceremony."

I turned away and sighed. This conversation was not going in the direction I intended. "Mrs. Rollings, I'm being very rude. I'm sure you must have plenty on your mind these days with your husband away so much and your son at war."

"Yes, of course, but I remain hopeful that the war will be over soon and my son returned safe and sound." She quickly caught herself and covered her mouth with her fingers. "Oh, my dear, how dreadfully callous and unfeeling of me. You who have lost so much. Please, forgive me."

"No forgiveness is required, I assure you." I couldn't help but shake my head as I listened to Jonathan's mother speak. She was so proper—so unlike Jonathan. It was easy for me to see where Grace got her gift for manners and propriety.

"My dear, you are far too kind," she replied.

"Thank you, Mrs. Rollings, but I assure you I'm not."

I was anxious to get down to business, but also nervous. I decided to inch my way into the subject by first asking about Jonathan.

"How is Jona . . ." I stopped mid-word and corrected myself. "Pardon me, I meant to inquire about your son."

Mrs. Rollings scrutinized my expression for several moments before answering. "He's fine, thankfully."

I smiled a half smile and looked away from Mrs. Rollings' penetrating gaze. "That's good," I nodded. I stood and pretended to admire one of the rose bushes. "And he's . . . safe?"

"Yes, Mrs. Hamilton. As safe as we can hope for in these times."

I nodded again, but kept my back to Jonathan's mother. "That's good," I said quietly.

There was an awkward silence for a moment, and then Jonathan's mother spoke.

"Mrs. Hamilton, I know of the sacrifice you made on behalf of my son. I imagine you would prefer not to speak of it, but I would be remiss if I didn't acknowledge it here in the privacy of your company."

I had to battle the lump in my throat to keep my emotions in check. "I love your son, Mrs. Rollings. I always have." I turned suddenly to face Jonathan's mother. She inclined her head and stared, gaping at me as though I had just admitted to some heinous crime. I figured I was on a roll now, and while I had her undivided attention I might as well tell her the real reason for my visit. I took a long deep breath before I began.

"Mrs. Rollings, I know you are immortal."

Mrs. Rollings' jaw dropped.

"I know about Cain and Abel, about the Lebas and Niaces. I know that God created other immortals when he created Adam and Eve, and that when Adam and Eve became mortal after partaking of the forbidden fruit, the 'other' immortals somehow managed to get trapped in Adam and Eve's fall from grace."

Jonathan's mother sat stiffly, her face expressionless. I paused briefly before continuing.

"I know about reclamation," I said, looking her square in the eyes. "And I know that soon, Jonathan and Grace will both go through a transformation process where their cells will reclaim their immortal nature."

I held Mrs. Rollings' gaze for a moment, but her blank expression made me uncomfortable so I looked away. There followed a prolonged silence that made the already awkward moment unbearable.

"Well? Aren't you going to say something?" I said abruptly. "Aren't you going to deny it and tell me I'm crazy?"

"Go on," she said quietly.

"What else do you need to hear? I know everything. I know the Lebas followed the example of Abel and the Niaces adopted the philosophy of Cain. I know about the council and the agreement between the two groups. And I know that there are others here as well, others known as Intruders and Possessors, and they—"

"Stop!" Mrs. Rollings stood suddenly, her face white. "I'm afraid I'm going to have to cut our visit short."

"Wait, please," I implored her. "Please don't send me away. I'm here because I'm desperate. I need your help."

"Mrs. Hamilton, I don't see how I can possibly help you. You're obviously very agitated and confused. It's no wonder, with the sudden loss of your father and being newly married and all, not to mention your new husband being forced to leave your side on your wedding night. Why it's—"

"This has nothing to do with my father's death or marriage or William or any of that! Please listen to me," I pleaded. "You must!"

Jonathan's mother started to turn away, but I grabbed her by the arm, determined to make her listen.

"Don't you understand? I'm not supposed to be here!"

The lump that had lodged in my throat suddenly burst into a series of uncontrollable sobs. "I'm from the future, Mrs. Rollings. Grace brought me here to hide me from a dangerous group of Intruders. Jonathan didn't want me to leave him, but Grace insisted that everything would be fine, but it wasn't fine. Nothing is fine. I couldn't travel because I'm not immortal like Grace, so she—or somebody higher up somewhere—put me in Eleanor's body. Eleanor was dying; you remember that, right? Nobody thought she would live, and then suddenly one night she was miraculously better. Think about what I'm saying. You must believe me!"

I stopped to catch my breath and tried to compose myself. Mrs. Rollings stared at me in disbelief. I could tell by the way her eyes dissected mine that she was trying her best to process everything I was saying and to decide whether I was sane or had completely lost my marbles.

"Even if what you're telling me is true," she held her hand up before I could interrupt her, "and I'm not saying that it is, why are you telling *me* this? And why *now*?"

"Because I need you to take me back!" I grabbed both of her hands and held them tightly. "Please, Mrs. Rollings, please take me home."

Mrs. Rollings stared at me for a long moment and then lowered her gaze.

"It's not that simple," she said, shaking her head. "If you know all this, then you also know that there are strict rules that forbid interference with—"

"Ugh!" I growled. "It's your damn *rules* that have kept me here for so long!"

Mrs. Rollings' eyes widened in shock. She freed her hands from mine and took a few steps backwards.

"I'm sorry, but it's true. Besides, Jonathan and I have already broken just about all the rules. He just doesn't know it yet."

Mrs. Rollings shook her head. "I don't understand."

"The day of the big scandal—you know, when I ran to Jonathan and kissed him—you remember, right?"

Jonathan's mother sat down slowly.

"I thought he was *my* Jonathan, the one from the future—the twenty-first century to be exact—but it wasn't him. It was *your* Jonathan. I just didn't realize my mistake until it was too late. I'm sure you can piece together the rest."

Mrs. Rollings sat quietly for a long time, staring blankly at the rose bushes. When she didn't respond I moved closer to her. She appeared to be oblivious to my presence, as though her mind was somehow miles away, completely detached from our conversation. I watched curiously as she continued to stare into the distance, devoid of expression. I waved my hand in front of her face, hoping to elicit some sort of response, but there was nothing.

"Mrs. Rollings?" I called hesitantly. Still nothing.

"Mrs. Rollings?" I called again, louder this time. Again, nothing.

When nearly ten minutes passed with still no reaction from her, I began to seriously worry. Perhaps she was having some sort of grand mal seizure. I remembered a student at my high school having one, and he was just as "out of it" as Mrs. Rollings. Only as I recall, he was clammy and vomited a lot. I was about to fetch the Rollings' housekeeper when Jonathan's mother suddenly snapped out of it.

"Mrs. Hamilton," she began, as if the past several minutes had not occurred, "even if what you're saying is true, there's no way I can help you—that any of us can help you."

I was dumbfounded by her nonchalance.

"But why?" I asked, disheartened by the sudden uneasiness in my gut.

"Because travelers cannot go forward in time—or more specifically, they can't travel to a time beyond their current timeline."

"But surely there are exceptions, right?" The small amount of hope I'd felt when I arrived was fading quickly.

"I'm afraid I don't have the answer to that. It's beyond our jurisdiction as travelers."

"Whose jurisdiction is it?" I asked, discouraged. "Can I speak to them?"

Mrs. Rollings shook her head. "I'm not sure there *is* a jurisdiction for something like this."

Just then, Mrs. Rollings' butler appeared in the doorway. "Pardon me, ma'am," he said in a gruff, yet kind voice.

"Yes, Robert, what is it?" Mrs. Rollings asked. I thought it unusual that she used his first name; Eleanor's mother and father would never have done that.

"This parcel has just arrived. I'm afraid it's from Mr. Rollings."

Jonathan's mother looked concerned as she took the letter from her servant. She unfolded the letter and read the message scribbled inside. A moment later, she turned to me, obviously shaken by what she had read.

"Please excuse me, Mrs. Hamilton. I'm afraid something has come up that requires my immediate attention." She handed the letter back to her servant and reached for my hand. She read my anxious expression and paused briefly. Choosing her words carefully, she said, "I will speak to Mr. Rollings about your situation as soon as he returns. He will know what to do."

I let out an emotional sigh of relief. For the first time in months, I felt a reason to hope. Relief washed over me with such enormity that my knees began to tremble.

"Oh, Mrs. Rollings, thank you! Thank you!"

"Please, don't thank me," she said quickly, "There's no guarantee that anyone will be able to help you. Now, I'm afraid I really must beg your pardon. Robert will see you to the door."

With that, Mrs. Rollings turned on her heel and disappeared into the house. Whatever news she'd received had obviously distressed her. It suddenly occurred to me that the parcel could have come from Jonathan; I had only assumed the letter was from her husband. An uneasy heaviness pulled at me. I wanted so much to know the content of that letter. But that was the last time I saw Mrs. Rollings.

When two days passed with no word from her or Grace, I returned to her home only to be met at the door by Robert, who politely informed me that Mrs. Rollings was indisposed. When I inquired about Grace, the response was the same.

The following week I tried once more to see Mrs. Rollings, but again was told that she was not receiving callers. Grace had allegedly joined her father in New York and wasn't due back for another week. Apparently, Mr. Rollings was working with several of Lincoln's constituents from the neighboring states, planning strategies for his reelection campaign. By now it had been nearly two weeks since my visit with Jonathan's mother, and the small amount of hope I'd felt when I left her house following our conversation had disappeared and given way to an unyielding feeling of dread. William would arrive any day now, and I knew that once he did I would have no chance of finding my way back to Jonathan—in this timeline or any other.

Sensing I had nothing to lose, I made one more attempt to see Mrs. Rollings and make contact with Grace. After recalling my dream from two weeks earlier, I determined to give fate a helping hand on the off chance that my dream was more than just a dream. There was no time for a trip to the cottage, so I quickly grabbed a blank sheet of parchment and using a quill and ink, sketched a crude rendition of my hands—Beth's hands. The sketch was rough and lacked dimension, but it captured the essence of what I was shooting for. Then, copying the sketch that Jonathan had shown Grace, at the bottom of the paper I scribbled, *"One of Life's Cruel Ironies . . ."*

I blew on the ink and fanned it until it appeared dry, then carefully rolled it inside the original score of "Eleanor's Theme." I tied the rolled parchment in place with the same crimson string that had held the blank sheets together when Grace first handed them to me well over a year earlier. Using a sheet of stationary, and choosing my words cautiously, I wrote a short message to Grace:

Dear Grace,

I wish to thank you for your kind words and well wishes on behalf of myself and Colonel Hamilton. I pray that someday you will understand how much your friendship means to me. Your brother seems to have a special regard for music. I hope you will do me the favor of giving this to him when he returns from the war.

Your faithful friend always,

Eleanor

I folded my note to Grace and tied it around the rolled parchment, then set it aside for the following morning when I would again attempt to call on the Rollings. I knew I was flirting with danger, but I didn't care. I would stop at nothing to get Grace's attention.

The sun was uncommonly hot that afternoon, so when Christine begged me to join her for a swim in the river, I happily agreed to go. With Lucinda in the role of chaperone, the three of us made our way down the path and through the woods until we arrived at the familiar bend in the river that had served as the family swimming hole for decades. Mrs. Weddington, who refused to join us (not that we thought she would), insisted on having the cook pack us a picnic lunch and some dry linens for the walk home later. We were in the midst of summer, and even though the afternoons were hot and humid and the evening air would not cool for several hours, Mrs. Weddington didn't wish to risk any of us catching a chill.

We wasted no time stripping down to our underclothes. As far as I was concerned, it was like swimming with our clothes on. I couldn't help but imagine what my companions would think of modern-day swimwear. It had been so long since I'd seen anyone in a swimsuit I'd forgotten that for the majority of my life, I'd had a tan tummy and legs.

We laid our clothes in three neat piles beside our picnic lunch and linens and then made a beeline for the water. Lucinda and Christine went in first; I stood knee-deep in the water and watched from a distance as they took turns dunking each other. The last time I'd been to the river was the day of my wedding to William, and I couldn't shake the image of him standing in the water, shirt soaked and clinging to his torso. He was, without a doubt, perfectly chiseled. I recalled the way William's eyes traced the shape of Eleanor's breasts through her soaked clothing, and a strange feeling of jealousy washed over me. There was no rational explanation for me to feel this way; what was it to me if William desired Eleanor? Yet, for some reason, this bothered me. Perhaps it was because it was further confirmation of how perfect Eleanor's body was, and knowing that my own could never equal hers. Besides, wasn't it just a little unfair that Eleanor was so naturally endowed and flawless? It's not like she had to work at it, either. Girls in the twenty-first century spent hours with personal trainers and months on special diets to even come close, and even then, the majority of them would still need plastic surgery to measure up to Eleanor's effortless beauty.

"What are you waiting for, Eleanor? Come in!" Christine called between girlish giggles.

"Be careful you two! The current is stronger here than you think." If I hadn't felt the words come out of my own mouth, I would have turned around to see who said them. I could only assume it was Eleanor who had spoken, and it made me uneasy to think she had surfaced so quickly without me sensing her presence.

"Don't worry, Miss Eleanor, I've got my eye on her," Lucinda replied.

"Let's use the rope! Can we? Please?" Christine called from the water.

Lucinda looked to me for an answer. "What do you say?"

I had no idea what they were referring to, so I nodded. Christine gave a gleeful yell and crawled up the riverbank toward an old mulberry tree that hovered near the edge of the water. I watched as she began climbing up the trunk of the tree. She reached for a large tree limb and swung her legs up onto one of its branches. A second later she disappeared behind the thick growth of leaves. Then, without warning, she came sailing out of the tree, hanging for dear life onto a long, thick rope that whirled her out over the water. She let go and plummeted into the river with a loud splash. She had entered the water from such a height it was several moments before she came up for air. When she finally did, much to my relief, she let out a holler that would equal the intensity of just about any rebel yell. Lucinda clapped with approval, and as soon as she was sure Christine was safely within reach of the shore, she swam out and used a long stick to pull the rope back to the base of the tree for another go.

The river's current was tricky—I could sense that much without going in very far. Judging by the pattern of the flow, it appeared that as long as we stayed in the deep pool at the elbow of the river, we would be fine; but if we ventured out too far, we would risk being swept away in the current. Lucinda and Christine seemed unbothered by the potential danger, but it was enough to keep my nerves on edge.

In spite of my edginess, when Christine motioned for me to take the rope, my response was automatic. Eleanor had obviously done this numerous times in the past and was not about to pass up the opportunity now, regardless of my inner pleadings to the contrary. Her life force was so strong I felt like a mere bystander, powerless of influence, mental or physical. So against my better judgment, I soon found myself high among the tree's branches, clinging on for dear life. I made the mistake of peering down at the water from the spot where moments before Christine had taken her leap. In reality, I couldn't have been more than twelve to fifteen feet above ground, but it might as well have been forty feet from my perspective. The rope was double-looped around the limb above me, which appeared to have been cleared of any branches or leaves, allowing the rope to slide easily back and forth along the limb's thick protrusion out over the deeper part of the water. It had obviously been used repeatedly as a "zip line" for years. I couldn't help but wonder what role William might have played in the mechanics of the setup, and for some reason, I easily imagined him spending the better part of some long-ago summer leading Charles and Miles in the endeavor.

I called upon my memories of high school physics to reason with Eleanor as to why this was a bad idea, suggesting everything from broken bones to rope burns; but while I was busy protesting, Eleanor was hitching her foot in the rope's loop and bracing us for takeoff. Without a second thought for our safety, she rocked forward and off we went. I dared not close my eyes, yet I couldn't watch, either. Instead, I did the only thing I could—I screamed.

We flew out over the water and at precisely the right moment, Eleanor released her hold on the rope and jumped. We hit the water with a bold splash and plunged deep below the surface before paddling our way up for air. Once safely above water, the thrill of the moment kicked in and like Christine, I let out a triumphant squeal.

For the better part of the afternoon, the three of us took turns plunging into the water's depths from the end of the swinging rope. Our confidence increased with each successful drop, and before long we began one-upping each other by finding creative ways to enter the water. The rush of adrenaline that occurred with each daring feat kept our energy and enthusiasm at maximum intensity until exhaustion finally kicked in and we lay sprawled across the flat side of a huge boulder in the sun to rest.

We absorbed the warmth of the late afternoon sun for several minutes before realizing we were all famished. I crawled down from the large rock and headed back to the spot where we had left our clothes and the lunch Mrs. Weddington had put together for us.

I was just about to reach for the large picnic basket when a host of blackbirds suddenly fluttered from their perch in a nearby tree and flew away squawking. A low rustling noise in the surrounding brush alerted my senses that someone or something was nearby. I stood, frozen, unsure if the source of the activity was human or animal—not that it mattered. Both posed a potential threat for which I was equally unprepared. My "fight or flight" instinct told me to run, but I couldn't move. I glanced back toward Christine and Lucinda. They were both sitting very still and even from a distance, I noticed the obvious fear in their expressions. Neither of them made a sound, but kept their eyes fixed on the movement in the bushes.

I bent down slowly and picked up a large rock, ready to strike at whatever threatened us, if necessary. All of a sudden, a wounded fox shot out of the underbrush and darted past me. I let out a started scream and sucked in so much air I began to hyperventilate. The fox paused briefly to acknowledge my distress and then hurried on his way down to the bank of the river.

I followed the fox's uneven gait until he was safely out of sight and then gave a heavy sigh of relief. I bent over and rested my hands on my knees, taking several deep breaths until my heart rate finally slowed and I could breathe normally again. Once composed, I stood and looked over at Lucinda and Christine. They were both standing and pointing in my direction. I couldn't make out what they were trying to tell me, but it was obvious that whatever they saw frightened them. I spun around quickly and found myself face to face with four Rebel soldiers.

Capture

CHAPTER 17

*J*udging by the look on the soldier's faces, they were not just passing through. The one closest to me let out a low whistle as he eyed me from head to toe. I stepped backward and hunted for the stack of dry linens Mrs. Weddington had sent with us. I started to reach down and grab one of the sheets when another soldier stepped forward and placed his foot on the stack.

"Afternoon ma'am," he said in a thick southern drawl.

"Please, sir," I said, trying to sound as though I presumed positive intent on his part. "May I?"

He shook his head slowly, and shot a quick look at his companions. "Boys, I think we done hit the mother lode." The two men standing furthest away from me laughed. One of them tipped his hat at me and offered a mocking bow.

"Woo-eeeh!" he mused. "She's as fresh as the summer day is long!"

I took a deep breath and struggled to hide the fact that I was trembling. "Sir," I said, addressing the one with his foot on the pile of linens. "I insist you remove your boot."

He let out a dark chuckle. "Now why would I want to do a thing like that?"

Frustrated, I stood up straight and shot each of the four men a determined glare. "Gentlemen, I suggest you take your leave this minute."

"My, my, missy," the first one began.

"That's *Mrs. Hamilton*, to you . . . Mrs. Colonel William Hamilton to be exact." I don't know what prompted my sudden response, but it flew out of my mouth with such deliberate contempt that it surprised all four of them.

"Whoa." The soldier standing on the linens removed his foot and let out a sneering laugh that made the hair on the back of my neck stand on edge. "Did you hear that Amos? We got us a colonel's wife here!"

"Yes, sir, I reckon we done hit us the jackpot."

I caught a movement out of the corner of my eye and turned around in time to see Lucinda and Christine approaching.

"Oh my! Boys, looky what we got coming," the one called Amos said as he motioned toward Lucinda and Christine. "That young'n there's a real peach. Yes, sir, a fine one at that."

"Leave her alone, do you hear me!" I ordered. "She's nothing to you!" I put my hand up and gestured for Lucinda and Christine to stop.

"Miss Eleanor!" Lucinda called as they got closer.

"Lucinda, stop! That's an order! Do you understand me?"

Lucinda stopped in her tracks and stood with her mouth open, gaping at me. "Miss Eleanor?" she repeated, confused.

"Lucinda, take Christine back to the house—right now!"

"Eleanor, no!" Christine yelled.

"Lucinda! Go!"

"Eleanor, stop! Please! I won't leave you here," Christine cried.

"Dammit, child, you'll do as I say!" I ordered. Lucinda and Christine both stared at me in shock. Our uninvited guests seemed equally stunned by my expletive.

Christine began to cry. "No, Eleanor, please!" she begged.

"Lucinda, send for Mr. Edwards. Do you understand me?"

"Yes ma'am," Lucinda nodded. With that, she yanked Christine by the arm and pulled her away.

"Run!" I yelled after them. Christine was still looking back at me and fighting Lucinda's determined grip. "Run!" I yelled again.

The man called Amos started to go after them, but he was quickly stopped by the man I ascertained to be the leader of the group. "Leave 'em be, Amos. We got what we came for."

"They'll be sending for help, you heard 'em," Amos argued.

"Won't do 'em no good," the leader replied.

"Elias is right, Amos," the third man spoke up again. "They won't find hide nor hair of us time they get here."

As soon as Lucinda and Christine disappeared up the path leading back to the house, I turned around to face the four men. "You best be gone when they get here." I tried my best to sound as though I wasn't frightened. "Men around here won't take kindly to your sort."

Amos stepped toward me until his face was just inches from mine. He turned slightly to one side and spat on the ground and then looked me square in the eyes. I wanted to wince at the foul stench of his breath, but I was determined to stand my ground. He grabbed my neck just beneath the jawbone and forced me closer to him.

"You got some kinda gumption, lady," he snarled. His breath was hot and rancid. "Makes me think you need to learn a lesson or two."

"That's enough, Amos," the fourth man said. Up until now, he'd been a silent observer. "We got our orders."

Amos spat again, but maintained his contemptuous glare. He licked his lips tauntingly as he shifted his gaze from my mouth to my breasts. "Captain didn't say we couldn't teach her a thing or two about manners."

"Amos has a point, Levi," Elias spoke up. "Ask me, we could all teach this one something."

He moved closer and slapped Amos on the back, sending another wave of Amos' repulsive breath in my direction. I started to gag against Amos's fingers, which were still clasped snuggly at the base of my jaw.

"You first Amos," Elias sneered. "G'on and get her warmed up for me, then I'll show her what it's like to be with a real man."

I stood erect, struggling against Amos' hold on me, but determined to maintain my resolve. I knew to try to outrun them would be futile, but I had to try something. I resolved that if I could somehow manage to hold them off until Lucinda could send for help, I might get out my predicament undamaged.

Amos laughed. "That'd be a pleasure, but after I get done with her, there won't be much left that's worth the gettin'."

Elias let out a low growl. "Nah, this one's got plenty for us all, don't ya honey?" He paused briefly and lowered his eyes slowly following the shape of my body. "Well, get on with it, Amos. Warm her up so we can all have a go at her."

A sickening chill surged through my veins. This went far beyond any horror I'd experienced with Bailey. I began twisting and pulling against Amos' grip, struggling with all my strength to free myself.

Amos let out a low chuckle and used his free hand to grab me from behind. He reached up and clutched the hair at the back of my head and then pressed his lips hard against mine, attempting to force my mouth open. I reached up and hit him square against the side of his head. I hadn't realized it, but I was still holding the rock in my hand, so I struck him with as much force as I could. He let out an angry growl that turned my remaining resolve instantly into fear. I knew I had crossed a deadly line.

Amos released his hold on me and without hesitating, drew back his hand and slapped me hard across my jaw, knocking me off balance. I immediately felt the warm sensation of blood coating my lips as I staggered backwards.

"Damnation, Amos! What do you think you're doing?" Elias grabbed Amos by the arm. "Captain'll kill you for that!"

"Elias is right, Amos," the one called Levi spoke up. "Captain said to use care with this one. We best get a move on."

Amos glared at me. "You boys go on ahead; me and the misses here got some unfinished business."

"That's enough, Amos!" Levi thundered. "We got our orders."

Amos shook free of Elias' clasp and challenged Levi. "I *said* I got some business here with the lady," he snarled.

Levi tilted his head and looked Amos dead in the eyes. "And I'm saying you lay a hand on her and Captain won't have to kill you, I'll do it myself."

While the men argued, I bent down and picked up one of the linen sheets and wrapped it around me, tucking it firmly in place under my arms. It wasn't much by way of covering, but it made me feel a little less vulnerable. Surely, it wouldn't be too much longer before Edwards showed up with help.

"Best pay attention, Amos. Levi's killed better men than you for a lot less," the unnamed man added. Then he reached for my arm. "Come along, ma'am. We don't want no more trouble here."

I pulled away and stood my ground. "Take your hands off me!"

"Listen ma'am," the unnamed man said quietly, "you're coming with us one way or another. We can take you by force or you can come along peaceably. Choice is yours. But I'm warning you, I can't hold these boys off much longer. Been a long time since they seen a woman pretty as you."

I don't know what possessed me to think that Eleanor's petite frame would be any match against the four Rebel soldiers, but I wasn't about to give in "peaceably" as the unnamed man suggested. I pretended to offer him my hand, but as soon as he got close enough to me I spit in his face and kneed him as hard as I could in his groin. The other three men roared with laughter as I turned away and started running as fast as I could. I felt like I'd won when the other three men made no attempt to follow me, but before I could put any significant distance between us, the unnamed man grabbed me from behind. I was stunned that he'd recovered so quickly from what I'd thought was a hefty blow to his manhood, but he reached down, swooped me up, and hoisted me over his shoulder in one smooth, effortless motion. Despite my flailing fists, which I drummed repeatedly against his back, he carried me much the same way he might have carried a gun over his shoulder. When I screamed for help, all four men laughed.

I had to think fast. "Okay! Okay!" I yelled. "I'll go with you! Just put me down!"

The unnamed man stopped and patted me on the rear. "That's a good girl," he jeered. "But mind you, you ever try something like that again, I'll let ole' Amos here have his go at you for sure. I'll even stand by and watch it happen. You understand?"

"Yes, yes!" I replied. "Just please, please put me down."

"Mercy me, Luke," Elias teased. "The lady actually said please! You done got her to beg."

Luke sat me down, but held onto my arm. "I mean what I said, ma'am."

I looked over at Amos, whose non-verbal expression dared me to try another escape.

Obviously, I had no hope of getting away from them, so I needed to figure out a way to outsmart them. I searched my brain, pleading internally for an idea—anything that might aid those sure to come looking for me. Then I had a thought.

"May I have a moment to relieve myself?" I asked, peering into Luke's eyes. Eleanor's biggest asset was her beauty; it was also her strongest weapon. Eleanor could disarm any man when she turned on her charm. I needed to buy time, and if that meant exploiting Eleanor in the process, then so be it. I'd apologize later.

"Can't let you do that, ma'am. You'll have to wait."

I gazed pleadingly into Luke's light brown eyes. "I promise I won't run away again. I realize I've no chance outrunning the four of you."

"I—" Luke's words seemed to catch in his throat. He hesitated for a moment and then nodded. "Amos!"

"Yeah," Amos replied, annoyed.

"You stand watch."

Amos chuckled. "Pleasure's mine." He started to move toward me, but Luke put a hand on his chest and halted him.

"I said 'stand watch,' that's all!"

Amos turned to the side and spat. I concluded that spitting was just one of Amos' disgusting habits. He muttered something under his breath and Luke lowered his hand.

"Well," Amos said to me, gesturing toward the bushes. "Get on with your business."

I searched for a clearing among the surrounding trees and brush, and then walked into the slight opening several feet until nearly out of Amos's view. I quickly gathered whatever rocks I could and went to work stacking the rocks so they formed an arrow. I knew it wasn't likely that anyone would see it, but I had to do something, and if the searchers ventured off the beaten path, then maybe I had a chance to at least point them in the right direction.

I reached under the linen sheet and tore a long strip from my undergarments. I carefully divided the strip into several square-size sections resembling small pieces of "toilet paper." As soon as I was satisfied that I had enough, I readjusted the sheet, tying it around my neck so my arms could move freely. I had learned four different ways to tie a sarong when my family spent a vacation in the tropics one year (one of the few times we'd had an actual vacation that wasn't a field trip). I had no idea at the time that the skill would someday come in handy. I tucked the square pieces of my undergarments securely in the folds of my makeshift dress and returned to my captures.

"Thank you," I said politely to Luke.

Luke tipped his hat and nodded. "All right, let's move."

None of the four men noticed when I began dropping the small cloth squares on the ground. I hoped that whoever came searching for us was familiar with the story of Hansel and Gretel and would recognize my clues. I knew it was a long shot, but I had to try.

The ground was hot and rough against the delicate bottoms of Eleanor's feet and I found myself silently cursing her for not permitting me to go barefoot around the estate. I was grateful for each spot of shady ground along the path, which helped with the heat but did nothing to protect me against small stones and sharp pine needles. I had to keep my eyes focused on the ground in order to strategically plan each step and avoid running thorns into my feet. I complained incessantly, but the four men ignored my numerous pleas to stop. They even ignored me when I suggested that if my feet started to bleed, it would help searchers track them quicker.

Turns out all my plotting was futile, for as soon as we crossed the edge of the Hastings' estate into the next Township, we stumbled across the bodies of four dead men strewn beneath the trees at what appeared to have been a campsite. At closer look, they appeared to be quite young, possibly in their late teens or early twenties. They'd been stripped of their clothes and from what I could tell, had been slaughtered in a vicious attack. Two of the men had suffered gunshot wounds to the chest. The third man had been stabbed, and judging by the amount of blood it looked like he'd been assaulted multiple times. The fourth man lay awkwardly bent against the trunk of a tree, his neck snapped.

Despite the swarms of flies and insects that now circled the bodies, the killings appeared to have been recent. The blood appeared to be fresh, at least it did from where I stood. It was a gruesome scene, and I immediately felt lightheaded and nauseous. Fighting back a sudden rush of dry heaves, I bent over and steadied myself against the trunk of a nearby tree. During the few times that I had volunteered at the

Marensburg hospital with Eleanor's mother, I'd seen men with broken and shattered bones, missing limbs, head wounds, and gaping holes from bayonet injuries; but in most of those cases, the wounds had been cleaned and dressed by trained medical staff. There were times, however, when every available volunteer was forced to serve as a physician's assistant due to the sheer volume of incoming wounded. This was particularly true in the days following the battle at Gettysburg. I suppose it was a blessing in disguise that Eleanor was still too weak to serve as a volunteer during those dark days.

Luke made it clear that our discovery of the four murdered men was no accident when he directed the others to remove their clothes and replace them on the men to whom they belonged. They wasted no time making the switch and retrieving their original clothing from beneath a pile of brush behind a large tree.

"What do you suppose these unfortunate souls were doing so far north?" Amos wondered.

"No telling," Elias answered. "No doubt they were scouting the area."

"You think Lee's planning an attempt to take Harrisburg?"

"Doubtful. Last I heard he's still fighting to keep his hold on Petersburg."

"Could be Mosby's men," Luke chimed in. "Could be he's planning another raid."

Levi's eyes widened with excitement. "You think that ole' 'Gray Ghost' might be somewhere nearby?"

Elias let out a sarcastic chuckle. "If he is, he ain't gonna take too kindly to us killing his boys."

Amos laughed. "He ain't never gonna know what hit 'em."

I noticed that Amos had dropped his southern accent.

Levi called over to Luke, who had walked a few feet away and was peering through the trees at something. "Hey Luke, you think they'll buy that these men were the ones to take the girl?"

Luke didn't respond right away, still focused on whatever it was he was looking at.

"Luke?" Levi called again.

Luke glanced over his shoulder at Levi and put his hand up to shush him.

"What is it?" Elias asked in a hushed tone.

The men stood silently waiting for Luke to respond. After several moments, he shook his head and turned around to face the men.

"What was it?" Elias asked.

"I'm not sure," Luke replied.

"Probably just an animal," Amos chuckled, and then looked over at me. "Lots of animals on the loose in these parts I hear. And what with fresh flesh close by, no tellin' how many of 'em there are."

"Nah, I don't think so." Luke shook his head. "It wasn't an animal."

"You think her sister and maid got someone in pursuit already?" Levi asked.

Luke removed his hat and scratched the top of his head. "I suspect it won't be long now," he replied.

Think they'll find the bodies?" Elias tilted his head toward the four dead boys.

"Gentlemen, I have no doubt. The lady here was kind enough to leave a trail that will lead them to this very spot." Luke shot me an appreciative grin. "Have to admit, it was a nice touch, ma'am."

The knot in the pit of my stomach twisted and my queasiness instantly deepened.

"Why are you doing this?" I shifted my gaze one by one to each of my kidnappers, hoping for some hint of compassion in at least one of them. "Look at them," I glanced over at the four lifeless bodies and shuddered. "They were just boys!"

Elias answered, "Go on, Luke, tell the little lady. Tell her what these *boys* would've done to her and her sister had they been the ones to find 'em splashing around in the river."

"That won't be necessary," a voice called from the distance.

I heard the sound of an approaching horse and a wave of hope gave me renewed courage.

"You see? They've come for me already." I looked past the men and started walking toward the man who was just coming into clear view. I recognized him instantly.

"James!"

James quickly dismounted and opened his arms wide to receive me. I hiked up my linen covering and ran speedily into his welcome embrace.

"Oh, James! Thank heaven it's you!"

James chuckled as he held me. "Of course it's me! Who else were you expecting?"

His reply confused me, but I was so relieved to see a friendly face that I ignored his curious comment. The fact that there were four horses trailing his registered slowly as I began piecing things together. James pushed me away slightly and looked me over. I winced as he brushed his hand along the side of my face where Amos had struck me earlier. James reached into his pocket and pulled out a handkerchief. He began dabbing it gently against my swollen and bloodstained lip.

"Who did this to you, honey?" he asked softly.

I turned slightly and pointed to Amos. "That one. They call him Amos."

James pursed his lips together and handed me the handkerchief. He stepped over to his horse and pulled his rifle from its holster. He walked toward Amos without acknowledging the other three men who stood watching in silence. Elias and Luke stepped aside to let James through, but Levi didn't move. I let out an audible gasp when I heard James call him by name.

"Step aside Levi," James said coldly.

"Let it go, Captain," Levi cautioned him. "Amos was only defending himself."

My hands flew to my mouth as it dawned on me that James was acquainted with my abductors. They'd mentioned the "captain" several times, but it never occurred to me they'd been referring to James. The uneasiness in my stomach worsened as I observed the exchange between James and the four men.

James pointed back at me. "Defending himself against a woman?" he asked incredulously.

Amos stepped forward. "Little vixen caught me square with a rock, she did," he complained, gesturing to the bloody welt on the side of his head.

James didn't hesitate. He swung the end of his rifle up and whacked Amos across the same spot on his head.

"James, no!" I cried, but it was too late.

Amos stumbled sideways and fell to the ground, clutching the side of his head in his hands. Devoid of emotion, James stood and watched as Amos groaned in pain. Then he stepped closer and slammed the butt of his rifle again into the side of Amos' head. I heard the sound of cracking bones and Amos fell limply to the ground.

"Oh, James!" I whimpered. "You killed him! You *killed* him!" I couldn't believe what was happening.

James turned around and faced his stunned onlookers. "Take care of this piece of trash," he ordered, "and then get the hell out of my sight."

"That wasn't the deal, James," Luke spoke up. "We brought her to you, just as you asked."

"My orders were for you to bring her to me *unharmed!*" James yelled. He pointed to my face. "You call that unharmed?"

"Nevertheless, we had a deal. We don't want no trouble here, so you just pay us and we'll be on our way." Luke didn't raise his voice, which almost made him more terrifying than James in my eyes.

James stared coldly at Luke for several moments and then muttered something under his breath. He continued to grumble as he walked past me to his horse and pulled a small bag from the side pocket of his carry pouch. He threw the bag at Luke.

"Now get out of here!" he ordered.

With that, the three remaining kidnappers quickly gathered their things and mounted the horses that James had brought for them.

Elias looked back and tipped his hat to James. "Been a pleasure, as usual!" he quipped and the three of them took off.

I was too stunned to speak. *As usual?* My mouth hung open as I turned to face James.

"James, what does he mean by 'as usual'?"

James smiled and took my hand. "Nothing for you to worry your pretty little self over," he remarked.

His patronizing tone infuriated me. "Who are those men?" I demanded. "Why have they brought me here? Tell me what's going on!"

James chuckled. "Relax honey. It's all according to our plan, remember?"

"What plan?"

James' smile widened. "The one where I rescue you from your would-be colonel husband and we run off together; now let's get along before all this . . ." he gestured at the five dead bodies, "will be for nothing."

An ominous chill flooded my veins. "Oh, James," I shook my head, "what have you done?"

"Come along, Eleanor," he replied, reaching for my hand.

I pulled away from him and folded my trembling arms around my waist. "Please James, just take me home."

James wrapped his arm around my shoulders and pulled me toward his horse. "It's okay honey. You're just upset by what happened today. In a couple of days, you won't remember any of this. Trust me."

I struggled to resist his hold on me, but it only made him pull harder.

"Please! Please take me home!" I begged.

"Shh!" James attempted to comfort me.

We stood next to his horse and James took my elbow, as if to help me mount. When I refused to cooperate, he looked hurt.

"Very well, Eleanor," he lowered his gaze dejectedly. "If that's what you want, I'll take you home. Here . . ." he reached for my arm again.

"Thank you," I replied reluctantly as he helped me onto his horse. A second later, he climbed on behind me and wrapped his arm snugly around my waist. He gave his horse a quick kick and took off—in the opposite direction of the Hastings' estate. I struggled against his hold, but with the horse on a dead run, it was all I could do to hang on.

James didn't slow his pace until we'd traveled far enough away that he knew I'd have no choice but to stop fighting him. I had no idea where we were, and judging by the changing colors in the sky, I knew it would soon be dark.

Oh Eleanor! I thought to myself. *What have you done? What have you done?*

Eleanor, who had disappeared in her usual fashion at the first sign of distress, now surfaced.

I'm sorry, Beth, I heard her say in my mind. *I didn't know. I didn't know!*

And this is the man you preferred to marry over William? I scolded her. *This cold-blooded murderer?*

Honestly, I didn't know. Eleanor started to cry.

I immediately rebuked her. *Oh no you don't! Don't you dare wimp out on me now! You have to help us get out of this.*

A long, frustrating silence followed. I assumed Eleanor had retreated to her usual hiding place in my mind when all of a sudden I felt a surge of renewed energy emerge.

What do you need me to do? Eleanor asked.

This time the long silence was mine.

I don't know, I finally said. *I honestly don't know.*

We had traveled for what seemed like the better part of an hour. I surveyed the setting sun and determined that we were heading in what I ascertained to be a southeastern direction. Somehow, we'd managed to completely bypass Marensburg.

Eleanor, where are we?

I'm not sure. Eleanor answered. *I've only been south of Marensburg once, but I was only a child. Mother and I spent the summer in Chambersburg visiting her uncle and his family.*

Do you think that's where we're headed?

It's possible, maybe, but this doesn't seem right. It seems like we're heading too far east for Chambersburg; but James isn't taking the direct route, so it's difficult to say.

Think Eleanor. Where else could he be taking us?

I'm sorry, I just don't know.

Well, if he is headed for Chambersburg, perhaps your mother's family will help us get back home.

I'm afraid they're no longer in Chambersburg. They went abroad shortly after the war broke out.

Of course they did, I muttered to myself.

What's that supposed to mean? Eleanor asked defensively.

Sorry, I answered. *You weren't supposed to hear that.*

James tightened his grip on the rope. "Whoa," he said, pulling reins back. The horse obeyed and quickly slowed to a walk.

"James, where are we going?"

"Somewhere you've never been, but where your arrival is eagerly awaited."

"What in the hell is that supposed to mean?" I demanded. I figured there was no sense worrying about social propriety at this point.

James laughed and squeezed me tighter. "Oh, Eleanor! You were most assuredly worth the wait!"

Something in James' tone struck a chord and my blood chilled.

"James, I don't know what you're planning, but this isn't right. I can't be with you like this—I don't belong here with you!"

"Eleanor my love, this is exactly where we belong."

The horse continued to plod along as the sun disappeared below the horizon and the sky behind us turned a bright shade of red. The horse was obviously undeterred by the anxiety I was experiencing, but when an unexpected sound in the distance caught my attention, the horse whinnied and began to rear backwards.

Eleanor, what was that?

Before she could respond, James made a quick turn to the left and spurred the horse into a fast run. "Hang on darling,'" he chuckled. "We're almost there."

"Almost where?" I yelled, but my words were lost in the wind as we sped through the trees. With the sun now far below the horizon, the first glimmer of stars appeared in the sky. The fast fading light made the path in front of us seem particularly dark and ominous. The trees shifted from green to black, no longer objects of beauty to be admired but dark creatures looming in the night.

Straight ahead, beyond the trees, I spotted a soft orange glow of light and caught the pungent odor of burning wood. Our horse must have recognized where we were because he suddenly whinnied and quickened his gait, without any encouragement from James. James pulled hard on the reins to maintain control.

Within minutes, we arrived at a large campsite. The orange glow I'd seen earlier came from several fires that were spread throughout the vast range of the camp. At first, I assumed we'd come upon a company of Union soldiers, and my mind started to relax. Although I had no clue where I was, I figured I was at least safe and among friends. But my relief was premature when I suddenly heard a blood-curling shriek in the distance.

"James! What was that?" I whispered frantically.

James reined his horse to a stop and dismounted. He reached up and pulled me down beside him, leaving the horse to graze. Placing a protective arm around my shoulders, he began to lead me into the camp. Horrible screams whirled through the air from all directions. At first, I was certain the high-pitched screeches were all female; but as we approached the center of the camp, I was able to discern that the frightening cries were both male and female.

My unsteady knees quivered as James pulled me along. I jumped at the echo of whips cracking followed by the anguished cries of men wailing in agony to a backdrop of hysterical laughter. Terrifying screams peeled through the air, followed by the rustling sounds of commotion and spontaneous eruptions of cheers. From directly in front of us, the ear-piercing screams of women paired with the pleading sobs of men sent a shudder reeling down the whole length of my spine. In every direction, men and women were in obvious torment while others groaned in heightened states of pleasure.

Paralyzed by fear and with nowhere to run, I dropped to my knees and covered my ears; but try as I might, I could not drown out the horrific sounds of pure evil.

"Get me out of here!" I squeezed my fists against my ears and repeatedly cried, "Please, James, get me out of here!"

James knelt by my side and pulled my arms away from my head. "Come now, love, you're missing the best part." He took a deep breath and groaned. "Ahh!" he hissed. "Do you hear it?"

I stared at James in shock. Another wave of laughter mingled with agonizing cries of torment and fear flooded the night. I shook my head violently back and forth, trying to repel the sounds. James lifted me from the ground and folded his arms around me, pinning my arms to my sides. Then he pressed his cheek against mine and whispered, "Listen, Eleanor."

The pattern of his breathing began to shift and his breath grew hot and heavy against my ear. "Mmm," he murmured over the continuous cries for help and the paralyzing screams. "That my darling is the Concerto of Human Suffering." He took another deep breath and slowly exhaled, releasing a low, hypnotic moan that resembled a human purr. "Don't you hear it? Pure unadulterated and unbridled passion. Anger, fear, desire, lust, pleasure, pain, revenge—they're all here, right here, right now." He tightened his hold on me. "Hear it, Eleanor. *Feel* it! Let the sounds of raw passion flood your mind until it completely consumes you and pierces your very soul. Sense its power! There's no sound more luring, more electrifying."

My heart pounded with fear and I started to heave in convulsions.

"That's it darling. *Yes!* You feel it too, don't you? I knew you would. This is what we've been longing for."

James slid his hands hungrily along my back several times and then reached up and untied the knot in my linen wrap. He pulled the twisted corners of the sheet free and backed away slightly, allowing the sheet to fall freely to the ground. I panicked as I watched his burning eyes consume my figure. I shoved him hard in the chest.

"Stay away from me, James!" I screamed. "You sick murderer!"

My clinging undergarments were still slightly damp and the moment the chill of the evening air hit them, I began to tremble. I don't know which was more violent, the effects of the cold air or the tremors that raged through my body from fear. James smiled sympathetically and picked up my linen wrap. He handed it to me with a polite bow and stepped away.

"Don't fret, my love. After all, I don't mean to frighten you; I only mean to help ease the way for you."

I had no idea what he was talking about.

"Why, James?" Eleanor spoke up, and instantly I began fighting back tears.

"Darling Eleanor, your beauty surpasses that of all women; surely you must realize that."

"But why? Why bring me to such a horrid place?"

James smiled and shook his head. "Alas, my love, a price must be paid before we can be together. It's the marriage of opposites—the ultimate union of beauty and beast, good and evil, or more specifically in your case, the union of virtue and vice. It's our version of the eight-pointed star."

I stared at him, trying desperately to make sense of what he was saying. James, recognizing the confusion in my expression, started to take my hand. But the moment he reached for me, I bolted. I had no sense of direction, other than to head back the way we had come. I no sooner began to run then one by one, shadowy shapes appeared in my path and blocked my escape. Each time I veered in a new direction, another shadow appeared. Fear caught in my throat. I wanted to scream. I struggled to find my voice. Before I knew it, a host of Intruders encircled me, all moving closer, closing the gap between us until a midst of darkness completely enveloped me.

As the ghost-like creatures drew closer they revealed human-like images, and I realized that each figure differed in appearance from the others in the same manner human beings possess physical traits that are uniquely their own. Some of the Intruders appeared to be female, although in most cases it was difficult to distinguish one sex from the other.

I spun around quickly and found James standing directly behind me. Once again, he reached for my hand and smiled.

"Come darling. You're exhausted from the ride. Let me show you to your tent."

Crippled with fear, I collapsed. James bent down and very carefully lifted me into his arms and carried me back into the camp. The eerie laughter and terrifying screams had diminished to an occasional groan or sudden outburst, but the haunting cries of pain had finally ceased. I shuddered as I imagined what might have transpired in the surrounding shadows. The absence of noise did not make me feel any safer; on the contrary, the forlorn cries and silenced screams overwhelmed me with a daunting sense of dread and hopelessness.

Beth, Eleanor called to me in my mind. *What were those . . . creatures?*

I couldn't respond. Up until now, I'd blamed Eleanor for everything that had happened today. I'd assumed that Eleanor had somehow pre-arranged to run off with James and leave her family, William, and the entire Hastings' estate behind; but I'd been terribly wrong in my assumptions. This abduction was not Eleanor's fault.

Beth, answer me!

How could I answer her? How could I explain the existence of such evil? How could I explain to her that in my quest for liberation, I had led her into the very jaws of hell?

Oh Eleanor, I lamented, *I've not only shattered any hope of reclaiming my life, but I fear I've inadvertently destroyed your life in the process.*

What are you saying, Beth?

I've focused so intently on trying to find my way home that I've sacrificed your future in the process.

Who are these monsters? Eleanor demanded. *WHAT are they?*

I can't speak to the rest of them, but the shadowy personages are called Intruders.

You mean like Bailey, the one who visits you so often in your dreams?

That caught me by surprise. She could experience my dreams?

Yes, Eleanor, I replied slowly. *Just like Bailey.*

"Here we are, love." James said as we arrived at one of the tents. He drew back the flap and carried me inside. "You'll find some fresh clothes over there in the corner, along with some of your personal belongings."

"My what?" I followed the direction of his gaze and saw that indeed, several items belonging to Eleanor were there, just as he'd said. James laid me down on a pile of neatly arranged blankets.

"You see, darling, I've thought of everything. Oh, I know it lacks the comforts of home, but I promise it's only temporary." James seemed exceptionally proud of himself.

I couldn't stop staring at the items in the corner. I recognized two of Eleanor's "at home" dresses, a pair of undergarments, some stockings, a pair of shoes, some hair clips, a brush, and a hand mirror.

"Wh . . . where did you . . . how did you . . . ?" I was too astonished to utter a complete thought.

James picked up the brush and began pulling it gently through my tangled hair.

"Lucinda packed some things for you days ago. I regret that she couldn't fit more into the bag, but I'm satisfied that this will suffice for now."

"That's a lie! Lucinda would never—"

"My darling Eleanor," James said smugly as he separated another lock of hair, "I've learned that most women would do just about anything in the name of love. It didn't take long to convince Lucinda that helping you run away with the man you love was a noble cause." He paused and stroked the side of my face.

His words struck a new chord of fear in me. "Oh, James!" I whimpered. "What have you done?"

James looked hurt. "I've only done what was asked of me."

"By whom?" I demanded, anger giving me courage.

James set the brush down and laced his fingers through my hair. "By you, who else? Haven't we always said that we'd risk any amount of danger if it meant we could be together?"

I started to get up, but James put his hand on my shoulder. "Darling, you're tired. It's best that you rest. I'm going to leave for a while, but I promise to return soon."

"James, why are you doing this? I want to go home. Please . . ." I put my hand on his, "please take me home."

James took my hand in his and rested it against his cheek. He bent down and kissed me tenderly on the forehead, then brushed his lips against my ear. "All our dreams are about to come true. Soon we'll be together, just as we planned, never to be separated again. Rest now my love."

With that, James disappeared into the night, leaving me alone to face the nightmares that were sure to come. I curled up into a tight ball and hid my face from the darkness. I was too numb to cry, too petrified to run, and too overcome with despair to fight—and this is how I remained until during the wee hours of the night, I finally drifted to sleep.

The Camp
CHAPTER 18

"Beth?" a melodious voice called from the distance. It was a woman's voice, but when I turned around to see who she was, there was nobody there. The trees along the side of the well-established dirt path rustled with new life. Their fresh green leaves, young and vibrant, seemed to welcome the steady flow of wind that gave them permission to dance and flutter without a care. Birds sang in animated harmony, announcing the arrival of another day.

"Beth," the woman's voice called again, this time from somewhere in front of me. But just as before, when I searched for her there was no one there.

"Are you going to sleep all day?"

The birds suddenly stopped their merry tune and the leaves fell flat, dangling lifeless from their branches. One by one the trees began to disappear, leaving behind a hollow darkness in their place until eventually, I was surrounded by nothing.

"Honey, you're going to miss your ride if you don't hurry!" The warmth of her tone was so familiar. It only took a moment for me to sort through my memory and recognize her, and the moment I did my eyes flew open and I shot up into a sitting position. I gasped for air and the moment I inhaled, my surroundings came clearly into focus.

"Whoa, shhhh, it's okay," my mother said smiling.

"Wh . . . ? Where . . . ?" I rubbed my eyes and shook my head against my fists.

"My, my," Mother quipped, "That must have been a doozy of a dream!"

I stared, dumbfounded, at my mom. I couldn't believe she was really there. I checked my emotions quickly, fearing that at any second I would discover I was the victim of some form of trickery.

My mom continued to act as though everything was normal. "I've got to get to work early this morning, so I'm afraid you're on your own. I left a cereal bar on the counter if you want it."

Mom turned to leave and then paused. She gave me a stern look and pointing her finger at me warned, "Don't you dare go back to sleep!" She pulled her eyebrows together in a tight line and shook her finger. "I mean it!" Then she grinned and turned toward the door. I couldn't bear for her to leave.

"Mom, wait!" I shouted. "Don't leave!" The words lodged themselves in the back of my throat so forcefully that I couldn't swallow or catch my breath.

My mom's face turned instantly serious and in a flash she was at my side. "Honey! What's wrong?"

I threw my arms around her neck and clung to her as tightly as I could. I couldn't believe she was really there. Several moments later, she reached around and pried my arms loose.

"Bethy, I can't imagine what's got you so upset! You've been looking forward to the first day of school for weeks now. What in heaven's name is the matter?"

"I what?" I scratched my head and frowned. *First day of school? What's going on?*

I backed away and surveyed my surroundings. I was in my old room—my room before the accident. I threw myself off the bed and flew to my book bag. It was propped up in the corner, right where I always kept it. My favorite jeans hung across the back of the chair in the corner along with a three-foot-high pile of clean laundry that had been there for days, waiting for me to fold it and put it away—a task I seldom found worthy of my time or effort. The bulletin board on the wall in front of my desk was covered in a collage of photos of my friends. Dominating the group were random shots of me with Adam, my boyfriend right up until a few weeks before my accident. Before—

I looked down at my left hand and stretched out my fingers. I let out a joyful sob and held my hand up in the air.

"Oh, Mom! My hand! It's well! And you're okay! And I'm home!"

"Uh, yes, Dorothy," Mom teased, referring to *The Wizard of Oz*. "Welcome to Kansas!" She reached out and held my hand in hers. "Now, how about you put on your red slippers and get ready for school before we're both late!" She turned a second time to leave, but suddenly remembered something. "When you get home this afternoon, I need you to wash the sheets in the guest room, okay?"

"Why?" I asked, surprised by how annoyed I sounded.

Mom pursed her lips and sighed. "I told you, your uncle is coming."

I burst into a wide smile. "Uncle Connor's coming? Here? Today?"

"Land sakes, child! What's wrong with you?"

"What did you say?" I asked, shocked by her choice of words.

Mother let out an exasperated sigh. "I said I need you to wash the sheets before Connor gets here to—"

"No, not that. The other thing you said."

"Beth, I'm about to lose my patience here."

"You said, 'Land sakes!'"

"So what? It's an expression. I say it all the time."

"I . . ." *Is that true?* I thought for a minute and chuckled quietly to myself. "I just don't remember you saying it before."

"Tell you what," she said, trying hard not to lose her patience. "Let's save the debate on semantics until your uncle gets here. Until then, get you and your sixteen-year-old, teenage-task-avoidance-tactics to school on time."

Oh! How I'd missed my mom!

I reached up and kissed her on the cheek. "I love you, Mom," I said, hugging her shoulders. She backed away and eyed me suspiciously for a moment. She nodded slowly and smiled.

"I love you too, Bethy," she said. "Now you'd best get to work on your hair or you'll never make it on time."

As I watched her leave, I thought it peculiar that she would make such a reference to my hair. I reached up and tried to pull my fingers through it. Something wasn't right. A nervous twinge quickened my pulse and I ran to the bathroom to see if my suspicions were real. I gasped the moment I caught my reflection in the mirror. The face in the mirror wasn't mine—it was Eleanor's.

"No!" I screamed, pressing my hands to the sides of my face. "No, no, no! It can't be!" But there was no denying what the mirror revealed.

"Eleanor," I shouted. I called again, louder this time. "Eleanor!" I listened closely to my inner thoughts, but the only thoughts I perceived were my own.

I reached down and grabbed the only thing that was handy— my hair dryer—and began beating it against the mirror as hard as I could. "No! No! No!" I cried repeatedly as I pounded the mirror into a thousand tiny shards of glass. When I was satisfied that I had sufficiently crushed Eleanor from my view, I threw the tattered hair dryer across the bathroom where it crashed hard against the wall and fell to the ground in pieces.

"Beth," Eleanor called. I turned around quickly and saw Eleanor's face, distorted by the irregular patterns of broken glass, staring back at me from the mirror. She reached out to me, and as she did her hand came out of the mirror and grabbed my arm.

"Nooooooo!" I screamed as loud as I could. In an instant, my eyes flew open and I found myself back on the floor of the tent where James had left me for the night.

Once I finally caught my breath, I buried my face in my hands and started to cry. I'd cried for the better part of an hour when all at once, I heard a woman's voice humming softly in the distance. I raised my head and listened more intently, hoping to discern where the humming was coming from. I knew it was impossible, but it felt as though the voice was coming from inside my tent. I sat frozen in place, fearful that my invisible guest might not be friendly; but when my visitor began to sing I was no longer afraid, for the voice that came to me in the dark belonged to my mother. She was singing an old song that she'd sung at my bedside for years when I was young. I often had nightmares as a small child, and many times in the wee hours of the night, my mom would sit by my side and stroke my hair softly while she sang the words that her own mother had sung to her. She told me once that the melody came from an old English hymn. And so, in the darkness of the night, I listened to my sweet angel mother's voice and found peace in the words that had comforted me so often as a child.

When in despair I strayed from Thee
Thou didst not hide Thy face from me.
And though I wandered on my own,
Thou camst to me and brought me home.
So in the darkness of the night
I'll ask of Thee to give me sight.
And through the midst Thy power break free
That Thou mayst light the path to Thee.
And through the midst Thy power break free
That Thou mayst light the path to Thee.

The sliver of sunlight that cut its way into my tent the next morning carried with it the promise of yet another blistering hot day. I raised my hand to shield the light from my eyes as I slowly rose to a sitting position. Eleanor's body was not accustomed to sleeping on the ground, and I felt stiff and achy in muscles I never knew existed. The moist trail of perspiration that had formed along my cleavage affirmed that not only was the temperature likely to reach the mid to high 90s, the humidity was on its way into the 90s as well. It didn't help that I'd gone to sleep in undergarments that had never thoroughly dried.

I retrieved the clean set of clothes that waited for me in the far corner of the tent and began to peel away the undergarments that were now plastered against my body like wet wallpaper.

"Ugh!" I groaned, as I wiggled out of my tattered underclothes and quickly replaced them with clean ones. Until now, I hadn't realized how accustomed I'd become to having Lucinda help me dress each morning.

Lucinda!

I pressed my fingers against my forehead and massaged my temples. *Lucinda, what in heaven's name were you thinking?* I wondered to myself. *What in the world could James have possibly said to convince you to do such a thing?*

The ray of sun lighting my tent widened when James appeared at the door holding two tin cups. "Good morning, love," he smiled as he let himself in uninvited. I started to protest, but the smell of coffee coupled with a familiar face made me think twice before sending him away. James' actions had been reprehensible, but regardless of how I felt about him at the moment, he was my only hope for protection in this strange and forbidding place.

I didn't respond, but took the cup of coffee when he offered it.

"You're looking rested," he said, and then gestured toward my dress. "I dare say you're a bit over-dressed for these parts, but I suppose that's to be expected from someone as refined as yourself. I fear you'll soon discover that . . . er . . . folks in these parts don't place much value on materialism." James grinned and scratched the back of his neck. "I think the word they like to use when referring to themselves is 'minimalists'; you'll understand why soon enough." James pulled back the tent door and offered me his arm. "Shall we?"

Though I refused his arm, I welcomed the opportunity to leave the tent. James chuckled and stepped aside. "After you, darlin'."

Once outside the tent, I took advantage of the opportunity to examine my surroundings carefully. We were in a heavily wooded area, much thicker with trees and brush than the areas circumventing the Hastings' estate. But the trees here were mostly deciduous, which suggested to me that we'd traveled to an area that was lower in elevation, which might explain the higher than usual temperatures and humidity. At least, that was my hypothesis; but the truth was, I knew very little about climates in the eastern parts of the United States—particularly during Civil War times. I was certain we'd traveled south, but how far we'd gone and where we were remained a mystery.

"It's very easy to get lost out here," James said casually as we walked. "There aren't any trails to speak of, other than the main path leading into the camp. And I'm afraid the wildlife is most unpredictable. So it's unwise to venture off alone and unarmed. Those who've done so have, er, well . . ." he shuddered, as if shaking off a bad memory. "Let's just say the animals didn't leave much for us to bury."

"James, where are we?" I asked, hoping his sincerity wasn't feigned.

"Difficult to say, exactly," he shrugged his shoulders. "I really couldn't put a name to it."

"Are we still in Pennsylvania?"

James laughed. "I suppose you could say that."

"Are we anywhere near Chambersburg?"

James let out a hearty laugh and shook his head. "Oh no you don't. Trust me, honey, the less you know the better."

A trail of moisture trickled down my neck. The entire base of my hairline was already soaked with perspiration and several strands of hair clung mercilessly to my skin. I reached back and worked to pry the strands free. James watched me with obvious concern.

"Don't fret, love. I'm sure we can find someone to help with your hair." He reached over and laced his fingers through the my hair. "Mercy, Eleanor! I don't suppose I've ever seen a more beautiful mass of hair. The good lord certainly has showered his favors on you."

I stepped to the side and stared into his eyes, unsure by his tone if he'd meant that last statement as a compliment. Hoping to make light of the moment, I replied, "I suppose that depends on the time of year."

James' eyes remained fixed on my hair and he reached again to stroke it with his fingers. Frustrated, I pulled away and then reached back and started to twist it into a tight knot. Eleanor's hair was exceedingly thick and wavy, but after searching the ground for a moment I was able to find a short stick strong enough to push through the hair I'd piled at the crown of my head.

"That's very impressive," James said when I'd finished weaving the stick through the twisted knot of hair. "I take it you didn't learn that at your poetry club."

I let out a nervous laugh. "No, I suppose not." I started to walk again, and James followed. After several minutes of silence, he reached over and pulled me to the side.

"Listen, Eleanor," he said, suddenly very serious. "I meant what I said about venturing off here. They'll kill you for certain if you try to leave."

My heart, which had remained a quiet bystander up until now, suddenly began to pound its disapproval. I stared at James for a moment as his words sunk in. "Who, James? Who are *they*?" I asked nervously.

James turned away and cleared his throat. "Eleanor, please don't ask me any more questions. All we have to do is give them one week. One week, love, and then you and I can be together for the rest of our lives. Free. Free of Marensburg, free of this place, free of everything and everyone keeping us from being together."

"James! What are you saying? One week of what? With whom?" The urge to panic that I'd managed to suppress, suddenly erupted into full-blown fear.

"It's the only way, love. The only way to guarantee our freedom and the ability for me to keep you in a lifestyle of comfort."

"Our *freedom?*"

"There you are," a woman's voice called from behind us. I spun around quickly and spotted a young woman, perhaps two or three years older than me, coming toward us. She stopped suddenly when she saw me and gasped. "Oh my," she said smiling, "you were right, James. She's beautiful." She looked me up and down before adding, "Oh, yes, James, she's perfect."

I turned back to look at James. His face was void of expression as he nodded in response. "Yes," he said quietly, "there's none who can come close to paralleling her beauty."

The woman's smile widened and she stepped forward to introduce herself.

"My name is Imelda," she said, holding out her hand. "I'm very delighted to finally meet you. James has told us all about you, but to be sure, his description of you hardly does justice to the real thing."

I couldn't respond. I simply stood in shock, quickly calculating the risk of running at that moment. James moved closer to me and put his arm around my shoulders. I didn't move.

"Imelda," James offered a polite bow. "May I present Miss Eleanor Louise Hastings."

I don't know what prompted Eleanor to do this, especially given the uncertain state of matters at the moment, but she suddenly jerked free of James' arm and, glaring coldly into Imelda's eyes, said, "I'm afraid there's been a terrible mistake. I am Mrs. William Carlton Hamilton. My *husband* is a colonel in the Union army. He will be most displeased when he arrives home and finds me missing. I'm afraid I must insist that you permit Captain Herman here to escort me home at once."

Imelda's eyes widened with her smile. "Why James, you didn't mention she was married—and to a colonel no less! This changes things."

"It changes nothing," James said, suddenly defensive. "It's a marriage in name only."

Ignoring his comment, Imelda placed her hands on her chest and sighed. "Oh, yes," she closed her eyes and drew in a long deep breath. "This is going to be an exceptional week." She opened her eyes and let out a gleeful laugh that set my teeth on edge. "Oh James, dear, you've outdone yourself this time."

"We have an agreement, Imelda. You promised me—"

Imelda cut him off abruptly. "That was before I knew she was already married. Tsk, tsk, James. I'm afraid the price for your freedom—and hers—has just doubled."

Imelda turned to leave and beckoned for us to follow. "Come along you two, you won't want to miss breakfast this morning."

James took me by the arm and urged me forward. When I resisted, he strengthened his hold. "Eleanor," he whispered, "please don't resist. Please. I won't let them hurt you."

"James, you're frightening me," I whispered angrily. "Please, just take me home. I don't want to be here."

James took a deep breath and shook his head. "Oh darling, I promise you, a week from now you will never want to see your home again. This place has a way of opening your mind to more possibilities than we ever could have imagined. Trust me, once you experience it, you'll never want to go back. It will change things for us, forever."

"I don't want to change!" I shouted.

Imelda glanced back at us and smiled. "Shall I send the others?"

"That won't be necessary, Imelda. We'll be along."

Imelda nodded once and smiled. "As you wish."

As soon as Imelda was out of hearing range, James grabbed me by the arm again and shook me. "Listen, Eleanor," his voice was harsh— almost desperate. "This isn't a game, do you understand? I made a deal with them in order to buy us a whole new life together, but if crossed, these people will not hesitate for one moment to kill you—or me, for that matter—and they won't do it quickly. Now, for heavens sake, do everything they say. That's the only chance we've got." His pleading eyes suggested to me that he'd gotten into something way over his head, and I realized that we were both in very serious danger.

"James, what have you done?" My voice shook with fear.

James pulled me into his arms and held me tightly. "Eleanor, please forgive me."

"No, James!" I pushed him away, "not until you tell me what is going on here!"

James stared at me, his eyes full of remorse. "I'm afraid I can't do that." He hung his head down and shook it back and forth. "Look Eleanor, I can't change what is; I can only change what will be. I promise, when this is over, if you still want to go home I'll take you back myself, and you'll never hear from me again." He raised his head and his eyes held mine. "That's the best I can offer."

I searched his gaze and sensed that he was telling me the truth. I also sensed that in spite of the fact that he had masterminded this elaborate plot to bring me here, my only hope for survival was to trust him—regardless of what horrors awaited me.

I followed James back to the camp where several others had gathered for breakfast. Imelda stood at a table between two men dressed in dirty Union uniforms. Both men wore long, untrimmed beards and one of them, the one with the longer of the two beards, was completely gray headed. Neither of the men appeared to be friendly. I counted twelve people standing in line, eight of them women. Strategically arranged logs formed a large circle that surrounded an oversized tent and the table where Imelda and the two bearded men were serving breakfast to those in line. Imelda greeted each person as they approached the table, but that's where the pleasantries ended. Others were seated on the logs— I counted six men and three women. None of them were engaged in conversation.

One of the women standing in line spotted me as James and I approached the camp. Her eyes were filled with a mixture of pity and warning. She made a slight movement with her head, directing my eyes to a tent at the far side of the camp. I quickly made a visual sweep of the camp noting a total of six small tents—tents presumably for no more than one to two people—and eight large tents that appeared to be big enough to sleep six to eight people. My tent was one of the large ones. I did the math quickly and realized that the numbers didn't quite add up. I looked back at the woman standing in line. She was still watching me, and again, she made a slight movement with her head directing my eyes to the tent in the back of the camp.

"Eleanor," James tugged at my elbow. "I suggest you get in line. There won't be another meal until late this evening, and as you can see, there are no servants to bring your food to you."

I ignored his comment about servants and focused on the part that he didn't say. "What about you? Aren't you going to eat?"

James scoffed. "I'm not exactly a guest, Eleanor. I have to work for my meals."

Imelda, who had been spooning some sort of hot "mush" into bowls, suddenly closed her eyes and began rocking slowly from side to side. She appeared to be in some sort of trance. Neither of the bearded men, nor anyone else for that matter, seemed to pay attention, as though this behavior of Imelda's was nothing unusual. But I couldn't take my eyes off her. After several moments, a satisfied smile spread across her face and she opened her eyes. Then she handed her serving spoon to one of the bearded men and excused herself. She crossed over to where James and I stood and addressed James.

"James, dear, there's been an unexpected . . ." she suddenly glanced over at me and took a deep breath, then turned back to James. ". . . situation. I'm afraid I must impose upon you again."

"No, Imelda. That's not part of the deal."

"Yes, yes I know, dear. But I'm afraid I must insist." Imelda's eyes fixed on James and instantly her piercing gaze became so intense it caused him to step backwards and nearly lose his balance.

"We have an agreement, Imelda," James said weakly.

"And our agreement still stands, but only after you fulfill one last . . ." Imelda shot me another quick glance, "assignment."

"And what about her?" James asked, inclining his head toward me.

"Why, she'll be our guest, of course."

"A *guest*," James let the word hang in the air before finishing his sentence. "And nothing more?"

Imelda smiled victoriously. "But of course. I'll take care of her myself."

James glared coolly at Imelda for several seconds, but she didn't back down. She returned his glare with a strange intensity that made James take a step backwards. It was as though the two of them were engaged in a silent conversation, the kind of conversation that everyone can sense, but no one can hear. It was a battle of wills, and it was clear that Imelda was winning.

A look of helpless resignation shone in James' eyes as he lowered his head in defeat. Having witnessed James so indolently bashing Amos in the head, I would have expected him to stand his ground against the likes of Imelda. I figured he'd at least put up an argument, even fight if necessary. I didn't expect him to acquiesce. But to my horror, James released a deep sigh and nodded.

"Okay. Where?"

"Chambersburg," Imelda replied, as if this was business as usual. "And you best hurry."

With that, Imelda turned and headed back to her spot between the two bearded men.

James looked down at me and shook his head apologetically. "Eleanor, it appears my breakfast will have to wait."

"What's that supposed to mean?"

"It means that this is where you and I part company—at least for now."

"What?" I asked, astonished by his unexpected announcement. "James, no, don't listen to her."

"I don't have a choice, Eleanor."

"What do you mean you don't have a choice. Of course you do."

James lowered his eyes and rubbed his hand across the back of his neck. "Eleanor, please try to understand. Imelda has . . . er . . . well, she knows things, things that could destroy everything for us."

"Us?" I nearly spat the word at him. "There is no 'us'!"

"Eleanor, don't say that. Everything I've done, everything I agreed to do—it has all been for us." James grabbed my shoulders and looked pleadingly into my eyes. "So we can be together and I can provide you with the kind of lifestyle you deserve—the kind you're used to."

"James, you're a fool!"

James released my shoulders and backed away. "Don't say that Eleanor." He shook his head slowly, his eyes suddenly wide. "I promise, as soon as I return and we can get out of here, everything will be different. I just need to do this one last thing and we'll be free."

"But why? Why do you have to do anything for *her*?"

James closed his eyes and took several breaths before answering. "Because Imelda paid for my services, Eleanor. And handsomely at that."

I was speechless. My mouth hung open, stunned by the implication of what James was saying. I searched his gaze and sensed that he was telling me the truth. But I also sensed that in spite of the fact that he had masterminded this elaborate plot to bring me here, my only hope for rescue was to trust him.

Satisfied by my silence, James cleared his throat and nodded. "Now then, if you'll excuse me, I've got to go back to work."

"James, wait! Please don't leave me here!"

There was a noticeable change in James' demeanor and he let out a sarcastic chuckle. "Don't worry, love, I'll be back soon." He paused, and then scoffed. "Who knows, in a few hours you may not even notice that I'm gone."

The spine-tingling chill I'd felt earlier returned and I sensed the veiled truth behind James' words. "James, take me with you! Please! I promise I won't make any trouble for you. I'll do whatever you say, anything, just please don't leave me here."

As if prompted by an eerie sense of unison, every head in the camp turned slowly toward the sound of our voices until all eyes were fixed on James. He smiled nervously and tried to ignore his audience.

"It's all right, Eleanor, you'll be fine, I promise." He bent down and kissed my cheek. I tried to pull away, but he refused to release me. He put his lips to my ears and whispered, "Whatever you do, don't let them see your fear."

I gasped and James immediately jerked me closer to him. "Eleanor, listen," he insisted. "I meant what I said. I promise I'll take you home just as soon as I return. But you've got to be strong. Do you hear me? No matter what happens, show no emotion. Understand? None!" His hold on me tightened. "Bury your emotions deep and you'll be fine."

Fear pounded its way through my blood and I began to tremble. James folded his arms around me and tried to conceal my shaking.

"Damn it, Eleanor!" he whispered in my ear. "They can sense your fear. They thrive on it! Now get ahold of yourself—"

"Is everything okay you two?" Imelda interrupted us. I had no idea how much she'd heard.

James backed away and smiled. "We're fine, Imelda. Eleanor just can't bear the thought of being away from me."

"We'll take good care of her, as you know." Imelda took me by the arm and waved James away. "Now off with you, Captain Herman. There's much work for you to do."

Imelda led me over to the table in front of the others. I watched James disappear behind the row of tents and the moment he was gone, I was filled with an ominous sense of doom.

"Everyone, this is Eleanor," Imelda announced to the group. "She's going to be joining us for a while—as our *guest*. I trust you'll make her feel welcome."

The onlookers paid no attention to Imelda's introduction. They each went back to their business without so much as a blink or a nod—with the exception of the young woman who had made eye contact with me earlier. The expression on her face was slightly different from the others' expressions. When she reached the front of the line, she closed her eyes and nodded. I had no idea what she was trying to say, but apparently her gesture didn't go unnoticed because Imelda held out her hand and covered the young girl's plate. Then she addressed the bearded man to her left.

"Lawrence, I'm afraid Miss Miriam isn't feeling well this morning. Please escort her to sick bay."

Miriam opened her eyes and stared blankly at Imelda. For a split second I thought I detected fear in her expression. The bearded man took Miriam's bowl and set it aside. Then he offered her his arm.

"Shall we, Miss Miriam?"

Miriam slid her arm through Lawrence's arm with a robotic-like movement and together they disappeared into one of the tents.

Resistance

C H A P T E R   1 9

*I*melda surveyed the disinterested crowd for a moment and then turned her attention to me. She took particular notice of the twisted bun on top of my head and smiled. She positioned herself behind me, then reached up and very slowly began working the stick out of my hair. My hair dropped and hung loosely at my back. Then Imelda threaded her fingers through my hair and began working the strands free so that my hair hung in their natural ringlets down to the middle of my back. She tugged on the ringlets, pulling them straight and then letting them bounce back into place. She did this several times, as if determined to show the onlookers how long my hair really was.

"Your hair is lovely, Miss Eleanor," Imelda said loud enough for everyone to hear. "I'm sure I've never before seen such natural beauty bestowed upon one woman. It is quiet unfair, would you not agree, for one woman to possess so much beauty?" She stepped around to face me and began working her fingers again through my hair, positioning it so that it hung forward so all could see. Then she turned to face the crowd.

"Who among us here wouldn't desire to come forward and comb their fingers through Miss Eleanor's silky curls? Is she not a vision to behold?" Imelda studied with interest the faces of the onlookers. "You there," she said, pointing to one of the women in the group. "Step forward, please."

The young woman's eyes widened and she hesitated. Imelda inhaled deeply and closed her eyes. "Oh, yes, it's as I suspected." She exhaled slowly and reached out, summoning the young woman to come. Then she continued to look into the faces of the onlookers. I got the feeling that she was somehow reading their thoughts, or at the very least, could perceive them.

"You," she pointed to another woman, "and you," she said to yet another. "Don't be shy, please, come join our newest guest."

The women glanced briefly at each other and walked over to where I stood. Imelda positioned the three women so that they faced the others who still stood with their bowls in their hands. Those sitting on the logs had stopped eating and were now watching with interest. Each of the three women who stood beside me would, in any other setting, probably be considered pretty in her own way. Each had long hair and wore it in a loose braid that hung down her back—common at the time among those in service or those of the working class. Of the three, none held a candle to Eleanor as far as beauty was concerned.

"Miss Eleanor," Imelda continued, "many who reside at this humble camp are very guarded when it comes to their emotions. They rather pride themselves on their ability to hide their feelings and bridle their passions. However, there are others among us," she chuckled, "and you'll meet them later," she made a gesture toward the tents at the back of the camp, "who do not share the same, er, self-control. On the contrary, they . . . express themselves much more freely."

Imelda walked over to the other bearded man and whispered something in his ear. He nodded and went into one of the nearby tents. When he reappeared, he was carrying a pair of scissors. Although I sensed a noticeable increase of nervous energy in the air, nobody exhibited any hint of a reaction. The bearded man handed Imelda the scissors and she turned again to face the spectators.

"I commend you for your commitment to guard your emotions so carefully, but these women standing before you now," she gestured behind her to the three women standing near me, "experienced an emotion so intense that they failed to hide it from me. Oh, not that I blame them;

their reaction was, after all, delightfully human. But look at them; could any one of them compare to our guest when it comes to beauty?" She turned and stepped in front of me.

"Miss Eleanor," Imelda spoke with feigned sincerity, "these women are secretly very jealous of you, but they are particularly envious of your hair. Here in our humble little camp, we are divided into two main groups—those who act, and those who are acted upon. I can't put it any simpler than that. These before you," she turned and waved to the onlookers, "like to call themselves resisters." She scoffed. "They believe as long as they guard their emotions well, they are exempt from choosing sides. Of course, in the end they all break. Everyone has a breaking point; the question is, what price are you willing to pay to keep from breaking?"

Imelda placed the scissors in my hand. "Which side will you take?"

I stared down at the scissors, unsure what she was suggesting. My heart pounded furiously against my chest, afraid that no matter how I answered, the results would be unbearable.

Imelda waited for a long time and when I didn't respond, she took the scissors from my hand, walked over to the first woman, and reached for her braid. She placed the scissors at the nape of the woman's neck and began cutting. Eleanor gasped so loudly and with such shock that I couldn't stop her. Imelda looked over at me and smiled as she continued cutting. When she stopped, she held the woman's braid high in the air for all to see and quoted from the book of Numbers: "And the priest shall set the woman before the Lord, and uncover the woman's head, and put the offering of memorial in her hands, which is the jealousy offering: and the priest shall have in his hand the bitter water that causeth the curse."

Imelda took the braid and said to the woman, "Hold out your hands." The woman, struggling to keep from showing any reaction, did as she was told, and Imelda laid the braid in her hands. The woman held her braided hair in her hands and then suddenly, as if caving in, she fell to her knees and began to weep. Imelda dropped behind the woman and rested her free hand on the woman's shoulder, drew in a long, exaggerated breath—and *moaned.* Then she went to work and began cutting more and more of the woman's hair, letting it fall in chunks to the ground. The harder the poor woman cried, the more aroused Imelda became, and the more wildly she cut. Wild-eyed and deranged, Imelda continued cutting, faster and faster with each snip—an inch here, two inches there, all over the woman's head.

"More! *More!*" She moaned as the woman continued to cry. "That's it!" She kept cutting. "Oh yes!" Hair fell in all directions, covering the ground around them until there was nothing left to cut. As if she were afraid she might have missed some, Imelda laid the scissors on their side, flat against the woman's head, and continued cutting as close to the scalp as possible, until the woman was virtually bald.

Wailing loudly, the woman slumped over in a wretched heap and sobbed, pawing pitifully at her hairless head. Imelda stood, panting, as she watched the disgraced woman with wanton pleasure, and then she burst into laughter.

"You see, Miss Eleanor? Everyone's emotions have a breaking point. Some emotions are so powerful they can't be suppressed," she scoffed, "not for long that is." With her appetite gratified for the moment, Imelda glanced down at the distraught woman and glowered at her with such disdain that it sickened my stomach.

What kind of evil is this? Eleanor asked in my mind.

I don't know, Eleanor, but please, please don't react. We can't get emotional.

But that poor woman! Beth, she's been debased in such a humiliating and degrading manner.

Quiet, Eleanor, I quickly ordered, *we don't know exactly what we're up against here. Don't give this crazy woman any ammunition that she might use against us.*

Imelda placed the scissors back in my hands. "Two others remain, each jealous of your hair and envious of your beauty—a jealousy offering is required. Who shall be next?"

"No, Imelda," I replied. "I won't play your demeaning game."

Imelda's evil grin made the hair stand up on the back of my neck.

"My dear, you will either act or you will be acted upon. The choice is yours. But before you choose, I beg of you to look carefully at the pathetic creature before you." Imelda glanced down at the wailing woman. "She couldn't hide her emotions from me, and you can see for yourself how she fared as a result."

Beth, please! Don't let her near my hair! Eleanor pleaded.

Stop it, Eleanor! I can't fight to hide both our emotions.

"Miss Eleanor?" Imelda was waiting for my response.

"This isn't my fight, Imelda." I said coldly.

Imelda grinned. "Oh, it's not? Well, we shall see." She took the scissors from my hands and went to the next woman. The woman looked at me with pleading eyes, begging me to do something to stop Imelda, but it was too late. Imelda grabbed the woman's braid and started cutting, just as she had with the first girl. The spectators in the crowd showed no reaction and made no attempt to stop Imelda as she cut through the woman's braid until just as before, she held the chopped off braid in the air and quoted from the Bible.

Imelda stood in front of the woman and ordered her to put out her hands. The woman stared coldly into Imelda's eyes and then spit in her face. Imelda's grin widened and again she drew in a long breath, closed her eyes, and released another repulsive moan.

"Oh yes!" she hissed. "Don't hold back dear. Give me more!"

The woman doubled up her fist, reached back, and slugged Imelda in the face. Imelda's eyes flew open, but she showed no sign of pain. The woman reared back, poised to strike again, but this time Imelda's hand flew up and she grabbed the woman's arm as it shot forward. Imelda twisted the woman's arm behind her back, forcing her into submission.

"Richard?" Imelda called to her bearded associate.

"Yes ma'am," he replied.

"Put this one in tent twelve."

"ma'am?"

"You heard me. She'll take Eldon's place in tonight's festivities." Imelda released the woman's arm and shoved her towards Richard. As soon as she was free, the woman took off in a dead sprint, heading straight for the woods. Richard started to run after her but Imelda stopped him.

"Let her go, Richard. She'll make a tasty feast for the animals."

I'd had all I could take. It was as if I were in a horror movie somewhere. "Who are you crazy people?" I yelled. "And you!" I pointed to the zombie-like onlookers, "why do you stand there and do nothing? Have you all been lobotomized or something? What in the hell's the matter with you?"

Imelda started to laugh again. "Oh, Richard! Remind me to reward

James with something special for bringing Miss Eleanor to us. Her emotions possess twice the power of any I've experienced yet."

Richard chuckled. "I'll give him the message . . ." he glanced at me and grinned, "right before I kill him."

"No!" I gasped.

Richard and Imelda each belted out a repulsive laugh.

Oh, James! Eleanor cried in my mind. *James, you wretched fool!*

Imelda's face grew suddenly serious again and she forced the scissors into my hands. "Make your choice, Eleanor! Act, or be acted upon!"

My response was the same. I'd never felt such contempt for another human being as I did at that moment. I struggled with every ounce of self-control I could muster to keep my cool and not reveal the hatred I felt for this woman.

"No," I said, determined not to cave into Imelda's demands.

Imelda raised an eyebrow and gave me an amused nod. "Very well, then." She took the scissors from my hand and handed them to the third woman.

"Act, or be acted upon!" she ordered the woman.

The woman looked nervously at the scissors. "I don't understand."

Imelda gave her a patronizing smile. "My dear, the choice is yours to make—Miss Eleanor's hair or yours. You decide."

The woman stared down at the scissors again. She looked up at me with pleading eyes that seemed to ask for forgiveness.

Beth, no! You can't let her! Eleanor cried.

Shut up, Eleanor!

Eleanor begged, *Beth, please!*

The woman walked slowly behind me and pulled several strands of my hair out to the side. She held the scissors up to the strands and placed the strands between the blades.

Beth! Eleanor cried. *Please, no! No!*

I stood stone-faced, determined not to care. My breath caught as I heard the scissors snap closed. I shut my eyes. When I felt the strands of hair fall back into place, I opened my eyes and gasped. The woman had taken hold of her own hair and was chopping off her braid as quickly as she could. Once cut, she held up her braid for all the onlookers to see. Then, with a smile on her face, she stepped in front of me and offered it to me.

"This is my jealousy offering," she said bravely. "It was prideful of me to be envious of your beauty. I won't be the one to take from you that which God has given so abundantly."

Imelda's expression fell instantly. The woman handed Imelda the scissors and knelt in front of her. "Do with me as you wish."

Imelda growled furiously. She grabbed at the woman's hair and began chopping off large chunks at a time. The woman didn't make a move. Instead, she held her head high and perfectly still, allowing Imelda free rein at her. Imelda chopped away until barely half an inch remained all over her head. Frustrated and angry, Imelda stomped on the ground, kicking the loose hair in a heated tantrum. The woman, head held high, continued to sit still without making a sound. She was totally calm, and the more animated Imelda became, the more at peace the woman appeared.

When Imelda finally stopped her tirade, I feared she would kill the woman; instead, she ordered the woman to get back in line. The woman stood and joined the onlookers who were still waiting in line for their food. I watched the woman with utter amazement as she proceeded to behave as if nothing unusual had happened. She glanced over at me and smiled. I stared at her, dumbfounded, and her smile widened. Never before had I witnessed such strength in a woman—such confidence— such character. She was perfectly radiant, astonishingly beautiful in a way I could never put into words.

Holding her hair in my hands, I returned her smile and then pressed her braid to my heart in a show of gratitude. Moisture filled the corners of my eyes and then I remembered James' warning. "No matter what happens, show no emotion."

Later that evening, Eleanor and I argued over what I'd proposed as an act of generosity in honor of the women who had suffered so much humiliation that morning.

Beth, no! Please! You mustn't do this to me! Eleanor pleaded with me.

But Eleanor, don't you see? We owe it to those women.

But, Beth! Eleanor whined. *I'll be disgraced forever. Shamed. I'll never be able to show my face in public again!*

Don't be so dramatic! I scolded her. *For heaven's sake, Eleanor. In* the twenty-first century, women cut their hair all the time! Jeez, it's just hair . . . it will grow back! Besides, I know how to—

It's my hair, Eleanor insisted. It's . . . it's part of my beauty.

You're wrong, Eleanor. Hair does not make a woman beautiful. You saw for yourself this morning when that last woman chose to sacrifice her own hair instead of yours. I've never witnessed a more beautiful act of kindness. It's who you are . . . what you stand for . . . that's what makes you beautiful.

Please, Beth, don't do this to me. I forbid it! If you do, I will never forgive you! Never!

Fine, I conceded, have it your way. I suppose I never really expected Eleanor to agree to my impulsive idea, but I hated losing—especially when I knew I was right. But consider this, Eleanor. What if tomorrow Imelda decides to repeat this morning's episode? What then? Would you really risk both of us being humiliated in front of all those people? Are you willing to give Imelda the satisfaction of hearing you cry? You saw what she did to that first woman!

I picked up the brush and pulled it through Eleanor's hair. I counted seventy-eight strokes before she finally responded.

Okay. Do it!

"You mean it?" I said aloud. I caught myself and then whispered, "Are you sure?"

Yes, for heaven's sake, just do it before I change my mind.

I picked up the scissors I'd snatched from the food tent earlier and held them up to Eleanor's hair. You're sure about this? I asked one more time.

Eleanor's life force rushed to the surface and took control. In a swift movement, she chopped off a large chunk of her hair and watched it fall to the ground. She gasped audibly when she saw her dark ringlets spread delicately on the ground. Then she started to cry.

Don't ask me again, Beth, she said. Just do it!

I marveled at Eleanor's brave determination and the defiance in her tone. I paused only briefly, understanding how difficult this was going to be for her. Eleanor attributed so much of her femininity to her hair. Her reaction as she stared at the spot where she had just cut her hair invoked such a feeling of guilt in me that I couldn't go through with it. I couldn't rob Eleanor of something so precious to her—all because I wanted to make a point and defy Imelda.

Beth, please! Do it now, before I lose my courage. Please!

You don't have to do this, Eleanor. It was selfish of me to guilt you into agreeing.

No. You were right, Beth. Those women were publicly humiliated because of my hair. This is but a small gesture on my part—something I can do to restore part of their dignity. Eleanor paused for a moment and I felt her resolve strengthen. *Cut it off Beth. All of it!*

You're sure?

Eleanor hesitated for a second before taking a deep breath and responding with a determined, *Yes!*

With that, I began carefully sectioning off her hair.

Eleanor, I promise to give you the cutest short cut of the twenty-first century! And you're going to love how it feels! Especially in this heat!

I spent the next two hours—late into the evening—transforming Eleanor's hairstyle from Victorian to modern-day Vogue. Even though she continued to insist through her tears that she was okay, I felt her sadness as if it were my own. The lump that lodged itself in her throat gave way to a pained sob as the scissors sliced through another section of her hair. It was too late for second guessing now, so I worked quickly. I knew that if I showed any sign of hesitation, Eleanor's remorse would be unbearable for both of us.

To speed past the initial shock, I made sure to cut off all her length first. It took a while, but eventually I was left with a short bob to work with. I was grateful that Lucinda had tucked a small mirror in with my things. Being able to see what I was doing helped me keep the cut even.

I was proud of Eleanor for holding onto her resolve as I clipped away. Once her length was gone and she acknowledged that we were well past the point of no return, her tears finally stopped and she became unexpectedly stronger. She even seemed interested in the process in a "looking through a peephole" sort of way.

Because Eleanor's hair was exceptionally thick and wavy, it took a long time to style it into layers, especially such short ones; but I feared if I didn't cut it short enough, Imelda would likely finish the job the next morning—if for no other reason than to just make a point. So I made sure to cut it as short as possible while still managing to keep it fashionable.

Rest assured, Eleanor, I said proudly when I was almost done, *you're going to rock this style! Trust me!*

Pardon me?

I chuckled to myself. *It's a figure of speech. It means that women all over will want to copy your new hairstyle.* I chuckled again. *I'm afraid they're going to be even more jealous of you than ever when they see how stunning you look with short hair.*

When I finally finished cutting Eleanor's hair, I used my fingers to style it into place. Then I cut a two-inch wide strip of cloth from my undergarments and folded it into a hair band. I tied the band around my head in a fashion similar to how girls sometimes wear their hair in the twenty-first century.

Once the intrigue of the process wore off, Eleanor was suddenly hit with the reality of what we had done.

Oh Beth! My hair! It's gone. It's really gone! Eleanor finally lamented. *Oh!*

Are you okay? I asked, fearing for a moment that I had managed to coerce her into agreeing to something she didn't really want. There was a long silence in my head. *Eleanor?*

Why are you tying a rag around my head? Eleanor asked, ignoring my question.

Consider it a fashion statement; sort of like an exclamation point on our act of defiance.

I feel so bald . . . so exposed, Eleanor complained.

I know, I said reassuringly, *but you'll get used to it, I promise.* I paused briefly then added, *I wish I could take you to the twenty-first century; there are fashion models with this same haircut—heck, some of them even shave their heads and they're considered some of the most gorgeous women on the planet.*

There was another long pause and then Eleanor said, *Will you tell me about your life some day?*

Eleanor's question surprised me. It never occurred to me to talk about my life; I suppose I'd somehow assumed that she knew everything she needed to know. I chuckled softly.

Yes, I answered. *I would like that . . . very much.*

I gathered up the longest strands of Eleanor's hair from the ground and smoothed them out with my brush. Then I divided the hair into three sections and started braiding. I cut two more segments from my undergarments—thin ones this time—to use as ties, and tied knots at each end of the braid. Satisfied that my work was finished, I lay down on the crude bed that James had prepared before my arrival and held Eleanor's braided hair against my chest as I began to drift to sleep.

Beth? Eleanor whispered.

What is it? I replied sleepily.

There was a silent pause before she answered.

My head's cold.

I chuckled and held Eleanor's braid tighter against my chest.

Eleanor's presence faded into the background as I lay in the dark thinking—trying to piece together everything that had happened. What had James meant by the union of virtue and vice? And what was the significance of the eight-pointed star he'd referred to? I didn't know James, but at one time he'd apparently convinced Eleanor that he loved her, and she thought she loved him, too. I couldn't decide if his role in bringing Eleanor here was his idea or if it was part of some perverse plan that was far more sinister than he'd foreseen. I got the feeling that James was merely a pawn in someone else's heinous agenda.

I was deep in thought when the screaming began.

At first, it was just solo voices intermittently piercing the night, more like cries for help than actual screams. Then gradually more and more voices started shrieking—so many that it was difficult to distinguish one from the other or whether they emanated from men or women. Some were cries of terror, others of pain; but what was most disconcerting was that again, mingled among the cries, were the sounds of drunken laughter that seemed to escalate as the cries grew louder. Just like the previous night, there were periodic explosions of obvious approval interspersed with cries of agony. My mind conjured up all sorts of images, all of them too terrible to imagine. I covered my ears and sank down in my blankets to drown out the noise. I feared that sometime during the night, one of Imelda's goons would come for me. I had no idea what their plan for me was, but whatever it was, I needed to be ready. And regardless of how terrifying or horrific it was, I had to keep my wits about me. I remembered what James had said about controlling my fear, so I found myself analyzing the emotions of the three girls who'd been exploited earlier. They were singled out because of their jealousy, but it was how they responded to Imelda that seemed to be the key. The first woman exhibited signs of fear and disgrace. The second women displayed definite signs of contempt and anger. The third woman, though nervous, showed a strong sense of determination, and even though she ended up submitting to Imelda, she did so in a manner that was anything but weak; on the contrary, she exuded strength the likes of which I'd never before witnessed.

Each of the three women's emotions triggered a specific reaction from Imelda which was very telling. She'd been intensely aroused by the first woman's fear, to the point that she'd lost all sense of control. When she'd finished debasing the poor woman, she looked down on her with loathing and contempt. The second woman's anger and subsequent attempt to defend herself by fighting did not seem to prompt the same level of passion in Imelda. Instead, Imelda's reaction was more cold and calculating. Then there was the third woman. She had evoked a much different reaction. After her unsuccessful attempt to humiliate and intimidate the third victim, Imelda acquiesced and ended up letting her go.

Try as I might, I couldn't get the image of these three women out of my head. Following Imelda's crazed rampage, the first woman had run to her tent, hiding her face in shame. God only knows the plight of the second woman who'd gone barreling into the woods. I hoped she'd somehow managed to survive the night, but I knew it was unlikely. There were too many wolves, snakes, and heaven knows what else lurking in the woods at night. I didn't worry about the third woman; she'd won the battle of wills this morning and seemed to be out of danger—at least for now. I felt a strong desire to see her again and speak to her.

Then there was Miriam. Lawrence had taken her to "sick bay," whatever that meant. Had her hair been cut too, or had she suffered some other form of humiliation? I couldn't bear the thought of what might have happened to her. She'd been punished because of me—they all had. Miriam had been trying to tell me something when she'd cut her eyes toward the tents at the back of the camp, something that Imelda did not want me to know. Blame it on morbid curiosity, but I had to know what was going on inside those tents. What was so important that Miriam would risk putting herself in danger?

The next morning, Imelda was nowhere to be seen. Miriam was back and by all appearances seemed to be okay. Oddly enough, she still had all her hair. She was standing with Richard and Lawrence, watching as people gathered for their morning meal. Some of the faces I recognized from the previous morning, but there were a couple that I hadn't seen before.

I was famished. Counting the day of my abduction, it was going on three days since my last meal. I thought longingly of Mrs. Weddington's lunch that I never got a chance to eat. I wasn't sure what type of "mush" they were serving us this morning, but I was determined to eat every bit of my portion.

James had promised to take me home if that was still my desire when he returned. His statement bewildered me; why would anyone choose to remain in such a wretched and repulsive place as this? What could possibly entice people to stay here? I was determined to find out the answer, no matter how frightening, and then I was going to figure out some way to free all the pathetic people being held here against their will—although for the life of me, I couldn't understand why they hadn't united to free themselves. As far as I could tell, there were no armed guards to stop them; so why didn't they rebel?

I'd walked out of my tent carrying Eleanor's carefully braided hair in my arms. I'd never seen Eleanor's hair in the outdoors, how it shimmered in the light of the morning sun. Contrasting rays of blue and copper reflected from her braid, making her hair impossible to ignore when the sun hit it. No wonder heads turned whenever she walked by! Imelda was right about one thing, Eleanor had been endowed with more than her fair share of beauty. I was not surprised when the onlookers gasped upon seeing me. They no doubt assumed I'd been disgraced by Imelda during the night—why else would Eleanor be sporting such a drastic change in hairstyle?

It wasn't difficult to spot the third woman in the crowd; she was the one with the same hairstyle as me—only sadly, hers was even shorter. Imelda had been careful not to leave more than a half inch or so all the way around the third woman's head—which was kind I suppose, given that she didn't stop until there was nothing left of the first woman's hair.

Unlike Eleanor, the third woman's hair was neither thick nor wavy, so it pretty much stuck straight out, resembling a straggly butch cut. I couldn't help but feel a little guilty as I approached her because I knew that even without her long, lustrous hair, Eleanor's beauty would still stop people in their tracks. The unfortunate woman number three was sure to feel self-conscious and insecure next to Eleanor.

Astonished onlookers stepped aside as I walked forward, determined to make contact with the woman. When she saw me approaching, she gasped and her hands flew up to her mouth.

"Oh, ma'am!" she whispered. "Your hair! Your beautiful hair! What have they done to you?"

I smiled and held my head up high. "This . . ." I held out my arms and offered her Eleanor's braid, "this is solely *my* doing!"

"But why?" She reached up and brushed her hand across her butchered head. "I—I let them do this to me that I might spare you such humiliation. Why—why would you willingly do such a thing?"

The woman's response surprised me. "Don't you get it?"

She shook her head in confusion. "Get what?"

I laid Eleanor's braid in the woman's hand. "This is my offering to *you*. You had the chance to save yourself from public humiliation, but you chose to save *me* instead. That was the most selfless act of kindness I've ever experienced."

The woman held Eleanor's braid up and inspected it in the sunlight. "Your hair," she sighed. "I saw Imelda's expression as she combed her fingers through it. She was so jealous—so envious of it! I knew she would find a way to rob you of it, it's how she is. And now," she stroked Eleanor's braid with her free hand, "now she's gotten just what she wanted."

"Oh no, no! You mustn't see it that way. This isn't about Imelda at all. This is about me wanting to honor you for what you did for me yesterday. Imelda didn't want to rob me of my hair, she wanted to rob me of my dignity. The two are very different! She wanted the pleasure of cutting it off herself and humiliating me in front of everyone here. You saw for yourself how aroused she became when she was cutting the others' hair. It was disgusting! No, this was never about hair—this was about our sense of dignity. When you denied her the satisfaction of demoralizing you, she became enraged."

The woman considered my words thoughtfully and then smiled. "She did throw quite the tantrum, didn't she?"

I laughed and the onlookers gasped. In unison, they stepped back another couple of feet. I ignored them and introduced myself. "My name is Eleanor," I said, offering the woman my hand.

"I'm Margaret," she replied, placing her hand in mine. She glanced quickly at the onlookers and then whispered, "We shouldn't be talking like this—it makes the others nervous."

"Why?"

Margaret shook her head. "Perhaps later?"

I studied her face for a moment, and then nodded. "Yes, of course."

Margaret started to turn away, but then looked back and gave me a sly grin. "It looks good on you, you know? That hairstyle."

I reached up and pulled at the short strands along the back of my ear. "Ya' think?" I chuckled sarcastically as I threw out another of my twenty-first century phrases; Margaret didn't seem to notice or care.

"I don't suppose you would make me one of those hair bands, would you?"

My smiled widened. "I'd be very happy to!"

I joined the others in line, well aware that they were staring at my hair when I wasn't looking. Each time I tried to make eye contact or speak, they would avert their eyes or turn away, ignoring any attempt on my part to communicate. When I reached the front of the line, Miriam handed me my bowl and I made a point to catch her eye. I shifted my eyes towards the tents at the back of the camp and then looked back at Miriam for some sign of acknowledgement, but she didn't so much as blink. She filled my bowl with what appeared to be some kind of wheat grains, but before she could finish, I released my hold and the bowl fell to the ground. "I'm so sorry." I acted surprised as Miriam and I both reached down for my bowl at the same time. "I'm such a clumsy fool sometimes!"

Miriam didn't say anything; she just nodded and tried to help me with the mess as best she could. She grabbed a rag from the table and wiped off the bottom of my bowl. Then she refilled it and handed it to me. I hoped that nobody noticed when I said thank you and her eyes flashed quickly towards the tents at the back of the camp. There was obviously something critical about those tents—something that kept the folks here in a zombie-like state of submission with no hope of escape.

Option Four

C H A P T E R   2 0

I ate my wheat grains in silence, careful not to eat too much or too quickly. I'd learned in school that eating whole wheat grains was murder on the digestive system when you weren't used to them. It's especially murderous—not to mention inconvenient—when you don't have access to flushing toilets or running water. Still, I was so hungry it required all my self-control to keep from devouring my bowl.

Not much went on in the camp during the daylight hours. It was as if the whole camp was asleep. There was no way all the excessive laughter and cries of agony during the night could have come from only those present for the morning meal. So where were the others? Were they sleeping in the tents? Was that what Miriam was trying to tell me?

Evidently, it was a daily ritual for everyone to meander down to the nearby stream during the heat of the day. Nobody hesitated or thought twice about stripping down to their underclothes in front of each other and bathing in the cool flowing water of the stream. The people moved together in mass, but did not make any attempt to communicate; they reminded me of programmed robots. Even when the women stood waist deep in the water with their undergarments soaked and pressed against their bodies, revealing far more than deemed appropriate, nobody paid any attention to them. Not only did this seem unnatural, it was creepy. Even in the twenty-first century, with hundreds of women lining the shores of the beaches in thongs and bikinis that left pretty much nothing to the imagination, no normal, healthy male that I'd ever met could resist staring at a woman in dripping wet clothes. Here, in a time when women wore enough layers of material in a single dress to make twenty modern-day outfits, it made no sense that so many women in wet underclothes wouldn't evoke some type of reaction from the men.

How much longer will I have to endure this? I asked myself, as I joined the men and women in the water. I was grateful for some relief from the blistering heat of the sun. Some parts of the stream were much deeper than others, and I couldn't resist the temptation to submerse myself repeatedly in the cool current. This stream was smaller than the one that flowed on the backside of the Hastings' estate, and it didn't run with the same power, but it was refreshing and a welcome distraction from the blistering temperatures of midday. I couldn't help but wonder where the stream led and what would happen if I coasted downstream. The thought was a tempting one.

"I wouldn't recommend it," a man's deep voice said. I whirled around to find Lawrence wading in the stream behind me. "Imelda says Chambersburg's been hit again; and this time they burned it clean to the ground."

"That's a lie!" I blurted. "There are no rebels around here." I suddenly thought of the four dead men at the rendezvous where James came for me. Was there any chance Lawrence could be telling the truth? I decided to call his bluff. "You're only saying that so you can scare me and keep me from running."

Lawrence winked and his mouth turned up into a sinister grin. "Be that as it may, it don't change the facts. It's miles to the nearest fort—and I doubt you'd last five minutes once those Rebel raiders got a glimpse of you. Some of 'em this far out ain't seen a woman for months, maybe even longer. Likely they'd turn on their own kind for a go at you. No, ma'am, you wouldn't last five minutes, fer sure."

I glared up at Lawrence's smug expression, searching for proof that he was lying.

"Then again, that's assuming you lived through the night. Lots of wild animals huntin' near these streams. They'd just as soon eat you as look at you." Lawrence squinted and held up his hand to shield his eyes from the sun. He looked me up and down slowly. "Yep, be a waste either way."

I started to head further downstream, but Lawrence grabbed my arm from behind.

"I ain't kiddin', Missy. You'll be dead by morning, or wish you were." He pulled on my arm but I jerked away from him.

"What's the trouble here?" Richard joined us in the water.

"What was the name of the little lady who tried to swim downstream from here?" Lawrence asked Richard.

"You mean the Pritchard girl?"

"Yeah, that's the one. What became of her?"

"Rumor has it they found her body somewhere up near Greensville, if I recall. Took 'em a bit to identify her."

"Yes'r, that's my understanding as well. Say, did they ever find the ones responsible?"

Richard glanced at me and chuckled. Then he turned back to Lawrence. "Some folks blame it on a group of rogue soldiers. Can you imagine such a thing?"

Lawrence let out a sarcastic laugh. "Now where d'ya suppose they came up with such a story?"

"Can't rightly say." Richard glanced over at me again. "Rumor has it they're in cahoots with the 'Gray Ghost' himself."

Both men burst into a simultaneous chorus of laughter. Then Richard continued his sadistic taunting. "You know, ma'am, it's a downright shame. Them Rebels just used that poor young girl up 'till she done died. Beats anything I've ever heard of."

"It's true ma'am," Lawrence's feigned concern for the girl made my stomach turn. He looked at the ground and shook his head mockingly. "Some say ain't no human could'a done that to another human."

As sickened as I was listening to the two bearded men banter back and forth, their rhetoric sparked a memory. I recalled the afternoon I'd gone into town with Eleanor's mother and overheard the two men by the post office talking about some girl's body that had been found near one of the neighboring towns.

"It's just like Harrisburg all over again," one of the men had said.

"The two attacks are nothing alike!" the other man had insisted. *"Listen to me, I was there! I saw the poor girl's body. She wasn't just violated, she was—"*

Was what? I wondered to myself. Could this have been the same girl that Lawrence and Richard were referring to? Surely not—surely Lawrence and Richard were just trying to scare me. And it was working. I couldn't begin to know the dark secrets hidden in this hell hole James had brought me to, but I resolved that I would survive until he returned and could finally take me home. Fortunately, James had a gun—he'd be able to protect us.

Figuring I had no alternative, I turned and headed back upstream and returned to the others, who were still splashing around in the water. Lawrence and Richard figured their work with me was done, so they slithered back to their respective perches near the stream's edge.

That night I had an unexpected visitor. I'd retired to my tent for the night and found Imelda waiting for me inside.

"What do you want?" I asked coldly.

Imelda chuckled. "Save your energy, Eleanor. You're going to need it. I came to let you know that tomorrow night is your night—it's a night we've all been waiting for ever since James first told us about you."

"What does James have to do with all this? What hold do you have on him?"

"Why, isn't it obvious, dear? James had everything to do with this. He's the reason you're here, and thanks to him we will all have an opportunity to feed on your emotions. I admit, I haven't looked forward to anything this much in a long time."

"You're crazy!" I muttered.

Imelda smiled. "Not crazy," she tilted her head to one side, "just hungry. Now rest up. You'll need your strength when we come for you."

Imelda started to leave, but I grabbed hold of her arm and spun her around to face me. "I'm afraid you're going to be disappointed, Imelda. You and your goons won't get anything from me."

Imelda laughed and patted my hand. "I love what you've done with your hair, Eleanor."

I took a deep breath, careful not to show any remorse. "Thank you." I replied simply.

Imelda stared at me for a moment and then asked, "Would you cut my hair like yours? Please?"

Stunned by her question, I simply stared at her, unable to voice a response.

Imelda retrieved the scissors from the corner of my tent and held them out to me. "Here!"

I stared down at the scissors and Imelda put them in my hand.

"Please," she said again, turning around so her back was to me. "Please do it!"

This was my chance—my chance to get even—to avenge the three women she'd humiliated and to avenge Eleanor, who'd relented after much coaxing and allowed me to cut off all her beautiful hair just to make a point. A sudden thrill of excitement rushed through me as I considered how much pleasure it would give me, how gratifying it would be, to cause Imelda the same kind of shame she'd inflicted on the other women.

My hands trembled as I reached out and unfastened Imelda's hair, which she'd twisted into a tight bun at the back of her head. Surprisingly, it fell all the way down to her waist. It was thicker than Eleanor's, but not as wavy; and though it was unusually soft, it did not hold near the luster and shine that Eleanor's did. I held the scissors to the hair at the base of her neck and thought about where to begin. The anger that stirred within me caught me by surprise, and suddenly, all I could think about was how badly I wanted revenge. I didn't just want to chop off all of this woman's hair, I wanted to hurt her—to scar her emotionally the way she'd no doubt scarred her victims. I wanted to make her pay for what she'd done—to disgrace her in every way possible. No, cutting her hair wasn't enough. I wanted to debase her, and then I wanted to kill her.

I grabbed a handful of her hair and held it tightly in my fist. Then I began cutting very slowly, I intended to take my time and savor every second of the pleasure I knew this act was going to bring me. I watched as the first few strands of hair floated to the ground—it was almost as though they fell in slow motion. Imelda knelt submissively in front of me. I dropped to my knees behind her and grabbed hold of another section of hair. I reveled in the sound of the snipping scissors every time another lock of her hair fell to the ground. I watched with satisfaction as the piles of hair grew bigger on the floor. Each clip of the scissors brought me such intense pleasure that my heart began to race and my breathing quickened. I tried to force myself to hold back, to make sure I prolonged her shameful ordeal. I couldn't wait to witness firsthand the mortification she would experience when she saw her reflection in a mirror for the first time once I finished with her.

The hatred I felt for Imelda burned hotter with every clip of the scissors. The more I cut, the hotter my hatred became. I hadn't realized how deep my contempt for her ran, but before I knew it, I was slashing away at her hair with such fury that I'd lost all sense of rational thought. I wasn't satisfied with chopping off all her length, I wanted to keep going—to keep cutting more and more, faster and faster. I was in such a state of heightened frenzy that Imelda's hair flew furiously in all directions; I wasn't even attempting to control myself any longer, nor did I intend to. I reminded myself repeatedly that she was getting everything she deserved, and that to leave so much as a quarter of an inch remaining was too good for her. If I'd had access to a razor, I would have shaved her head in a heartbeat. I wanted to rob her of every ounce of dignity she possessed, to take it from her the way she'd taken it from the others. So when there was nothing left for me to cut, I did as she had done and laid the scissors on their side and cut as closely to her scalp as possible. I was in such a rage I couldn't stop until I was certain anything resembling hair was gone.

When nothing but skin remained, I screamed out as loudly as I could, frustrated that I hadn't debased her enough. I stood, panting and out of breath. A stream of blood trickled from Imelda's head where I'd cut too closely to her scalp. This gave me such a rush of satisfaction that I reared my head back and screamed again, hungering for more.

"Ohhhhh," Imelda moaned, still kneeling on the floor at my feet. Then she began swaying back and forth, moaning deep in her throat. I watched her for a moment with amusement; then suddenly the thrill was gone and I wanted her out of my sight. My work was done—and yet for some reason, I still wasn't content that she'd suffered enough.

"Oh, Eleanor!" Imelda sighed hoarsely. "That was amazing! *You* were amazing!"

Imelda's response baffled me. Amazing?

"I'm afraid I underestimated you."

Imelda stood slowly, her knees wobbly. She pulled herself up straight and when she did, the temperature inside my tent began to drop dramatically. She closed her eyes and took several deep breaths. When she opened them again, they had turned into two lightless, yellow orbs.

"Bailey!" I gasped.

Bailey began to laugh. There was no doubt the evil laugh was his, even though it came from Imelda's body. "Hello, Beth Anne!" he mused. "Miss me?"

I stood paralyzed with the scissors dangling from my hand.

Bailey released a dark chuckle. "I must thank you for tonight. I had no idea you were capable of such unbridled passion. You're even more than I'd hope for!"

"What . . . how . . ." I looked down at the scissors in my hands, "When did you—"

Bailey bellowed with laughter. "Oh my, you really didn't know, did you? Oh yes, that makes this even sweeter than ever."

"What are you talking about? Makes *what* sweeter?"

"Why, your unleashed emotions, of course. I've waited your whole life to experience your passion; and tonight, you gave me the sweetest sampling imaginable. You, Beth, were most certainly worth the wait and ooohhh, judging by your ferocity a few moments ago, I can only imagine the pleasure that tomorrow night will bring."

Pleasure? I was confused. *What pleasure?* "But . . . you . . . Imelda, I didn't—"

"But-but-I-I, Imelda this, Imelda that," Bailey mocked. "Really, Beth Anne, are you always at such a loss for words? It's rather annoying, wouldn't you agree?"

"Stop it!" I demanded. "You're not making any sense. This . . ." I waved the scissors at Imelda's hairless head, "has nothing to do with you! This is about Imelda—about revenge! The only one who experienced *any* pleasure tonight was me! I gave Imelda exactly what she deserved!"

Bailey released another loud roar of laughter. "That you did, my dear. That you did. But don't think for a moment you're the only one who took pleasure in Imelda's debasement." Bailey shook his head slowly and pointed an accusing finger at me. "I have to admit, you impressed me. I thought for a moment you were going to kill her."

"I . . . she . . . I was just—" I stammered, trying to find words.

"You can say it, go ahead. You already admitted that this was about revenge; I wasn't about to stop you—even if you did end up killing her. After all, isn't murder the ultimate act of vengeance?"

Bailey's haughty smirk made me squirm. The fact that I'd done anything that had pleased him this much was disconcerting. "I wasn't going to kill her," I said defensively, "I just wanted her to pay for what she did to those three women."

"Let's not kid ourselves, Beth. Revenge emanated so strongly from you that I could taste it—and so could you. Admit it—it tasted sweet, didn't it?"

I glanced down at the scissors and a cold chill ran through my veins. Suddenly, they felt very heavy. Had anger and revenge so consumed me that I actually might have killed Imelda? I shuddered at the thought. The weight of the scissors pulled against my fingers and I slowly released them and let them fall to the ground.

"You see, Beth, we're not so different, you and I."

"You're wrong, Bailey. I'm nothing like you."

Bailey started to laugh. His shadowy figure oozed its way out of Imelda's body and once free, her body slumped to the ground in a motionless heap—just like Eric's had the night he attacked me at Jonathan's ranch. Bailey's disembodied spirit stood before me. In the dim light of the lantern, it was difficult to discern exactly where Bailey's spirit ended and the darkness began.

"Look at her Beth," Bailey gestured toward Imelda. "Tell me it doesn't please you to see her stripped of all her power."

I stared down at Imelda's body—she suddenly seemed so frail and fragile. How could this pathetic woman lying on the floor of my tent have been the cause of so much humiliation? Then, with unimaginable force, I remembered what Jonathan had told me about possessors. I'd felt so guilty after Eric died, blaming myself for his death, and Jonathan had tried repeatedly to reassure me that it wasn't my fault. Now, with sudden clarity, Jonathan's words flashed to the forefront of my mind.

"The possessor would have killed Eric no matter what happened with

you. It was his plan from the beginning to use Eric's body to get to you and then dispose of it. He would have taken you by force either way—if not through Eric, then through someone else."

My breath caught in my throat. *"Through someone else."* The words dangled in my mind. *"Through someone else."*

I knelt down beside Imelda's limp body and rolled her on her back. Her glazed-over eyes stared blankly toward the canopy of my tent as I checked for her pulse. It was weak, but at least she was alive. Imelda had been used, just like Eric, by an entity with absolutely no regard for human life—and I had played right into his hands.

"You used her," I whispered remorsefully.

"I suppose that's one way to look at it. But then again, so did you, didn't you?"

"You stole her soul, just like you tried to steal Eric's."

"You're boring me, Beth. Eric is ancient history," Bailey chuckled. "Or I guess in Eric's case, it's more like future history. Hard to keep it all straight, what with traveling and all. I have to hand it to your boyfriend, though; it was a great idea hiding you from me in the past. It took a lot of effort to figure out where you were; but lucky for me, I had time on my side."

"But Intruders can't travel, so how did—"

"Come now, you can't expect me to reveal all my secrets, can you? I've found that if you want something badly enough, the rules just don't apply." Bailey laughed, "I learned that one from your precious boyfriend."

"What do you want, Bailey?" I asked coldly.

"I want what I've always wanted. I want what's rightfully mine. And as far as I'm concerned, that includes you!"

"Why me?" I said wearily. "What am I to you?"

Bailey chuckled. "Let's just say I have a score to settle and, well, claiming you as my own is part of the deal."

"I will never be yours, Bailey. I made that clear the night you killed Eric."

Bailey roared with laughter. "That, my dear, was mere child's play. What you gave me tonight," Bailey moaned, "that was only a sample of what you and I can experience together."

"I gave *you* nothing!" I insisted.

"You're wrong, Beth. You gave me access to your emotions. It was incredible! *You* were incredible!"

"No!" I cried. "That's not what I did, I was—"

"That's exactly what you did!" Bailey interrupted. "You lost control of your emotions. It's okay—all humans do eventually. The moment you made the decision to avenge those girls, the instant you cut through those first few strands of Imelda's hair, you opened a door that allowed *me* access to your emotions. Whether you intended to or not is simply irrelevant. The stronger the emotion, the more powerful the passion; and for me, the pleasure was two-fold. At the same time that I was feeding off your emotions, I was unleashing my own passion through Imelda's body. It was gratification unlike any I've ever experienced—to be both the giver and the receiver. Incredible! And now? Well, it's like a drug, Beth. I want more!"

"You make me sick!" I nearly spit the words at him. I loathed Bailey. "You listen to me, Bailey, you'll get nothing more from me. Nothing! Do you understand?"

"Careful, Beth Anne. Your anger is my key to access!"

"Thanks for the warning," I said sarcastically. "Now get the hell away from me!"

"Um, not so quick, my dear. You see, I've got something you want, something you want more than anything in this world, and I'm quite certain you'd be willing to pay a hefty price for it."

"What are you talking about?" I demanded. "There's nothing you could possibly have that I want!"

Bailey let out a low chuckle. "All right, have it your way then." He began to recede into the night air, and then all of a sudden he was directly behind me. "Enjoy the rest of your stay here, Beth . . . as our *guest.*"

I despised having to lower myself to his level, but I had to know.

"What is it Bailey?" I demanded. "What is it you have that I supposedly want so badly?"

Bailey didn't answer for several moments. He began slowly circling the room and then floated right up to my face, his yellow eyes peering intently into mine. He smelled of death—pungent and repulsive. Refusing to back down, I stood fixed in place and waited for his response. He finally laid his cards on the table.

"I can get you home," he said tauntingly.

I stared blankly at his eyes, determined not to react.

"James is coming to take me home any day now."

Bailey backed away slightly and continued. "I can take you back to the twenty-first century—back to your beloved Jonathan, your family, your friends, everyone." Bailey paused and allowed his words to sink in before continuing. "All you have to do is say the word and I can have you back home within two days."

I let out an audible gasp and Bailey smiled.

"Yes, Beth. I am your *option four*."

Bailey had struck a nerve and he knew it. He had the upper hand in this bargain for he understood how badly I wanted to go home, to have my life back, to be with Jonathan again. He held all the cards—he knew it, and he knew that I knew it.

"And I suppose all I have to do is sell my soul to the devil, is that it?"

Bailey floated away, bellowing with laughter. "Oh my dear, don't be so dramatic! It's nothing as sinister as that." He circled around me several times before again stopping in front of me. He slithered right up to my face and hissed, "All I want is one night."

"Never!" Eleanor spewed the word without warning, but Bailey persisted.

"One night, Beth! And then, by sunrise the following morning, you'll be home and back in Jonathan's arms."

Home? Was that possible?

No Beth! Eleanor cried. *Don't listen to him.*

But Eleanor, he said he could get me home.

He's lying! Please, Beth, you know he's only trying to trick you.

I knew deep inside that Eleanor was probably right, but what choice did I have? What were my options if I refused him?

"And if my answer is no? Then what?"

"Then you survive as a guest in our camp and James will take you home—home to your colonel husband, that is—and you'll never see your family, your home, or your lover again. The option is yours, Beth. But know this, each night that you refuse my offer the stakes will increase."

"What's that supposed to mean?"

"It means that my patience is wearing thin, and you have a decision to make before sundown tomorrow."

"What do I have to do? Share my bed with you? Is that what you want? Like the night at Jonathan's ranch when you wanted me to pretend I wanted you?"

"Please," Bailey scoffed. "Don't insult me, Beth. That was child's play. This goes way beyond our escapade at the ranch."

"I don't understand; what do you want from me?"

"I want you to let me *be* you for one night. To give me full access to all your emotions and the freedom to act on them at will, nothing barred."

It took me a couple of minutes to process what he was saying and to consider the implications. Bailey wanted me to give him carte blanch to Eleanor's body for one night, so he could do what? Eat, drink and be merry? Party? Feed on the negative emotions of others the way he'd fed on mine with Imelda? Is that what was happening every night in this camp? Was that the reason for the screams and excessive laughter?

"I can't do it, Bailey. I can't give you free rein to Eleanor's body—it's not mine to offer."

"Foolish girl! I already have free rein to Eleanor's body. Don't you understand that if I wanted to defile her, I could do so anytime I please? I already have access to ten healthy male bodies out there—all of them licking their lips and begging me for a shot at her. But I didn't bring you here for that. I brought you here so I could help you get home."

"For a price," I added.

Bailey cocked his head to one side. "It's a small price to pay for what you'll receive in return, don't you agree? After all, we're talking about what, eight hours of access for an entire lifetime with those you love? I consider that incredibly generous on my part."

Imelda groaned and began to stir.

"You think on it," Bailey said smugly. "I'll be back for your answer tomorrow at sundown."

Bailey closed his eyes and his shadowy shape began to morph into a whirling funnel that hovered over Imelda's body. A moment later, Imelda was on her feet.

"Good night, my dear," Imelda said, or rather Bailey did; to be honest, I couldn't be sure. But it was definitely Imelda's voice speaking to me, not Bailey's. I had to remind myself that Imelda was not the enemy here.

Bailey and Imelda left and not long after their departure, the screams began. It was the same as the two previous nights, so once again I found myself covering my ears and singing my mother's hymn to drown out the noise. I was moments away from sleep when I heard Eleanor's voice in my mind.

You have to do it, Beth. It's the only way.

Eleanor, you have no idea what you're saying. Bailey's evil, he's—

Yes, I know. I'm well aware of what and who he is. I know he frightens you because you have nightmares about him all the time, but I'm not afraid of him.

Then you're more naïve than I thought. You saw what his influence did to Imelda—

No, Eleanor corrected me. *I saw what his influence did to you! He doesn't have the same power over me.*

Eleanor's take on Bailey surprised me. *Eleanor, listen, whatever this obsession is that Bailey has with me, it doesn't involve you. Besides, what if I took him up on his offer; what then? I go back to the twenty-first century and you're left here to fend for yourself in this hell hole of a camp? No. Absolutely not.*

Eleanor was quiet for a moment and then continued. *At least one of us would be happy, Beth. If you don't go back, then we'll both be stuck here in this god-forsaken place.*

We're going to get out of here, Eleanor, I countered. *One way or another, we're getting out!*

And then what? You're going to hang out with me for the rest of my life?

I started to snicker.

Why are you laughing? You know that's what will—

I'm not laughing about that, Eleanor. I'm laughing because you just used the phrase, 'hang out.'

Eleanor started to giggle, then she turned serious again. *I want you to go, Beth. I want you to have your life back. You deserve to be happy.*

And what about your life, Eleanor? Don't you deserve to be happy too?

The man I thought I loved betrayed me—betrayed both of us, she said sadly.

What about William? He loves you Eleanor, really loves you.

It was several moments before Eleanor responded. *I know. But when Lucinda tells him I've run off with James, that I've disgraced the family name, he'll want nothing to do with me. That's why you have to take*

Bailey's offer. There may not be much hope for my happiness, but there's still a chance for you to have your life back.

My answer's no, Eleanor. Period.

Eleanor didn't respond.

I pulled the blanket around my shoulders, surprised by the cooler temperature. The past two evenings had been hot and muggy, but tonight there was a slight chill in the air. I was just about to doze off for the second time when Eleanor spoke again.

What's it like where you're from? she asked.

Did you have a coke or something? Why aren't you tired?

A coke?

I chuckled playfully. *It's a fizzy drink that makes you stay up late and pee a lot. I used to drink it all the time.*

There was a short pause before Eleanor resumed her questions.

How did you know you were in love with Jonathan?

I laughed to myself. Jonathan and I would disagree on the answer to this. In my mind, I didn't realize I was in love with him until Christmas Eve; but according to Jonathan, I was in love with him much earlier in our relationship.

I don't really know, Eleanor, I finally said. *I just knew that when I was with him, I felt happy; and when we were apart, I missed him.*

So it wasn't love at first sight?

No, I chuckled. *It was more like "awe" at first sight.*

Oh yes! I heard him playing Chopin's Etude in E, and I immediately felt a connection between us that I couldn't explain. It wasn't love; I hardly knew him but I was drawn to him, to his music. I could have sat and listened to him for hours. He is terribly good, isn't he?

He's amazing!

Eleanor paused for a moment. Then she said, *That song you wrote, you wrote it for him, didn't you?*

Yes.

What is it called? she asked.

I chuckled quietly. This was definitely a story for another day.

Um, don't take this the wrong way, but Jonathan refers to it as "Eleanor's Theme."

Oh! Eleanor seemed genuinely surprised. *You mean he thinks I wrote it?*

Yeah, something like that, I laughed. *Now, do you mind if we continue this conversation tomorrow? I really need to get some sleep. Apparently I've got an Intruder to fight tomorrow, and I'm going to need my wits about me.*

Oh, sorry. I'll be quiet.

Thank you.

There was a long silence, and I figured Eleanor had wandered to wherever it was she went when she disappeared from my mind, so I nearly jumped through my skin when she suddenly spoke again.

I travel too, sometimes, she began. *Not like what you did when Grace brought you here, but like when you travel in your mind and see things, hear conversations that you never could have heard. I sometimes wonder if Mrs. Weddington isn't right about us. Maybe we are possessed by some demon—or maybe we're witches—*

Oh good grief, Eleanor, there's no such thing! Now for the love of Pete, would you go to sleep?

I saw him watching you, you know.

Saw who?

Bailey. I saw him in your bedroom—at your uncle's house. He was in your mirror.

A sudden rush of goose bumps covered me from head to toe. *You saw him?*

Yes, and that wasn't the only time. He followed you to the cellar in your uncle's basement. He didn't like it when he discovered that I could see him. He tried to scare me away, but I refused.

When did these episodes begin, Eleanor?

Shortly after you arrived. Sometimes, when you think I'm "hiding" as you so often call it, I'm not hiding at all; I'm visiting you in the future.

I thought about this for a moment—and about all the times in the future when I had felt Eleanor near. I'd convinced myself that it was her ghost that was trying to communicate from beyond the grave—that her presence was connected to Jonathan. Perhaps I was wrong.

Eleanor, I'm beginning to think that the connection between us goes much, much deeper than either of us knows.

Unexpected Visitor

CHAPTER 21

There was no sign of the sun when I finally emerged from my tent the next morning. The sky was grey, completely clouded over. The thick moisture in the air told me that rain was on its way, and probably lots of it. I was grateful for the cooler temperatures, but I remembered how terrified I'd been the year before when the summer storm season struck. I immediately thought of Eleanor's little brother, Christopher, and recalled how we'd buried him right before being hit by Marensburg's roughest storms of the summer.

The camp was empty this morning, not a soul in sight. With the sun obscured by the clouds, I had no way of discerning what time it was. There was no sign of food at the mess tent, so it was either extremely early or very late; either way, my appetite would have to wait. I decided to head down to the river, wondering if perhaps that's where the others might be, but there was no one around. Thunder rolled in the distance, confirming my suspicions about the rain.

I walked from the river back to the camp and took a quick inventory. Three of the small tents were missing, along with two of the large ones.

That's curious, I thought to myself. Eleanor, do you see this?

I see it, she replied quickly.

Hmm. I wonder.

Eleanor read my thoughts. *I was thinking the same thing,* she remarked.

With no one around, this was an opportunity for me to find out the mystery of the tents at the back of the camp. I approached the first of the six remaining tents and before poking my head inside, called to see if anyone was around.

"Hello? Is anyone in there?"

No one responded. I glanced around the camp quickly, making sure I was still alone. I pulled back the flap that covered the opening to the tent and slowly poked my head inside. What I saw made me immediately jump backwards with a gasp. My hands flew to my chest in an effort to calm my exploding heart rate. When I finally caught my breath, I took a second look. I counted eight motionless bodies lying side-by-side across the width of the tent. A closer look confirmed that they were the bodies of three women and five men. Two of the men I recognized from the previous two days, but none of the women looked familiar to me.

Common sense told me that if these were dead bodies, the tent would stink, especially given the hot temperatures of the past two days. I inched my way into the musty tent, which was thick with the stench of human body odor. Being careful to make as little noise as possible, I approached the first of the bodies and bent down to check his pulse. He was definitely alive, although his heart rate was much slower than what should have been normal. I repeated this process on the remaining seven bodies and in each case the results were the same—lower than normal heart rates, averaging around forty beats per second for the men and fifty or so for the women.

What's wrong with all of them? Eleanor whispered. I thought it humorous that she was afraid someone might hear her.

I'm not sure; it's as if they're all in a coma, I responded. *Or worse.*

Worse?

Look closely at them; they look like Imelda did when Bailey left her body.

Oh Beth! You're not suggesting that Bailey is using all these people the way he used Imelda?

No. I'm afraid what I'm suggesting is far more frightening.

I crawled out of the tent, grateful for a breath of fresh air, and replaced the flap. Then I proceeded to visit each of the remaining tents. All of them housed people in a similar state—alive, but unresponsive.

Bailey isn't the only Intruder here, is he? Eleanor muttered.

No, I replied. *I don't think he is.*

Beth, what is this place?

Well, I can't be certain, but I think we're part of an entire camp full of Intruders—or using Bailey's word, a legion of them.

What have they done to these poor people?

I thought of Eric's fate the night he fought off Bailey, and I thought of Uncle Connor's description of what was happening in pockets of the United States in the twenty-first century—crimes that Uncle Connor was convinced were being committed by Intruders. According to Uncle Connor's explanation, the Intruders were using the bodies of criminals to prey on innocent victims, after which the Intruders would shed their borrowed bodies and move on to their next conquests. In Uncle's Connor's account, the host bodies did not survive the intrusion, and they decayed at such rapid rates that their deaths appeared to precede any of the crimes they'd committed. Uncle Connor had referred to their plan as "brilliant."

I don't know, Eleanor, I finally answered. I just don't know. But assuming these are all innocent victims, then where are the corrupt ones?

Maybe they've moved on, Eleanor suggested hopefully. *Maybe they're finished here, and they have moved on to set up camp elsewhere.*

Perhaps, I replied, *but I doubt it.* I began piecing parts of the puzzle together in my mind; but no matter how each scenario played out, the shuddersome outcome was ominous.

Imelda had alluded to some grand, culminating event to take place, something for which she found me ideally suited. A knot twisted in the pit of my stomach. I was on the brink of something unfathomably terrifying, and though I vowed to remain strong, I was beginning to lose hope.

Eleanor, I'm afraid what we're experiencing here is the calm before the storm.

You think they're coming back?

Oh yes, I replied, *they're coming back, and my guess is they're not coming back alone.*

You mean they'll be bringing in more innocent victims?

As if on cue, a flash of lightening flickered in the distance, followed a few moments later by a loud roll of thunder.

No. Not this time, Eleanor. I took a deep breath and sighed. *Judging by these tents, I would conclude that they've gathered enough victims.*

Then what? Who?

I suspect that tonight they'll bring in some very eager and willing participants, most likely the vilest evildoers imaginable—evildoers that make Amos and his lot look like good guys.

Oh, Beth! No!

Another bolt of lightning flashed across the darkening sky, followed seconds later by a crashing boom of thunder and the first drops of rain. The storm had arrived.

That's what Bailey meant by upping the stakes.

There was another explosion of light, this time accompanied by a roar of thunder so strong it shook the ground; and then the heavens opened and bucket loads of rain gushed down on the camp.

Beth, you have to say yes to Bailey's offer. It's the only way. Why should we both perish?

Listen to me, Eleanor! We will never give in to Bailey's demands! You hear me? Never! We will fight him—him and every other foul creature in this place.

Eleanor started to cry.

Don't you dare get soft on me now, Eleanor! I need your help to fight through this.

But Beth, Eleanor sobbed, *we can't win this fight.*

Then we'll run.

Run? Where to? You heard what James said; we'll never get away.

Lightning and thunder continued to split the sky, sending down sheets of rain.

Listen, Eleanor. I'll be damned before I'll let anyone defile you. Do you understand me? We'll run and we'll fight and should we die in the process, then so be it—but we'll die together, and we'll die on our terms, not theirs! Agreed?

Eleanor hesitated only a second before giving me her answer.

Agreed!

I went to work gathering whatever supplies I could find while rummaging through the tents. An overpowering sense of urgency spurred me to move as quickly as possible and to search only for items necessary for survival. In the mess tent, I managed to find a few bags of dried beef sticks, some oats, a role of thin wire, a couple of flint sticks, and some candles, which I tucked into the pouch I'd made by folding up the skirt of my dress. I grabbed two metal cups and threw them in as well. Then I hurried back to my tent and grabbed the scissors. Using my discarded undergarments from the night I arrived, I quickly folded them into a sling, tucked the supplies inside, and tied them to my waist. I started to grab the lantern, even though I knew it would be useless once it ran out of oil, but I decided against it, afraid that its light would give me away. I rolled up one of the blankets; it wouldn't be good for much once it became drenched from the rain, but I figured I could always toss it if it became too cumbersome.

Ready? I asked Eleanor.

Yes, for heaven's sake. Let's get out of here.

James had brought me in through a small clearing behind the mess tent. We'd been off the main trail for a quite a while before arriving at the camp, and by my estimation we'd traveled eastward from the south-bound trail. But given the dense cloud cover and pouring rain, I had no way of determining my direction. If I could somehow make it to the main trail, it might increase my chances of survival. I was well aware of the fact that this wasn't a failsafe plan, but it was the best idea I could come up with. I'd have to take my chances and hope for the best. I'd meant it when I told Eleanor that I'd rather die than allow myself to be violated, and although I was prepared to die if necessary, at the same time I was very determined to live.

Shielding my face from the rain, I headed for the clearing behind the mess tent. The ground was too saturated to provide any hope of tracking prints—animal or human. My goal was to get someplace where I could take cover for the night and protect myself from the storm. I didn't want to venture too far into the woods until I could figure out what direction I was heading. I'd hoped that the storm would let up and I'd be able to use the sun as my guide, but the rain was falling in a steady flow, and judging by the clouds it wouldn't end anytime soon.

Fortunately, the lightning and thunder had passed through, and judging by the length of time between flashes of light and the rumblings of thunder, I guessed it to be about five miles away. That was comforting, given that I'd always been taught to stay away from trees in a thunderstorm. With the sky growing darker, the lightning seemed much brighter. Each time it flashed it cast threatening shadows among the trees which made it feel as though the trees were coming to life.

I'd feel much better if we could make it to the main trail before the sky turns completely dark, I said in my mind, not sure if Eleanor was listening.

It's too far, Beth. We came in on horseback, and even then, it was more than an hour before we arrived at the camp. On foot it would take much longer.

Darn! If only we had a compass. Then at least we'd know we were heading in the right direction. The last thing we need is to end up traveling in a circle and finding ourselves back at the camp, I grumbled.

Look for moss, Eleanor chimed. *My father always told me that moss grows on the north side of a tree.*

Yeah, my father used to say the same thing, but he also said to be careful because in densely wooded areas, the moss can grow just about anywhere. I don't suppose you'd know where I could find a needle and a cork, do you?

There was a momentary pause and then Eleanor laughed.

No, really, it's a trick I learned camping one year. If you take a sewing needle and rub it in your hair, it magnetizes. But you need a cork to float it on—and the water can't be moving.

Silly Beth, I'm laughing because I can't imagine anyone having to use that trick in the twenty-first century—you with all your modern conveniences. We made compasses all the time when we were kids. We were forever getting lost on the estate, but we usually just used a hatpin and a leaf.

Leaves I can find. Any idea where I might find a hatpin?

Would a roll of ferrous wire do?

I'd forgotten about the wire. *Eleanor, you're a genius.*

I collected a couple of leaves and used the metal cups I'd brought to collect rainwater. It didn't take long for the cups to fill to overflowing, but I had to remain sheltered from the rain long enough for my hair to dry or I wouldn't be able to create the static electricity needed to magnetize the wire. With my hair so short, it didn't take long. I cut a small piece of wire from the roll, rubbed it against my hair, and then floated it on a small leaf in the metal cup. I watched with anticipation, but the wire didn't move.

What'd I do wrong? I asked in my mind. *Maybe my hair wasn't dry enough?*

I doubt it; a little moisture in the hair usually helps.

I stared down at my crude version of a compass and searched my mind for ideas. Then a thought suddenly occurred to me.

Eleanor, what do they make cups out of in your day?

I don't know, silver I'd guess.

That explains it. The silver in the cup must be interfering with the magnetized wire.

So what do we do now?

We'll have to create a puddle deep enough to float our leaf.

Within no time, we had the compass working. It was quite magical, actually. Without thinking about it, I looked up to the sky and whispered, "Thank you."

As grateful as I was for the sense of direction, I found that we had to repeat the process several times in order to maintain our course. There was no other way to determine if we were moving in a straight line. Still, it gave me something specific to focus on rather than letting my imagination run amuck with conjured images of what lay in store for us if we happened across a pack of wolves, or worse, were caught by Bailey and his followers.

Soon it was dark and I knew I'd have to stop and look for shelter. I found a tree with a large trunk and snuggled up to it, settling in for the night. I unrolled my blanket and tried to situate it so that it kept the rain from hitting my face. Rolled into a tight ball, I tried to make myself as small as possible so as not to be easily noticed when Bailey's goons came looking for me, which I knew deep down they would.

In spite of my obvious discomfort, I must have drifted off to sleep at some point because I soon found myself carried away to a familiar hillside overlooking the same large field surrounded by rolling hills that I'd visited numerous times in my dreams. The sun was warm and showered its rays along the tips of the long, flowing blades of grass that covered the slopes. Bright orange and purple wild flowers peppered the rolling hills and I watched with curiosity as bees danced from flower to flower, unimpressed and unthreatened by their audience. The feeling of despair and intense loneliness that so often overcame me when I visited this place was now gone; in its place was an indescribable feeling of peace. I waited patiently, confident that in a few moments, I would no longer be alone. I knew this scene well. I knew that very soon, Eleanor would make her way to the top of the hill and join me.

Just as she normally did in my dream, Eleanor arrived dressed in a creamy, antique white gown that flowed freely from her waist in such a manner that she appeared to be floating. She carried with her a brightly lit candle in one hand and in the other she held the same familiar scepter that she would soon pass to me. I, too, held a candle that burned with equal fervor.

Eleanor held out her candle to me and motioned with her eyes for me to raise my candle to hers. When I did, both candles ignited into a brilliant, glorious light that nearly blinded me. Rather than turn away from the light, an unexplainable compulsion urged me to stare into it. As I did, I noticed thousands of tiny crystals glistening in the flame. The crystals danced in a circular pattern, swirling in an upward movement that forced my gaze toward the sky. While I was thus gazing, the sky seemed to open and a golden spiral staircase appeared. I watched excitedly as a white-haired man in a white suit descended the staircase and stood before me. I recognized him immediately from my previous dreams.

"Eleanor, Beth," he greeted us both, "it's so good to see you both here, together. Well done," he smiled pleasantly and nodded his approval. "Well done, indeed." He turned slowly as if to climb back up the stairs.

"Wait!" I called. He turned toward me and smiled. "Please don't go," I pleaded. His expression filled instantly with compassion. "I'm afraid I can't stay," he replied.

"Please," I begged him. "Please take us with you. Please don't leave us here alone."

"Oh, Elizabeth," he said as he began climbing the stairs, "my dear Elizabeth, you are never alone."

With that, he proceeded up the stairs. The sky folded inward and just as quickly as they had appeared, the staircase and the man in the white suit disappeared from view.

Eleanor stepped quietly away from me and as she did, the flames from our candles gradually receded into two thin trails of pure white smoke. Eleanor handed me her scepter and then took her candle and floated away. I glanced down at the golden scepter and studied it carefully. Etched delicately along its sides were three, eight-pointed stars.

With my left hand, I held the scepter high into the air. Instantly, the sky turned black.

Lightning bolted down with hateful vengeance and struck the scepter. Rapid successions of roaring thunder followed, coupled with crackling sparks of light. The scepter burned in my hand, but I clung to it, determined not to let go. But when I could stand the fiery pain no longer, I dropped to my knees and let the scepter fall to the ground.

"It's not easy holding onto vain hopes, is it?"

The blood-chilling sound of Bailey's voice pervaded the air and his shadowy mist of a personage soon hovered over me. I looked up toward his dull eyes; though still yellow, they were as lifeless and hollow as ever.

"My hope is not vain," I grumbled.

Bailey bellowed out an evil laugh. "You pathetic fool! You don't believe that any more than I do."

"You're wrong, Bailey. I do believe!" Even as I said it, I felt doubt flood through my mind. I wanted so much to believe—why was it so much easier to doubt than to trust?

"Shall I presume then, that you've decided not to go home?"

Not wanting to humor him, I decided not to give him the satisfaction of an answer. "You can presume whatever you want, Bailey."

Bailey chuckled. "As you wish," he replied. "But here's a truth you can rely on—before dawn breaks, you will beg me to make you mine, for I am the only one who can call off the evil that lies in store for you tonight."

I refused to acknowledge Bailey's hideous threat.

"Sleep well, Beth Anne," Bailey mused as his shadowy mist slithered away.

A loud burst of thunder shook the ground beneath me and my eyes flew open in a sudden panic. I pulled the drenched blanket away from my face and listened through the now hammering wind for signs of intruders—both human and non-human. Lightning continued to provide flickering glances of the surrounding area, and thunder pounded its angry warnings repeatedly with each thread of light.

I rose quickly, ready to bolt at the first hint of danger. But my efforts were in vain for the next flash of light revealed my worst fear—I'd been discovered. Lightning flashed again, illuminating Imelda's face as she stood staunchly before me. Behind her were three men, none of whom I recognized; but in the brief, momentary flashes of light, I could tell they were evil.

"As promised boys, she's yours for the night," Imelda grinned wickedly. "Do with her as you please, but whatever you do, do *not*, I repeat, do NOT kill her!"

Imelda cocked her head to one side and raised an eyebrow. "Enjoy the evening, Beth," she smirked.

Lightning flashed and a loud explosion behind the three men sent the top portion of a pine tree crushing to the ground. In unison, the three men and Imelda spun around to see what was happening and as soon as they did, I tore off into the woods, leaving everything behind.

I ran as fast as my legs could carry me over the slippery, uneven terrain. I only had about a ten-second lead, so it wouldn't take long for them to catch up. I did my best to evade them, but I knew it was only a matter of time before one of them would have his nasty hands all over me.

The one advantage I had was that Eleanor was small and agile. She could hurdle limbs with ease and dunk under low branches without slowing her pace. Loaded with adrenalin, I urged my legs onward, ordering them to move faster and push harder, a command which, to my surprise, they obeyed. The men chasing me sputtered out expletives, cursing the ground and the rain and their mothers as they continued in pursuit. I knew they wouldn't give up, but I was damn sure going to give them a run for their money.

I ducked under a low-hanging branch on the next tree and darted quickly to the side, leaping over a large protruding root. I had scarcely landed when a man's arm suddenly grabbed me and pulled me down into the mud. I started to scream, but immediately his large hand covered my mouth.

Terrified, my arms and legs thrashed in all directions as I fought to free myself from the man's iron grip.

"Eleanor, stop!" a familiar voice whispered harshly. "Stop! It's me!"

I froze, holding my breath as I watched the men who were chasing me stumble their way over the large root and then pause briefly to determine which way I might have gone. Fired with testosterone, they decided to split up and continue their search. The man who had hold of me pulled me against his chest as we lay on the ground, camouflaged by the mud.

"It's okay," he whispered against my ear. "I've got you!" He breathed a heavy sigh of relief. "Thank heaven I've got you!"

I twisted my head against his arm and looked up at his mud-stained face. The moment I realized who it was, I broke down and began to sob. My whole body shook in uncontrollable spasms as he did his best to shush me.

"Shh!" he whispered, pulling me closer. "I'm going to remove my hand now, but you've got to be quiet, understand?"

Still shaking, I nodded and he released his hold on me. "Oh, William!" I sputtered between spasms. I threw my arms around him and buried my face against his neck. "Oh, William, you came for us."

"Us?" William whispered, confused. I knew I'd slipped, but it didn't matter. All that mattered was that William was here, and that meant Eleanor and I were both safe. William put his arms around me and held me against him. He waited until the three men were safely out of sight, then urged me to my feet.

"We don't have much time, Eleanor. They'll double back in a few minutes and be right on our tail. We have to move quickly."

I nodded and William grinned.

"What?" I whispered.

William's smile widened as he looked me over. "The clothes are iffy, but I love what you've done to your hair," he teased.

Eleanor threw herself at him and kissed him hard on the mouth. William returned her kiss passionately, but after a moment, he pried her arms from around his neck and backed away.

"There's no time for sporting, Eleanor," he breathed. "We've got to go."

"Not so fast, Colonel Hamilton." The distinct sound of a gun cocking was clear, even through the distortion of the rain. We turned and found Imelda standing with a rifle pointed at us. "The lady belongs to me."

William put his hands out, showing that he was unarmed. I spotted a pistol in his side holster, but there was no way William would be able to grab it in time.

"I've got no quarrel with you, colonel. It's her I want." Imelda held up the rifle and took aim at me. "Just step aside and I promise I won't hurt her."

William's eyes darted around quickly as he considered his options.

"Come along, now, we mustn't keep the others waiting," Imelda ordered.

I glanced up at William and nodded, motioning to his gun with my eyes and hoping that he understood; then I stood on my tiptoes and kissed his cheek.

As soon as I was halfway to Imelda, she suddenly switched her aim from me to William and pulled the trigger. I spun around, horrified. William was on his knees, gun in hand.

"William! No!" In an instant I was at his side and he lowered his gun. I looked him over frantically, trying to see where he'd been hit. In anger, I grabbed his gun, spun around, and filled Imelda with bullets. Imelda's body teetered with every entry and she fell to the ground.

"I'm pretty sure that was unnecessary," William said quietly.

I turned around, shocked that he could make a joke at a time like this.

"Unless I'm mistaken, the bullet I put between her eyes should have done the trick."

"Wh . . . ? William, you . . . but—"

"I suppose one can never be too sure, but there is a war on, and it's almost a crime these days to waste bullets." William held out his hand and I gave him the pistol.

"You're not hurt?" I stared at him, stunned.

"Of course not!" he replied, as if deeply insulted by the insinuation.

I breathed a deep sigh of relief. "Oh, William, I thought for sure she'd killed you!"

Almost immediately, the ground shook furiously as Bailey's shadow rose from Imelda's lifeless body. He roared with anger.

William sprang quickly to his feet and threw a protective arm in front of me. "What the hell is that?"

"Oh, that?" I said gesturing towards Bailey, who'd made his personage much larger than usual. He was obviously very unhappy to lose his access to Imelda's body. "That's Bailey."

Bailey's shadowy mist churned, conjuring up a powerful wind that jetted the rain into tiny horizontal pellets. Fortunately, it wasn't raining as hard as it had been; but once caught in the ferocity of the wind, the pellets felt like sharp needles piercing my body.

"Face it, Bailey, you've lost this one," I yelled, trying to shield myself from the shooting rain.

I circled in front of a stunned William. He was wide-eyed and gaping at what he saw.

"I'm so glad you're seeing this, William," I hollered into the wind. "It will make explaining things so much easier."

Bailey released a ferocious growl and pulled his shadow inward, revealing his human-like features. The wind died down and the rain instantly returned to its vertical path. "Oh, we're far from done here, Bethy," he said coldly.

"Bethy?" William shook his head, confused. He looked like someone just waking up from a bad dream.

As if they'd been secretly summoned, all three of the men who'd been chasing me earlier stepped out from behind the trees. One of them held a knife in his hand. William raised his pistol and aimed it at the man with the knife.

"Hm," Bailey chuckled. "By my calculations, you've got one bullet left, thanks to your overzealous wife. That won't be enough to save both of you." Bailey's yellow eyes glared at William, then he turned back to me. "You should have accepted my offer, Bethy."

Bailey glanced at each of the three men who had closed in and now surrounded us. "Kill her first," he charged them. "But," he scoffed, "feel free to take your time—and make sure her soldier boy watches."

As soon as Bailey gave the order, the man closest to me lunged forward and threw me to the ground. I didn't see exactly what happened next, but there was a gunshot and I heard William groan. The man who'd grabbed me suddenly slumped forward and fell to the side with a gunshot wound to his head.

William reached up and yanked a knife from his shoulder just as the one who'd thrown it ran forward and jumped him. Both William and his attacker tumbled to the ground in hand-to-hand combat—William with the handicap of a wounded shoulder which his opponent took advantage of repeatedly.

The other man came for me. I stood, ready to fight, knowing full well he'd have no trouble leveling me with one blow. The rain had subsided to a light shower, which made it much easier to see what was happening. Figuring I had nothing to lose, I reached down and grabbed a large stick and braced myself. I swung at the man as he came toward me, but he simply grabbed the stick from my hand and slammed it against his thigh, easily shattering it into two pieces, which he cast aside. His eyes grew wild with anticipation as he reached for me. I struggled against his burly arms, but to no avail. Within seconds, he twisted my arm hard around my back and forced me face first against a tree. He used his free hand to tear at my skirt.

"Let her go," a man's voice ordered. There was a gunshot, and my attacker whirled me around in a chokehold. James stood a few feet away, holding his rifle in the air. "I ain't too keen on repeat'n myself, so you best do as I say!" he ordered.

The man holding me grabbed my throat, threatening to choke me. James pulled his rifle to his shoulder and aimed it right at us. William was still fighting off his own attacker, and by the looks of it, he'd finally gained the upper hand. Both men appeared to be a bloody mess from what I could see. I shifted my eyes back to James, who still held the rifle aimed at my attacker and me.

"You're bluffing," my attacker sneered. "You can't kill me before I snap her neck in two."

James didn't budge. "Maybe not, but either way, you die."

The man holding me hesitated, as if considering his chances against James's rifle.

William grunted loudly and I watched from the corner of my eye, horrified, when he shoved the knife deep into his opponent's chest and then yanked it upward. His opponent's eyes widened and his breath gurgled hoarsely in his throat as his life drained away and he slouched to the ground. William stood, panting; then turned and made a quick appraisal of my predicament.

"James, don't," he cried hurriedly. "He'll kill her."

I struggled against my attacker, stunned that William knew James by name.

"I 'spect he will," James answered. "But he won't live long enough to know it."

The man holding me shifted his gaze back and forth from William to James. He tightened his hold on my neck, and the minute he did, James cocked his weapon.

"You ever seen what a Minnie does to a person?" James asked.

William took a deep breath and moved a couple of steps closer. My attacker squeezed his hand into my throat, causing me to gasp for air. William stopped, but didn't take his eyes off me.

"Ain't like a musket ball; Minnies are ragged shaped bullets that tumble somethin' awful in a man's body. Don't just break bones, shatters 'em to pieces. Not so bad going in, but nasty business comin' out."

William studied the man carefully; he must have noticed a slight change in his expression because he played on James's words. "He's telling the truth. I've seen plenty of soldier's insides shredded by the likes of a Minnie."

"I'll make a deal with you," James offered. "You give the colonel here back his wife, and I'll put down the gun. Then you and me can have a go at it, man to man. What d'ya say? That way, I figure you at least got a thirty percent chance of living."

James stared at the man for a moment, then smiled and laid down his gun.

The man holding me growled and cast me aside like an unwanted toy. William caught me before I fell and pulled me behind him. James grinned as he and my attacker squared off in an even heat—unless you consider size a factor; my attacker was twice James' size.

"Go on you two—get out of here," James ordered.

"James, no," I cried. "He'll kill you!"

"Colonel, would you please get your wife out of here before she insults me again and makes me regret saving her?"

William pulled on my arm. "Come on Eleanor, you heard the man."

The Choice
CHAPTER 22

*B*ut William, I don't understand how you can just leave James behind," I complained. William and I had been arguing about this for nearly half an hour as we stopped to rest the horse and stretch our legs. The slowly brightening eastern sky told me the storm had passed and dawn was on its way.

"James can take care of himself, Eleanor. I have every confidence in him."

"How can you be so sure? And by the way, how do you two know each other?"

"Which of those would you like me to answer?" William chuckled. "My darling wife, are you always going to be this argumentative?"

I started to laugh, but I was having a difficult time understanding how William could be so unconcerned about the man who had pretty much saved both our lives. "Yes, William, I am argumentative—especially when you're being so stubborn about this."

William bent down and kissed me on the mouth. When he pulled away, he was grinning.

"What?" I demanded.

"Eleanor, I probably know James better than you do."

"That's ridiculous. How could you possibly—"

"I always make it a point to study my competition."

"You what? You *studied* him?"

William laughed. "Although you caught me a little off guard with the Rollings kid. That one came out of nowhere."

"But . . . there's—"

"Figure it's a good thing we're finally married. No telling how many others I'd have to compete with if we'd waited any longer.

My mouth hung open; I couldn't find the words to reply. William folded his arm around my shoulders and gave me a gentle squeeze.

"James is going to be all right, Eleanor. He's highly trained in hand-to-hand combat and I imagine it didn't take long for him to finish that man off. I'm just glad *I* didn't have to fight him."

I slugged William in the side. "Whatever!" I said, using my best Southern California drawl.

William chuckled and shook his head. "Now then, you and I are going to get ourselves good and rested, and then you're going to tell me what in the hell just happened back there and how it is that my wife goes by the name of 'Bethy.'"

"William, wait," I said, resting my head against his shoulder. "Before we . . . er . . . rest," I cleared my throat nervously, "I need you to understand something."

"What's that?"

"I never intended to run away with James."

"Eleanor, don't. I know all about James's plan and how it went awry."

"You do? But how? "

"He found me, Eleanor; he found me and told me everything. I would have ordered him hung on the spot if he hadn't agreed to take me to the camp where he'd left you. Even then, I vowed to have him court-martialed as soon as you were safely home."

"But you changed your mind?"

"No, not exactly. James has a certain set of—let's call them *skills*— that could prove very advantageous for the Union right now."

My curiosity got the better of me. "How so?"

"Meade needs someone who can infiltrate Mosby's Raiders. I figure James is about perfect for a mission of that sort."

"I see." I thought about that for a moment, and then asked, "Is Mosby the one responsible for what happened in Chambersburg?"

William looked confused. "How do you know about that?"

So, I thought to myself. *The bearded men weren't lying about that.* I wondered if the rest of their story was true as well. If so, then—

"Eleanor?" William was still waiting for me to answer.

"The men at the camp told me the Rebels had burned Chambersburg to the ground. Is it true then? The Gray Ghost is here?"

"The part about Chambersburg is true, yes. But Mosby wasn't responsible for the raid. Best we can tell, Mosby is still in Virginia."

"Then who's responsible?"

"The order came from General McCausland. He claimed he was there to raise money in order to compensate the Southerners who lost their homes during Union raids. When they didn't raise the money, McCausland gave the order to burn the town."

"William, that's terrible! Was anybody hurt?"

William cleared his throat and scratched the back of his neck. "We don't know yet, but this was an act of vengeance, Eleanor, and I've learned that revenge more often than not leads to the worst kind of destruction."

Instantly, I thought about Imelda and how my overwhelming thirst for vengeance had caused me to lose all sense of reason. "Oh William," I said, shaking my head. "Those poor people."

"Thankfully, not all Confederate officers share McCausland's same lust for revenge, so a good number of people were able to escape without harm, but—" his voice trailed off.

"But?"

William took a deep breath. "Some of the soldiers took liberties, Eleanor, terrible liberties with some of the women. They abused and violated them in the worst ways known to men—and some of the younger women were taken captive."

I gasped. "William, no!"

William pulled me closer to him. "When James found me and told me where you were, I was afraid . . ." he paused and traced the side of my face with the back of his fingers. "I was afraid the raid on Chambersburg and this place James told me about were somehow connected. I didn't wait for orders, I got on my horse and just . . . ." William slowly shook his head.

"You came for me," I said quietly, finishing his thought.

William nodded. "Yes. I didn't realize at first that James was following me, I was too focused on finding you. When he finally caught up to me, he offered his help."

A lump formed in my throat. I realized that Eleanor would be moved by James' act of gallantry on her behalf.

That doesn't make James a hero, Eleanor, I said in my head. *His impetuous behavior nearly got us killed.*

I know, she replied softly. *I know. But I don't want him to be punished, Beth. He behaved foolishly, but he made it right in the end.*

Yes, I'll give him credit for that.

"Eleanor?" William's voice startled me.

"Yes?"

"James will be okay. I'm certain of that."

William seemed to guess what Eleanor was thinking and she responded before I had the chance.

"And after the war? What will happen to him then?"

"I suppose we'll have to wait and see." William reached up and caressed the side of my neck and touched my hair (what was left of it) with the back of his fingers. "Now then, enough about James. It's your turn."

I knew that William wanted me to explain everything that had happened at the camp—my hair, among other things. I also knew he had a whole lot of other questions, the answers to which would lead to even more questions. I wasn't sure where to begin, or how much I should tell him—how much I *could* tell him. But one thing was certain, if I was going to spend the rest of my life married to William, he had the right to know what he was signing up for. I'd have to find a way to tell him the truth and hope he wouldn't have me committed. He'd seen Bailey with his own eyes, so at least he would know I wasn't making that part up. I decided to start small and leave the rest for later.

William helped me onto his horse and then climbed up behind me just as the first rays of the sun peeked over the eastern horizon. They cast brilliant hues of purple, orange, and pink across the sky. Sunrises were always the prettiest after a storm.

We began the long trip back to Marensburg, and while we rode I told him about my abduction and the horrors of the camp. I assured him that my virtue remained untarnished, and that seemed to bring him a tremendous sense of relief. I explained what Imelda had done to the three women and how I cut my own hair as a token of gratitude for Margaret's sacrifice on my behalf. I described the terrifying cries and screams that occurred during the nights, and the state of the bodies that lay motionless in the tents.

William promised me that as soon as he delivered me safely home, he would take a group of his best men with him and wouldn't rest until he'd rescued every one of the victims we'd left behind. This gave me some sense of relief since I was struggling terribly to come to terms with the fact that Miriam, Margaret, and so many others were still held hostage in such a horrible place.

Several times during our ride back to Marensburg, William pulled me close to him and rested his chin or the side of his face against my hair. At first I thought he might be lamenting that I'd cut it all off, but later he confessed to me that he loved how the short cut looked on me. He said it made me look regal and sophisticated. I'd laughed at his comment, suggesting that love was indeed very blind.

We arrived home by sundown and were greeted excitedly by Christine, Lucinda, Mrs. Weddington, and Mr. Edwards. Despite their efforts not to comment, all four of them gasped when they saw me. Up until now, I'd held myself together and, surprisingly, so had Eleanor; but as William helped me down from his horse and started to walk me toward the house, my legs folded and I fainted in his arms.

When I came to, I was in my bed—not the bed in my old room, but the bed in William's and my room. Lucinda and Christine hovered near my bedside. They were both relieved when they saw I was awake.

"Oh Eleanor," Christine cried, "thank heavens you're home safely! We've been sick with worry these past few days. I was afraid I'd never see you again!"

"William?" I croaked. My throat was exceptionally dry and before I could say more, Lucinda handed me a glass of water.

"He's gone, Eleanor," Christine answered.

"*Gone?*" Eleanor's heart sank.

"He said he'd made you a promise and he intended to keep it." Christine looked over at Lucinda and something unspoken passed between them. They were obviously hiding something from me. I searched their expressions, looking for a hint.

"How's Mother?" Eleanor asked, suddenly nervous.

Christine shot Lucinda a quick glance and then smiled. "She's the same, Eleanor. Nothing's changed."

"Then what is it? What are you keeping from me?"

Lucinda looked at Christine and made a gesture with her eyes. "You might as well tell her; we can't keep him waiting all night."

"Night? Who? Keep who waiting?"

"It's Mr. Rollings, Eleanor—Jonathan. He's been waiting downstairs all day to see you."

"He's *what*?" I struggled to sit up.

"No, Eleanor, you have to rest for a few more days." Lucinda placed her hand on my shoulder and urged me to lie back down. "It's doctor's orders."

"What doctor? Land sakes, what's going on here? How long have I been asleep?"

"Shh!" Christine said quietly. "You're not supposed to excite yourself. It could bring back your fever."

"What fever? Would somebody please tell me what's going on?"

"Eleanor," Lucinda began, "you've been asleep for three days. Colonel Hamilton said he couldn't delay his leaving any longer, but he wrote you a note and told us to give it to you as soon as you were strong enough."

"And Jonathan?"

"We don't know. He showed up early this morning with a handwritten invitation from Colonel Hamilton asking him to pay you a visit. Apparently, there's some scandal about why Mr. Rollings came back to town so suddenly, but the colonel didn't pay it any mind. He sent for him sure as day—I saw him write the invitation himself."

Christine picked up where Lucinda left off. "The colonel is worried sick about you, Eleanor, afraid you might, you know, end up like before when we thought you were going to . . . well . . . die. He couldn't bear leaving you in such a state, but he insisted on keeping the promise he made you. He was in an awful state of worry. I think it broke his heart to leave you before he knew if you would pull through. Then he got some notion to send for Mr. Rollings."

"I don't understand." I shook my head, trying to make sense of everything they were telling me. *Three days? I said to myself. I've been asleep for three days?*

"Supposedly it's all in the colonel's letter. Here." Christine reached for an envelope on the bedside table and handed it to me. Then she and Lucinda stood up and started to leave. "We'll give you some privacy. Ring us when you're ready."

I stared blankly at William's letter for a moment, and then slid my finger under the flap to break the wax seal that held it closed and started to read.

My Darling Eleanor,

The fact that you are reading this confirms that once again my prayers have been answered and you are well. Would that I were there to see for myself, but I am bound by duty to settle the score with those who held you against your will, and to see to it that all those responsible receive due justice. It pains me to my very core when I think of all you must have endured. Would to God I could have spared you from the unspeakable atrocities. You have my word that I will not rest until the others are freed and safe.

Seeing you ill again reminds me of those agonizing weeks last year when we came so close to losing you. I discovered in those dark hours how much I love you and how desperately I want you to love me, but it is your happiness that matters most to me.

It is for this reason that I have sent for your Mr. Rollings. I'm sad to report that he is not in good standing with the Union army at this time, but that is of no consequence to me. I will leave it to him to explain, should he choose to do so.

I want you to see him, Eleanor, with my express permission. In fact, I insist, for contrary to what I previously thought, I can never be happy with you as my wife if you are in love with another man, or if you think yourself to be so. Therefore, I am offering you your freedom. Should you decide your heart truly lies with your Mr. Rollings, I shall apply for an annulment and release you from our arrangement. As for me, you will always hold my heart.

Yours Sincerely,

William

I read William's letter several times, stunned by how deeply his words moved me, and confused by how conflicted I felt. I loved Jonathan, there was no confusion there, but at the same time, I was drawn to William in a way I couldn't explain. The fact that he was willing to put my happiness above his own, no matter the cost, was the ultimate affirmation of his love. As I lay there pondering this, it suddenly hit me that William's letter was never intended for me. It was Eleanor who William loved, and it was her happiness he wanted more than anything else.

Oh Eleanor, I sighed. *He truly does love you.*

I love him, too, Eleanor replied.

I know. How could you not love him?

No, Beth, I mean I really, really love him. When we were hiding in the woods, I was so scared; I honestly believed that it was only a matter of time before the worst would happen, and all I could think about was how much I wanted to go home—to feel the safety of William's arms around me, and to be his wife. When I looked up and saw his muddy face, it was the most beautiful face I'd ever seen, and I thought that maybe, just maybe, God was giving me a second chance to do things right.

I didn't know how to respond. What could I say? Eleanor had every right to her feelings, and she had every right to be happy with the man she loved—and who loved her so deeply in return. What was I to do? If I chose to be with Jonathan, then I would rob Eleanor and William of their life together. But by staying, I risked losing Jonathan forever, and I wasn't ready to make that sacrifice. Everything I had fought for, everything I'd dreamed of, revolved around my longing to be with Jonathan, and if I'd lost my chance to be with him in my time, then I'd be darned if I would give up the chance to be with him now.

I'm sorry, Eleanor, I said regretfully.

There was an uncomfortable silence for several moments before Eleanor responded.

I know you are.

A light rapping at the bedroom door tore me away from my thoughts.

"Excuse me, Eleanor," Christine remarked. "What shall I tell Mr. Rollings?"

In spite of the sadness I felt for Eleanor and William, my heart skipped a beat at the thought of finally being with Jonathan—of finally being able to accept his proposal without regard for propriety or rules to hold us back. The thrill of knowing I would soon be in his arms propelled me to an instant recovery, but I wanted to do this right—I wanted it to be our moment—I didn't want to share it with the entire household.

I climbed out of bed and quickly scribbled a note for Christine to deliver to Jonathan.

Jonathan,

I meant everything I said to you about the two of us being together in Wyoming. That is where we fell in love, and it's where our future lies. Meet me at the cottage first thing tomorrow morning and I'll explain everything to you. Then, you can decide if you still want me.

Even if Jonathan's morals cautioned him against a rendezvous with a married woman, I knew his curiosity would get the best of him and he would want to hear what I had to say. Besides, putting him off until the next morning would not only give me time to bathe and make myself presentable, it would give me time to figure out what I was going to say once he got there. As a precaution, I sealed my note with wax before handing it to Christine to deliver. I didn't want anyone to know what I was planning—they would all try to stop me. I could sense Eleanor's sadness, but I had to push her feelings aside and focus all my energy on seeing Jonathan. Every time a thought of William crept into my mind or a twinge of guilt plagued me, I pictured how happy I would feel when finally in Jonathan's arms. It occurred to me that I wasn't thinking things through thoroughly, but I'd had the annoying habit of overthinking things in the past and for once—just this once—I didn't want to think about what I was doing; I just wanted to follow my heart.

I had a terrible time trying to fall asleep that night. I suppose after three days of rest it wasn't unusual to experience some form of insomnia, but I was also excited to see Jonathan again and couldn't help but do several practice runs in my mind. The problem was, in every scenario I was left with the guilt of knowing I'd destroyed the happiness of two people I cared about very much. In the busy hours of daylight, I could distract myself from these bits of conscience, but in the quiet hours of the night, I couldn't ignore my feelings of remorse. I tossed and turned for most of the night, fighting with myself and trying my best to rationalize that I was doing the right thing.

But if it was the right thing, why did I feel so ashamed?

Morning arrived, and although my resolve had weakened during the night, I was still determined to meet Jonathan as planned—if for no other reason than to tell him how much I loved him and then tell him goodbye.

When I arrived at the cottage Jonathan was already there. He had let himself in. My heart pounded furiously with anticipation as I dismounted and made my way down the pebble path to the partially open door. Jonathan was standing on the far side of the room staring at Father's painting of Annabelle. He smiled and looked up when he heard me, then his eyes widened and his jaw dropped as he fixed his gaze on my hair.

"Whoa!" he said, shocked.

I automatically reached up and fussed with the hair behind my ear. "It's a long story," I chuckled.

Jonathan shook his head and blinked as if his eyes were playing tricks on him. "I . . . uh—"

"I know, you hate it, don't you?"

He replied quickly. "No, no, I'm just . . . I mean . . . I wasn't expecting it."

"Nor was I." I dropped my head, suddenly very self-conscious and uncomfortable. Jonathan's reaction was so different from William's. Why did William have to be so perfect?

"I'm sorry, Eleanor. You just took me by surprise, that's all. Why the drastic change?"

It hadn't occurred to me that Jonathan didn't know what had happened. Apparently, William had left that part up to me. A little warning might have been nice—at least I could've been prepared.

Hah! Finally, a flaw in Colonel Hamilton! I thought to myself.

Stop it, Beth, Eleanor scolded me. *William's the whole reason you're here.* I didn't realize she was listening to my thoughts, but I should've figured as much; after all, my meeting with Jonathan would likely impact the rest of her life. Besides, she was right; if it weren't for William, neither of us would be here.

Jonathan must have misinterpreted my silence because he began making small talk.

"Who is Annabelle?" he asked, glancing back at the portrait he'd been admiring earlier.

I scoffed quietly at the irony of Father's painting. "She was someone very special to my father."

Jonathan raised his eyebrows with obvious curiosity. "Caption here says, 'Tribute to Lost Love.' Does that mean what it implies?"

"You mean was he in love with her?" I watched Jonathan's expression carefully before answering. "Yes. Very much so."

"You mean, all this time, he—"

"No," Eleanor quickly spoke up. "It was a long time ago, before he met my . . . my mother."

Jonathan nodded. "Curious that he kept this portrait of her. I suppose the caption speaks for itself, then, doesn't it? It's sad, don't you think?"

I shook my head and brushed off his statement. I hadn't come here to discuss Eleanor's father and his lost love.

"Jonathan, a lot of things have changed since you and I were together last,"

Jonathan raised an eyebrow but his gaze remained fixed on the portrait of Annabelle. "You mean like the fact that you're married now?"

I lowered my eyes. This wasn't going to be easy. "Yes, I suppose."

Jonathan cleared his throat and looked up at me. "Eleanor, why am I here?"

"It was William's idea," I replied awkwardly.

Jonathan shook his head. "I don't understand. *What's* William's idea?"

I stepped toward Jonathan and reached for his hand. As soon as I did I realized I wasn't wearing my gloves. I suddenly wanted to tar and feather the person who had invented gloves!

Eleanor laughed.

You knew, and you didn't warn me, I accused her.

"Eleanor?" Jonathan held my hand in his and everything about his touch seemed warm and familiar.

"I think we'd better sit down, Jonathan. There's a lot I have to tell you."

Jonathan and I sat next to each other on the small couch and I spent the better part of the next hour explaining everything that had happened, beginning with how Eleanor's father had blackmailed me into marrying William. In my account, I made sure to include the fact that our marriage had never been consummated—a bit of information that didn't go unnoticed by Jonathan. I told him about the camp and about the women who'd had all their hair cut off because they were envious of mine, and how I'd decided to cut my hair so that no one else would be disgraced the way those women had been. I described the horrible things I'd heard and seen while I was being held there, and how close I'd come to being killed.

Jonathan was stunned. "I don't know what to say, Eleanor. I'm so sorry. I had no idea."

"How could you?" I replied. "I'm lucky William found me when he did."

"Yes, of course!" Jonathan nodded. "But pardon my confusion; I still don't know why your husband sent for me."

I pressed my lips together and scratched my head. "I'm getting to that." I couldn't bear to look at him while I said the next part, so I turned away. "Jonathan, William knows that it's you I love. He's known all along. After everything that happened, he decided that he couldn't share me with you any longer."

Jonathan put his hand on mine. "What are you saying?"

"William has offered to have our marriage annulled so that you and I can be together." I was suddenly very nervous, afraid that Jonathan might have moved on already and that I was sharing all this with him in vain. "That is, if that's what we truly want."

Jonathan was silent for what felt like several minutes before asking, "Is that what *you* want, Eleanor?"

I was trembling and couldn't bring myself to say the words out loud. I nodded, worried that Jonathan might elect to reject me. I couldn't blame him if he did.

Jonathan put his fingers under my chin and forced me to look at him. One glance into his deep blue eyes completely unnerved me. "Are you sure?" he asked quietly.

All I could do was nod, unable to put my feelings into words. It occurred to me that Eleanor might be holding me back, but before I could get very far in my thoughts, Jonathan pulled me to him and kissed me passionately. The feeling of his lips on mine ignited a fire in me that melted away all my ability to think rationally.

"Eleanor," he said when he paused for a moment so we could catch our breath, "let's get married!"

My heart was racing so fast that my answer was barely audible. "Yes!"

"You mean it?" Jonathan backed away suddenly. I wasn't ready for him to stop kissing me, so I answered by pulling his mouth back to mine.

BETH! Eleanor shouted in my mind! *Stop!*

Go away! I shouted back at her.

YOU STOP THIS MINUTE! Eleanor insisted with such authority that I had no choice but to obey her.

"What!" I said, frustrated.

"What?" Jonathan replied, puzzled.

I shook my head. "I'm sorry, I thought I heard something."

Jonathan grinned and caressed my nose with the side of his finger. "I'm sure you did."

"Don't tease me, Jonathan, please. It's not funny," I whined.

Jonathan pressed his lips tenderly to mine and kissed me again.

Beth, please make him stop. I'm still married!

"Fine!" I snapped.

Jonathan pulled away, "Fine?" His perplexed expression was almost comical.

I let out a frustrated sigh and stood up. Jonathan stood as well, and I could tell by the look on his face that he was flustered. But I wasn't going to have a moment's peace as long as Eleanor was in my head.

"Forgive me, Eleanor, my behavior is out of line, I—"

I shook my head abruptly. "Don't be silly, it's not you, it's me."

"I don't understand," he said, still confused.

"Jonathan, we need to do this the right way. I owe that to El . . . I mean, William."

"Are you sure you're okay, Eleanor? You seem a bit out of sorts."

I let out a nervous laugh. "I'd say that's a pretty fair assessment."

"Well, it's no wonder with all you've been through."

I needed Jonathan to understand—why was it so difficult for me to explain myself? Jonathan misinterpreted my hesitation. "Perhaps you need more time to be sure what you want."

"No," I said quickly. "I know what I want, Jonathan." I put my hand on his arm. "That's not it at all."

"Then what?"

"William's a good man, Jonathan. He's kind and caring, and he's going to be terribly hurt by all this. I want to be as considerate of his feelings as I possibly can. He deserves at least that much from me."

"I understand, of course. Tell me what you want me to do and I'll do it."

Jonathan wasn't going to be happy with my next statement, but I owed so much to William that I refused to cause him further disgrace. "Jonathan, I can't see you until the annulment is final."

Jonathan started to protest, but I pressed my fingers to his lips. "Please Jonathan, it's the only way."

Jonathan closed his eyes and nodded. He reached up and pulled my fingers away from his mouth. "Of course, you're right."

"Thank you for understanding."

"It's just that, well, I—"

"Yes?"

"I can't stay around here, Eleanor."

"I don't understand. Why not? The annulment shouldn't take that long, should it?"

Jonathan cleared his throat and shook his head. "It's not that. It's . . . me. I . . . left my post suddenly, and I have to go back and try to make things right. I didn't exactly have permission to come back here. The sooner I report back, the less likely they are to shoot me on the spot."

"Oh Jonathan, don't say that!"

"It's true, Eleanor. They've executed men for less. They'll be especially harsh on deserters on account of what's happened in Chambersburg and what's occurring in Petersburg."

"You're not a deserter, Jonathan. Surely they know that."

"That's why I've got to go back. I have to make it right."

"Then that settles it," I declared.

"Settles what?"

"We wait. William will get the annulment, and you'll make things right with your superiors. Then you and I can get married and leave this place for good."

Jonathan folded his arms around my waist. "You'll wait for me, then?"

"Oh, Jonathan, you silly fool. Of course I'll wait for you! I'd wait for you for eternity if I had to."

Jonathan bent down and kissed me. "Eleanor, you have just made me the happiest man alive." He kissed me again, and then grinned.

"What?"

He stared at me affectionately. "I like your hair."

Jonathan and I parted with our plan carefully choreographed. I hated waiting, but I owed it to William to do things in as honorable a manner as possible considering the circumstances. As anxious as I was to begin my life with Jonathan, I still had to find a way to reconcile my decision with Eleanor. But as soon as Jonathan was gone my guilt set in, and I was overwhelmed with the burden of knowing that by running away with him, I was robbing William and Eleanor of their life together. Worse than that, I was forcing Eleanor to leave her family and loved ones behind and live the rest of her life in the shadows—bound through me to a man she didn't love. I was doing the same thing to her that I couldn't bear going through myself. My leaving with Jonathan would be the ultimate act of intrusion on my part.

Guilt tormented me for the next several days as I fretted over how I would break the news to William upon his return. Eleanor was apparently giving me the silent treatment because in spite of the fact that her life force was a constant presence, no matter how many times I tried to communicate with her she refused to respond. I missed her companionship so much that by the end of the second week, I began to question whether I was making the right decision. I realized that in the course of the past year, I had come to care for her very deeply. She was part of me—more than that, she was my friend, and I loved her. In a way, she and William were like family to me, and the thought of betraying them both was more than I could bear.

The choice wasn't an easy one, and regardless of the rationale or how badly I wished to avoid it, the outcome was the same. I had an agonizing decision to make—and no matter how badly I wanted to avoid it, somebody was going to get hurt.

Bittersweet Goodbyes
CHAPTER 23

"*I* thought I might find you here." Christine's voice startled me. I was sitting at the grand piano in the ballroom. I'd been there for at least an hour, but I couldn't bring myself to play. I turned around and motioned for Christine to join me.

"I wish I could play as well as you," Christine lamented.

I chuckled and nudged her with my arm. "You could if you'd practice more."

Christine ducked her head. "I bet you don't know this, but when you come in here to play, I can hear you all the way upstairs. Sometimes, when I'm supposed to be doing my studies, I just curl up on the sofa in the sun room and listen to you. The music carries me far away, and the next thing I know, time has disappeared."

I gave her a melancholy smile and shrugged. "No, I didn't know; I know what you mean though, about being carried away."

"Eleanor, I don't know what happened to you when you were taken away, but you seem so different now that you're home, so . . . sad I guess."

I raised an eyebrow. "It's the hair," I joked, but Christine wasn't laughing.

"When those men took you away, I thought I would never see you again. Oh Eleanor, I thought you were dead!" Tears streamed down Christine's cheeks. "Then, when William brought you home, I thought I should never beg God for another favor as long as I live."

I wrapped my arm around Christine's shoulders and wiped away her tears. "Oh, Christine, it's okay now . . . everything's okay."

"But that's just it, everything is not okay. You haven't been yourself at all since you've been home. I'm afraid—that—that you were—hurt or something."

"Don't worry about me, Christine. I'll be fine, you'll see."

"Will you tell me about your hair?" Christine asked. "What happened?"

I shook my head. "Please don't ask me, Christine." I reached up and stroked her hair. It was so lovely—so thick and long. "I really prefer not to talk about it."

"Was it bad, Eleanor? The place they took you? I mean, really bad?"

"Yes."

Christine frowned. "Would it cheer you up if I played a song for you?"

I smiled fondly at Christine and squeezed her hand. "Why, yes, I would love that. What song will you play?"

"It's a surprise . . . well, sort of." Christine stood up and reached for the music on the top of the piano. She placed the all too familiar score in the resting place in front of the keys and then nudged me to the side and placed her hands on the keys. The score was mine—written just as I remembered—only at the top of the page someone had scribbled the title, "Eleanor's Theme."

Christine's interpretation of the music was crude, but her determination was admirable. "Oh bother!" she frowned, frustrated. "I can't do it as good as you."

I laughed, and for the remainder of the afternoon Christine and I sat together at the piano and played. I don't know what possessed me to do it, but I decided it was time to teach Christine how to play Three Blind Mice—Beth style. Christine laughed as I told her stories about a young girl who once lived with her father in a small house with a big piano, and how the father and his daughter played piano wars.

Then I did something really daring; I played Debussy.

"Pardon me, Mrs. Hamilton," Edwards said, interrupting our little impromptu piano recital.

"What is it, Mr. Edwards?" I asked.

"Miss Rollings has come to call. Will you be receiving her this late in the afternoon?"

I couldn't believe it. "Miss Rollings? Grace?"

"Yes, ma'am. I can ask her to call at a more appropriate time if you'd—"

"No! No, Mr. Edwards. Of course I'll see her. Please bring her to the garden room."

Mr. Edwards looked shocked. "Ma'am?"

"You heard me, correctly, Mr. Edwards. And please ask Mrs. Weddington to have a snack tray delivered."

"Yes, Mrs. Hamilton, as you wish."

Christine recognized that I needed to speak to Grace in private, so she excused herself and went upstairs.

Grace was dressed in a lavender silk tea dress, which suggested that she'd been making calls most of the day. As usual, she was the picture of perfection.

"Thank you for seeing me, Mrs. Hamilton." She smiled and extended her hand. She obviously noticed my hair, but didn't say anything.

I squeezed her hand and replied, "Please, you needn't be so formal."

"Mrs. Hamilton, I'm afraid this is not a social call."

Grace's tone stunned me. "Grace, what is it?"

"May we sit?" she asked uneasily.

"Yes, please." I motioned for her to take a seat next to me on the sofa.

"I'm afraid I'm not very good at this, so if you'll please permit me, I'll just speak my mind."

I nodded for her to continue.

"Mrs. Hamilton, our family's honor has been shattered and my poor Mother shunned by those whom she once considered her friends."

"Oh, Grace! No! What has happened?" I reached over to take her hand, but she moved it away from me—subtly of course. Grace was not one to offend overtly. "Whatever it is, please tell me and I will be happy to intercede on your mother's behalf."

"Mrs. Hamilton, I'm here to ask you to promise me that you'll have nothing further to do with our family."

I gasped. "Grace! I don't understand. What's going on?"

"Jonathan informed me that you plan to have your marriage annulled so that you may run away with him. Is that true?"

I stared, bewildered by Grace's harsh tone. "William and I have discussed it, yes."

"Mrs. Hamilton, what you do with your life is your business, but when that business involves Jonathan, then it becomes a whole new matter. Jonathan has behaved dreadfully ever since you decided to make sport of him. He has lost all sense of duty—to his family, and now even to his country. He refused a marital arrangement formerly agreed upon, abandoned his post with the Union without authorization, and is now pursuing a married woman. His behavior is deplorable and . . . well . . . it seems you are of a propensity to encourage him."

"Grace, please, I—"

"That's not all, Mrs. Hamilton. My fiancé's family has withdrawn its offer of marriage and has forbidden us to have any further contact."

"Oh, Grace, no! I-I don't know what to say."

"You sit here with your high position, your land, and your money, and you think you can play with people however you wish—after all, the rest of the world is only there to satisfy whatever whims you might have at the time."

"Grace, please. I'm sorry. It's not like that at all! I didn't know any of this would impact you."

"That's just it, Mrs. Hamilton. You are not prone to think of anyone but yourself."

I stared at Grace in utter disbelief. I had never known Grace to be so unfriendly and offensive. "That's not true! I've thought of nothing else since I got here," I caught myself, "I mean, since that day with Jonathan."

Grace shook her head and half smiled. "Mrs. Hamilton, the sad part is that you've somehow managed to convince Jonathan that you love him, so much so that he won't listen to reason."

"But I do love him; you know that. You said it yourself at the Ball."

"And as I recall, you denied it. I watched you dance with him, and I watched you dance with Captain Herman, and then Colonel Hamilton. Honestly, if I didn't know better, I'd say you loved all three of them. That's not love, Eleanor, not lasting love."

"Oh, Grace, if only I could make you understand! Nothing is what it seems."

"I asked you that night not to trifle with my brother's feelings. I'm afraid I'm not asking you now—I'm insisting. I've already lost one brother; I cannot bear to lose another!"

I gasped. "You what? What brother?"

Grace covered her mouth quickly and then rose. "I'm sorry, Mrs. Hamilton. I do not wish to overstay my welcome. I really must get home."

"No please, please tell me what you meant by that. What brother?"

"I must go. Please, Eleanor, you must never speak of this conversation again—not to me, not to Jonathan, not to anyone."

With that, Grace turned abruptly and left the room. She ran down the two flights of stairs to the main entryway where Mr. Edwards met her and escorted her to the front door. I stared in shock from the top of the staircase as I watched her leave.

I tossed and turned all that night, more confused than ever, contemplating every plausible explanation for why neither Jonathan nor Grace had ever mentioned having a brother; but try as I might, I couldn't come up with a reason—none that made sense anyway. The more I speculated, the harder it became to fight the feeling that I had been betrayed in some way, betrayed in the sense that Jonathan could keep something like this from me all this time. I suppose it was possible that their brother had died young, like Eleanor's little brother, and that by the time I met Grace and Jonathan in the twenty-first century, it had been so far in the past that neither thought to mention it. That was the only explanation that made any sense. Rather than torture myself with further speculation, I determined to ask Jonathan the next time I saw him, despite Grace's emphatic insistence that I never mention our conversation.

It wasn't just the news of Jonathan's brother that troubled me—I could deal with that easily enough—it was the entire tone of Grace's visit. She had all but accused me of being a wanton woman, and she blamed *me* for pretty much everything that had gone wrong in her family. I didn't know how to handle that, so instead, I stewed over it and lost sleep.

The next morning, William came home.

I'd been outside taking my morning stroll through the gardens when I heard his horse approaching. He reared up on his horse when he saw me in the distance and tipped his hat to me. I'd been holding a set of clippers in my hand along with some freshly cut roses, but upon seeing William, Eleanor tossed everything aside and ran off to greet him. Her life force emanated so strongly that I was powerless to stop her.

William dismounted and opened his arms. Eleanor flew to him and threw her arms around his neck.

"You're well," he smiled. "I'm glad."

"And you? Are you also well?" Eleanor asked.

"Darling, I couldn't be better now that I'm home and can see you've recovered."

Eleanor accompanied William into the house. I was the third wheel, and I was a little concerned by the fact that they were acting as though I wasn't there.

William had a bath and then joined me in the drawing room. I have to admit, the sight of him took my breath away; he cleaned up nicely.

We sat in the drawing room for most of the morning while William recounted everything that had happened. He explained that by the time he'd arrived at the camp, the only people who remained there were a handful of willing participants.

"We searched every tent and all of the surrounding areas, but we saw no signs of anyone being held against their will."

"And Miriam? Margaret? Did you find them?"

"No, I'm afraid not. When we inquired of their whereabouts, those present pretended they'd never heard of them. It was all a bit too innocent looking, if you ask me. Whatever *did* happen there, they've covered their tracks well."

"I was afraid of that."

"We did make a gruesome discovery at what appeared to have been a camp of sorts a few miles south of where I found you, but I doubt it has anything to do with the camp you were at."

"How can you be sure?"

William scratched the back of his neck. I'd learned that he did that every time there was something he didn't want to tell me—but knew he had to or I'd pester him to death until he did. "We found . . ." he cleared his throat and took a breath, "human remains that were, er, well, there wasn't much left to identify."

I sucked in too much air and had to compose myself. "Oh no, William, that's horrible! You don't think, I mean, you don't suppose that Margaret and Mir—"

"No, Eleanor. I don't see how it could be either of them."

"Why not?"

"These remains had been there for a long time—months I would venture to guess."

William's assertion was understandable, of course, but he didn't know what I knew about Intruders and what happens to a human body once an Intruder abuses it.

"Don't worry, Eleanor. We'll find your friends. I've notified the authorities in the surrounding areas and they've promised to continue the search for them.

"Thank you, William." I smiled a half smile and distracted myself by taking a sip of tea, which by now was cold. Then I thought about James. When I asked about him, William laughed.

"He's fine, Eleanor, I told you he would be."

"Where is he?"

"I suppose he's somewhere between here and Virginia, possibly even Maryland."

"Why Maryland?" Eleanor asked.

"Remember those *skills* I mentioned him having—and that special assignment I told you about? Well, let's just say that right now he's on a 'mission' and leave it at that."

Mrs. Weddington arrived with a tray full of fresh fruit and sweet breads.

"It's good to have you home, Colonel Hamilton," she said.

William took the tray from her hands and smiled. "Thank you, Mrs. Weddington. That will be all."

I watched with curiosity as William dismissed Mrs. Weddington. He was normally not so quick to dismiss the servants without first inquiring about their day and their children and their dogs and the weather. The servants all loved him because he was so congenial.

As soon as Mrs. Weddington left the room, William turned to me. "Eleanor, please don't hold me in suspense any longer. I must know if you've made your decision. Did you see Mr. Rollings?"

"Yes," Eleanor responded.

"And?"

"And Mr. Rollings has gone back to his post, William."

"That wasn't my question, Eleanor. You know what it is I need to know."

I struggled against Eleanor's life force for my voice, but she was too strong for me. Apparently she had been saving her strength for this moment, because I suddenly found myself without any control.

"All you need to know is that Jonathan is gone, and I am here."

William grabbed both of Eleanor's hands. "You've decided then?"

"I'm your wife, William."

"That's not good enough, Eleanor." He turned to walk away and Eleanor's heart dropped.

"William, wait, please." Eleanor began to panic.

William stopped, but he didn't say anything and he didn't turn around.

"I love you!" Eleanor said softly.

Oh geez, Eleanor! What are you doing?

William turned around and grinned. "You love me?"

Eleanor, don't, I pleaded, but my plea fell on deaf ears.

"Yes, William."

"Then you don't want an annulment?"

"No, you silly man. I don't want an annulment."

Eleanor? Hello? Remember me? Am I invisible here or something?

William's smile widened and even though nothing was going my way, I had to admit that it pleased me to see him so obviously happy.

There was a subtle shift in William's expression—something in his eyes as he held out his hand for Eleanor. "Come here, wife."

Uh oh. This is going to get awkward.

Eleanor placed her hand in William's, and together they climbed the stairs to the bedroom.

Hey! Is anyone out there listening? Eleanor, you can't do this to me! I insisted.

Shut up, Beth!

Oh good, you do hear me. For a minute there I was worried.

Go away! Eleanor ordered.

Eleanor, you can't do this!

I said, GO AWAY!

We reached the top of the second flight of stairs and headed down the hall to our room. William didn't say a word, but as soon as we reached the entrance to our bed chambers he reached down and scooped Eleanor up into his arms and carried her over the threshold.

Ah, come on! That's so not fair! Why was he so dang perfect?

Once inside the room, William bent down and kissed Eleanor tenderly as he set her back on her feet. William's kiss would have unnerved even the strongest of resolves. I was trying my best not to pay attention to the smoothness of his lips, the gentle caress of his fingers on my face and neck, and the alarming brightness of his blue eyes; but heck, any girl would be hard-pressed to ignore this man. I was in trouble here, and I knew it. If Eleanor and William made love, then all bets were off. There'd be no hope of an annulment and no hope of me ever being with Jonathan again.

William wasn't in any hurry. He explored the back of Eleanor's neck with his lips as he slowly began unhooking her dress.

Oh no, not the neck. Ah geez, not the neck!

I was holding my ground, barely, but Eleanor was a complete gonner. She'd lost all sense of resolve, if she'd ever had any, and she was doing a heck of a job ignoring me.

Once unhooked, William slid the arms of Eleanor's dress off her shoulders and like magic her entire dress slid to the floor.

Holy cow, how'd he do that?

Before he went to work on Eleanor's corset, he reached up and began unbuttoning his shirt. Eleanor turned around and to my astonishment, she pushed his hands aside and finished the task. In no time, William's shirt was completely unbuttoned and hung open, revealing exactly what I had witnessed during that afternoon when we were playing in the river—William was ripped.

He backed away slightly and gazed into Eleanor's eyes. "Tell me again, Eleanor," he whispered.

"Tell you what?" Eleanor smiled.

"Tell me you love me."

Eleanor reached up and stroked the side of William's face. "I love you, William."

William's breathing quickened and he pulled Eleanor close and kissed her passionately. He was just about to untie her corset when all of sudden, an explosion of thunder shook the room, followed by a bright flash of light. Acting on reflex, William shoved me to the ground and threw his body over mine.

"Oh, crap!" a familiar voice exclaimed. "I can't believe I got it wrong again!"

What? I couldn't believe my ears. *It couldn't be!* I struggled against the weight of William's body to try and catch a glimpse of our untimely visitor—to see for myself if I was imagining things, or worse, if I had completely lost my mind. I blinked several times to regain my vision after being blinded by the explosion. William stood quickly to confront our rude intruder.

"How did you get in here?" William demanded sternly.

"Oh, hey dude, my bad. I didn't mean to interrupt anything here. I seem to be having a little trouble with my math calculations."

"Carl?" I said when I could finally see again. "Oh, Carl! Is that really you?" I ran to him and threw my arms around him. "Oh, please tell me you're real—please say you're not a dream."

"Who the hell are you?" Carl pried my arms away from his neck.

At the same time, William shouted, "Who the hell is Carl?"

"Carl, it's me, Beth!" I shook Carl's shoulders as hard as I could.

"Bethy?" Carl exclaimed, scratching the top of his head.

"Bethy?" William echoed. "Eleanor—what's going on here? Who is this awful-looking man, and who the hell is this Bethy I keep hearing about?"

"Eleanor?" Carl said, ignoring William's outburst. "Geez, girl, you look nothing like your picture. Of course, you had your clothes on in your picture, and your hair was a lot longer."

"Picture? What picture?" William stepped back and buttoned up his shirt. "Eleanor, I demand you tell me who this man is and why he's in our bedroom!"

"Bethy?" Carl did a swift survey of our bedroom and the state of our clothing. Then he cast me one of his infamous ornery grins. "Girl, you've got some splainin' to do!"

"Oh, Carl! It really is you! I can't believe it! You're here! You're really here!"

"Yep." Carl's eyes grew big suddenly. "Uh oh."

I turned around just in time to see William land a punch square on Carl's jaw. Carl staggered backwards several steps holding his face. "Dude! What's your problem?"

"William, stop it! You stop it right now!" I shook my finger in his face.

"Would somebody please tell me what the HELL is going on here?" William roared.

I could tell he'd long since passed his tolerance threshold.

"And for the love of God, Eleanor, how many more men am I going to have to fight off of you?"

"Oooh, somebody's had a bad day," Carl teased. William started for him again, but I grabbed his arm.

"William, stop! This is Carl. He's harmless."

"Harmless?" both William and Carl said at the same time.

"Oh shut up, Carl! You know what I mean." I pursed my lips and looked at William. "Carl's my cousin, William. Carl, this is William."

"Pleasure's mine," Carl said, still rubbing his jaw.

"What cousin?" William asked, suspiciously.

"Um, Beth?" Carl interrupted. "Just curious. Who's William and why is he undressing you?"

"Carl! Would you shut up!?"

"I'm Eleanor's husband, that's who I am."

"Husband?" Carl raised his eyebrows in surprise. "Oh, man, Bethy, you're in some deep trouble here." He wrinkled his nose at me. "Husband? Are you serious?"

"Eleanor, would you please tell me who this Bethy person is?"

"Oh, William," I sighed. "William, I'm afraid this is a very long story!"

"Well, then, I guess you'd best get started."

I suddenly felt lightheaded and sick to my stomach. The room felt like it was spinning around me and I had to grab onto the bedpost to steady myself.

"Eleanor? What is it? What's wrong?" William was at my side instantly.

"I—I don't know," I stammered. "I feel like I'm—"

Before I could finish my statement, my knees buckled and I dropped to the floor. All of a sudden, my head felt like it was in a vise. I hunched over into a ball to try and alleviate the pain. I reached up and grabbed my head with both hands, closed my eyes, and started to scream. A heavy weight pushed against the top of my head and worked its way downward past my face, neck, shoulders, and on down until it finally exited from the tips of my toes.

When the pain finally subsided, I stood up, and William gasped.

"Whoa! Now that's not something you see every day!" Carl stated.

William's face was a horrified mask. I followed his gaze and noticed Eleanor's body lying on the ground.

"Eleanor!" I called, but she didn't respond.

"William, do something!" I insisted.

William looked at me as if he were seeing a ghost. His eyes shifted back and forth from Eleanor to me, and then back again.

"William, please!" I implored him. "You have to help her."

"Is she dead?" Carl asked. He started to kneel down next to her, but William pushed him out of the way.

"Leave her alone!" he ordered. William cradled Eleanor's body in his arms. He kept glancing up at me and then looking back down at her. "What are you?" There was a biting edge to his voice.

"I'm Beth. Now would you please forget about me and help Eleanor!"

William looked down at Eleanor's motionless body and paused. He cocked his head to the side and listened.

Eleanor made a low groaning sound and started to stir.

William breathed a deep sigh of relief and pulled Eleanor to him.

"William?" she said weakly.

"Yes, I'm here. I'm here."

Eleanor forced a smile and opened her eyes. When she saw me, her smiled broadened.

"Beth?"

I hadn't realized it, but I'd been holding my breath. As soon as Eleanor said my name, I released a loud sigh of relief.

For the next couple of hours, the four of us talked. It was actually more like an interrogation—Carl and I talked and William asked questions. Surprisingly, William kept an open mind, and before long his sense of humor returned.

"I'm rather pleased that I don't have to kill you," William said to Carl.

"Uh, that makes two of us. Actually that makes three of us. Beth here needs me in order to get home.

"Speaking of going home, why didn't anyone come for me after I'd been here for two weeks?"

"I tried, Beth. But you wouldn't come with me."

"What are you talking about? You never came for me. Nobody did."

"Well, granted I got my bearings a little mixed up,"

"What? When?"

"At the cemetery, when Eleanor's little brother died."

My mind flashed back to the day we buried little Christopher. "The storm . . . but I thought—"

"Look, all I know is that one minute I had ahold of you, and the next thing I know someone else is pulling you away from me. If you'd have listened to me . . . I kept telling you to trust me and let go, but you had to get all stubborn on me, and—"

I hauled off and slugged Carl as hard as I could, forgetting that I no longer possessed a physical body. Carl feigned being hurt when my disembodied fist floated through his arm. Then he laughed.

"Well, this is certainly inconvenient!" I sneered. "Just you wait, Carl, until I get my hands on you! For real!"

With that, the room exploded with laughter.

Carl let us talk as long as he could before cautioning me that it was time for us to leave.

"There's something I don't understand, Carl. Why you? Why didn't Grace come for me like she promised?

Carl's expression fell instantly and his face grew very serious. "She wanted to, Beth, but she . . . ," Carl hesitated and I knew he was hiding something.

"Carl, what aren't you telling me? What is it? Is she okay?"

"Beth, Grace is fine. It's Jonathan." Carl shook his head back and forth slowly.

"Jonathan! What's wrong? What is it?"

"He's been hurt, Beth."

"Hurt? How? How bad is it?"

Carl reached for my hand. "It's bad, Beth."

"No! Carl, no!"

"Grace wouldn't leave him; not even for you."

"Oh, Carl!" I started to cry. "Please, take me to him. Please!"

"Say goodbye to the lovebirds here and we'll be on our way."

William and Eleanor both stood when I did. I wanted so much to hug them both, but with my life force now bodiless, I couldn't hug them any more than I could slug Carl.

"William," I smiled. "Someday I'm going to write a book about you. You are a true super hero! I'll miss you terribly!

"And I you," William replied. "Especially now that I know it was you who caused me so much grief!"

I laughed. "Don't underestimate your wife! Eleanor can dish it out every bit as well as I can."

William chuckled. "I've no doubt about that!"

When I stood before Eleanor, I couldn't find the words to say goodbye. Tears streamed down Eleanor's cheeks. "You gave me my life back, Beth. I shall never be able to repay you for that."

"I will always look for you in my dreams," I smiled.

"Yes, and I'll know just how to find you," Eleanor grinned.

"How?"

Eleanor laughed. "You'll be the one who's not wearing gloves."

"Oh Eleanor," I longed so much to touch her. "I'll always love you!"

"And I you," The words caught in her throat, and she reached out as if to stroke my face.

"You ready, Beth?" Carl interrupted. He never was very good at goodbyes. "Just think ladies, if Beth ever becomes a traveler, you can come back and visit."

Hard as it was to tear myself away, I couldn't bear to wait another minute. Jonathan needed me. "Take me home, Carl. Take me home to Jonathan."

Carl nodded. "Come along then," he said, motioning for me to stand next to him.

"Beth?" William said as I started to leave.

"What is it, William?"

"I shall pray for your Jonathan—the same way I prayed for Eleanor."

William's words touched me so much that I wanted to cry, but of course, I couldn't.

"Thank you, William," I nodded, and then reached up and blew him a kiss. "Thank you."

"Ready?" Carl asked.

"Yes, please. Let's do this!"

"All right then, cousin. Let's get you home."

Epilogue

*J*onathan never re-joined his unit in Petersburg. By the time he made it back, he discovered that General Lee's forces had pushed their way through the Union stronghold along the western trench line in an effort to reclaim access to rail lines and much needed supplies for the Confederacy.

Upon learning that the western trench line had been compromised and that numerous Union soldiers had been killed in the raid, Jonathan blamed himself for not being there to fight alongside his men. Racked with guilt, he joined Grant's troops on the eastern trench line and fought valiantly under an assumed name for the duration of the Union siege.

After months of devastating trench warfare, General Lee succumbed to Union pressure and began a retreat that would eventually lead to his surrender at Appomattox in April 1865.

Jonathan did not return to Marensburg a hero, despite the fact that he had served honorably for the remainder of the war. While the majority of the citizens of Marensburg paid little attention to his momentary lapse in judgment, the upper echelon of Marensburg society turned up its nose at the Rollings family. The social and emotional impact were so humiliating for Mrs. Rollings that Mr. Rollings sent his wife and daughter abroad for a season while he managed his business affairs from his New York office.

The Rollings family never returned to Marensburg; except, of course, for Jonathan, who came back at the end of the war in the hope that Eleanor had waited for him as she'd promised. Upon arriving at the Hastings' estate, he was greeted by Christine, who was practicing her sketching while sitting on her favorite log near the bank of the river.

"Good day, Miss Hastings," Jonathan called to her. He tipped his hat and bowed politely.

Christine looked up at him and smiled. "I wondered when we'd see you again, Mr. Rollings."

Jonathan removed his hat and cleared his throat. "I was hoping you'd tell me where I might find your sister."

"I'm afraid she's gone, Jonathan," Christine replied, using Jonathan's given name to imply that she was privy to Eleanor and Jonathan's relationship. "She and Colonel Hamilton left on a belated honeymoon just a few weeks after the war ended.

Jonathan's gaze dropped to the ground and he nodded in understanding. "I see." After a silent pause he chuckled and looked back up at Christine who was watching him intently. "Then he changed his mind about the annulment?"

"Annulment?" Christine looked at Jonathan questioningly.

"Never mind. I thought Eleanor might have said something to you about it."

Jonathan's obvious disappointment plucked at Christine's heartstrings; she couldn't help but feel sorry for him.

"Won't you come inside with me and have a beverage and some refreshments?"

"Thank you, Miss Hastings, but I'm afraid I've intruded on your privacy long enough."

"Then at least follow me to the house. Eleanor left something for you before she went off with Colonel Hamilton. She wanted me to give it to you if you came back."

"I don't understand. She left something for me? What?"

"Please, come with me."

Christine gestured for Jonathan to follow her, and regardless of his angst, his curiosity would not afford him the luxury of leaving without knowing what Eleanor had left for him.

Once inside the Hastings' mansion, Christine excused herself, leaving Jonathan alone with his thoughts. When she returned she was carrying a letter and some pages of rolled up parchment tied with red string.

"Thank you," Jonathan said when Christine handed them both to him.

"I debated as to whether or not I would give these to you, but it seemed important to Eleanor that you have them."

Without hesitating, Jonathan broke the seal on the letter and began reading.

Dear Jonathan,

By now you will have heard that I've gone away with William to begin my life as Mrs. William Hamilton. This will surely be difficult for you to understand, particularly after our last meeting. I wish I could explain everything to you now and prevent you from heartache, but fate must have its say in our futures.

You must trust me when I tell you that things are not as they may seem at this time, and though you may come to the conclusion that I have trifled with your emotions, please know that I never meant to hurt you. You will find your true love again. I promise. And when you do your memories of me will fly away into nothing more than a bittersweet chapter in your life.

I want you to have the portrait of Annabelle. I left it for you in the cottage, along with a couple of the sketches you admired during our time there. The sketches are of no real consequence and are yours to do with as you wish, but I would ask that you indulge me in one last favor. Please take proper care of Annabelle's portrait and see to it that its meaning is not lost, for I will treasure every moment you and I shared together.

I leave you with this final promise. Remember the warrior's tale from Grace's bracelet? Love will come to you again through another. When you hold the musician's flawed hand in yours, you will know that your true love has returned for you.

Until then, fare thee well, and may happiness be yours forever.

Eleanor

Jonathan fought back the pain that was swelling in his chest and did his best to hide his emotions from Christine.

"Are you all right?" Christine asked as he folded the letter and slid it carefully into his pocket.

Jonathan cleared his throat and nodded. "I'll be leaving now, Miss Hastings."

"Would you like to leave a response for my sister?"

"Thank you, no. That won't be necessary."

"Very well then," Christine said, motioning toward the door. "Please give our regards to your family."

"Thank you, I will."

With that, Jonathan took his leave. And though he opened the rolled pages of parchment while walking down the wooded path that led to the main road, it would be several years before he learned to play the piano well enough to play Eleanor's Theme.

Jonathan never went back to the cottage to retrieve the portrait of Annabelle and the sketches Eleanor mentioned in her letter. His anger wouldn't allow it. It wasn't until well after the turn of the Century that a package arrived for him at the Rollings' ranch in Wyoming. There was no return address, only a handwritten note taped to the back of the portrait of Annabelle. The note simply read, *True love is never forgotten.*

As the decades went by, Jonathan only returned to Marensburg once—to visit the grave of his brother. On that day he approached the grave slowly, not with the reverence and longing you would expect from someone remembering a deceased loved one but with deliberation and defiance—the kind born from pure contempt. He knelt beside the headstone placed more than a century and a half earlier and pulled back the weeds that had long since overgrown and concealed the unimpressive spot that marked the end of his brother's life. The etchings made in the stone were barely legible due to the elements and the passage of time, but with some effort and in the right angle of light, he could make out most of the words:

Maxwell Buford Rollings
Beloved son and brother
1840–1862

Jonathan traced the numbers with his index finger and pushed against them as if he expected to draw blood from the battered gray stone.

"So brother," he said scornfully in a voice so low it almost sounded like a growl. "You've decided to claim your birthright after all."

Watch for the exciting conclusion of
The Birthright Legacy **in**

Coda

TheBirthrightLegacy.com

"What was I thinking?" Hattie Arrington grumbled as she surveyed the endless stacks of research papers and lab reports that lay sprawled across her kitchen table. Shaking her head, she let out a frustrated sigh. She was beginning to seriously question her sanity, not to mention her common sense. "You'd think I'd know better by now," she mumbled quietly to herself. In her defense, she had hoped that requiring additional labs on her term papers would force her students to grapple with evidence and include more findings in their research reports. Instead, her well-meaning intentions had created a lot of unnecessary work for everyone—especially her—and a task that would normally require only a few extra hours each afternoon had morphed into a monstrous undertaking. The fact that she hadn't slept well for the past several weeks only added to her frustration and fatigue. She had chosen to ignore the warning signs, and she knew it was only a matter of time before her body would give in to exhaustion. With another sigh, she tossed aside the green marker she favored for making notes on her student's assignments and reached for a sip of coffee. She made a mental note to eliminate the extra lab requirements from next semester's syllabus as she drank.

"Bleh!" Making a sour face, she spat the cold coffee back into her mug. "Why?" she exasperated. "Why do I do this to myself?"

Her husband James lowered the book he was pretending to read and watched his wife quietly as she removed her reading glasses and pressed her fingers against her temples to release her tension. Increasing the pressure, she made circular movements against the side of her head, then rubbed along the shadowy moons beneath her eyes. She looked up briefly and caught James watching her.

"Don't you dare say it," she warned.

James raised a sympathetic eyebrow and bit his tongue. Under normal circumstances, he would seize this as an opportunity to tease Hattie by saying something clever or sarcastic, knowing that a healthy dose of humor would lighten her mood. But for the past few weeks the air in their home had been thick with anxiety, and instead of their usual playful banter, James found himself walking on eggshells, nervously sidestepping Hattie's uncharacteristic mood swings and bracing himself for the next time she would take her frustration out on him—something that rarely happened in their relationship.

This wasn't the first time James had seen his wife look so haggard and tense. Hattie had a knack for placing unrealistic demands on herself and biting off more than anyone could possibly chew. Even so, James knew intuitively that it wasn't the stacks of ungraded term papers and lab reports that were causing his wife's erratic behavior and sleeplessness. Something had changed.

"Can I get you something?" James asked hesitantly. He chewed on his lower lip and wondered how much longer he could sit silently by and watch his wife suffer. Eventually, when she finally snapped, she would tell him the truth about what was really troubling her; but waiting for her to confide in him was spiking his own anxiety and driving him crazy.

Hattie forced a tight smile. "Can you get me two weeks on a deserted tropical island?"

James inclined his head and cleared his throat to cover a sarcastic chuckle. "My love," he said teasingly, "you'd never endure the peace and tranquility of a deserted island in paradise. No phones? No computers? No laboratories? You'd implode before sunset on the first day."

"Hah! Bet me!" Hattie scowled. She pulled her mouth into a tight line and flipped her hair behind her shoulders. "You think you know me so well, don't' you, Mr. Smarty Pants?"

Even though there was an edge to her voice, James recognized a familiar glint in her eyes that he had come to appreciate and adore during the eighteen years of their marriage. This was the first hint of humor he'd seen from Hattie in weeks. He raised a hopeful eyebrow and tried not to smile—just in case he was wrong about the glint. Generally speaking, Hattie was a fun-loving, easy-going woman. Always the optimist, she usually faced the challenges and uncertainties of life with an inner strength and faith that was, for the most part, unshakable.

Except when she was keeping secrets.

James had first noticed the dark circles under Hattie's eyes about three weeks ago. Then last week he had observed the first signs of wrinkles forming around her chin and along the corners of her mouth. He'd even spotted a gray hair or two. Subtle changes such as these were to be expected among average women approaching their forties; but Hattie was not your average woman. Hattie was immortal—and Immortals don't age. At least, not in the same way mortals do. The secret Hattie was hiding this time was taking its toll on her and sucking away her everlasting youth and vitality. That could only mean one thing: Hattie was experimenting again.

Early experiments involving genetically-based immortality had always been, for the most part, harmless and unsuccessful, so James had indulged his wife by supporting her when she approached him about writing a grant for extended research and development in the science of biological immortality. He figured Hattie would quickly grow bored with the tedium of data collection and analysis and eventually move on to explore some other fascinating area of research. He couldn't have been more wrong. Hattie's research for isolating the genetic codes for immortality had become more than just another hobby, and knowing that recent advancements had given scientists hope that a major breakthrough was eminent only added to her tenacity.

But Hattie's fascination with biological immortality wasn't what troubled James; it was her propensity to take unnecessary risks—that, and her determination to take the experiments to the next level without proper precautions or authorization. All experiments involving immortality were highly classified by the government to forestall exploitation by "fountain-of-youth" fanatics: but where Hattie's peers' experiments were legal, Hattie's were not. They were off the logs. Her work involved finding a way to reverse the process known as reclamation—or in layman's terms, a way to keep those predisposed for immortality from becoming immortal—at least temporarily.

Hattie and James weren't typically prone to having serious arguments, but the topic of biological immortality had been an escalating source of contention between them ever since their daughter Beth's fourth birthday. That was when Hattie discovered that her little girl was communicating with Intruders—evil entities who had aligned themselves with a faction of immortals known as Niaces. Hattie believed the only way she and James could protect Beth from the wicked designs of the Intruders was to keep her from ever becoming immortal—and that meant they had to find a way to reverse the process of reclamation. Hattie and James fought repeatedly over the validity of the research and the risks involved in the experiments.

"There is absolutely *no solid evidence* to support the contention that reclamation can be suppressed," James had argued when Hattie first told him her plan.

"I'll find the evidence," she insisted.

"Well, you can't find something that's not there."

"If modern science can isolate genes and manipulate DNA to the point that they can prolong the life of human cells, then there's got to be a way to reverse the procedure."

"Safely?" James snipped sarcastically.

"Safely!"

James' face turned red and his nostrils flared. "And then what, hmm? What's next Dr. Frankenstein? Will you develop a serum that predetermines a person's lifespan? Wanna live to be a hundred? No problem—here's a pill! Prefer to die a little younger? Well then, step right up and select your year of choice."

"Very funny, James! A bit over the top, don't you think?"

"Obviously, but you get my point."

Hattie let out a long breath. "We both knew there'd be risks, James; we knew our offspring could become immortal. That's what happens when mortals marry immortals. You said you were willing to—"

"I know *exactly* what I said!" James interrupted. "And what I said did *not* include risking your life—or the life of our daughter."

"I would never risk Beth's life! Don't you see? That's exactly why *I'm* doing this."

"It's too dangerous, Hattie. If something were to happen to you, Beth would be left without a mother . . . and I . . ." James' voice dropped and caught slightly, "I'd lose the love of my life."

His fear was tangible as he pleaded with his eyes for Hattie to understand. He sensed that something terrible could happen to her. He slowly dropped his head for a moment, then raised his eyes to meet hers again. "At least promise me you won't test the serums on yourself until you're certain they're safe."

Hattie met his gaze and held it. When she finally nodded, she knew she was making a promise she wouldn't be able to keep. Her expression softened. "James, if the tables were turned, if you were in my place," she hesitated briefly, "wouldn't you do exactly the same thing?"

He lowered his eyes. It did nothing to calm his fear, but he realized she was right.

She pressed when he seemed lost in thought and didn't answer her right away. "James, wouldn't you?"

James shook away his memories and refocused his attention on the matter at hand—Hattie's restless behavior.

"What in the world are you thinking about so intently?" she asked.

"Nothing much," he replied, swallowing hard to hide his emotions.

Hattie rolled her eyes. "Oh, my mistake. Of course it's nothing. Otherwise I'd have to accuse you of actually ignoring me."

James chuckled. He adored his wife's sarcastic sense of humor. He leaned forward, resting his elbows on his knees, and scrutinized Hattie's expression. Yep, the glint was definitely there. Hattie blushed and fidgeted slightly in her chair. It amazed her how after all these years he could still unnerve her with a single glance. He had a gift.

"Come here, woman," he said, using his James Bond voice and trying his best to sound seductive. He had met Hattie while stationed in England prior to his first covert operation as a Navy Seal, and when Hattie had questioned him about his upcoming mission, he had dazzled her with a sexy impression of James Bond as he gave her intentionally vague information.

"Stop it, you!" Hattie shook herself free of James' stare and reached for her glasses. Pretending to be disinterested, she casually raised an eyebrow. "I don't have time for your 007 games right now."

She picked up a pile of lab reports and bounced them gently against the table several times until they formed themselves obediently into a neat stack which she placed carefully in front of her. James waited for her to pick up her pen; when she didn't, he knew he'd successfully managed to distract her. He pointed a come-hither finger at her and gestured the same way James Bond might have summoned one of his romantic liaisons.

"I said come here, woman," he said in a husky English drawl, successfully masking the humor in his voice. But there was no mistaking the mischievous glimmer in his eyes as he continued to bait her.

Hattie positioned her elbows on the table and made a tent with her fingers. She was tired. She had mounds of term papers and lab reports to grade, and the miserable secret she was harboring was aggressively eating away at her insides. But in spite of all that, her husband had managed to arouse her to the point of distraction, darn him. She rested her chin on her thumbs and considered her options.

"And what if I don't? What then, Commander?"

The corner of James' mouth slowly curved up into his signature one-sided smile—the smile that had won Hattie's heart and still made it skip a beat nearly twenty years later.

"We call that a challenge where I come from," he said evilly. "Do you have any idea what the consequences are for disobeying an official command?"

Hattie faked a yawn. "Oh, please, Mr. Bond, not the hot tar and feathers again."

James' frown made Hattie giggle. "I could have you court-martialed for that," he teased.

Hattie shook her head and waved away his comment. "James Bond would never say that."

"Hmm," James' frown deepened. "Quite right my dear." He took a deep breath and tossed the book he'd been holding onto the coffee table. "My darling, you leave me no other choice." He stood casually, unfolding his muscular frame to its full height, and moved purposefully toward her, making a conscious effort to ignore the deep shadows under her eyes.

"And what choice might that be, Commander," she said loftily. "Do tell."

James reached for her with strong arms and pulled her to her feet. He brushed his fingers lightly along the outline of her cheek. "I am highly trained in the art of persuasion," he said in a low, sultry voice as he moved his fingers down her face and along the curve of her neck. "You of all people should know better than to resist."

Hattie tried to manage an alluring smolder for her husband's benefit. His warm breath on her lips almost destroyed her reserve, but standing up made her realize just how tired she really was. Her mind and body suddenly felt totally disconnected.

James chuckled at his wife's pathetic attempt at seduction, but there was no mistaking the hollowness behind her eyes. *A little time together will help her sleep,* he thought. He reached low on her back to pull her to him and kissed her forehead lightly, then slid his lips down her cheek toward her mouth.

"James!" Hattie was barely able to utter his name when her legs suddenly stiffened and her body went rigid. She drew in a desperate breath of air and clutched frantically at his shoulders as she struggled to maintain her balance.

James pulled her tighter and tried to steady her, momentarily confused by her reaction. "Hattie! Hattie, what's wrong?"

Hattie's body started trembling, lightly at first and then convulsing in thick shudders. Her wild eyes cried out for help, but the more James tried to calm her, the more violent the convulsions became. She twisted wildly against his hold, clawing at his shirt and fighting furiously to free herself from his grip.

"GET AWAY FROM ME!" she howled.

James released her and took an astonished step backwards. Once free, Hattie fell to the ground and began clawing at her face.

"Hattie, stop!" James ordered as he pulled her hands away.

Hattie's eyes widened. "No!" she bellowed. She grunted and groaned and continued to fight as if against some unseen force. Her hands flew out in front of her; her fingers flexed and fanned in unnatural contortions. James had witnessed Hattie's seizures before, when she had offered herself as a human guinea pig for the serums her research team had been testing, but those seizures were never this violent and usually lasted only a few seconds.

"Hattie!" He pressed his hands tightly against both sides of her face and shook her. Her eyes searched blindly for his, shifting in and out of focus so quickly he couldn't connect with her gaze long enough to communicate. "Hattie, look at me!" he ordered. But as soon as her wild gaze met his, she began gasping for air. James shook her again. "Breathe!" he demanded. "Breathe!"

Red-faced and panicked, Hattie's mouth flew open, but there was no intake of air. Her eyes grew wilder, desperate, begging for James to help her. Finally, she managed to wheeze one word. "Bag!" Then her eyes rolled up into her head.

James understood immediately. He raced toward the bedroom. A moment later he returned with Hattie's leather science bag. He flipped open her cell phone and hit the call button as soon as he found the number he needed. A man's voice answered immediately on the other end.

"What did you give her?" he demanded without formality. He listened for a moment and then tossed the phone away. He dumped the contents of the leather bag on the floor, scattering apart several vials, test tubes, and syringes so he could read the notations along the sides of each container. Finding what he was looking for, he quickly inserted a syringe into a vial and drew up what he hoped was the appropriate amount of anti-serum. He'd done this before, usually in milder concentrations, but there was no time right now for second-guessing himself. He tapped out the excess air. Then holding the syringe in his mouth and grabbing scissors from the bag, he tore open Hattie's blouse and cut away her bra to expose the area directly above her heart. He tossed away the scissors, took a deep breath, and with a desperate cry, plunged the needle into Hattie's heart, emptying the contents of the vial directly into her blood stream. As soon as the vial was empty, he pulled out the needle and threw it as hard as he could against the far wall.

Exhausted, he rolled onto his back, glanced up, and in spite of claiming to be an atheist, silently summoned the powers of heaven to help his wife. Then he waited.

That night, Hattie slept.

About the Author

California native Melinda Morgan's novels reflect her love of the mountains of eastern Idaho and Wyoming. She lived in Idaho in 1980–81 and enjoyed the grandeur of the Tetons, an area that is significant to *The Birthright Legacy*. As a displaced homemaker and single mother of four, she went back to school and in 1998, received her BA in Liberal Studies from California Baptist University. She then went on to earn a Master's Degree in Education and Administration from Azusa Pacific  University—all while teaching full time and raising her children. In 2002, she married Ron Morgan, who is also an educator and musician.

Melinda has worked in education since 1998 as a teacher, staff developer for the K12 Science and Math Alliance, Teacher on Special Assignment, and assistant principal. While writing *The Birthright Legacy* books, Melinda has drawn upon her experience as a language arts and science teacher to tell stories that have scientifically intriguing plots and endearing characters. Melinda is also a classically trained pianist, and her love of music is a motif woven throughout the pages of *The Birthright Legacy*. Her performances landed her on the Piano Players Guild's National Role with a superior rating for five years in a row.